WINTERHORN

Book I of the
TOKENS OF BENEVOLENCE
Series

Written and illustrated by
BAICULESCU OVIDIU NICOLAE

For might and magic believers.

TABLE OF CONTENTS

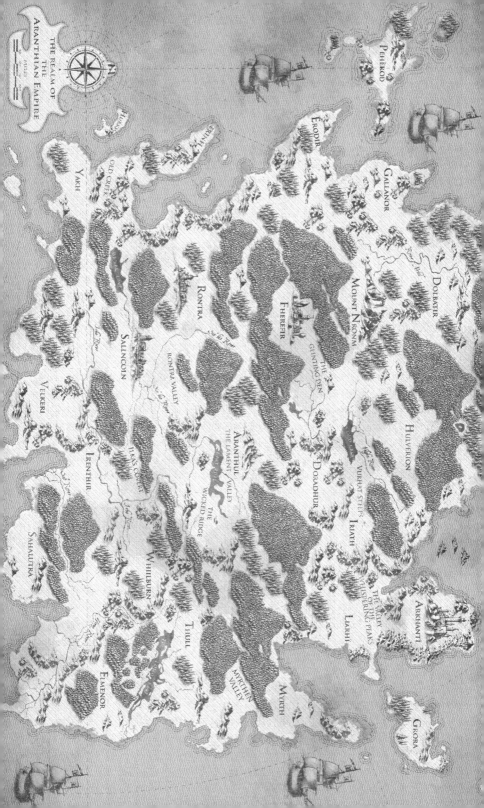

CHAPTER I

THE LONELY TOWER

Jaro / Guzheraak

"The wizard can wait!" Jaro bellowed his frustration to the skies with a heavy voice while fighting the strong and cold blasts of wind in mid-air.

The young Drakhahoul had only recently been recruited into the services of Arkhanthï and his first task was the defence of the citadel's far, eastern gate. If at first the task presented itself somewhat interesting to him, after a couple of weeks he became annoyed with his role. There was barely any action involved, except a repetitive and dull taking-up-to-the-sky, scan the surroundings and then back to the tower or the ground. An unworthy activity for a dragon. A waste of time. He was never allowed to venture too far, none of the dragons were. And if any of them tried to leave the two, distant rows of walls, the magical wards would prevent them from doing so. Yet, often he had indulged in a few escapades as high as he could reach, but only when the other Gholak guards were not around.

Felduror, the wizard right-hand of the dragon king, had reproved him multiple times already, always threatening to make an example of his bad behaviour with a severe punishment if he were to continue with his misconduct. Though, he had never actually done anything. So many threats had been issued by the old man, that the dragon had turned almost fearless to his idle words.

However, there was a more pressing matter that concerned the young dragon; someone was spying on him and reporting back to Felduror. He always came to the same conclusion as to which of the four guards was telling on him, but he could never actually prove it.

For no particular reason, other than the fact that orcs have always hated dragons, a rancour had gradually grown between him and a Gholak that went by the name of Guzheraak.

Guzheraak was an orc champion who had proved himself as commander of the front contingent in every battle he had led at the wizard's commands. To any other beast in the realm, his brute scarred-face and tall, muscled body instilled terror and demanded respect. There were very few among his own race that would dare contest or disobey his orders. Yet, he was not a real match for the young dragon.

At thirty years of age, the Drakhahoul was well-muscled and thrice the size of the Gholak. He was one of the most skilful flyers, even if he was the youngest, and was also able to wield some magic. But that was not what made him distinct. All dragons were born with the ability to wield the power of the mind and they also had a specific power to exert control over natural elements. That Jaro had these abilities was no exception. Though, while others were capable of breathing fire, ice, or could control the winds and summon other unnatural elements to their aid, Jaro's ability was different. Very different and unlike any of those known by the ancient dragons; he could breathe poisonous vapours. This was such a rarity that many of the elder dragons initially thought there was something wrong with him, yet in time, they realised it was his aptitude to gather toxic elements from his surroundings and use them. And so, his name became Jaro-the-Venomous, hatched from the egg of the dragoness Sereri-the-White, who herself was the right-hand of the wizard, Felduror.

But the fact that Guzheraak was outmatched by Jaro did not

placate the orc's anger. On the contrary, to the eyes of the young dragon, he had only become more imaginative when it had come to blemishing Jaro's attitude towards the empire. The orc-brute had always found a way to irritate and infuriate him.

Jaro shook his head forcefully, while propelling himself even higher with his powerful wing-strokes. It served more to shake the fury growing inside himself, stirred by the memory of the orc's challenging face, rather than achieving new height.

The cold air appeased his mind. Up here was rough and challenging, though he liked it nonetheless. He liked to feel his body ache with the soreness of his muscles as they throbbed after long hours of fighting nature's blows. Surrounded by solitude, it was him against the winds. Like his mother, the ice dragoness, cold felt like his natural environment, a place where his body thrived. And, although he had never known his father, he liked to think that it had been his as well.

The Arkhanthï's citadel was only a tiny speck from up here, where he practiced his flying skills in the strong and harsh early-spring currents. The winds were so cold that ice was continuously forming and cracking upon his strong scales; layer upon layer formed and broke with the effort of his strong wings. It was one of the best practices a young dragon undertook, to strengthen the mind and body.

It was time to return to the tower.

With a swift drop and a series of circular glides, he landed back on it. A potent thrust of his wings shook the ice off his body and he regained his bearing with a couple of long deep breaths. Once composed, he scanned the surroundings, feeling somewhat guilty that he had abandoned his duty in search of exercise once again, only to hear steps approaching on the stairs below.

From behind the creaky wooden door that led to the top of the tower, Guzheraak appeared with a defiant smile. "Once again, 'bandoning your post, Jaro!" the orc exclaimed leaning on the stone wall, his perfidious glare inspecting the panting dragon.

Jaro knew then that this brute was the spy.

"And why would it be of any concern to you? Have I ever failed in doing my duty?" asked the dragon.

"We both know very well that small 'scapades, while on duty, do not result in a just punishment for you, *mighty* creatures," Guzheraak retorted, "an orc gets decapitated while a dragon gets a mere reprimand. Like it has already happened many times. We both have witnessed it, if you recall." His smirk turned sharper, his eyes narrower.

"Could it be that we're not alike? That Drakhahouls hold more importance to the empire's cause than Gholaks?" Jaro replied sharply. "Everyone knows that having a Drakhahoul as a king, bothers you orcs a great deal – more than I could justify, I could add."

Guzheraak scoffed and tilted his head, clearly offended. He appeared troubled by the dragon's words.

"Of course you hold importance to the dragon king, just as we do to the wizard. Felduror knows how to compensate the services of his faithful and loyal orc comrades. Under his sole command the powerful foot-force of our armies could make anyone bow to our powers. Even you, the mighty Drakhahouls." A grin formed on his fanged-face as the orc took a step towards the dragon. "Do you think that the few dragons that still live in the citadel could defeat the hordes of Gholak armies?"

There it was again, the challenge on the orc's face. Those four overgrown, sharp fangs that bent over the pale skin of his cheeks and chin, almost as if he was biting his own face. That angry light in his small eyes, the fearless spark that made Jaro lose his temper every time.

Against his pounding heart and the venom-glands that instinctively started to swell inside his throat, the dragon forced himself to composure and restrained himself from spitting acid in the brute's face. He let out a low, guttural growl of dissatisfaction.

"What is that I have ever done to you, Guzheraak?" he asked. "Have I ever offended you? If that is the case, let me remedy and put an end to this petty quarrel that does no good to any of us."

The orc spat on the ground in disgust and moved away from the wall, slowly and confidently approaching the dragon. "It's not what you've done, dear Jaro, it's what your race is doing to this empire by the simple fact of existing." The orc's voice became more irritating, his words louder.

What was that scent the dragon felt emanating from the Gholak's skin? And was that a provocative bearing on his swollen chest and tight fists?

"The Drakhahouls?" Jaro managed to say instead. "What are they doing to the empire?" He stood to his full height, slowly advancing towards the orc, meeting his stare. "It is because of our race that humanity has found a better and safer life and we all can live in peace."

Another step.

"It is because of us, that this empire has thrived and reached the state in which you came to pledge your allegiance."

Another step.

"It is because of us you're even here, orc!" Livid, Jaro was now standing over Guzheraak, his full stature shadowing his small opponent.

The orc did not falter, nor did the grin of overconfidence vanish from his marked, pale face. His right hand tightened around the hilt of his sheathed blade and he took another, confident step towards the dragon. His breath was now dewing over Jaro's cold snout scales.

They were standing face to face, intently awaiting the other's move.

The orc's leather suit crackled beneath his chest and metal plated shoulders as he tightened his hand around the handle of his deadly sword. The skin around his nose and mouth trembled with anger as it started revealing the full length of his boar-like fangs.

The dragon's throat throbbed vibrantly and Jaro felt the veins on his long neck pulse in accordance with his anger. A grumble vibrated deep inside. His talons pushed and splintered the hard stone of the floor, while the roar inside his throat grew deeper. His opened maw emitted a glowing-green light and timid wafts of vapour.

Guzheraak seemed to have appreciated the seriousness of the dragon's carriage and took his hand up to the blade's pommel.

"We shall see." He swiftly turned away and slammed the door behind him as he descended the tower's stairs.

Jaro shook off his fury, and waited for his heart to cease drumming inside his chest. This time had been very close, he had almost let the venom out. A strong bitter taste of metal and acid permeated the inside of his mouth and throat and he had to swallow repeatedly to make it fade.

The bold behaviour of the orc always managed to make him lose control. The thought infuriated him more now that he had failed to compose himself yet again. Every time he intended to ignore his threats and every single time he failed. He did not like that Guzheraak knew which nerves to hit – it could get very dangerous, very fast.

Though, after a few moments of fighting the negative influence left by the encounter, Jaro managed to calm himself. Half of his day's guarding-shift was complete and he decided that the second half would suffice to forget and put the unfortunate affair behind him.

He spread his wings and let out a shrieking roar that echoed through the valley. With a vigorous pounce he launched himself from the tall tower taking to the air, this time to do his duty.

Guzheraak returned to the hall where all the orcs met when off-duty – if duty could be called having to stay idle in the hope that another conflict would break out. More than three years had passed since the wizard had had a real need of his Gholak armies, and then too, it had been for way too short a time. The orcs now found themselves getting fat and growing lazy, having to fulfil petty tasks between the two rows of walls.

A gathering of drunken Gholaks, spiritedly arguing by the entrance, stopped at the sight of their chieftain, clumsily saluting with their quivering bodies and half-opened eyes. He pushed the unlucky one standing in his way, making him tumble in the mud, to the enjoyment of the others who started laughing loudly. Once past the entrance, he walked the long corridor that led to the tavern built inside the enormous hall. A snoring orc, fallen asleep on the counter, got shoved to the ground accompanied by the empty pint that broke over his head, failing to wake him. After sitting comfortably in his new seat he lifted his finger in an attempt to order the strongest mead, which arrived just before he looked at the barkeep on duty. He smiled, pleased that everyone knew their place in here, and took a long sip of the strong liquid.

Meanwhile, to his left, a small orc was staring. Guzheraak knew that he followed him like a shadow wherever he went, where access was possible for such an insignificant creature. He was his chieftain after all, his protector, and Pakto knew better than to disturb the champion orc. He'd have to wait for Guzheraak to call upon him or look at him before imparting the news or prepping for any sort of task his master had planned for him.

Though, this time he wanted to let the creature wait for a moment, he didn't want to hear his irritating voice just yet. But, the small creature – actually the smallest Gholak in the entire camp, the one that would bring shame to their notoriously, terrifying race – slowly craned his head from behind the chair, and bothered his field of vision.

"So?" Guzheraak grunted annoyed, not even deigning his slave with a look.

"Master," bowed Pakto. "I've ve-verry good news. I've found someone that'll be able to helps us in aur causs."

"Us?" replied the chieftain, looking down at the smaller creature. "There is no us in this, creature. There is only me, while you… you can thank me for being my slave. You see that nobody dares pick on you any more, now that you work for me. Be grateful for that!"

The small orc shrunk under the counter and Guzheraak raised his finger to ask for a second round.

"Yes master, 'm verry grateful to your lordship." Pakto bowed again. "Howeverr, the one in question," and he closed in to avoid being heard by the others, "is an acolyte and can procurre the potion you requested, and can be verry, verry discreet about it. He only asks forr a small amount of coin in exchange forr his serrvices."

"Good. I shall like to meet him. Arrange for it, Pakto! Tomorrow at dawn, by the well," Guzheraak replied while getting off his chair. "And, here," he gave his pint to Pakto, "you can finish this!"

"Thank you, masterr," replied Pakto.

As Guzheraak departed he turned his head. "And don't forget to pay for it," he said and then left.

The next day, before the first crack of light, Pakto was waiting at the well accompanied by a cloaked human.

Many stories told that the abandoned well was haunted by the ghosts of those that perished in its depths – many centuries ago, in a time of war when Arkhanthï did not even exist, the tribes that invaded the lands decided to drown or leave their enemies to die of starvation. It was said that their laments could still be heard to this day, and, although the water was still pure and aplenty inside, nobody dared to approach the doomed place. Time had decayed it and allowed nature to take its course, making it a very distinct landmark. Overgrown ivy and other rampant plants had taken over the entire place, externally as well as inside the shaft, covering every single rock, piece of rotten wood and rust-eaten metal. A piece of the broken roof had collapsed inside the shaft and was hanging dangerously by the chain and bucket. On windy days, the dried-out well would hoot a ghostly noise that would echo through the walls of the hills in between, making those that knew the place avoid it all the more.

The early spring still carried the cold bite of winter air and the fog was so thick that it was hard to see more than few feet ahead. The uneven candle-torch Pakto used, only made visibility worse – its beam of light spread on the moist billows of fog and bounced back, glowing into their eyes. They had to kill the flame to make it there in time, and still Guzheraak had not arrived. He was never late.

The hooded man let out a small cough which Pakto ignored, absorbed in checking the surroundings in lookout for his master. Yet, the coughing worsened.

"Are you well?" Pakto asked.

"I am. It's only the cold air. I should be fine if we do not linger much longer in this soggy weather." The man somewhat recovered, though he still swallowed with difficulty.

"What's all this fuss?" the rasping, deep voice of Guzheraak came from behind the well.

They both turned around on their heels, surprised, and looked at the big Gholak.

"So you are the one that will help me, human?" he impatiently asked, circling the small man who barely reached the height of his chest.

The man did not move and stood quietly when the orc took the hood off his head and bent sideways to inspect his features.

"What's your name?" Guzheraak asked.

"I am called Dharamir, my lord," the man replied.

"And has my slave told you what I require?" Guzheraak demanded, pleased to sense fear in the man's voice.

"Of course, my lord. I'm to provide you with an alteration potion for you to take the shape of anyone you wish, as well as the voice. But, I…" the man hesitated.

"You what?" Guzheraak asked loudly.

"I… I need to know in advance exactly who you're going to transform into, otherwise the potion will not work."

Guzheraak gurgled, "It is not I who needs the potion, it is him." He pointed at Pakto who was just as surprised as the trembling man in front of him.

"Me, masterr?" asked Pakto. "Why would I need it and who should I transforrm into?"

"Quiet creature," growled Guzheraak, "you shall do as I tell you. Besides, you will be transforming into me. Isn't that what you've always wanted, to have a great body of an orc champion? To be a proper Gholak? Well this is your chance!" His grin widened.

Pakto let out a noise of amazement that Guzheraak read as excitement and gratification.

"Wizard, I'll be needing him to look and sound like me, for at least half a day, that is all you need to know. Can your potion achieve it or should I be looking elsewhere?"

"I shall do as you bid, and my alter-potion will work for the time requested. Though, I will need the coin in advance. You will find the potion in a flask at this very spot in two days' time." The man indicated to an aperture in the well's wall.

"Mh," Guzheraak groaned and forced his gaze deeper into the man's eyes, "if you just think to trick me wizard, I shall come find you in that fetid stinking little hut where you came out from, and make you wish you were never born. Here's your coin!" He placed a leather purse filled with golden coins in the wizard's small hands.

The wizard nodded and darted into the fog, not even taking the time to count the coins.

"Masterr, what do you have in mind forr me?" Pakto then asked.

Guzheraak exhaled a steamy breath. "You'll have to speak with Jaro during his shift, pretending to be me. He has insulted our ruler, Felduror, one too many times and I think he deserves punishment for his insolence. I will be hiding in the tower and as soon as he says something wrong, I shall come out and expose him. This way it is not only my word against his anymore."

The small orc appeared confused for a little while and then he brightened up and smiled. "I will be looking just like you, masterrr?"

"If that wizard's potion is good for something, certainly," Guzheraak replied, drawing pride out of the little orc's tearful eyes.

Most likely the dumb creature was feeling honoured beyond belief for being granted such an opportunity, he thought.

After two days, Pakto brought to his master a pear-shaped flask, filled with a thick, purple liquid, which he had retrieved by the well. There was a tiny string that held a note, and Guzheraak read it aloud;

My Lord,

I am pleased to provide you with the finest of my potions. But for it to be effective, you need to drink it in the same instant as your servant, and not a moment before having spilled two drops of blood, each of you, in the flask. Give the blood time to dissolve and then the magic will take effect instantly.

Your humble servant, D.

"Simple enough," said the big orc, taking out a double-edged dagger from his well-furnished belt. "Give me your hand, Pakto." He extended his big palm towards the smaller orc.

Pakto hesitated, allowing a whine to abandon his mouth, and Guzheraak pulled him forwards with a sudden move.

"Be brave, creature, you're about to become me." Guzheraak laughed and slashed the skin of Pakto's palm, letting two drops fall into the little flask.

He then cut himself too, an even wider gash, and smiled as he allowed two bulky drops of blood to mix into the potion. Once the second drop reached the still fluid, the concoction started swirling vigorously for a long moment and once it stilled itself again, it turned into a dark and vivid purple.

"Put a bit in your mouth, but don't gulp it yet! I'll tell you when," Guzheraak said.

Pakto did just as bid, his face paler than before.

Then, Guzheraak sipped his bit of potion, kept it under his tongue and once ready, he lifted the little orc's mouth with his fingers so they both swallowed the potion at the same time.

Pakto was shivering now as he gulped down the liquid. And after two blinks he fell to the ground, eyes rolling over. Guzheraak tried to laugh at the orc's weakness only to find himself unable to speak or move; he could only hear the heavy thud his own body made as he collapsed to the ground.

They woke sometime later, dazed and confused in the same humid air.

There was no pain as Guzheraak lifted himself with dizziness, to a blurry vision. Pakto was puking with vigour, crouched on the ground. His clothes were torn to shreds, leaving the turgid muscles of his renewed-body protrude impressively. His hair was longer and darker.

He was bigger. Stronger.

"Impressive!" Awestruck, Guzheraak reached out and touched Pakto's back.

He bent to measure with both hands how wide that torso was and started laughing while aiding the befuddled Pakto to his feet.

"How marvellous this body is," he continued.

Pakto swallowed confused and looked around his own, new body. He weakly chuckled with surprise as soon as he saw his big palms.

"Masterr," he managed to say before he swallowed twice, "this is magical…" his words trailed to a brief silence, and a quick exchange of glances, before exploding into wild laughter.

Guzheraak joined in the glee. The more Pakto laughed, the harder it was for him to stop; they sounded just the same, a very awkward, but pleasant sensation to witness. He bent with palms on his knees, breathing slowly and trying to break the laughter that was getting the best of both of them.

"I am you!" Pakto failed to detain the tears of laughter that started falling from his eyes.

"No, I am you!" added Guzheraak, losing at another miserable attempt to be serious and compose himself.

The laughter was genuine and cleansing and it took them a long time to calm themselves and regain some self-control. Even more so as Pakto kept pulling a funny face that made it hard to stop.

When the laughter subdued completely, they continued to marvel. Pakto continuously looked around himself, stretching and kicking his legs and checking the muscles on his veiny arms, chest and stomach. He did not appear bothered to be almost naked.

Guzheraak appreciated how the potion had worked and was struck to see his twin-body flex and perform as well as he knew he could, in front of his own eyes. He also appreciated the determination and content of his slave, who no doubt would do as he was told, to please him. Most certainly he himself would, if places where exchanged and he had been granted such a unique opportunity to demonstrate himself.

He then imparted the last details of the meeting, that would soon take place between Pakto, embodying him, and Jaro, who was about to start his guarding shift. There was no time to waste and they had to be quick to reach the tower.

Once there, they stood hidden and waited for the dragon to take to the air on his scouting routine, and only then, made their way to the top.

As decided, Pakto had to wait on the tower's platform to greet the dragon upon landing, and Guzheraak would hide behind the wooden door, within hearing distance.

Not long after, the Drakhahoul returned and landed with a loud thump on the square blocks of white stone.

Oh, how he wished to see his slave's face right now, Guzheraak thought. Pakto had never stood face to face with a Drakhahoul, very few Gholaks had ever been allowed to.

The gust of air hit at the door as Jaro, seemingly welcomed the orc with a threatening pose, as usual. But there were no words from his slave, and he wondered if the potion had transferred any of his own courage and nerve.

"Gholak." The dragon's voice was loud as it bounced around the top of the tower.

No reply came from Pakto.

"Have you come to apologise?" continued Jaro, in a more defiant tone.

Speak you coward!

Guzheraak measured it was taking Pakto too long to reply, and feared that his plan would fail. The only consolation was that the dragon did not see, nor sense anything wrong; the potion was working.

"I..." Pakto cleared a wavering voice, "I came here to tell you that Felduror has been far too kind towards your race and has always placed your kind above all others. It's only fair that you should ask forgiveness for your insolence and all will be well among us."

Very well. If courage was not completely transferred with the potion, certainly his knowledge has, thought Guzheraak as he appreciated the orc's words.

"My insolence? You dare talk to me like that, orc?" Jaro almost barked.

Very well, indeed.

Guzheraak was pleased to imagine how easily it was for him to anger the young dragon. He envisioned the Drakhahoul swelling his chest and moving his long neck and those bat-like wings, like he had always done when threatened and upset. From there, it was easy to lure the beast into a false step.

That image made him smile cunningly behind the door while he searched for a slit to be able to witness the sight.

He found it. Not too big, just wide enough to see half of the dragon's body at one end of the tower's opening, and just a small portion of Pakto's.

Something was wrong.

Pakto did not speak anymore, he appeared still as a statue.

Amazingly wrong.

He could almost see the usually green-yellow eyes of the dragon, turn black as tar; it had occurred in the past, but briefly, way briefer than now.

Olive-green fumes were uncontrollably released from the dragon's nostrils, accompanied by a frightening growl that shook every stone in the tower.

To his annoyance, the hidden Gholak found himself gulping nervously at such a terrifying sight. He couldn't imagine what it felt like to witness it first-hand. He had to admit that he did not want to be there, not now. Almost feeling sorry for his ignorant servant, he crouched to check lower on the slit, as the dragon lowered his neck. Most likely there were tears in Pakto's eyes and he was wetting his new robes, unable to speak or say a thing that might spare his life.

It's far too late now, comrade, he confessed.

With a sudden step and a twist of his long neck, the Drakhahoul snapped at the frozen orc as if it were a rotten twig. His powerful jaws made a loud cracking sound as they closed in on the long-haired head and swallowed it briefly in his big mouth, only to spit it to the ground as soon as it had been cleanly cut from his neck.

Guzheraak swallowed nervously, his fingers curling into a shaking fist.

Pakto's headless-body fell to the ground heavily and almost instantly, like a hallucination, he slowly started to shrink and turn into the usual, harmless body of the deformed creature he had always been.

Unworthy to be called a Gholak, though your sacrifice will not be forgotten. Guzheraak allowed his thought to fill him as he witnessed the despair and frustration of the dragon.

The realisation of the ruse forced Jaro to an ear-splitting roar that made the tiny pebbles bounce on the floor. It echoed around the valley as the muscles of his limbs started desperately to shake, perhaps overwhelmed by the inexplicable deceit. He kept it alive for as long as his lungs allowed. There was a sad vibration to it. The green-yellow eyes returned as his howl faded and Guzheraak was sure that those were tears that started forming in his eyes.

The dragon lowered his head. Was that shame? Was it fear? There was no possible justification for his action which would definitely earn more than mere reprimands. Guzheraak knew then that Jaro would try to flee and so he anticipated him by kicking the door to splinters.

Jaro felt like he was waking from a bad dream, a nightmare. The proud smile of the orc who had stood in front of him could've infuriated the wisest of the mighty beasts. Yet, the sight of the beheaded small orc made him retreat from his threatening stance. Blood was spreading in a puddle and almost reached his left paw's claws. He retreated back a step further.

"How is this possible?" Astonished, Jaro did not need a reply to read the trick out of Guzheraak's face.

He had been deceived, a malevolent trick, too low even for such an unimportant creature like an orc.

There were steps on the stairs, multiple steps reaching from below and the smirk on the orc's face grew wider. Jaro hesitated, confused by what was happening.

"Bear witness, acolytes," the orc spoke proudly, as three acolytes came through the broken door, "this Drakhahoul has killed a harmless messenger, whose only fault was to deliver a message on my behalf."

The fake sadness in Guzheraak's voice was as palpable as the morning's thick blanket of fog. If any of the orcs had to die, then this one was supposed to.

"Bind his wings and let his mightiness, Felduror, as well as our enlightened king Belrug, know of such a miserable affair. He shall be trialled on the spot." The orc champion pulled a bull's horn from his belt and started blowing with all his might while the acolytes bound the dragon's wings, preventing him from taking to the air.

From the high tower the sound of the horn echoed vigorously in the surrounding valleys and after its last bounce died down, a roar of warriors lifted in response. Every orc in the empire would be compelled to present himself when the horn of battle was rung.

The three acolytes succeeded in binding the two mighty wings of Jaro with a spell and were now descending the stairs to run and take the news to the citadel.

"What have you done?" In utter disbelief and sorrow, the voice of the dragon sounded worn.

"You should've known better than to mess with me," came the reply of the proud orc as he checked behind him, as if to confirm they were indeed alone.

A mingle of feelings entrapped the young dragon's body. His mind painfully pounded inside his skull and the only thing that kept him from biting off the insolent orc's head was the revolting sensation he had experienced only few moments before. No one had ever warned him of such a shameful feeling; taking an innocent life. How could he have ever been such a fool to fall for the deceitful scheme of the cunning orc? A part of him told him to run and save himself, yet another was keeping him still as a stonewall. Although deep down he wanted to escape, among the throng of thoughts that were constantly crossing his mind, he considered jumping to his death from the tall tower.

Such is the shame I have to live with. I am a disgrace to the entire Drakhahoul race.

Heavy steps of rowdy running orcs announced the stampede that was on the way. They must have moved in hundreds, and they made Jaro's ears pulse achingly, their heavy metal-boots crushing the tussock-patterned plains around the tower.

Too long had they been idle and too silent had these valleys been without a war to quench their thirst for blood. The occasion would be like a feast to manifest some anger, a long-subdued anger. The horde let out enraged calls and cries, so terrifying that would make any brave Drakhahoul falter.

But Jaro was not afraid anymore. He had renounced the brief urge to flee and abandoned his big head to rest on his forelegs. From where he stood, he stared without a blink in the lifeless eyes of the decapitated head. There was no light and passion in those grey irises, there was no hint of treachery.

Who knows what he had been promised to take part in such a devious plan? he wondered as sorrow filled his tearful eyes, compelling him to fix on the staggered expression, frozen in the moment of death, on the small orc's face.

Just like himself, the helpless orc had been another victim of Guzheraak's deceit. Though nothing seemed to matter anymore.

The army had reached the tower and the orcs piled into an angry crowd of fetid beasts, their weighty scent inebriating for Jaro's sharp senses.

From the many growls, yells and howls a single voice reigned, compelling the others to follow. A unified and guttural chant soared in the air as the throng of Gholaks started invoking the ancient name of their past, present and future chieftains – a battle cry used to instil fear before a battle; 'Gharrakuul, Gharrakuul, Gharrakuul,' leader of all. The earth trembled as they stomped their feet on the ground.

Undoubtedly enthralled by the sound, the champion orc approached the edge of the tower and filled his chest at the sight of the faithful warriors. He lingered wordlessly, apparently basking in the disgraceful moment, which he most likely considered a triumph.

He lifted his right fist, high in the air. The rowdy horde stopped chanting.

"Brothers," the orc commenced, "you're gathered here to bear witness of a tragic misfortune. Our brother, Pakto, my dearest servant and friend, has been killed in cold blood by a Drakhahoul. Eaten alive."

An angry growl of the horde lifted in the air and Guzheraak had to insist for it to desist.

Jaro watched, almost lost in his own reasoning.

"Brothers," the orc continued, "I invoke the highest court of the Aranthian empire to judge as it seems fit the heedless dragon. Although I do hope that an example shall be made, as no life is bigger than another, independently of how big or small a beast one is."

His words instigated another unanimous chanting of agreement, raised to the air accompanied by vigorous clapping, weapon smashing and heavy stomps on the ground.

Every single being that lived between the two rows of walls must have trembled in fear at that sound. The humans that shared the lands with the orcs, most likely kept quiet and hid in the safety of their homes, fearing for their lives and those of their children, unaware of what occurred.

The acolytes reached the citadel. Jaro could tell by the sight of the other Drakhahouls who were flying in haste towards the tower. At the head of their battle-formation, Belrug-the-Black, the dragon king, biggest of them all. He was leading the others to witness his misfortune. Alongside him, his mother, Sereri the white dragoness, who was carrying the old man, Felduror, the powerful wizard. He was the most devoted servant of the empire and counsellor to the dragon king himself. He was the one to fear.

Jaro returned his gaze to those small, dead eyes, trying to reach deeper and only when Belrug arrived above the tower, did he manage to stand and follow attentively as his king prepared to land.

The tower was wide and strong enough to withstand the weight of multiple dragons, though Belrug's body made it appear very small. He eclipsed everyone around him, casting a long, dark shadow over the entire area. His thick wings lifted all the dust and small gravel that Jaro had broken upon his many landings, forcing all the others to cover their eyes. Upon his landing the tower shook as if moved by an earthquake and the king had to spread his wings again to rebalance himself. Sereri had already landed and let the old man descend to safety, while the other dragons scattered upon the hills nearby and among the throng of orcs below, definitely not pleased by such company.

Compared to his king, Jaro was but a tiny chick and he could not take his eyes off Belrug's strong legs. They reminded him of the ancient oaks he had seen in the green forests of Orethill.

"What happened?" The king's voice resounded powerfully in

the valley.

Guzheraak who had never met the king in person, nor the wizard, rushed kneeling in front of them both.

"Your highness, I witnessed this horrific –"

"I didn't ask you, brute!" The king's voice exploded and snapped at the orc making him bow lower.

The wizard then approached King Belrug and whispered something.

When the king continued to speak after, his voice was softer, "And who might you be, warrior?"

Surprised by the sudden change, Jaro watched as the orc lingered in his stooped position, seemingly perplexed.

"I am Guzheraak, your mightiness," the orc said, eyes locked on the pavement.

"Raise and speak up!" commanded Belrug with the same peaceful tone.

Guzheraak did as bid and said, "I call for justice to be served. My brother in arms, Pakto has been killed in cold blood, by Jaro-the-Venomous and we'd all like a fair trial so nothing of the sort ever happens again."

Belrug-the-Black turned his gaze upon Jaro who, ashamed and lacking words, dared not to look in his king's eyes.

"Is that true?" demanded the king.

Compelled by the direct question, Jaro lifted his head and, with tearful eyes, nodded at the king. Eager to see a glimpse of hope and comprehension in those big, brown eyes, Jaro lingered a moment. He knew he had to make his king see what really happened. So, he then tried to use the power of his mind to speak with him and him alone; a power all Drakhahouls shared.

My king, I have been deceived and I beg forgiveness. My only fault is that I did not see clearly the trap I was falling into.

Awkwardly, nothing came back, as if the mind of his king had been shut to any external interference. It was deserted of his mighty presence; a deep, dark, empty cavern. He tried again, but nothing still and then he turned desperately to find Sereri's eyes, his mother's. Yet the white dragoness turned away with a discouraging gesture, confirming her disappointment. She denied him even a comforting look.

Desperation engulfed the young dragon and he turned his head to the white stones of the floor again. He decided that words would achieve nothing where his thoughts had failed.

"Then so be it!" added the wizard, moving closer to the young dragon. "You shall be trialled as we stand." His loud voice could be picked up by the orcs gathered around the tower that started yelling in agreement.

"Highest members of the assembly here gathered; Sereri-the-White, King Belrug-the-Black and myself, Felduror, as the sole representative of the wizard community of Arkhanthï, shall judge you and decide upon your fate."

The horde of Gholaks started growling and pounding with whatever they happened to have in their hands; swords, axes, bottles. The rumble was so loud that one could not hear himself even if he shouted. It was only when the white dragoness lifted herself in the sky and growled with colossal strength, that the myriad of orcs ceased their racket. The scorching flames she spat in the air illuminated her scales as bright as the sunlight, making her body shine with blinding sparks. The powerful roar was as piercing and powerful as ever and every other sound in the valley bellow ceased.

Silence was restored and her threatening stance, perched on the edge of the tower, made sure it would be kept.

"Very well," added then the wizard, "what is, in your opinion, a just punishment for Jaro-the-Venomous?" He exchanged glances with both the older Drakhahouls. "I would not like death to deprive us of such a mighty being, yet I consider few alternatives satisfactory enough for us, as well for the horde of warriors. And, might I add, we would not want any of them angry."

"Exile," suggested the king with a strong voice.

"And, would you agree, wise dragoness?" Felduror asked Sereri.

"Blood of my blood, the punishment must be fair and I would not let my mothering instincts cloud my judgement. I must agree with my king," she replied.

"Mother where would I go?" Jaro, awoken with worries by the implications his exile would bear, started to argue.

"Silence," growled Belrug, making the young dragon draw back.

"I must say," continued Felduror, "although I find it just, I think it's not enough. We should consider a life has been lost, whereas, if exiled, Jaro could live a normal life and soon leave this behind. Not to forget that this would also risk exposing us all. Behind the walls we are safely protected by our wards and hidden from the rest. Now is not the time to start revealing ourselves to the humans, or the dwarves and the elves. And how is this setting an example that everyone is as important to the empire? How is this fair for the Gholaks?"

The wizard's words stung and made Jaro feel like there was no hope of escaping certain death. He thought he had seen a proud and brief nod of consent, coming from Guzheraak who had retreated to a corner far from everyone's gaze.

"The only alternative to death, which as you can see, my friends, I'm so desperately trying to avoid, is to rid him of his powers that have caused already so much harm to his troubled soul," the wizard continued.

"Take his reasoning away and leave him as plain as an ordinary beast? A goat, or a sheep?" Belrug replied dismayed.

Felduror approached him and looked up at the giant dragon, gently placing his hand on the giant foreleg. "Yet, I think it is better than death. Is it not, my king?"

A silent moment passed.

"If that is the case, then I suppose it is," the king replied shifting his leg away from the wizard's hand.

"My king, I beg of you…" Prey to his own fears, Jaro begged as he violently started shaking in the king's own shadow.

Mother please!

Ignited by fear, a state of chaos ruled his mind and body.

Belrug did not look at the young Drakhahoul.

"If that's your wish, my king," added Sereri.

Seemingly concentrated on considering the request, the wizard took his time to reply.

"Then it is settled. And who would you consider should proceed with the spell?" Felduror then asked.

After another odd moment of silence, the dragoness

answered, "I shall do it!"

"Very well," replied the wizard.

The king stood silent.

Sereri moved closer to Jaro, who shivered in fear uncontrollably when she nodded her readiness. The three judges allowed her to start and then followed in, closing their eyes to conclude the spell.

As if summoned, everywhere around the valley clouds started to gather out of nowhere, threatening the tower and its surroundings with an abnormal blanket of darkness. Silence reigned as the three conducted the magical binding. The blind horde of orcs below, stood equally as quiet. They knew better than to interrupt a spell.

Jaro was in a state of pure terror. The agonising shakiness was beyond his control just like the raw fear he had never felt before. His body did not know what orders to follow from his contaminated mind and he found himself squeezed against the walls of the tower, unable to run. The tears in his eyes blurred his vision to a point of blindness. His gaze was lost in a far-away world, deep inside his own soul, where more and more, an invisible, friendly force dragged him closer.

Mother is that you? He sensed her presence like a warm hug. A hug he craved to receive, yet even the memories of those few moments that actually had happened, were starting to drift away. His last words caused a violent disruption in his already-confused mind, as he exhaustingly lost any sense of what he was doing.

He soon forgot what he wanted to say. He didn't remember his name anymore, and with the realisation came a desperate need to growl, to let out his muted fury and shout his anger and frustration at everyone around. Alas, he could not. The friendly force was now a face in his imagination, an unrecognisable one that was too close for him to move away from. He was compelled to look at it and had to stare attentively. Maybe he would understand who that friend was.

Friend? with a last abrupt shiver, the word blurred before consciousness left his mind and he fell numbly to the ground.

A piercing growl exploded as both Sereri and King Belrug lifted their heads toward the darkened sky. The other dragons, perched wherever they had found space upon landing, lifted to the air and joined the growl with trembling strength. The valley echoed with the lament of the Drakhahouls and every creature down below stood breathlessly in fear.

When the dragons left for the citadel, no one dared to cheer or chant. A few yells were soon subdued by far away growls of the younger dragons.

Felduror looked down to the horde of orcs only to address them to discharge with a brief 'Justice has been served.'

The sky was starting to clear and the sun slowly lay tepid rays on the deserted valley. Small wafts of fog lifted from the cold, furrowed terrain – ploughed by the angry orcs and their heavy boots. Coloured birds and furred animals were fighting over seeds and insects, unearthed by throngs of feet. In the middle of the feeding frenzy, the solitary tower was lit by the day's dying sun. It was like the sky above wanted to soothe the fate of the young dragon, the only consolation he had. There would be no guards for the day and perhaps for many days to come, as on that doomed side of the empire, by the lonely tower, nobody would dare enter anytime soon.

In the same spot where he had met his fate, on that very stone-tile, Jaro was resting. He was not dreaming, he was not thinking, he was sleeping his first sleep as a plain beast.

CHAPTER II

THE FIRE

Lorian

The late-summer sun was still standing strong, against a surprisingly clear sky over the village of Sallncoln. It was a good day for me to join my grandmother and my two brothers gathering berries and collecting firewood in the nearby forest. It took Nana a long time to convince both Henek and Kuno to come help us – they were never happy to join in our petty chores – but she insisted it was necessary if we wanted to have a decent stash of jams and marmalades for the fast-approaching winter.

Firebreath, our horse, was with us, untethered from the cart he had pulled, and bound by a tree with a long rope. He looked happier than us while nibbling at whatever bush pleased his appetite, sheltered by the shadow of a tall maple tree.

The berries' shrubs were not too abundant, yet they were rich with tasty fruit, which I could not avoid sampling every once in a while.

"More to the bucket, less to the mouth," my grandmother chided me in a playful manner from where she stood, concealed by a tall bush few feet away.

"But, they're delicious, Nana," I tried to justify myself, "and how did know I was eating them?" I asked.

"There's no need to see, we can all hear you!" replied Kuno, who was furthest away from us.

"It's true." Henek let out a chuckle.

They were almost done filling the cart with twigs, branches and logs good for burning, while Nana and I had only filled a couple of small wooden buckets with berries. There were still plenty on the tallest branches, enough to fill at least another bucket. Unfortunately, neither I nor her could easily reach them. Grandmother was not that tall, and even if I was taller, I had some difficulty too, given my condition.

A birth imperfection the elders had said, an imperfection that unquestionably represented much more than that to me and my family. It was a defect that had taken from this world far more than it had brought; my mother had died giving birth to me. Soon after her, my heart-sick father. Sometimes I wished it had been me instead of her, though my grandmother insisted that nobody was to blame. 'You're nobody's main reason for unhappiness', she often said. While her words always cheered me, I never knew what my brothers really thought of me. We seldom talked about my condition and they never upset or mocked me over it. Nor did they willingly mention anything about our parents. With father gone as well, they respected our grandmother more than anyone else, and I often suspected that she kept them in line for me rather than allowing them to speak their minds.

And so, after sixteen years with the same condition, I thought I had grown accustomed to it, I thought I would learn to live with it. But I wasn't sure I was. Almost every time my knee ached or sent a spike of pain through my body, I would become upset and incapable to accept it.

"What is wrong, son?" asked Nana, clearly worried to see me massage the bulge on my left knee.

"Nothing, just a bit tired," I replied.

As a matter of fact, the long climb to reach the good crop of berries had taken its toll on my weak leg.

"Then rest, there is no need to strain yourself," she continued as she joined me to sit on the soft patch of grass.

Her voice always succeeded in making me feel better. She

always knew how to cheer me up.

"You know," she started again, "I never told you this. You remind me a lot of your mother. She used to be just like you are now. She'd turn away from whatever her chore was just to stop and think on her own little problems for a time. And when asked what was wrong, she'd try to lie that everything was well." Nana smiled.

Her honest smile was contagious.

"If anything has been passed onto you from her, I think it is her confidence and cheerfulness. Nothing would ever get her down or make her really upset. She'd face the grimmest circumstances and carry on, sharing hope to everyone around. You might not see it, but I do." Her wrinkled hand stroked my knee gently, right over that bulge.

Her confession delighted me a great deal. I knew there was no point complaining, that I had learned. And I also knew I could not let them down, my grandmother, my brothers and the memory of my unknown parents. Besides, my body was pretty well muscled compared to others of my age, and I could still walk and briefly run, even if not very fast.

We sipped some water from the waterskin and got back to our feet, motivated to fill at least another bucket. But, just as we did, a loud noise lifted itself in the valley making Firebreath neigh nervously.

Henek and Kuno dropped the piles of wood they carried and ran to the edge of the hill, where the village could be seen. We were not that far from it, and from where we stood, quite high on the southern forest, Sallncoln could be seen entirely, big as a fist.

"Fire, fire!" they both shouted.

We reached them as fast as we could and gaped at the sight. Chaos ruled over our quiet, little village. Tall, vicious flames devoured the buildings as if they were made of candle oil and sulphur. Like ants chased away from their anthill, people were running for their lives, chaotically trying to grasp whatever precious things they could save in their escape.

Nana let out a fragile cry.

The flames rose higher than the village's tallest building, the tower, which had been built in the ancient times of raids and wars. Luckily, the ancient structure was situated at the edge of the walls, safe from any damage. Sadly, everything in the centre was engulfed by flames.

Most of the people were heading towards the lake, as were some of the animals that had managed to escape.

"Let's go!" said Henek, and leaped ahead downhill on the dangerous side of the mountain.

Kuno followed with the same haste, careless of the bramble ahead.

Although my intention had been just the same, I could not leave Nana behind, scared and alone. So, we quickly gathered our things in one place, made sure Firebreath was properly tethered and retrieved the path that descended to the village.

The enormous bell of the tower started ringing loudly, tallying to the chaos and fear around.

We helped each other by holding hands and she started crying and mumbling something that only she could understand. Her anguish added to the loud clanging of the bell and my inner anguish; Elmira.

Heavens, please keep Elmira safe!

There was no point in ignoring the apprehension that had clutched at my stomach with sharp claws, as soon as I saw the flames. Elmira was an occurring thought in my daily routine.

Being a cripple has never been easy for me, and I was the only one with the condition in our village. I tired more easily than others, and was often cut from games that involved much activity and physical effort. That made bonding with other children my age quite difficult and I was always the one left behind. If things hadn't been unpleasant enough for me already, in time I also became the ridicule of their boring days, and that took me further away from the desire to have a real friend. I liked to say I was used to it, but most of the time I was sad and did not comprehend why I had to be different. Many times, it bothered me a great deal but, in time, I'd learned to cope with it. I became accustomed to watching them play from a distance.

But my childhood had not been all sorrow and sadness as in my solitude, a similar soul became isolated like myself. Her name was Elmira and she was the youngest daughter of our neighbours, who lived few houses north of ours, near the wall. Perhaps it was her inquisitive nature and the fact that she did not feel the impulse to run every time she wanted to play. Or perhaps, it was that deep inside she felt alone like myself, that allowed us to become very close friends. My childhood days turned brighter and I soon forgot about my bad leg as she never seemed to mind being my friend. She was kind to me.

Almost nine years ago, having been forced to flee their own village far in the west, where the clans' feuds had turned into a merciless war, she and her mother had abandoned the horrid place to look for refuge. In the conflicts, her father and three brothers had perished. In time they had tried building a normal life, if that could be possible after such a loss. The peacefulness in the eventless, quiet Sallncoln, aided their cause and soon allowed them to settle. Elmira and I became friends rapidly. So had Elmira's mother and my grandmother. We were often together and did most things in each other's company. I taught her how to fish and she soon became better than me, more patient. We often went gathering fruit near the edge of the forests, where we were allowed to venture alone, and helped each other with various hard chores that either my grandmother or her mother imposed on us. We shared a common passion for books, a rare and luxurious custom in our village where most weren't capable of reading or writing. Thanks to Inga, the broom and basket maker, who had travelled to many places, there were only few tomes in our village, and she entrusted me and Elmira to become the privileged guardians of them all. We read their heroic quests until we knew them by heart, often pretending to be the champions and queens of the tales recounted. We understood each other like nobody else did.

If initially the other children mocked us for our peculiar friendship, in time they became envious because of it. Elmira grew into the most beautiful girl in Sallncoln; her origins gifted her the brightest red hair, a rare sight in our village. The fiery hair contrasted to perfection her striking, blue eyes, making me fall for her like a rotten pear off a tree branch. Our childhood friendship instinctively and harshly transitioned into something else, something bigger than us and we understood we wanted to be together, forever. Such was our infatuation that earlier in the spring we promised our love and swore that we'd get married when the time was right. To seal my words and prove my love, I gave her a precious possession from my unknown mother; an iron ring. There was no value to it except for what it meant to me; the one thing that could possibly remind me of her, and I was happy to give it to Elmira.

Our infatuation and persistence, and perhaps our teenaged stupidity, managed to convince our family members of our serious intent. My brothers were actually even more surprised than the rest of the villagers, not ever thinking of me as being 'such a charmer', to put it in Keno's words. That only encouraged us to anxiously start planning our future.

As if pulled out of a day-dream, I found myself at the edge of the village. Nana was not crying anymore and appeared more resolute. The loud ringing of the bell had stopped as well. A flagging wave of heat and smoke welcomed us, accompanied by shrieking flames that ate at the buildings.

Many people were fighting the fire. Borr, the butcher, was efficiently throwing dirt and sand from a sand pile, previously gathered in front of his house. Others rushed about with buckets of water, while some took wounded people and animals to safety.

It appeared that the fire had started from the centre, where the damage was worse.

"We need to check the house!" I said to my grandmother.

She nodded and we picked up our pace, walking at a safe distance from the flames.

Our agonising walk toward the northern side of the walls, made me wonder if our village had ever before experienced a similar calamity. Nothing came to mind, except a few small fires, some flooding and plenty of cruel raids from the west, though the latter hadn't occurred for centuries and nature's wrath had yet to reveal itself so violently.

I felt the hand of my grandmother strongly pulling at mine. She stood in complete shock, her face fixed to the left, on the ground, where, to my consternation, an extended hand was visible from underneath a beam and other burnt rubble. Fear chilled my burning body for an instant and I felt cold sweat dripping over my back, underneath my shirt. It was a house of someone I knew.

"Dear soul," Nana whispered.

"May he rest in peace," I replied as I coldly pulled her away from the sight.

We took a shortcut that led directly to our cottage; a narrow and dangerous passage.

Had it been completely swallowed by the fire?

Once there, we realised with anger that indeed, our home had been reached by the voracious flames; a portion of our cottage's roof was slowly burning, threatening to collapse. The fire must've spread from the stable, which stood further to the left, and which was almost entirely burned to the ground.

I feared for our beast but there was no time to ponder. Henek and Kuno were already tackling the fire with buckets of water and a blanket.

I ran towards them and climbed the ladder that was already on one of the two giant, rain-water barrels – we kept two barrels for rain-water, that would be otherwise used in the driest days of summer, for our garden and beasts.

Nana reached us and placed herself at the bottom of the ladder. A working chain was soon established, with me on top of the barrel, taking water out and passing it to my grandmother, who passed it to Henek and then to Kuno. He had the arduous task of getting as close as possible to the flames and dousing them with water.

When we were done, the cottage looked like a late autumn tree; skeletal and smouldering on one side, while the other was almost completely intact. It would carry the smoky scent for many days to come, impregnated in the walls, furniture, clothing and every other object inside.

"We need to collapse the stable to make it safe!" Henek suggested.

"Aye," replied Kuno with a cough.

A brief pause, to catch our breath and drink some water, and we were ready.

The unsafe walls collapsed safely to the ground with the

smallest effort. We checked through the wreckage for any dead animals, yet we could find none. There was no mistake that our two goats, one sheep, two pigs and many chickens and ducks had managed to escape unharmed.

"The fence is broken, here," Nana called to us. "Most likely the stubborn pigs raced through the wooden-poles and saved every animal enclosed."

I let out a loud chuckle, which encouraged Henek and Nana to join me; we knew whose task it was to retrieve the fleeing animals.

"Damnable beasts. I shall enjoy your meats when your time comes." Kuno shot his disappointment to the sky, while kicking at the rubble.

The brief pause encouraged us to spend more time in securing the cottage, making sure it was not in danger of falling or igniting again, and once we knew it was safe, and our intact kitchen was locked, Kuno went to find the beasts.

"We should go now towards the market, it seems they've had it worse there," suggested Nana.

"Yes, but first," I started, "I need to go check on Elmira. I'll meet you there."

"Surely you should. Meet us by the market! And be safe!" Henek suggested, hearteningly.

I couldn't have waited for a better opportunity. I couldn't wait at all. The thought that haunted me since the very first scream, made my heart pound harder the closer I approached her house. I feared for everyone I knew. Especially, I feared for Elmira.

Their house was not too far from ours, and it took me only a short time to get there. To my relief the house was completely intact from the angry fire, being one of the closest to the northern edge of the forest. Yet, there was nobody around and the door was shut; the only sign that someone had been there were the wet walls splashed for protection. Their beasts, apparently calm, were gathered around their stable waiting to be fed. Confused and a little less worried, I walked to their closest neighbour, a rope-maker, who told me that he had seen them leave the village and that he would be keeping an eye on their animals. Glad that they were apparently safe from harm, I went to meet Henek and my grandmother by the market.

From what I could see between the rows of damaged and undamaged houses, the surrounding village's walls were still strongly standing, undamaged. They were too far for the fire to reach.

Once I reached the widest streets of the village, I was astonished to see that, among the many burning houses and stalls and huts, the hall was miraculously still standing. With not so much of a threat from a single spark, it even sheltered many of the wounded villagers and some beasts.

The hall was the centre of our village. Together with our market, it was the only place where we had the chance to see everyone from Sallncoln assembled in the same place. It was used for important events such as duels, weddings, conflict meetings, disputes amongst the villagers and battle strategies in case of raids, which luckily ended almost a century ago. It was a big and solid building that extended on two levels, the second floor only being used as a standing arena to watch the gathering from above. That was generally occupied by those that had no say in the matters discussed; their only participation being by cheering and heckling. We never had any major disagreements except regular scuffles amongst the most passionate supporters that generally solved themselves with a pint of ale later the same day and probably forgotten the next.

"A miracle." Nana distracted my astonished inspection as she called from inside the hall where she was aiding other women tend to the wounded.

"Indeed," I replied, "where is Henek? What can I do to help?"

"Near the market, they need help there!"

And that was the case, as the fire was still hungry and fierce on this side of the village. People were franticly running about, some with water buckets, some with wooden poles to fix the structures that risked collapse and some carrying the wounded to safety.

I spotted Henek among the men, shouting orders and helping as best as he could, but I continued ahead. I followed the line of men that formed towards the well and offered to replace the man that was drawing water. He did not let me beg, and I was happy to see him smile, appreciatively.

Chaos still ruled and soon fear and adrenaline gave way to exhaustion. The unbearable heat allowed terror and anger to persist through the heavy smoked-air and nobody knew what had happened or if we were still in danger. Between one bucket and another, some recounted their version and opinions on what had transpired. Yet none appeared to make sense; a fire that big could not have started from the market, an unattended leaves fire-pit or a barn.

The people who initially fled towards the lake, found the courage to return and give a hand. Everyone was fighting the fire. Even the few drunkards of Sallncoln, who were perennially stoned at breakfast, midday and supper, sobered up with cold water and were doing their best to help.

Everyone was doing as much as they could and more, and determination to make everything safe and help everyone gave us courage and lightened our minds from darker thoughts.

What mattered was to extinguish the fire.

Our numbers overwhelmed the strength of the fire and the general panic. We made good progress in a relatively short time. Though, everyone was tired and scared. Many bore heavier signs of their fights against the fire; heavy bruisers, deep cuts, burns, broken fingers, toes and limbs. Those were all marks that would be carried throughout their lives, making sure the day would never be forgotten.

Every fibre of muscle in my shoulders, legs, neck and hands was agonising. If my knee had hurt me during the day, I could not recall. The bruises and blisters on my palms were hurting more than anything else. I even had difficulty unclutching my fingers from the instinctive fist they were tending to form.

The dangerous flames were finally extinguished and there were only the hot embers that needed tending to. It would take us the whole day and probably part of the night to make the village safe from the flames, I reckoned. Though I was glad it was almost over.

"How you faring?" heaving Henek asked, as he joined me for a mug of fresh water.

"I'm well. Nothing hurts too much, everything hurts the

same," I laughed, making him smile as well.

"What happened here? It can't be an accidental fire? Someone must've set it up!" he said.

A depressing sight surrounded us. The thick, dark smoke had cleared and we could see further away, as much as the buildings allowed. Some of the houses were beyond repair and completely gone, few were still standing and many, towards the edge of the forest, had been spared entirely. The unscathed hall stood like a new sculpture among the decayed and burnt buildings around it. It was as if the fire had started from there, but that could not have been possible.

"I have no clue; we should ask the elders. I think I saw Parelh at the hall. Nana's there too." My voice was hoarse due to the smoke I had inhaled.

"It's a good idea," he replied.

Now that the fire was gone, almost everyone was heading toward the hall. Given the circumstances, it was still nice to see children play amongst themselves, between the wounded and the crowd, careless of what ensued. Though, the anger and frustration sculpted on adult faces, was threatening and concerning. Soon there'll be a harsh reckoning; many had lost their homes, their animals, and some had lost members of their families.

Someone was talking at the gathering, making the incomprehensible sea of noises, cease. It was Parelh.

"There will be no reckoning today!" he started. "Nobody knows what happened and nobody is to blame at this time. All we need is for everyone to stay safe for the night and, if in strength, help those that need most help. Secure your homes for the night if you can, and find shelter at your neighbours if you cannot."

His words captured the attention of everyone, just like he always did, and only the laments of the wounded and a few children's cries could be heard against his words.

"The hall and the market stalls that still stand, are for the wounded. Anyone wishing to help through the night, is welcomed to stay here!" he concluded.

There were no arguments and no complaints as the

murmuring slowly lifted itself around the hall and people started moving away.

Henek and I reached our grandmother inside the hall. Those who decided to remain and help for the night, were being given orders and suggestions from the other elders. There would also be two shifts of watchmen and, given the circumstances, I could only agree with their decision. Kuno, who had just reached us, offered to do the first round with Henek, while I decided to stay with Nana.

Before my brothers departed to their assignments, a quick dinner was prepared at the hall, for those that would spend the night there; bread, onions, cheese and salted meat was more than enough to fill up on lost strength.

"Are you okay, Kuno? Your hands are shaking," I asked.

"My hands are fine, only a bit tired." He smiled with a half-full mouth, lifting his left hand in front of his face for closer scrutiny.

The charred-smudged face with his food-swollen cheeks, that had bread coming out of one corner of his mouth, made us all smile quietly. We were glad that none of us had been harmed and even if the dire situation did not allow for it, I felt happy.

"He's tough as a mule this one!" replied Henek chuckling and giving a tug on Kuno's shoulder. "Now up we go, brother, we need to reach the camp." Both got to their feet and started towards the eastern walls.

Me and my grandmother arranged the bed and the chair that was to be ours for the night, and went to assist to tending the wounded.

The seriously wounded and the unlucky souls that had perished during the day had been moved inside a building neighbouring the market. Besides them, everyone else was being brought to the hall. It was big enough for us to fit in, comfortably separated from each other; a few beds had been brought from nearby houses or salvaged from the flames, and there were plenty of chairs and blankets on the floor.

Our task included tending light wounds; burns, cuts, bruises and some broken limbs. Most of the people treated were serene and glad to be alive, given the circumstance, and only one screamed with horrible pain, when his leg had to be amputated. Witnessing the entire procedure, with the corner of my eye, made my skin itch and my forehead sweat tensely.

After assisting those in more pressing need, we took on feeding those that had minor injuries. It took a while to walk around the erratically arranged bunk beds and finish our rounds, but in the end, we managed well and the place finally fell quieter. Everyone had had their dinner and been tended to, and by the time we finished most of them were already asleep.

It took us more than three, long hours and I felt exhausted and in desperate need of fresh air.

Even as I started contemplating the idea of laying my aching spine flat on a bed, an itch formed in the back of my mind, carrying me unwillingly outside the hall. I took advantage of the air, which filled my lungs with stinging freshness, and learned that the itch was not related to my body's need for air. It definitely felt invigorating, though my legs kept carrying me through a dark alley downhill, and I only understood what it was about when it was too late; I found myself inside the room where the heavily-wounded and the dead were being kept overnight. I froze before I could take another step, neither inside nor out. The fresh air of the night vaporised, leaving in its stead a warm stench of medication, urine, blood and candles; the reek of death.

I was compelled to fill my lungs with the stench, for my mind would not let my body escape the horrid vision; the dead bodies of people I knew, lying on the floor, most of whom were not even entirely covered from sight.

Horror engulfed me, making my body prevent me from taking in any air when I spotted Eadric's body amongst those that awaited their final bath before their departure from this world. The sight of the *tyrant* that had tormented my childhood with his many pranks and mockeries caused by my defect, had an instant effect on my heart and mind. My heart started beating fast and unsteadily while my mind forced me to relive moments of our times together. Unpredictably and surprisingly, it was not the unpleasant reminiscence I had experienced; I did not see any of his bad behaviour and I did not hear his angry voice shouting at me without provocation. All I could see was another child that wanted to play and have everyone's attention. My sight blurred and I felt cold drops trickle down my cheeks. I gulped nervously and all I wished for was to run. Though before I could even turn, two hands grabbed me strongly by my shoulders.

"What in heaven's name are you doing here, Lorian?" Fiera, the fisherman's wife, whispered angrily at me, her round face with those dark, small eyes failing to make of her a frightening sight.

"I..." the tears started falling faster on my face and they couldn't stop.

She hugged me with her chubby hands and pulled me to her wide chest.

"You shouldn't have come here, lad!" She whispered as she stroked my hair, clearly displeased that I had to witness such a sight.

I held her tightly, thinking it was that, perhaps, what a mother's hug would feel like. Only when I had no more tears to cry, did I remove myself from her embrace. No words had been needed, none that we could have voiced and instead we had looked in each other's eyes before I ran back towards the hall.

Inside, everything was calmer, quieter and felt more optimistic, if that was possible. Nana and a few other women talked quietly, seemingly grateful of how the day had ended, given everything that had happened.

When she joined me, we retired to our assigned beds and lay down; the best thing that had happened to me for the entire day. *Finally, resting. Finally, silence.*

No more screams and shouts or babies crying or playing. My eyes felt heavy and the blanket was awfully comfortable and warm. It had taken me a sigh to fall asleep though it felt like a minute afterwards that I bounced up when a hand touched me.

"You did a good job today, cripple," said Kuno, who arrived with Henek from their guarding round.

I had no idea if minutes or hours had passed and before I decided to strike back, I realised what he had said. He actually praised me, something that had only occurred twice from his side during my lifetime. I knew he meant it well; his kind words were rare but honest, his offensive ones were ample and meaningless.

I smiled aimlessly in the candle-lit space and acknowledged the one positive fact about the whole day; a compliment from one of my brothers. Happy about myself I chose to let my gripe pass and slur a 'thank you' instead. It would've been far too easy to get him back; he was already asleep on the double blanket he had chosen for a bed.

My grandmother was on a chair by the bedside, apparently not able to asleep.

She was softly muttering some indistinct words, almost like a song when I took her hand, "Are you alright, Nana? You have been awfully quiet. What's the matter?"

She stopped humming and took a slow breath. She then unfolded the blanket from her shoulders, and abandoned the chair she had preferred, to come and sit closer to me on the bedside. With a swift gesture, she covered our backs with the blanket in what appeared to be more a gesture of preventing the others from hearing us rather than keeping us warm from the chill of the night.

She grabbed both of my hands in hers and said, "I know where the fire came from!"

CHAPTER III

WINTERHORN

Lorian

"A long, long time ago, when my parents were still alive," my grandmother started with a soft whisper.

I was always enthralled when her stories started with passion and intensity, even more so now, as her tearful eyes were gleaming with a touch of sadness.

"They often took me and my sisters to Naghnatë, the village's healer. She was very good with plants and herbs and she was also a very entertaining storyteller, which was the reason why kids often gathered around her house in the hope they could be entertained or shown a trick. But everything about her indicated she was a witch – much later I came to learn that. The way she looked, dressed, behaved and talked; the foul smells inside her hut emanating from odd looking jars and pots containing curious-looking creatures. All seemed to indicate she came from a different time, foreign to our own. One evening, during the spring celebrations, she gathered all of the villagers around the big fire and told us the story of the Drakhahouls and the tokens of benevolence, a story of magic and dragons, which in that cold night frightened even the bravest of men. That's the only time she told us where she came from and that she was three hundred and seven years old." Nana smiled.

"Three-hundred-and-seven years old?" I exclaimed in a daft whisper. "You haven't told me this story before, Nana."

"Well, according to her this is not just a story. Dragons did exist and still do to this day. I've never seen one of them, yet I don't see any reason not to think that other creatures might have walked the earth than those we know. And yes, I'm certain she was of an unnaturally-long age, I saw her."

"How –"

"And stop pestering me and let me get to the point before I forget it!" she snapped at me.

"So, where was I? Oh yes! Naghnatë recounted she came from a faraway place called Arkhanthï, a very difficult place to reach and be granted access to. In that period of time, men and animals lived a very different life than we know it; they were not master and servant, so she said. They were all equal and, to everyone's surprise, king of all the land was not a man, but a Drakhahoul; a mighty dragon, whose name was Yrsidir-Two-Tails. He was so big that when he spread his wings the whole Arkhanthï castle was covered in shadow. Nobody dared to challenge him and nobody had reason to, because the dragon was a strong and fair ruler, of the purest and noblest heart." Nana paused briefly.

I followed attentively, her story was different to the ones she normally recounted.

"For many, many years the city thrived and flourished and everyone lived happily, though the king's powers were fading with age. So he approached his advisor, a wise and powerful elder wizard, Felduror, to whom Naghnatë was a student herself in the arts of magic. Now, the dragon, according to the witch, asked the wizard for advice on what to do to keep peace and harmony in his realm. Felduror was a cunning serpent, dreaming of being king over the beasts and humans himself. He had once considered animals to be inferior to the human race, let alone to enlightened minds such as his. So he suggested that the king not only gave his blessing to the new successor, but he'd also have to aid his reigning years by sharing some of his own powers to whoever he considered fit to entrust with such a gift. Obviously being the king's advisor, Felduror, the wizard, hoped that the dragon would choose him. Fortuitously, that was not the case, for Yrsidir-Two-Tails had decided to give one of his talons to another dragon, Belrug-the-Black, a younger and auspicious Drakhahoul." Nana stopped with a querying face.

"What?" I asked.

"Do you remember what the tokens are? I know you've read about them. You and Elmira never stopped talking about them," Nana asked.

"Of course I do," I started, "some called them dragon stones, some called them tokens and some called them artefacts. Whatever their name, they are the same thing. They are part of a mighty creature's body, willingly offered towards creating a powerful stone or artefact. The parts can be as small as tears or blood drops and as big as claws, scales, fangs or even whole fingers and they will be encased within a common object and instilled with some of the powers of their owners."

A noise from outside made my grandmother stop and look around alerted. Once she was sure there were no prying ears she continued.

"Good," she said with a smile. "To the new possessor they'd be of great help and importance and throughout history, the witch said, there have been only a handful of times that this happened. So, the dragon king had chosen a younger dragon to rule and take his place, while he would retire in solitude for his remaining days. But he did so after having fulfilled his promise. From his talon, a master dwarf-smith crafted the Blight-Stone, which the young dragon wished to encase in ember and place at the centre of his wonderful chest plate."

"Whoa," the soft exclamation left my mouth against my will.

Nana smiled briefly and checked the surroundings once more.

"At this part of the story the witch was angry and stern with her words, I recall it very well," Nana continued. "She said that the magnanimous king hadn't considered that the young dragon's mind could be easily corrupted by the adverse influence of Felduror, the wizard. So, he departed for unknown places never to be seen again while Belrug, the young black-dragon, became king over Arkhanthï's territories. The astute wizard had been ready for such an event and didn't have to wait long to initiate his evil plan. He used all his powers in preparing an unusual concoction that was served in low measures to the new king. This special potion was not aimed in killing the dragon, only in weakening his mind, confounding and clouding his judgment. Although physically he was still strong, his mind was not. Thinking he was ill and dying, the new king summoned the wizard for help. Alas, this only made it easier for the wizard to fully insinuate himself inside the mind of the helpless young dragon, binding his mind to his own will. Weak and defenceless Belrug-the-Black soon became a puppet in the powerful wizard's hands. Or so the witch believed." Nana broke off her story.

From the hall's entrance, which stood opposite our bed, I could clearly see sharp shadows being cast on the muddy ground by the full white moon, seated above our village like a restless guardian. Glistening ruts marked the streets like scars on a battlefield while steaming embers continued to release the heat trapped within. The screams, the agony and the crackling of the fire heard throughout the day, were now a tiny persistent noise in my ears that refused to go away no matter how hard I tried to yawn. Although it had been a long and exhausting day I did not want to sleep, not until I heard the end of the story.

My grandmother drank some water then continued.

"Belrug-the-Black had grown weaker and the cunning wizard had finally put his hands on the Blight-Stone. With it, he became unstoppable; he became Belrug himself. His mind was of his own but his body was that of the mighty black dragon, the king. To the eyes of the Aranthians, the king had been miraculously cured. In truth, the king was fading, trapped inside the wizard's mind. Felduror, in the body of Belrug-the-Black, convinced everyone that the king, had been poisoned by an evil force using these powerful artefacts forged across millennia, dragon stones that needed to be retrieved and brought to him to be destroyed. He then declared that anyone who opposed him would be considered an enemy of Arkhanthï and therefore tried for high treason. Almost everyone was thankful that the king recovered so they naively accepted his words, unsuspecting of the wizard's plans. Only a dozen loyal servants reluctantly consented, secretly determined to understand what was really going on. They were the most loyal followers of the former king, Yrsidir-Two-Tails, and together they formed the Drakonil Order." Nana tilted her head and moved closer to me. "And who do you think was part of that order?"

"Naghnatë!" I said.

"That's exactly what she said, that she had been there from the very beginning. She had been one of the wizard's acolytes, and very soon found out that his heart was not pure and so, she slowly stepped away from his apprenticeship. She also said that, of the many dragons that roamed around the northern lands, very few remained at the citadel, but many more decided to run away from the wrath of the mad wizard. Those, she considered, were the ones that knew what really happened, and still cowered away, not wanting to have anything to do with his evil plan. Similarly, the dwarves have been the second to take their leave, suspicious about the wizard's corrupted nature. They retreated inside Mount Nrom, the Mountain of Iron. To Felduror none of this mattered, the futile threats of the hiding dwarfs or the absconding dragons were not a real hazard to his plan. All he wanted was to find the powerful and precious stones and be unrestricted in his scheme."

"And what has today's fire to do with all this, Nana?"

"Patience, I'm getting there," she replied.

"The witch told us that the first token of benevolence the wizard had found afterwards, was the Lux or the Stone of Light, a powerful dragon stone made hundreds if not thousands of years ago. Many believe it to be one of the very first to be created and that it contains the last teardrops of a dragoness called Irridae-the-Brave. A dragoness who suffered a deadly wound on a battlefield against some wild beasts, and decided to give her tears, imbued with her Drakhahoul powers, as a token of benevolence to the queen of the elves, Loreeia, a beloved friend and faithful fight companion of the dragoness. The elven-queen had the tears placed inside a necklace which she wore wherever she went. And so she did for many years until a similar fire, such as today, fell upon the citadel in the forests of Elmenor. You see, the elves are creatures of strength, with inhuman endurance, and skills, so that day none of them perished during the fire. Only, Loreeia inexplicably lost her token. Naturally, everyone had their suspicions that the fire was the wizard's doing, but the elven-queen did not want to break the peace that at the time ruled amongst the realms. According to Naghnatë, the Lux made the wizard even more powerful; where any other light failed, the Lux succeeded, and so he ventured beyond the darkness, into the depths of the Earth, and summoned to his service the faithful Gholaks, which as you know…" Nana trailed off, seemingly waiting for me to confirm it.

"They are the uglier, taller and stronger variety of the common orcs," I added with certainty, replicating the words she preferred using in her recounts.

"Exactly so." Nana smiled and all of a sudden, her face became firmer. "The witch's story conveyed, that during the ill-fated day a great fire had descended upon Elmenor, the elven city where the elven-queen was residing. You see, Lorian? Fire descending from the clear sky just like it happened to us today, here in Sallncoln!" My grandmother's breathing appeared heavier than before.

She clenched the mug at her side before draining all the water from it.

"The witch understood that in order to find the artefacts, Felduror had to use the power of the Drakhahouls, who were able to scout and unearth the precious stones. They had a special power to sense the tokens and when they found one, they would spit flames from the skies to reveal and isolate the place. Of course, being forged through magic, they could not be destroyed by dragon fire nor by any other fire or metal for that matter, though they could be revealed from where they were hidden. Only magic, the witch said, could undo what has been done through magic!"

I sat silently bemused; I saw the damage the inexplicable fire had done, but I couldn't believe that such a dragon stone was hidden in our village. Who on Earth had ever lived here and was powerful enough to own an artefact? And what kind of a token was it? I had so many questions I was eager to find an answer to.

"The witch ended her story saying that nobody to that day knew how many artefacts the wizard had found, nor what kind of powers they held. She said that the entire world would have to suffer and no army would become powerful enough to stand in the wizard's way if everyone ignored the seriousness of these threats."

"Nana, what happened to Naghnatë? Is she still living in your old village?"

"I left that village many years before you were born. I hardly think there's anyone still living up on that cold mountain," she replied.

Her words loitered until a shiver ran down my back and made me jerk and realise how sore and rigid my body was. I yawned and stretched, grasping forlornly, that it was already dawn.

Kuno woke up and curiously asked if we slept at all, shaking his head in confusion when understanding that we hadn't. He went outside the hall shivering in the frigid air, soon followed by Henek.

There were many things that still rang loudly inside my head as grandmother lifted herself and went talking to other women that quietly started to gather inside the hall. I assumed they were assessing how many lives had been lost.

At her return she suggested that we should go home and rest, now that others had come to help.

On our way home, I diverted once more towards Elmira's house which did not make me find anything new; their place was just as it had been before, locked and safe. A clear sign they had left and a promising portent of their well-being, though it still made me wonder where could they have gone.

There was no more smoke puffing from the burnt embers of our cottage, even if the air was still damp and rich with the scent of fire against the cold of the morning. Kuno was already inside the undamaged kitchen trying to fix us breakfast among the pile of things we previously placed inside. The kitchen was situated on the right side of the house, right under the attic room, which was my little room.

Many objects lay on the floor, irregularly placed in a rush after being taken to safety from my brothers' room that sadly suffered the most damage. My grandmother and I were silently contemplating the damage that our cottage had suffered, measuring in time and coin the amount of energy it would take to rebuild. One side of my brothers' room was completely deprived of walls. Yesterday it had seemed only a small portion of the roof to have been damaged, today we comprehended that the main beams were charred and useless, and that embers still fumed in the cold air of the morning. Part of the roof had collapsed and shattered Henek's bed while Kuno's had been miraculously spared by the fallen beam, which prevented the ceiling rubble from causing further damage. The fire hadn't caused too much destruction internally but, alas, there would be plenty of work to do in order to restore the room completely.

Henek reached us not too long after, Firebreath pacing at his side, happy to be in our company again.

The four of us had Kuno's breakfast with tea, bread, butter and jelly, eggs and cheese. We silently enjoyed each other's company, grateful that none of us had been harmed. After we finished our breakfast, I helped clean the table, thanked Kuno for the food and climbed in my tiny, smoke-smelling, warm attic-room and fell dead asleep on my beloved bed.

I woke up late afternoon, my aching body feeling wearier than before. My head started spinning as soon as I got up and I had to prop myself against the roof's beam to recover from the flimsy ordeal. There were noises down below, and as I descended the ladder to the kitchen, I saw it had been neatly cleaned. My grandmother was cooking a vegetable soup while my two brothers were quarrelling about what needed to be done to repair the missing walls inside their room, which already was in better condition – they had temporarily fixed the missing walls with wooden boards externally and tanned skins internally.

"Look who's up!" Nana said with the same pleasant voice that used to wake me every morning. "Come give me a hand chopping some herbs, it's almost ready!"

Before I could start helping, I went straight to the water bucket and gulped breathlessly a couple of full mugs of clean and fresh well water. I then splashed my face with the cold liquid.

"What does the rain-water taste like eh?" Kuno said as he propped against the kitchen door, chuckling and inciting Henek behind me.

"Oh, leave him be, Kuno, like you never tasted it before! Now, off you go if you want to eat tonight." Nana hushed them before I could even reply.

I had forgotten that the fresh well water had been used against the flames.

Wordlessly, I started helping Nana, a little embarrassed that I did not recognise the raw taste of rain water in my hasty yearning to satiate my thirst. Though it didn't take long before Henek came asking for a hand to move the big, fallen beam.

The heavy piece was not broken, and with a pulley, and a lot of effort, we managed to connect and fix the standing walls. From there, adding smaller braces, spread sideways across the ceiling, would be an easier task to add stability to the house. What mattered was that at day's end, their room would be sorted for the night against the rain and wind.

My blistered hands held well enough but not without opening and burning my skin, reminding me to apply some ointment to help them heal. I went rummaging amongst my grandmother's balms and picked what I knew would help ameliorate my burning hands; knitbone and mint. The sharp smell reminded me of the many times grandmother had forcefully delivered it to me, for those bruises and cuts I procured as a child. Once past the burning sensation, I wrapped some gauze made of clean cloth and went back to the kitchen, where everyone was gathered around the table.

The vegetable soup was surprisingly cleansing for body and soul, probably the weight of the past day's events made a simple stew seem something out of the ordinary.

Once finished, my brothers went straight to bed, strained by the long hours of guarding and the efforts put into fixing their room. Since I had rested during the late morning and into the afternoon, I happily took on the cleaning of the kitchen and feeding the beasts which had been gathered for the night in their temporarily-fixed pen – Nana told me that Kuno had done a very fine job retrieving and bringing them back to safety, losing nothing but his patience.

On my return, Nana was still busy cleaning. There was something unnerving about the way she moved and I strongly doubted she had slept at all. Every time she was worried and concerned about something, she behaved just as she was behaving now.

She approached the stove and picked up the big pot of boiling water. As always, she needed her favourite tea to help her rest. The strong mint, linden and camomile scent imbued the air of the entire kitchen.

"Come sit with me for a while, Lorian!" she said.

She poured tea in two mugs and went by the fireplace where, from the pile of firewood, she took something wrapped in a ragged cloth. I attentively followed her slow moves while blowing on the steaming brew. The faint lights springing from the candles and the stove were not enough to make out the shape of the wrapped object.

I grew ever more impatient.

"This belonged to your grandfather." She sat close to me, grabbing the wool blanket that was used as a bolster on the table's bench.

"What is it?" I whispered, my eyes fixed on the wrapped object, though she had already disclosed what the ragged cloth protected inside.

A beautiful, old knife that had a stag's horn as a handle. One I didn't know she had. She held it in her hands and I could hear the voice trembling with emotion.

"This is Winterhorn!" She handed it to me.

It was an object of fine workmanship. Surprisingly heavy for its size, not bigger than both my palms put together head to head. The tattered horn had been smoothed by the haft to allow the hand a comfortable grip while the butt evolved in two small antlers, still dangerously sharp. The tip of the blade curved slightly upwards and the spine was thicker than a normal blade. I softly moved the tips of my fingers to feel the blade and instantly regretted my decision; the sharp metal snipped the rough skin on my finger's tip.

"It's still sharp!" Nana exclaimed with a giggle.

I pressed my finger on the ragged cloth to stop the bleeding from the little cut, but a drop had already dribbled on the shiny blade. I grabbed the corner of the cloth and wiped the blade clean only to reveal that the blood had crept into a small marking of some sort; a tiny symbol that looked like a snail shell.

"What's this, Nana?" I said pointing my finger at the symbol.

"I don't know!" she replied pulling the knife closer. "I've never seen it before. I wonder how I could have missed it? You know this is not just a simple knife," she put her warm hand on my shoulder, "it may look like one, yet it is not. Although I never actually believed it, I thought it was all a contrivance by your grandfather, and only too late it all started to make more sense!"

I was always lulled by her sweet words of my grandfather. It always seemed as if he were a different type of man, one seldom seen nowadays.

"This was his favourite hunting knife. He carried it with him wherever he went. I remember the day he had it made, like it was yesterday." Nana appeared happy and serene as a vision of my grandfather filled her mind and soul. "At that time, we were living in Velkeri and were secluded from this unknown-side of the world by the dangerous peaks of Mount Velka. Winters there were never easy as we were quite high compared to the mountains you can see around Rontra. During one of our last winters there, the cold was so sharp it could bite at hard rock and leave a mark. The winds froze everything in their path and we barely survived." As if struck by a shiver, Nana jerked a little.

She hunched and cupped the mug of tea and took a long sip. I replicated her gesture.

"To this day I have still to live a winter as cold as that one. The bitter wind howled and veered as a rabid beast for endless days at a time, like a presage of the doom we were about to endure. The snow was packed almost as high as the houses' roofs making it impossible to move around. Often, weak huts collapsed under the weight of weeks' snow and cleaning them was an arduous task. We had to dig tunnels in the snow between the houses and the forest where we went for firewood. We had been trapped for many weeks by the cold weather and were dangerously low on provisions. Our livestock had been consumed already or had been claimed by the cold snap and we were surviving on wheat, spices, and bad fruit. So Dhereki, your grandfather, after much convincing and commanding, gathered a handful of other strong men in the village and decided to go hunting even though they knew there were no odds of finding anything alive. Yet, they had to try." She sighed intensely.

I was silently imagining my grandfather, another bit of information about him I did not have before.

"It took them four days to return. I continuously cried for two, thinking him to be dead, a victim of that wretched winter. Luckily on the fourth evening they returned and, not only that, they brought back a beautiful, sturdy stag big enough to feed us all for weeks. What first were tears of sadness became tears of joy." Nana started weeping again.

I placed my hand over her shoulder and she smiled at me through her tears.

"Oh, how your grandfather was praised that night, and for days to come! For he had not only found and killed the stag with his spear, but he had managed to convince the others to continue after almost giving up hope on their third day. The waiting agony and hunger was over and we finally had meat to regain our long-lost strength. We stayed up all night sorting and preparing the meat in rations for the weeks to come. And here is where I wanted to get to, my dear." She took time to refill her lungs as well as lift her spirit.

"That night, your grandfather told me that the stag came to him, and spoke to him. A most unsettling confession. At first, I thought he had suffered some unseen injuries due to the cold, and I didn't know how to react. So, I stood there listening to him, not daring to believe his babbling. He said he felt ashamed and dishonoured that he didn't fight for his prey, though he was happy nonetheless that it had happened. He insisted on telling me that the stag had taken control of his thoughts, and had directed him to where it was hidden. Guided by strange emotions and thoughts that weren't his, your grandfather had been told that the beast was dying and it would willingly give his skin, flesh and blood for saving the lives of others. The only thing it asked of him in return was that your grandfather should keep part of his horns as a testimony to its thoughtfulness. That it would do him and his family nothing but good if he accepted the token and he would only gain by such a gift.

"After that night, the days started to get warmer, the wind was softer and quieter. We could even hear birds chirping in the forest, leaving their winter nests for small insects that slowly started to appear along with the first buds. We never hoped to have an early spring that year; not after that sort of winter. During those days your grandfather fashioned himself this knife, with the help of the smith. He said it gave him a sort of single-minded feeling and a power of concentration that he had never felt before. His skills improved considerably. There was no game that he could not hunt alone. His strength had doubled or tripled and he never tired. Imagine that! He was able to swim across the Basak Lake from one side to the other." Her voice was filled with pride.

"Across the lake with no boats to aid him?" I was astonished, thinking of the imposing size of Basak Lake.

Even on a clear day one could barely see the other side and few people had ever dared venturing in those marshy-green and perpetually-cold waters – often claimed to shelter long snake-shaped fish, as few of the fishermen in the village stated.

"He had even taken down a giant black bear whilst on a deer stalking spree, and not with a single scar. I say! A giant full-grown black bear, single handedly?" The glimmering in Nana's eyes displayed brief bouts of happiness, though soon, too soon, sadness returned.

"It must've taken some serious blindness on my part not to believe there was something about this knife. Something way beyond our imagination. I've been a fool to doubt it all along. I was young and I believed magic did not exist. I only thought that he found all that energy from being able to provide for the whole village in time of need, when nobody else could."

"Oh, Nana," I offered and she smiled weakly at me and patted my hands.

"He later told me that the same dream disturbed his nights for weeks at a time." Nana's eyes were wet again. "He'd see the stag, just like that time in the frozen forest, yet it was not wounded and dying anymore; it stood in its full strength taller than before. It wanted to know if its token was being kept safe and that it was very important not to let anyone know about it, lest they try and steal it. It was his and his alone, only to be given away to someone he completely trusted, if ever such a time should arrive. And I think, that time has come."

Her crying was pure regret as she moved her hands without purpose over the heavy knife. This wasn't like the other times she had told me or my brothers about the grandfather we had never met. There were times when she recounted stories of great deeds but never revealed too much. And on all those many occasions she hadn't felt so sad and alone.

Unable to think of something that might cheer her up, I shifted my attention to the blanket that slowly started slipping from our backs. I raised it up and put it on her shoulders. She appeared to recover and wiped her tears.

"Before he died, he said to me something that only too late I've come to comprehend. He said, that in the grimmest of moments, I should give this to the most needing of our children, or our grandchildren, 'if we'll ever be blessed with any', to put it in his own words." She chuckled bitterly. "He mentioned it was of vital importance to understand its powers, and if in doubt, that I should help the one to find the right path to the truth. He specifically mentioned Naghnatë, the witch in our village, and only now I come to understand that this indeed is not an item of common knowledge. His words stayed with me ever since, and their meaning was never clear, not until last night." She took a deep breath and reached towards the mug that she emptied in a single quaff.

"I wish I had known him, Nana!" I confessed, trying to envision what it would have felt like to be taught by him.

"You would've liked him very much, and he would've liked you, too! Alas, he died before you were born. I've always thought that Henek might need this knife the most, because you know Kuno; he has always been a strong and tough lad, healthier than most."

"And luckier I might say," I added, thinking how fate always seemed to favour him amogst us all.

Nana laughed. "Very true. Yet, when you arrived to this world everything changed." She sighed, patting gently my left knee. "You were the tiniest little thing when you were born. Always writhed with that bad leg of yours, but don't be mistaken, son, I feel no pity for you because of that! I know you can achieve great things, nevertheless. A bad leg is not the same as a bad head."

"I know, I know," I assured her, knowing what sort of speech that would lead to.

"So I want you to have it! I know that you alone can understand its meanings, you've always been as sharp as a tack and have pestered me with endless questions." She smiled and handed me the knife. "Here, take it!"

"Thank you, Nana!" I said, and grabbed the knife from her hands with improved curiosity.

Although it was hard to believe what Nana said, the knife felt oddly lighter than before. My fingers started tickling with a curious perception that moved hastily across my whole arms reaching the top of my head. I scratched the itching sensation out of my hair and smiled. The cold, grey blade seemed to glow softly with a blue tint and I blamed my watery eyes and the lack of natural light.

Could it be true? Could grandfather had come to know magic, just like the stories Elmira and I kept dear at heart? And mostly, could this dagger have anything to do with the fire?

"Do you think Naghnatë is still alive?" I asked, keeping my eyes on the sharp blade.

"I could not tell. Last time I saw her was in Velkeri, when I was little older than you," she replied, seemingly confused by her thoughts. "Now that I think about it, there might be someone that might know more."

"Who?" I asked.

Nana let out a giggle. "His name is Alaric, a very passionate and peculiar man. Curious how my old mind works these days…" her voice trailed off before continuing. "Some years ago, I can't recall how many, I had the pleasure of making his acquaintance. He was very determined to find her too, for his 'own reasons' he told the people at the market. By mere luck someone sent him my way when he enquired, and I only told him that I met her when I was very young, nothing more. But he insisted that, if ever anything changed, to be kind enough and let him know. He also promised very generous recompense. I wonder how the poor fellow is doing these days. You could go and meet him, if he's still alive!" Nana suggested.

"Where should I go? Is it far?" I asked.

Somehow, the idea of leaving home at such short notice was scarier than the dragon tales I just heard.

"He told me I'd find him deep inside Ilka's Covert, by the streams on the hills."

"That's at least two-days' travel east. And given my leg, might take me even longer," I complained.

"Yes, at least," she replied with a smirk on her face, "yet on horseback, I think that it can be less than a day."

"Really, Nana? Can I?" I jumped from my seat, almost knocking the two mugs to the ground.

The excitement of riding Firebreath made me restless and impatient for dawn to come. In that instant I decided that the experience was worth the trouble, even if it proved to be a mere there-and-back journey.

Firebreath was the most precious of our possessions; a long-haired, black, Myrthen steed, one of the strongest and tallest horses in our valley. And also, one of the most expensive; he had cost Nana and my two brothers months of their income. And he was totally worth it. Many had come asking with mare-mating offers and we had light-heartedly declined each one of them. We had plans on getting a new mare, but had never found the proper match, and after the latest events I was doubtful we could afford one.

I was never allowed to ride him, of course. I only had the privilege of cleaning, feeding and taking him in or out of the barn and, on rare occasions, I was allowed to exercise him in the yard. Obviously, that was not what I had done whenever I was left alone with him, and I was sure my grandmother had her suspicions about the few occasions I rode him on the hills of Rontra and upstream of the Sir'hio River, pretending I had only taken him to graze fresher grass along the river.

Excitement distracted me from what Nana was saying. I had

to shake my head to concentrate.

"Of course you can," she assured me, "and I'll make sure your brothers don't argue."

I could not wait for dawn to come; I was about to ride Firebreath again.

CHAPTER IV

THE OLD MAN

Lorian

An entire day had come to an end and I was still walking astray. The dense brushwood within the forest forced me to pace alongside Firebreath as, with dread, I realised we were lost.

After having ridden across the valley and followed the Sir'hio downstream, I found myself in an unknown woodland of taller trees and denser undergrowth. The only guidance I had was a faint sound of flowing waters, foaming over the rocky bed somewhere to my right.

Noisy birds accompanied my every move, hiding in their dry nests above my head and I was content to have the forest's shelter from the rain. The summer's end has been suddenly announced by the arrival of the autumn rains, way earlier than the previous year. My journey couldn't have been planned for a worse time. Although the shower had not been too rough, it proved quite persistent, and I had been cold for the entire day.

The sensation of walking on dry, dead leaves and needles was pleasant and reassuring, even if the light underneath the canopy was dangerously reduced. Fortunately, I finally got an opportunity to light a fire and warm myself. Its amber light revealed how tattered and torn my boots had become.

"They definitely need some mending," I mumbled to myself wiggling my toes as soon as I'd liberated my sore and cold feet.

The fire's warmth was a welcoming sensation, thumping at my skin through wet clothes. Alas, the soothing sensation only allowed space for another, crueller feeling; hunger. It let itself known with a loud gurgling of my stomach, disturbing the thoughtless Firebreath as he neighed, while gnawing. Maybe I could carry on wet for another day, but I definitely could not ignore the hunger for much longer.

With some agitation, I rummaged once again inside the saddle bags, hoping that something had escaped my previous inspection.

Perhaps a slice of loaf? Dare I say some cheese?

No, nothing, just minuscule crumbs and a couple of ants.

"How did you two get here?" I puffed them outside, flipping the bag in anger.

The dagger that Nana had given me, dropped with a heavy thud between my legs, unfolding halfway from its bundle. I could see its sharp tip sparkling in the fire-light, almost entrancing me to a full stop. I hurried to wrap it again and placed it back into the saddlebag.

A terrible mistake, to take only that little food that I had decided to pack. Still, there was no point in blaming myself for such a poor decision at this point.

There had been a few handfuls of sweet and delicious berries during the second part of the day, which luckily spread around in abundance on this side of the forest. Unfortunately, they hadn't been enough to satisfy a growing appetite for sustenance. I had to eat proper food and I knew exactly what I needed to look for. All I had to do was to reach the tall patch of cedar trees I spotted up ahead, surrounded by a thin area of grey poplars, and there I'd have a good chance of finding some fresh red-pine mushrooms.

"That would be very nice indeed for my little fire, don't you agree?" I said to my horse, imagining how well-received the delights would be for my noisy stomach.

I had to take advantage of the remaining light of day, and

quickly grabbed my boots which I had propped near the fire; they were warm but still wet. Disagreeably accustomed to the disturbing feeling of wetting my dry feet again, I secured the fire, tethered the horse to a pole and went on my pursuit.

A few hundred feet ahead, the forest altered radically. The thicket dwindled considerably, leaving many open spaces where the pine needles coloured the forest bed. There was more light on this side and it looked like the perfect spot to find what I was looking for.

I stopped in the middle of the closest open-patch and tried to accustom my eyes to the change in colour tones. I knew it would take time to spot the precious mushrooms so I closed my eyes and took two long deep breaths, pleased to notice how the scent of the wet pines pervaded the air and overwhelmed the other mild fragrances.

The evening air was warm. The rain had reduced so only a few drops penetrated the thick crowns of the pines, splashing to the ground, each sound muffled by the soft blanket of needles.

There you are!

It didn't take too long to find the scrumptious delights often hidden underneath bonded clusters of needles that required patience to clean and avoid losing too much of the precious, succulent mushroom-meat. Thinking of which, had I been home it would have bothered me a great deal to clean – often having to chop entire portions off the mushroom because of that thick and stuck blanket of dirt and needles that was hard to separate – but not now. Hunger had transformed me into a patient *hunter* and I was determined not to waste anything. Surprisingly, they grew in abundance here and against my recalcitrant stomach I took the time to clean each and every one.

I returned to my dying-fire with a pile of cleaned, fat milk-caps, which I couldn't wait to eat without any spices or salt, in itself a culinary irreverence.

Rekindling a bigger fire proved easy and my cooked-to-perfection dinner was delightful. I could finally take off my boots again and let them dry for a while.

There was no point returning home with no light and I decided to spend the night, sheltered by the same bush until the morning. The thought did not bother me much; it wasn't the first time I had to spend a night outside, especially in summer. Besides, I had my bow and a well-stocked quiver with me, even though I knew there wouldn't be a real need of its deadly arrows. Very few night-predators hunted on our lands, and there were none that could harm a human. The bears had been long extinct and the last pack of wolves had been hunted down and directed miles away many years ago, when they had endangered the herders and the sheep they took grazing for months at a time in the nearby hills.

Thinking about dangerous animals made me ponder at what Nana had said. My grandfather had been able to take a black-bear down. If that was true, he must've had magical help of some sort. There could be no other explanation as those were terrifying, giant beasts, that used to be hunted in parties of dozens of people. Borr, the butcher in Sallncoln, still kept the head of one he had acquired from some travellers, framed above his counter inside his store. The attraction of very few people in our village, the nightmare of most. Its wide-opened maw was big enough to put my head inside, and still move it freely about. I could barely embrace it entirely from ear to ear.

Almost without realising it, my hands reached for the cloth that covered the odd-shaped weapon, and started to unfold it. I did not desist. It was mine, yet I still had to understand its meaning, or use it. Even if it felt enjoyable in my hand, my mind was reluctant to share the same pleasant feeling. It filled me with the same sense of weakness and inquiry instead. Did the fire have anything to do with my grandfather's knife?

I passed my finger along the gleaming blade and, as if in response to my motion, it appeared to spark brighter for a moment. The same tickling sensation lifted itself from the tip of my finger to my wrist, and then quickly up, over my forearm and shoulder to end over my head. I smiled aimlessly as the itching sensation trailed over my arm's hair.

Though the brief moment of concord vanished with haste and no anticipation; my mind shifted me wildly back to the moment of the fire in Sallncoln. Raw, disturbing memories flashed across my body making my skin crawl with hundreds of imaginary spider bites. I recalled people's screams and the boisterous noises of the scorching fire, loudly biting at metal, wood and flesh.

I jumped to my feet, fighting the impulse of covering my ears with my hands. While circling barefoot the small bush that would be my shelter for the night, I remembered every face of those I saw lay naked and dead at the market's stalls. With horror I comprehended I might not make it back to Sallncoln for the last goodbye, as their funeral would take place in the morning. The realisation bothered me a great deal.

"That dreadful fire!" I heard myself weep.

Yet, like a veiled hit, accused long after it had happened, a second pang hit at my stomach with reinvigorated vehemence; Elmira.

I dropped the knife on the ground, failing to contain the wretchedness that slowly took control of me.

On my third attempt on finding them, right before departing, I've learned from their neighbours the same thing that Nana and my brothers had supposed; that they must have probably returned to their village. But it did not make any sense to me, there was no reasonable explanation why Elmira and her mother would return to the place that had taken so much from them. And I strongly doubted that Elmira would have done so without first telling me. Something else had happened, of that I was certain, and it must have been about the fire.

The consideration made me more resolute to understand what it all meant and if, indeed, it had anything to do with that Naghnatë witch.

After a dozen more circles around the same shrub, I finally recovered the knife and sat down by the fire. My knee was hurting, a good distraction and a reminder to properly rest, if in the morning I wanted to look for the old man.

Loud chirpings delivered me to a nippy dawn after a rough night. I yawned widely and lengthily, considering how lucky I was that the fire had died after my clothes had managed to dry to a decent state and there had been no more rain during the night. I did not feel soggy anymore.

"Slept well, my friend?" I brushed Firebreath's long mane, content to see him dry, rested and still nibbling, "Do you ever stop eating?" I chuckled and untethered him.

With determination, I gathered my belongings and continued my journey.

The intermittent sun soon started to cast bright rays, making the dawn unthreatened by imminent rain. The clouds were moving fast and were light enough to dissolve in the ray's beam; spending another day in the rain was something that could've seriously risked my resolve.

I crossed the wide patch of pines, where I had collected my dinner the previous night, and not long after, I reached a fortification of brushwood. A long barrier of thick, living bramble and undergrowth was blocking my way to either side. It was unnaturally congregated as if to make a growing wall, denser still than the thicket at the forest's edge. It was so dense that I feared I'd have to continue without the horse, and dreaded I'd have to circle it and waste more time. The positive thing was that I could the hear rushing waters louder than before. A reassuring sound, I was getting closer. There was no mistake, the place was the Ilka's Covert, a place I had never visited before, yet often heard of its unusually tall trees and the multitude of sweet rivulets that fed into the main river, the Irhe.

I picked a sturdy twig to help me cleave myself a path through the plants but even with my hardest blows, it was impossible to penetrate.

"Aaarrggg!" I yelled my frustration and launched the useless rod to one side with what was left of my violence.

Two long intakes of air and I calmed myself, briefly considering the sole solution at hand; I'd have to circle it to reach the rushing waters. Though as far as I could see the wall continued with the same distribution and magnificence.

When I turned to pick Firebreath's bridle, a twig snapped behind the thick bramble.

"Who's there?" I promptly asked, hand on the saddlebag that kept knife.

No reply came, even as I became certain of a presence.

"What are you mumbling there, lad?" Unpredictably, a croaky

voice came from behind me.

I turned around to see the face of a small, old man. He was wearing a long robe that reached to the ground and in one hand he had a walking cane, which he gripped tightly. What he lacked in hair over his almost completely bald head, he made up for with his long and properly trimmed grey beard. His slight stooped back did not make him a proper hunchback and nothing of him betrayed his age.

"You almost scared me to death, kind sir," I offered, slowly recovering from my fright.

"As you've very much done to me, young sir!" he retorted, obviously disturbed by my intrusion.

"I didn't know," I tried to argue.

"That I lived here?" he scoffed. "And how could you? Still, I'm most certain that you'd made it your undertaking to take down my fence, had I not come to its rescue."

He looked keen to show his disappointment.

"I apologise, it was not my intention," I stammered, "I didn't know this was a fence, I'm only looking…"

"Bladder, boy! Of course you knew, what else could it be? Have you seen anything of the like before? I very much doubt that."

His serious face and reproaching tone made me very uncomfortable.

Under his scrutinising eyes, I slowly reached for the reins of the horse and tried to find an excuse to leave.

Though, his altered tone surprised me when he continued, "But it is a very fine wall, don't you think?"

His serious grin turned into a wild smile, showing all his remaining teeth.

"Excuse me?" I asked, unsure if he was mocking me.

"Now come on, lad. I was just teasing you, cheer up! Barely anyone comes this way, ever. I thought I'd try and scare you a little."

"I see." I was not sure I had an explanation for the sudden change of temper.

"Now honestly, was I believable? Did I scare you a little?" He craned his head closer to me, carelessly dodging Firebreath's nose and placing one of his thin hands over the horse's forehead.

Miraculously the horse did not even flinch at the touch. I was starting to believe that he was not right in the head and prayed he was not the man I was looking for.

"Of course you did," I said, quickly changing the subject, "Would you happen to know a man named Alaric? I came a long way to find him, and I'm afraid I am lost."

"Isn't this the most fortuitous day? Someone looking for me. How lucky am I?" he snickered, while hopping jubilantly from foot to foot. "Name's Alaric Eamon Beorth; at your disposal, young sir!"

"Lorian Garr." I grabbed the hand he extended and shook it, surprised at the strength he offered.

"Nice making your acquaintance, Lorian! Now, what can old Alaric do for you? Do you require a map, a formula, dare I say, write a love letter?"

"No, none of that. I know how to write and read quite well, thank you very much." My reply came out sharply.

"Oh," he murmured, turning more serious, "then what?"

"I need counsel on an important matter. I've been told that you might be able to help me find someone, an old woman that went by the name of Naghnatë."

His face became blank. The name most certainly was familiar to him, but I could not comprehend why the sombre stare, nor the silence that followed.

"Naghnatë, you say?" His words trailed with a long humming before he continued, "I believe there's no hope for such an endeavour. She doesn't want to be found!" His tone elevated as he almost shouted his disdain.

With imprecision, he started to move, small steps back and forth as if deciding whether he wanted to stay or leave. He pushed his pointy cane into the ground and took out his anger on a smaller twig at his feet. He wasn't content until he had broken the rotten branch in half.

"I believe old Alaric cannot help you much, lad! This may be something for a wiser being," he mumbled and moved away from me.

"But, wait! What do you mean?" I followed him. "I know the

name's familiar to you. Why would you not impart what you know of her?"

"Because…!" His tone was irritated, his pacing faster.

"Because, is not an answer! An educated man such as yourself should know better."

My witty remark made him stop and turn.

Nana had mentioned that the man had struck her as an educated scholar, perhaps a clerk, or at very least a scribe. And that must have been the case since he had offered to help me with a map or a love-letter.

"Boy, trust me when I say this! You do not know what are you meddling with. Turn back and go home before you spend another night in the forest." He started to walk again.

I was baffled, "Did you…"

"Of course I knew you were here. I should know whenever someone intrudes into my forest. It's my home, what did you think?"

"Wait!" I pulled at the horse's reins.

"Go home!" he kept at his diatribe as I reached him.

"I won't go home, I need to know where I can find her and then I'll leave," I insisted.

He did not reply. However, nor did he insist on sending me home. Instead, he followed through the shrubberies and trees with impressive deftness, apparently unbothered by me following him.

To my surprise, he had a lively pace. I was struggling to keep up with him, mainly because of my stubborn horse, but also because of my bad knee.

Being further back gave me the chance to take a better look at him. Soon I realised that what initially had appeared to be a white-grey tunic was now the most detailed robe I had ever seen. The rays cast by the leaves' filtered light made the fine embroidered details twinkle lustrously. There were subtle, golden double-lines, crossing around its base, sleeves and neck. His waist was bound around by a thick leather belt with small pockets all around, some bulging with small things within while others were empty. The belt had odd bumps over its surface, undulating and elegantly flowing around its surface, like the scales of a big lizard's skin. Remarkably, the stick he was holding and aiding his stride with was not the simple rod I initially thought. There were markings all around it, from the very bottom to the very top, which ended in an entanglement of little branches that covered a dark-red stone. In my rushed pacing, I thought the stone was pulsing with light. What a nice rod that was, I marvelled and wondered inquisitively how a defenceless old man could carry such fine things without worry.

Just as I was trying to get closer so I could see the stone, he said without looking at me, "So, what do you want with the witch?" He slowed his pace, though he did not stop.

"There's been a fire in Sallncoln, an inexplicable tragedy which claimed many lives. Some of us have reason to believe it has to do with the tokens."

He stopped and found my stare. "Are you another of those filthy pilfers that thinks he can find a token with my help? Don't lie to me, be honest! I've had enough of you people –"

"No, I am not! I am from Sallncoln and…" with hesitancy I decided it was best to be honest with him, "as a matter of fact, I think I have one of my own."

His intense gaze turned to a muddled one and, by the time I had lifted the bundle and unfolded the knife from my saddlebag, his face was contorted with curiosity.

"Mind if I have a closer look?" he whispered, pointing at Winterhorn.

I extended my hand and, as soon as his spindly fingers touched the handle, his face shifted to complete astonishment, "By all beards, son, it is true what you said. Look at the boundless mark!"

"How do you know it?" I asked.

"Oh, I…" he interrupted himself briefly, "it's a long story."

There was sadness mingled with bright sparks of joy reflected in his eyes. His wrinkled and honest face seemed less happy than before as he moved his fingers over the knife. A sad expression overwhelmed with ease his brief moment of elation.

"These are things that are far more valuable than silver, gold or any other precious metals and stones," he explained. "They go beyond human nature and our ability to comprehend. Objects that can heal wounds, cure diseases, make you stronger, taller or even younger, and also can make you walk faster." A faint smile curved upon his lips as he looked at me.

"Do you know what the boundless mark means?" I ignored his remark.

"Once I thought I did. I saw one many years ago and I thought I'd never see one again before my time arrived," he said with a candid smile. "Where did you get it? Does it have a name?

He must have noticed my hesitation.

"Not to worry, if this is indeed a true token then it's useless in my hands," he said hurriedly.

"It belonged to my grandfather; he named it Winterhorn. Though, as of what it does or if it still does anything, I'm totally unaware."

"This is a very lucky day for me, lad. A lucky day indeed. Here!" He handed it to me with both his hands. "And I would very much like to hear its story and hopefully shed light on some of the questions you might have. However, I do not know where Naghnatë is, and that is the plain truth."

I sighed. He appeared honest to my eyes. If he could not help, then all I could do was return to the village and try to find a better way. Perhaps, the elders knew more and they could point me in a different direction. Curiously, I was reluctant to leave the place just yet. There was something about his words that made me want to know more.

"How does one know when or if a token still has powers?" I decided I'd spend a little more time with him.

"Oh, their powers never fade, only their masters' will and strength to yield them does!"

The revelation ignited my hopes, not that I had actually tried to understand what the knife did, but to me it still felt and looked like a butcher's knife.

"Before you ask anything else, why don't we walk towards my home and you recount me everything you've seen about the fire?"

His invitation to impart whatever he knew was something I could not refuse.

The long walk inside a forested hilltop, soothed my spirits.

After having recounted the events again, I felt uneasy and saddened. I had no desire to relive the vivid and painful memories and, at times, I could still feel the scorching heat brushing against my face. Surprisingly, he said nothing more after I was done. His silence loitered, in tandem with my aching soul.

The sun had lost its early intensity and allowed the clouds to gather and impart a feeble rain. Small drops of water pattered above our heads, though inside the forest, few drops managed to reach us. They were patterning erratically on the surface of the many rivulets' water and on the sodden ground, where the leaves above allowed them to penetrate. I counted at least three little veins of water on our way up; they descended the mountain with haste, trickling their perennial presence with weak sounds.

When I thought there was nowhere else to climb, we turned to the right side and soon after reached an opening on the tip of the peak. It was not a very tall mountain, yet it was quite steep and my knee was starting to feel the strain.

His house was rather narrow and tall, with two floors and odd-looking chimneys with no visible shingles on the brown wooden roof. Its walls had been painted a duck's egg green, which was nothing one would see in Sallncoln, but I did not mind it at all. On the ground, all around the house, there were pumpkins of all sizes, shapes and colours and on almost every single one of them there were candles; some almost melted to the bottom and some longer than my forearm. A tall and wide, old oak tree shadowed the house. It blanketed the ground surrounding it with many leaves that, up here, were already starting to fall.

Near the house there was a small stable where a beautiful black horse and two goats were enjoying some hay. There were some chickens and a pair of geese and everything around the place was clean.

"This place is beautiful!" I exclaimed.

"Thank you kindly! I like living this high. It gets cold most times of the year, but I've plenty of wood. Now, fasten your horse and come round the house, we should eat something. I caught I nice trout last evening, before learning there were intruders on my lands." He chuckled.

I did as bid and then reached him behind the house where everything was made of grey rock, including the table, the long benches to its sides and the fireplace itself. The only bit made out of wood, was a sturdy structure that roofed the table for wet days.

"I could do with a hand on peeling some potatoes," he said.

The sack of potatoes was already near the table, and I took the opportunity to use the knife. Confirming my initial impression, its weight was unmatched; I could move it with tremendous ease, almost like a feather and the agility with which I handled it was far uncommon to my skills. It was as if the knife moved of its own accord, guiding my hand and correcting my actions.

"In they go, lad!" Alaric placed a wide cooking pot on the table and was waiting for me to add the chopped tubers.

The cleaned trout, salted and covered in herbs was garnished to perfection and everything went inside a special aperture to the side of the stone-stove.

Our lunch was ready in a flash; there was bread, cheese, wine for him and water for me, and the fuming trout with the melting potatoes.

"Since the dawn of time," the old man broke the silence, "when Drakhahouls soared the sky and walked the Earth, humans and animals lived a very different life; a peaceful life. There were unspoken rules and hierarchies and men and mighty beasts were equals and rulers of all. Every species would do their part for the benefit and prosperity of the both. Humans would build cities, invent new machineries to aid and alleviate the hard labour that the earth required, cultivate the lands and grow cattle to feed themselves as well as the mighty dragons. The dragons would share their wisdom, knowledge and protection, for there had always been evil forces trying to separate the two. They lived in harmony and thrived beyond imagination. Such was the bond between them that the dragons started to share the most precious of their obscure secrets. And it was in such times that the wisest of the Drakhahouls –"

"Irridae-the-Brave!" I said, convinced of my knowledge.

"He-he!" he chuckled, still chewing on a big chunk of the

trout's tender meat, "Irridae-the-Brave was not even born in that time, lad. This goes further back in time than you can imagine. No, the wisest dragon, as the true-tales recount, was called Algudrin-the-Bold, the bold being given specifically for this cause, because nobody had ever dared to share this much knowledge with humans – which in all honesty are far inferior to Drakhahouls. He was a forest dragon. His scales were of the brightest green, his eyes a burning orange. A strong and fearful creature he was, but he had a weakness; he wanted humans to be as perfect as dragons. Their alliance had always thrived even though there were moments when humans would reach their limitation in comprehension; things that for dragons were plain as day would not make sense to humans and that was because of the impossibility and limits of humankind, to think clearly. At least, that was what the dragon thought, so he decided to impart some of his knowledge to his best human friend Medoris, a master builder. He tried teaching and educating him in any possible way a dragon knew, for as you know dragons were capable of spoken words as well as communicating with their minds. It was as if Medoris were a new-born baby incapable of fully understanding what was said to him. For many years Algudrin tried and persisted in his endeavour and for the same amount of years he failed. But one day a witch came to him – as this was not a secret anymore, Algudrin had consulted many wise dragons and dragonesses and news had spread – and this witch offered to aid his cause. She offered to impart a method where knowledge could be shared from Drakhahouls to humans." Alaric paused to lick his oily fingers in a cacophony of gratifying sounds, unpleasant to my ears.

"I see," I added.

"So she told the dragon to willingly incise his own skin and allow a few drops of his blood fall on a simple river stone that would be later used by his human friend. Though he would have to pay attention and decide what sort of knowledge his blood should share. And so the dragon did. Willingly, he spilled a few drops from a painless cut, and the human, Medoris soon became a wiser man. He crafted himself a necklace which held the stone inside – the Blood-Stone – and soon he started to understand

and read the dragon's mind like he never had before. He was even able to control natural elements like light and water. Of course the dragon had only transferred some of his vast powers, and that was more than enough to contaminate the frivolous mind of humankind. Medoris achieved many great deeds and built some of the ancient cities that still hold today, many of which are still to be discovered, yet in time people turned envious of him and started to desire what the master builder had achieved. Great kings and queens of many races were willing to pay mountains of gold to get their hands on the stone or anything similar, and many times had they tried to get it, not listening to reason nor considering that in their hands it would be useless. Who would've imagined that such a pure gesture of friendship and benevolence would one day become the downfall of the friendship between Drakhahouls and humans?"

Another long lick.

"Medoris had lived a long and marvellous life and his death sentenced the blissful alliance between men and dragons to a cruel and sudden end. After his death, his two sons started to fight over the priceless artefact causing the death of one by poisoning and the banishment from the lands for the other. The Blood-Stone still held powers entrapped in its core for the direct descendants of Medoris, so the banished son soon became a powerful ruler of the lands he had fled too. Alas, the dragons were torn apart. Many had never agreed in first place to Algudrin's determination of sharing the sacred knowledge and now they had the reason to exile the dragon too from their fraternity. They condemned him to a solitary life away from his kin. Alone and abandoned to fate, Algudrin tried for many years to find the son of Medoris and convince him to put an end to this unfortunate affair but he managed to avoid and escape the dragon. When Algudrin picked up a trail, the son of Medoris was always a step ahead and so, in time, was the Blood-Stone lost. Nobody knows where the stone is or if it still exists, though many have tried to find it and none have succeeded," he concluded.

Luckily for me, he had no more fingers to lick.

"And what if one found the stone, would its powers be of any use to a new master?" I asked.

"That is a very good argument. The answer is yes and no. If the one that finds it is a direct descendant then yes, it might work, if not it won't, unless one was a wizard or a witch. You see, the beauty of humanity's slow minded nature is that in time thinkers and wizards had found ways of binding the will of these artefacts and make them respond to a new owner, with altered powers, but they could work nonetheless!" He stopped and gulped some wine.

I took the time to wet my dry lips with the water that he had poured in my mug.

"Centuries have passed and the Blood-Stone turned into a simple story, much like the ones you've probably heard already. Luckily, the original connection between man and beast did not easily fade. Eventually other animals, under different circumstances of threat, danger, friendship, had decided to gift tokens of benevolence to humans and I think this has to do with the Blood-Stone as well. I am most confident about my theory," he pushed his head closer to me as in trying to conceal his words, "when Algudrin-the-Bold made the first stone, he transferred some of his powers, unwillingly, most certainly, to the realm of which he was part of, the beasts, the animals of all kind, and so, this power now lies within every single breathing beast; the power of benevolence."

"Oh," I murmured, thinking of the stag that Winterhorn was part of.

"Of course, it takes some wits about the animals to be able to do it. I don't suppose frogs are able to make anything else than croaking in the ponds. Perhaps they do, who knows?" He placed a spindly finger on his lower lip and turned his head toward the cloudy sky as if pondering what he just said.

He murmured something to himself and for a while he started moving his hand on his long beard.

"Bah! I'd like to see that," he said all of a sudden turning his eyes on me.

There was no point in trying to enquire about his lost thoughts, so I patiently waited for him to continue.

"The wizards and the witches had always had their hands in these matters, and for such they have always desired the stones, some for good and candid reasons such as understand their true nature and comprehend more about the worlds from which the Drakhahouls arrived, but many for the simple desire of power and governance. Medoris and his deeds had been almost forgotten when Irridae-the-Brave gifted the Lux-Stone to Loreeia, queen of the elves, many, many centuries later. And nobody truly knows how many artefacts have been granted, or what powers they held and where they could be found. Only the dragons can sense them as they are the forefathers of these tokens." There was sadness in the old man's voice, his passion and excitement brusquely fading with his words.

"Alas, Drakhahouls have been gone for centuries," I added.

He started laughing loudly, his eyes turning to slits. "No they aren't, they're only well-hidden and out of our reach, but I know exactly where to find them!"

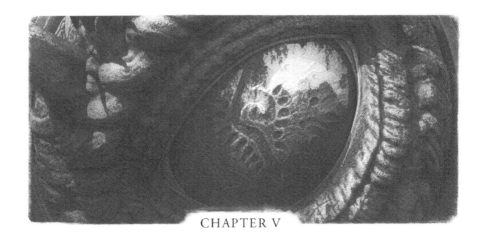

CHAPTER V

THE BOUNDLESS MARK

Lorian

Alaric's revelation put an end to our copious early-meal. His words rung stridently in my head and I could barely contain myself from demanding more details. Nor could I decline his demand of help when he asked me to give him a hand cleaning and preparing the table for making bread – a custom he repeated every two or three days during the week.

"If you will, would you fetch a bit of flour from inside?" he asked once the table was cleaned. "There's a coffer behind the door to your left. You'll find two jute-bags with white flour and a bowl already in one of them. There's also a sieve somewhere, use it and sift the bowl full to the edge and bring it here," he said, determined on rekindling the fire.

Once through the main entrance of his house, I was startled to find it completely different than what I imagined. What initially had been a kitchen, was now a lecture room with very few spots occupied by common things like jars, pots and cooking tools. The rest of the space was home to scrolls, quills, inkwells, books, maps and tomes. The table hadn't been used to dine upon in a long time as indicated by the colourful set of goose-quills and papers that lay, spread across its surface. Other parchments were set on the chairs as well as on the floor. I dared not touch anything even if I was intrigued to check what one of the maps on the table was bestowing. Its bulk was held in place by heavy, smooth river-stones and tiny wooden sculptures of horses and towers.

I found the two sacks of flour and started sifting it into the bowl, but my eyes were elsewhere.

A slanted writing of beautiful letters at the top of a parchment spelled 'The Aranthian Empire' in the common language. Underneath, right at its centre there was a big, white castle with five towers that had red coloured roofs. Masterfully drawn on top of it, in black ink, was a Drakhahoul symbol outlined with its bat-like wings and flame coming from his mouth and nostrils, its size wider than the entire citadel. From all the names written on the parchment many had cross or circle marks in red ink; Dolbatir, Callanor, Mount Nrom, Hulverion, Myrth, Grora, Thull, Doradhur, Rontra, Velkeri and many others. Besides the forests, rivers, mountains and lake symbols there were other black ink scribbles, indicating quick and rushed notes freely placed across the yellow tinted map with various orientations. Of all the location names, almost at the edge of the paper, one was encircled with both red and black ink and it said, 'Elmenor' and something written underneath in a language I did not recognise. I interrupted my task and craned the head closer to it, trying to make up the shapes.

Sadly, the old man's voice called from outside, "What's taking you so long, lad? Want me to come get it, myself?"

"Found it!" I yelled back, brushing off the bits of flour I unwittingly spread on the map.

With the clear image of the map still in my mind, I joined him by the fireplace. He was already set on making the dough, the water bucket, salt, and oil at his disposal.

"I started as a very young lad to look for her," he started, with the briefest look at my face and a quick gesture to snatch the bowl from my hands. "I was born in the big northern city of Dolbatir, very far from here, high north. Beyond that place lie the unknown and untravelled seas. Naghnatë, as I came to understand much later on, travelled to spread these tales, that many had believed to be mere children stories. Though, they aren't!" He shifted his position, the bowl was moving on the table.

I extended my hands and held it.

He continued swiftly, "She arrived with a group of merchants from Arkhanthï, looking to trade for our goods with their leather merchandises; bags, garments skins and boots, and all sorts. Yet, one could tell she was foreign to trading as she barely considered any living soul during her trades. Only once dusk had descended upon the city and the market had broken on the fifth and last day, that she had lit the fires and started recounting her tales. It was a custom of the merchants, see, always to celebrate the ending of their trading with a big feast. It was on such a day that I saw her, and I recall it as if it happened yesterday. And what has haunted me for all these years was not her enticing voice or the depth of her story, but the look on her shabby old face." Alaric paused.

Although keen to know more about the dragons, I was also curious to hear more about the witch.

"She stopped and stared me as if she were talking only to me. It felt like her voice could touch my mind against her words, which were directed to all of us. I knew I had to find her the moment she laid eyes on me. I was young and wanted to achieve great deeds, just like everyone else. And just because it was me she had looked upon, it made me feel I was different and more important than the rest. I've always had this liveliness and strength about my convictions that I couldn't see in others, and I knew that was my call. Alas, you see what good it did." He pointed his sticky hand to his figure.

"Is it true that she is very old? Nana says she's at least three hundred years old."

"Well, so she said. I think her story is always the same, even if the purpose is unknown, more reason for me to enquire, so I considered. It took me a while to overcome my fears and finally decide to change my life, and only a couple of months after the tradesmen had arrived in Dolbatir, I departed in the search of the witch. Me and the family's horse, Fleck. First, I went west, towards the city of Callanor, a seaport populated with many foreign folks and peculiar people. I never quite fancied that place to be honest, the sole place where one can find means to travel towards the western worlds. To my displeasure, I was only able to learn that the traders had left the month before my arrival and they were headed south, to the peaks of mountain Nrom. Now, Mount Nrom, if you have read your stories, has been occupied by a dwarfish colony for centuries, and by the time I visited, the king was no other than Hegor Strongfist, the tallest of all the dwarfs I've seen."

"You met the dwarf king of Nrom?" I interrupted him, surprised to hear him mention the name of one of the characters in my grandmother's tales.

The story had it that Hegor had not achieved his greatness because of his peculiar size, but he had managed to accomplish what no other dwarf had ever dreamed of doing. Born into a poor and simple family, he had gained his right to rule and be king of all dwarfs in the iron mountain of Nrom, by challenging the rightful heir to the throne, who had always been corrupt in his opinion. He had been granted the right to the challenge, though hadn't been allowed any weapon whilst the rightful heir had picked an axe. Against all odds, he had fought and defeated the oldest son of the defunct king with only few scratches, barehanded.

"I did, as a matter of fact!" continued Alaric, "and not in the best fashion, I might add. Dwarfs have different rules, with which I was not acquainted when I was your age, and if you want to venture on this path, you might as well learn of those you might want to meet, because it could save your skin. I arrived at the mountain of iron on a dire rainy day in spring, and asked the keepers of the gates if I could, in exchange for coin, of course, shelter for a day or two, not wanting them to know my true purpose. They obviously accepted my coin and invited me to the common caves inside the mountains. I get you are familiar that dwarfs are jealous of their homes and secrets and only few outsiders had ever been inside the mountains in those days. That had always been a sacred rule passed on from generation to generation. Yet, they had a problem. Since always reluctant to venture in the open world, preferring the lightless cold rooms of stone to the sunshine on their hairy skins, they were cut from the most common trades of goods so they decided to make their households partially reachable for travellers and traders. This way they could take advantage of the goods being taken to their doors without having to go outside. So with the minimum effort they made a smaller village inside of the mountain secluded from the core of their burrowed dwellings. Generally, these galleries were as big as our common villages on land and had everything one needed but they were confined from the rest of the mountain halls where the king and his people lived. Therefore, shelter for me and my horse was obviously in the common rooms, at a young woman's wooden-hut. Now that I think about her she was quite nice and kind, and offered definitely cheap lodgings." His face betrayed a quirky smile.

From his expression, I sensed there was more to the story – a romance perhaps - but my smile must have betrayed my thoughts as he quickly changed his expression and moved on.

"And dammed be my curiosity, I could not keep myself still for too long and after the first day, I started enquiring about the witch, not knowing that the dwarfs would not allow wizards, witches and magical works inside their homes. Soon enough I found out about it, though, when the word spread that I was looking for trouble. On my third afternoon I was taken by the dwarf guardians to the dungeons, one of the deepest levels of the mountains. It took me days to plead my case to the commanders of the that place and after they realised I was not a wizard I was granted permission to be heard by the king himself, which would decide my fate." Alaric looked at me and a smile broadened on his face, his eyes wide. "He was every bit as the tales recount; broad shoulders with strong arms and legs and robust hands as big as boulders. He was almost as tall as any given human, and being in his presence only made me shiver in fright. His royal deportment and strong voice only made me shrink under his throne when he had ordered me to serve a full moon of labour in the mines with the other dwarfs that had been punished for various causes, like larceny and other lesser crimes. Later I learned from the guards that my sentence was rather light, since magical issues had always been punished with death by being buried alive within stone – a ghastly practice if you ask me, but they had always believed that this way the mountain would be grateful for the sacrifice and make their realm prosper and thrive." He shook his old body as if to cast away the shiver of displeasure.

Nervousness showed in his kneading of the dough inside the bowl.

"Those were the hardest days of labour that I have ever endured. A new mine was about to be opened and we were supposed to follow a vein of iron that supposedly lead to an empty chamber of ore deposits. I had food, water and shelter and being young and strong, I could not complain, even if I could not keep up with the laziest of the dwarfs. They seemed to be like ants; tireless, hardworking and it was almost impossible to bend their humour in any situations." Alaric stopped himself abruptly. "Most importantly, never try to outdrink a dwarf! You'll be long asleep and probably have awoken back up before they've reached their fill."

I nodded at his advice, almost amused by his worried glare.

"Either way, after the full month of hard work expired, I was to meet the king again. He seemed to look at me in a different light, a more approving manner since there had been no complaints about the duties I fulfilled. The last words I heard from him were that magic was not allowed in his realm and he did not want to have his people stain their minds by those who venture in magic exploration or vague ideas. And in order for me to never forget it, he *generously* arranged to have my skin marked with everlasting inks. And so, I got myself this." Alaric slowly lifted the sleeve of his long robe and showed me a dark blue marking on his forearm in a shape similar to an adorned key.

"What does it mean?" I asked staring at the odd shaped mark.

"Outlaw, in dwarfish. This is a reminder that I'm not welcome anymore in the city inside the Nrom mountain as long as he is king, and probably not welcome in any dwarf colony for what I know. I reckon it could've gone worse." He quickly covered his forearm and moved to throw a log inside the stove.

"As a matter of fact, I think it could have gone worse!" I

added.

"Indeed, the joy to be free was bigger than any remorse or grudge I could hold against his people. Lucky to escape alive, I didn't mind the idea of not returning to that cold, grey mountain at all, so I left with all haste. Though, I still hadn't learned the whereabouts of the witch and so I decided to continue southeast, to Doradhur. And after three weeks' travels, with only a handful of halts in villages and small towns that I stumbled upon, I reached the mighty city of Doradhur. Little did I know back then that I was about to spend three years in that place! On my very first day, while I enquired for shelter at the alehouse, I learned of Naghnatë's whereabouts; confirmed by regular consumers of spirits, and then by common villagers. I had been told that she had come to the city and left after the same five customary days of market, just as she had done in Dolbatir. They mocked and laughed when they spoke of her, as nobody cared nor believed her stories of dragons and wizards; they only considered her a crazy old hag. Yet nobody knew where they were headed, nor did they care.

"Having travelled for so long, I decided to stay for a while, and the next day I started looking for work and ways I could earn some coin to provide for me and my horse. That is when I met Takahok and the very thing that had fed my passion for the dragon stones and the tokens for the rest of my years to come; my first and only token of benevolence!" He paused and drank some water and indicated at my belt. "That and your knife, the Winterhorn, of course. They both share the same mark, lad! The boundless one, it's unmistakeably somewhere around, and from what I can tell, is not fashioned by the smith who crafts the token, no, it's fashioned by magic."

I gaped in awe, thrilled and impatient to have another look at my knife's mark.

"As I was saying, Takahok was in need of an assistant to tend to his herd on his property which was located just at the edge of the citadel, and I seemed to be the right match from the many listed for the part."

"What was the token called?" I interrupted.

"Still called, Lorian," he corrected me by lifting his grubby finger, "its name is the Rose of Ice, and it has this particular name because of the peculiar skills its master had and the uncommon creature it derives from. Takahok is the most experienced hunter these lands had ever seen; I have been fortunate enough to witness it with my own yes. Probably now he's too old, though he had always been that skilled, long before his token. We became quite close being of similar age and interests, more or less. On many occasions he taught me how to spar with blades and how to draw a long bow. Soon we both joined on hunting trips and it was on one of those days he showed me the Rose of Ice and recounted how he had earned it. It was kept in a special pouch around his belt plated with thin and tough iron sheets. It was a container worth its treasure. The rose was but a fist-full item of a curious transparent object which roughly resembled a rose. Minute ice-splinters darted outwards all over its surface, which even if they appeared delicate, they weren't. It was of the brightest white, sparkling with its own light as if made of snow and ice that never melts. Inside, there was a tusk of a fox that he had chased for many years, and when he had finally caught and killed it, the fox's spirit had appeared and congratulated him for being the only human in centuries able to capture the essence of the winter foxes. It was then that it had offered its token of benevolence; a magically crafted rose, fashioned from the very ice where the lifeless body was laying," Alaric explained.

I squealed with marvel.

"He told me that its powers gave him unhuman strength, him and him alone – making my hopes of having one of my own, instantly die. These powers, he said, manifested especially in winter by sharpening his wit, stealth, sight, smell and stamina as well as resistance to the cold, this being one of the strengths of the winter white-foxes. I have witnessed him hunting and I can tell you it was a sight for sore eyes. He ran as fast as a hare and anticipated almost every move of his prey; it was something I could never tire watching. Almost unfair for the poor animals that never managed to escape. Yet, he was a fair man and a good soul, he never abused his powers nor did he take from the forest more than he needed. He often went against those that did not respect nature and abused the power of their ingenious machineries to hunt and kill almost to extinction entire colonies of boars, rabbits and deer.

"Perhaps that was the reason the winter fox had chosen him…" I started but got interrupted.

"Precisely so! A guardian of the forest of a pure and uncontaminated spirit." He added. "With that, obviously, came a lot of envy and he earned many enemies in exchange. In all conscience, to me it looked like a simple object, of course of very fine craftsmanship and uncommon beauty. In all honesty, no powers could be sensed by holding it or just looking at it. Back then I did not know that the objects had to be granted to be of any use, so I started dreaming of obtaining one myself. This late discovery together with the good coin I made in his service, delayed me from my path for two more years, until I came to realise that nothing more could be obtained from my lingering in the city. So I bid my farewells, with plenty of sadness and reluctance to leave a true friend, and decided to proceed north-west, towards Iriath since it was the nearest town, big enough for me to hope I'd be able to learn something about the witch." He took another sip of water and filled a second cup for me as well.

I thanked him and drank the water, ensnared by his story.

"But to no avail, since as in every other place I visited I was always late by a matter of days, weeks or months and I could not find anything useful about these wretched stones. She had set me upon a goose chase, unwillingly perhaps, although at times I doubted that too."

"Do you think she might have wanted you to look for her?" I enquired.

"I think she might've wanted help on finding the stones. I've considered it at length; every time I failed it came to mind. Maybe she was only enlisting oblivious young souls, whom she involved with her glamour and stories. Eventually one of us could fortuitously stumble upon a stone at some point," he replied.

His words rang in my years for a while and my face most surely betrayed my obvious concern; I could see it upon his frowned forehead.

"Oh no, do not disquiet yourself! I'm in no cahoots with the witch or anyone else. And even if I were, I'd not know where to find her, nor do I have an interest in giving her your token. It's not mine to give!" he assured me.

"For a moment I thought it was all a trap," I confessed.

"Bladder, no! Not while I still have my wits about me. At any rate, I doubt I was alone in this, there must be others. All the villages and cities she visited over the years; I doubt it was only me that fell for it. It can't be! That seed she planted in my ears with her story, was growing inside my mind. It was like a sickness that I carried everywhere I went, one that sporadically liked manifesting its presence with raw bursts of reinvigorated energy."

I did not know what to say, or if there was anything I could add to aid his troubled expression.

"I was lost. For many days I did not know where to start again, having stayed too long in Doradhur. Luckily, everything was about to change; a lad in Iriath, one of the workers of the market, mentioned that he was sure Naghnatë had lived in Arkhanthï for a long while and most likely someone there might be of help. I never known anyone that ventured that far north. For the people in Dolbatir, Arkhanthï was as far north as anyone has ever dared venture."

I gulped some more water while Alaric paused briefly to recollect his thoughts, his hands slowly bending and poking the dough.

"Odd, old tales recounted the same thing; the citadel was not a hospitable and friendly place where everyone was accepted and as such, nobody cared or dared going there. The tales mentioned that few were those that managed to get access and the same tales recounted that none of them ever returned. Yet I did not care at the time. It was my sole option so I had to see it with my own eyes." He chuckled, passing his hand between his wispy beard. "Travel itself was an arduous task. I had plenty of resources and much coin from Takahok's service, but few were those willing to aid me in my journey even for my precious gold. The farther I ventured the fewer people I met. Undoubtedly the weather did not help for anyone to easily settle comfortably and live a decent life, but I still consider that weather alone was not the cause for such desolation. I carried on and together with

Fleck, after weeks of travelling and getting lost in the vast, desolate and cold planes, we made it to Arkhanthï." Alaric filled his lungs with fresh air and took a long exhale before continuing. "The walls surrounding the citadel and the gates are so high you can barely see the tips of the tall structures from underneath their shadow. The citadel is built upon a high rocky peak and all around it there are shallow hills and small patches of bush woods and, to one side, a dark-green and tall forest. The closest mountain one could climb and look upon the castle is too far out to be able to make out anything inside. I was convinced for many years that something was happening in there, and as hard as I tried, I never managed to gain entrance. The human guards at the gates never listened to my motives, they just forced me to leave!"

I could see his frustration still consuming him after all this time. He manifested it with a series of hard punches in the dough.

"I made several attempts to gain access, thinking that different guards might be reasonable enough to let me in. It never worked. They all followed the same instructions not to let anyone pass the gate. So I decided to linger nearby to see if that was true. I should have known better; camping outside in the nearest, small blotch of birch trees, was a harsher task. Odd forces were continuously coercing me out and prevented me from staying. I could not light a fire! The wind seemed to be working against me and against all odds it'd come out of nowhere to kill my fire, even on the sunniest day. The beasts inside seemed reluctant to accept my intrusion too. There were no big animals, fortunately for me, yet the swarm of small birds and beasts made all sorts of interminable noises whenever I tried to sleep. I've also lost my horse, my Fleck! My fine and stubborn Dolbatir breed."

I swallowed nervously, the tension in his words made me wonder what the situation must've been like for him.

"My first night there, I ran away after only few hours; scared and frightened of that evil place. Though, I was not that easily downbeat. The following night I convinced myself to try again. I did last longer, but I wasn't able to last the full night, neither awake nor asleep. With few other attempts that followed during those weeks, I had the same number of failures, and without my horse and almost without any food left, I felt less convinced of my plans. So I left for Liarhï, few days south of Arkhanthï, which without my horse took me six entire days. I was certain I could learn more about the citadel and the people that lived inside from there. To my surprise this woeful town was almost as inhospitable as the forest itself. A ruthless ruler had everyone subdued and almost poisoned me. If it hadn't been for a lovely young lady that took my young, good looks to her heart and eyes, I would've died then and there."

The obvious sorrow was nesting on his old, white brows and he took a long sigh while stooping his head over the stillness of his hands. A sad thought occurred to me, a dreadful image of an old me, who just like him, was regretting the choices that had broken a promised love or a missed opportunity. I quickly gulped down all the cold water and shook my head heartily, disbanding the doom my consideration would cause.

My gesture rekindled his spirit.

"North from Doradhur is a miserable place to venture, young Lorian. In time I thought I would learn the secrets of the citadel of Arkhanthï, yet I failed. Years passed as I moved from town to village, and from village to town. East to west, north to south. And every once in a while, I would brace myself again for a new attempt on spying on the citadel, and always with the same outcome. That place is cursed I tell you!" There was anger in his words now.

I stood in silence feeling compassion for his tormented past.

"In time I gave up looking for Naghnatë and started gathering as much information as I could about the tokens. From the many people I have met during my travelling years; menders, healers, wood choppers and warriors, I have learned, through their stories and recounts, about odd facts and curious places which I deemed worthy of consideration." His enthusiasm seemed to be rising again.

"That's why you have many scrolls and maps inside your home?" I asked.

"Indeed. I noted and scribbled every bit of information I could gather. I'm a proud master of the quill, I must say. This passion of mine, for words and paper, has only helped me keep track of everything I reckoned was worth conserving."

The intense working of the dough was done. He covered the wooden bowl with the bread-ball inside and placed it near the fireplace.

Then he meticulously cleaned his hands. "Come! I might as well just show it to you!"

With haste I followed him inside and allowed him to share his cache of scrolls, maps, letters and books.

He started listing the names of the places he had visited, passing a finger on the map, pointing at the most obvious ones and rummaging with his eyes around the tall shelves when he mentioned others.

They were countless; places I'd never heard of and places I'd only heard in the stories of long lost treasures. I wondered how one could have accomplished so much and still feel dismayed. I could only marvel. This was the farthest I'd ventured, a mere day on horseback, and I was already homesick.

"There are so many!" I exclaimed in awe.

"Yes, there are! Our world is bigger than this valley, way bigger," he laughed, "but mind you, it's also a very dangerous place. I will spare you the details of my life's work, we wouldn't have enough time to go through all of my findings. Suffice to say there are many unexplored places, places of riches and magic and ancient beings that few attempted to visit. If that might come of interest, you know now how to find me." He winked at me with honesty.

I took to heart his generosity and continued flatly, "And where would you start looking for the dragons?"

"Then, if the Glinting Den cannot interest you, nor its cache of diamonds, then I can show you this." He pointed a thin finger on the Drakhahoul symbol at the side of the map.

"Arkhanthi?" I asked.

"Isn't it obvious? Why would they keep it so secret and protected?" he replied.

"There could be many reasons," I tried to argue.

"Oh lad, if only you could see that place. You'd instantly know it."

I was still not convinced.

"Would you take the chance of greeting someone when that someone felt the need to build another row of walls around his home, and keep its gates protected day and night? Clearly the man does not want to be disturbed, and clearly the closest cities inside the Aranthian Empire are well under his political influence. Can't be otherwise."

"True," I whispered, not sure what to think.

With dexterity and haste, he unrolled a blank scroll from under the thick pile of parchments on the table, took his quill and ink and started to make the rough shape of a map.

"All the land you see right here on this map, was commonly known as the Aranthian Empire. Every race was freely and equally allowed to live and prosper within its lands and it has been so for millennia, when Drakhahouls thrived on Earth." He pointed his thick quill on the dragon symbol drawn above the five red-roofed towers of the Arkhanthi's citadel. "The divisions between races and the land they occupy afterwards, has only been made rather recently, once the balance and peace had been broken. If you ask me, I'd say that the Drakhahouls shouldn't have made any artefacts at all. It was a mistake to trust mankind with such powerful yet treacherous gifts. Look how many wars and conflicts there have been from then until now! And for what, I say? The yearning for power and desire for wealth?"

I couldn't agree more. Every single major conflict, battle or war that our parents, grandparents and their ancestors had lived through or heard about, had come about from the desire to own more. To some extent, even the most trivial of quarrels had a material-related problem to them. The clans that formed Sallncoln were the perfect example, having fought and argued over land ownership, fundamentally, for the entire existence of the village. To these days, the direct descendants still carried their obfuscated anger and discord amongst each other and only kept it at bay because of what another war would mean for its people.

"Nevertheless," Alaric continued, having evaded his resentment, "these lands now are divided amongst humans, dwarves and elves, with a vast majority of human settlements."

I watched as he made three circles on the map.

"There are only a few dwarf cities left inside the Aranthian Empire; Mount Nrom, which as mentioned is also known as the mountain of Iron where King Hegor Strongfist resides; then we have Callanor, which, because it is close to the western sea, is becoming more a human city than a dwarf one, and then, a bit under here, there is Erodir which I have only heard there have been dwarfs living there. On my single visit to the city I could see no other race but humans; different races and regions tall and short, though no dwarf. The last one is a bit south from mount Nrom and here we have the citadel of Fherefir, which truth be told, I doubt there are any dwarves left there either." He lingered a moment over the name he had just written and softly blew some air to aid the dark ink dry on the amber paper.

I was impressed with the care he offered to the art of lettering; from the few circles and words scribbled on the parchment, each stroke and letter had the same intensity and inclination making the entire word pleasant to the eye and easy to understand.

"On the other side of the map," his quill marked the names on the right side of the scroll, "we have, or had, I cannot confirm to the information's reliability, we have the elven cities; Elmenor, to the very south, Thull somewhere around the middle, here, then on this edge we have Myrth and up north we have the island of Grora."

I nodded at his enquiring glance.

"None of which I have been able to visit! If Arkhanthï is closed to outsiders, one can at least approach the outer walls and be told off. Elmenor, instead, as well as the other three cities, are entirely forbidden to any race except the elves. Nobody has succeeded in crossing the dense forests that surround the citadel and, from those that had ventured there, nobody had returned. The elves are cunning and can also be very dangerous if they want to be. They are also very secretive and rarely seen. Though, I do not believe for one second they've vanished, even if they never wanted anything to do with any other race that wasn't theirs. And I wager they'd share none of their knowledge on any matter related to the tokens, dragons or magic. Probably they wouldn't tell you the right direction if you'd got lost either!" His phrase that ended with a chuckle soon faded into an incomprehensible mumble.

His frantic stutter made me smile, though I had to withhold the laughter when his face turned red while cursing breathlessly under his beard. He reminded me of Numaluk, the oldest man in Sallncoln, that could keep at his grumble for the entire day, if one dared to keep him company for such a long time.

I shifted on my chair with a bit of noise, and Alaric took it as a hint to continue.

"Mh-mh," he cleared his throat, "the elves have always preferred to keep to themselves and stay neutral for as long as they could, unless the matter involved them directly, which it never occurred except for very few occasions that time itself cannot recall. And what you already know, the story about Loreeia and how she has been deceived by the wizard, is not one of those occasions, as they didn't lift a finger against the evil old wizard, they only accepted their defeat, retreated to their forests and kept silence. Argh…" Irritated by those particulars he let out another typical, old-man growl of complaint, only briefer this time.

Another fact on which I silently agreed; from all the stories I have read and been told, the elves were seldom in them. Few were the exceptions when rebellious characters of their race ventured into our world and allowed humans to interact as well as be let into some of their secrets, though mostly they kept to themselves caring for their lands and protecting their lengthy existence while keeping it safe and isolated.

"And this is what I can quickly surmise. Of course there are many, less important places, hidden caves and treasure maps, which I hope we'll have the opportunity to discuss." His words were a direct invitation to linger further.

"Perhaps another time?" I tried to be as polite as I could.

"Some other time, then," he replied unshaken by my decline, "either way, the most sensible attempt for your endeavour would be to try and gain access to the citadel of Arkhanthï. I strongly believe that all our questions will be answered if you gained access!"

"If only it was that easy to reach it and charm the guards, but I would like very much to meet you again, one day." I honestly hoped he could see I was serious about my suggestion, even if I was more than keen to return home at the present time.

"At least you could keep this!" He rolled the small scroll he had just sketched, tied it with thin string and gave it to me.

"Thank you, Alaric! I really appreciate it and I hope I can bring news of my findings, optimistic news. If only it were that easy to know what to do with a token of benevolence." I smiled ironically.

"I thank you, Lorian Garr of Sallncoln. It was my pleasure to acquaint myself with such a passionate and fortunate young man. And I'm very certain you will, and something tells me sooner rather than later!"

CHAPTER VI

THE CITADEL

Felduror / Ghaeloden

Thick unscathed walls, high as mountains, surrounded the white castle of Arkhanthï. Taller still, four round towers guarded it at each corner of the square-shaped city and a fifth stood tallest in its middle. Just like a warrior of stone that had endured through wars and time itself, the erection stood tall and shone brightly between the pale landscape of the early autumn. A sight that could take the breath away from most, even if Felduror, the old wizard, could not care less.

The citadel had been built on one of the tallest summits in the valley of the Whispering Peaks, a strange and ancient rock formation where wind caused the exposed rocks and their crevices to whisper with almost comprehensible words. It was said that the fearless King Arkhan himself had taken shelter amongst the rocks after an unfortunate day of hunting. His men, dogs and horses had been slayed or forced to scatter for their lives by a furious beast of the forests. Having lost his sword in an attempt to kill the beast, and being isolated from his remaining guards, the king had retreated among the rocks and there he had remained hidden for three days without food or water. Hungry, weakened and frightened, before the edges of insanity, he had solemnly vowed that if he were to be spared, he would build a citadel on top of those hostile rocks worthy of his worse enemy's praises. When he had lost every hope, on the brink of the fourth day, a party of his subjects had finally found and rescued him. True to his promise, once he had recovered, he had ordered his master builders to come up with new plans for a new city; the citadel of Arkhanthï. The marvellous citadel had taken many years and resources to be finished, and its founding-father never had the chance to see it completed – he had died few years after the works had commenced, on another battlefield. Yet, his promise had been fulfilled.

Although many years had passed, the beauty of the place appeared untouched. It was as if time and weather could not lessen the magnificence of the ancient city. On the contrary, it appeared enhanced by it or, perhaps, the evil wizard had used spells to protect its ever-shining presence and preserve its splendour.

The dark red tiles canvased the roofs of all structures which contrasted the whiteness of the marble walls with a pleasant distinction of tones. A multitude of red and black standards flew frantically in the soaring wind, their flapping lifting a loud chorus in unison. Today, the fast-moving clouds allowed the sun to briefly shine its feeble rays and bounce back almost with the same blinding intensity, yet, its strength betrayed the cold that started to persist on the lands of the north. The rains had started angrier of late and the falling droplets fell like little ice-arrows bouncing on the stone-paved floor and walls.

Whilst the four external towers were of a somewhat normal fashion, used to garrison the guards' brigades, workforces and archers that maintained and protected the citadel, the impenetrable main-tower was of a more peculiar manner. It evolved thinner and rounder by each floor and had a dragon-landing structure all around its summit, enforced by metal structures that dug within the stone's surface.

It was the wizard's favourite building of the entire city. He hardly ever visited the other four, as well as any other insignificant constructions inside and outside the walls, unless in their dungeons there were prisoners that needed visiting. The importance of the middle tower wasn't provided by its majestic proportions, being the tallest and widest, but mainly because of what it enclosed.

Its tall and painted windows filtered the light on every level springing a flecking spectacle on the marble floor, which was of a different, rarer quality. Many rooms for many purposes lay symmetrically on a repeated pattern throughout the height of the tower. From the wine cellars to libraries, underground prisons, kitchens, storage and sleeping rooms and many secret rooms, which few were allowed to enter and fewer still knew of their existence, the tower had everything necessary to last for years of conflict in the unlikely and unprecedentedly event that the citadel came under siege.

The initial project, under the specific instructions of King Arkhan himself, had originally only a row of high walls, not far from the core of the five towers. It allowed for plenty of space for houses, markets and garrisons to be built. And, as soon as the new king, Belrug-the-Black had been crowned, the wizard had made a new request; to raise a secondary row of walls around the citadel, many miles away from the first. A request granted without a blink, given his influence upon the dragon's young mind and therefore on every one of his loyal subjects. In the common people's eyes, his request had appeared like a simple purpose of protection, yet he had known then as he knew now his true intentions.

Firstly, he meant to prevent any outsiders coming within sight of the main citadel, therefore unable to see what really happened inside. This allowed the few Drakhahouls that still lived within, plenty of safe space to hunt without being seen, given that the distance from the second row of walls to the citadel was such that even the biggest of them appeared the size of a small sparrow. Secondly, the vast space that divided the rows of walls allowed the lands to be shared by his farmers and his warriors. The farmers were humans, and were those whose families maintained the beauty of the realm, growing cattle and crops and all the necessities for the citadel and the empire to prosper. Closer to the walls, quite far from the human settlements, were the armies and these were made by the Gholaks, which had been summoned by Felduror himself from the deepest caves of the earth.

Although temptation and natural instincts of the orc brutes was to pillage and destroy, they blindly followed every order of his, and never once had there been any major conflict or quarrel between humans and orcs. They were settled in four major colonies, each of them guarding the four gates of the external walls; the eastern, the western, the northern and the southern gate. Gholaks never complained about rain, snow or sun and as long as they had food and ale, they rarely sent their chieftains with new requests to the wizard and the dragon king. Their perpetual presence around the citadel, made some of the mighty beasts perturbed, and not without reason as the two races never got along well, so in time most of the Drakhahouls had distanced themselves from the citadel. Many had retreated to the far-away islands of the east, lands impossible to reach by humans and many still to be discovered. The only dragons that remained were the younglings hatched from Sereri-the-White, who was the oldest Drakhahoul, but still young in dragon-years at four hundred years old. Given that she was the only eldest dragon at court, King Belrug being around two hundred years younger, the younglings knew almost nothing of the story – she had agreed to withhold various notions and events of their past considering, as Felduror had insisted and suggested, it was for their own good. That was of course until they grew older and memories of their long-lost relatives, as well as those still alive, started to mingle. There was still plenty of time before any of them came of that age and wisdom. They were growing freely, if free could be considered those restricted miles between the walls, where they could hunt. They were secluded, even if they felt protected from the outside world and lived and grew with no true knowledge of their history. Young as they were, they did not seem to miss or wonder about anything at all, and they kept providing their services as guardians of the citadel while enjoying their lives.

Of late, there was always silence inside the main tower, more so in the highest rooms, where any sound was dampened by levels upon levels of the thick structure's walls. The always-busy kitchens and the underground prisons with their frantic sounds were imperceptible up there, and only the gust of always-cold wind reigned over all sounds.

Felduror was stooped over an inclined desk, his nose almost touching its surface whilst carefully examining an ancient scroll through a golden magnifying glass. His long thin finger carefully followed marks of red ink painted on the fragile parchment. For restless nights at a time he'd find himself looking upon the same yellowed parchments, standing in the same room, barely eating anything and only drinking his own turbid teas.

Today, he was feeling his lower lip flutter more agitatedly; a restless sign of frustration and tiredness and his old bones ached, unaccountably so. As always, every once in a while, he would dictate something without ever taking his eyes away from the important scrolls, to a servant-clerk.

Tired of remembering everything he deemed worthy of note, he had personally selected the peculiar amanuensis amongst many others of his race. His name was Nuuk. Yes, he remembered it today, but more often he did not. He called him creature instead, since he was an imp. The odd-looking creature, that from afar could be mistaken for a lean child of eight or so, up close could alarm many brave people and, in some cases, cause disgust. It was the craggy skin of his wrinkled face and his big ears that caused it, while the small and almost deformed bat-like wings were almost tolerable. Unfortunately for him, the wizard could not take any chances and he had bound the wings of the little creature with a thin, threaded-white filament which dug quite deep in his hard skin. One could easily be mistaken in thinking that the thread could be easily broken, yet its fibres were imbued with magic, unbreakable without the proper spell.

Today the wizard could not recall precisely why he had inflicted such punishment in first place, clearly the little creature was not a real threat, weakened by years of servitude and his binding spells. Nor could he recall the reason for the fresh, dark-purple bruises, that covered the creature's neck and arms. Were they another sign of his appreciation? Had the creature upset him recently?

He could not remember.

The brief look upon the silent servant almost made him ask a direct question, then another thought slipped in and he quickly ignored his impulse.

"Mhh, I wonder. Could that be one of the olden locations?" He broke the silence thinking about the last bit of map he had inspected.

How many times had he thought he was close to an answer? How many times had he misled himself? Another clueless row of questions invaded his uneasy mind.

The reflective moment quickly passed and Felduror was delivered into the same big, gawking eyes of his servant.

Just like countless days before, the helpless creature stood still and mute, attentively following his every movement. Sometimes he thought that the imp was unable to talk, something to be appreciated, especially for such a skilled master of quill and modern and ancient tongues, the creature had surprisingly proved to be.

Felduror held back an otiose smile, recalling now why he had chosen this little creature, and for the same reason he would not let him think for a moment he was of any worth. Instead, he barked his order, "Summon Ghaeloden, creature! And be quick about it!"

Fear was good, fear was safe, he considered as he listened to the desperate bare feet distancing on the marbled floor.

Ghaeloden-Three-Horns was one of the strongest among the young Drakhahouls of the citadel. He was also the last one to pledge allegiance to King Belrug-the-Black. Though he knew it had all been a charade; he could not be fooled by what really transpired in the empire. For as far as he could recall, he had always disliked the wizard. An innate instinct, just like the desire to fly, only far less enjoyable. He was always on alert when it came in having to deal with the wizard's devious ways.

On this cold late-summer day, the dragon was resting and cleaning his fangs after a swift hunting which consisted of a couple of sheep. Delicious, scented tender-meat, were it not for the wool that always stuck in his tall teeth. Luckily, he was stood by his favourite spot, which always soothed his many annoyances; the pond. None of the others had a liking for the quiet place, yet he enjoyed laying his wide, crimson stomach on the soft patch of moist grass. Given that his thick-scaled skin did not allow neither cold nor heat to penetrate easily, he enjoyed the pond in whatever weather the days provided. The silence and the stillness of the water the sunny days delivered, nurtured his soul and allowed his thinking to become clearer. He couldn't care less if the others wanted to claim the spot now, he would not allow it. It was his, and his alone.

Built at the same time as the citadel, the pond was placed on the lowest level, and reflected the whole castle in its pure lime-green water. Compared to the dragon, it seemed nothing more than a puddle, but for the human gardeners that maintained it, it required quite a laborious effort. They had to allow only a precise number of plants to grow and of a specific type, which they tended weekly. Therefore, the perfection of their work was pleasantly in accord with the dragon's undisclosed opinion. The biggest part of its size was taken by a cattail cluster in one corner which provided shelter for the singing frogs and smaller fish. Scattered all over the water's surface, there were a dozen or so wide water lilies which blossoming in this year's spring had caused annoyance for Ghaeloden; everyone had wanted to witness their marvel, inexplicably some of the Gholak brutes included, and the place had always been crowded. Other smaller plants and water weeds were carefully allowed to multiply and each provided further balance to the overall charming aspect.

Among all vegetation, the most beautiful was the most recent shrub; a pair of water hyacinths. The plants had appeared rather like an ordinary water-shrub for months, much to the dragon's irritation. He had considered it to be the sole disagreeable addition, which unbalanced the pleasantness of the entire pond. Yet, the last month of summer he had changed his mind; the bloom of the plant had demonstrated its unexpected and true essence. Few marvellous purple-bluish flowers had sprung with an unexpected beauty, their sweet and delicate aroma permeating the entire area around the pond and tantalising the dragon's senses. The event had been very intense and, unfortunately, very short lived, yet he had been seized completely by their beauty and their fragrance like he was a meagre, brainless insect. Even the fish of various dimensions and colours appeared to have changed their habit of scattering whenever he moved, since most of the time he was still as a plant himself.

As he thought back to that day, he noticed the same group of fish languidly swimming undisturbed under his big shadow. Today they were looking more curious about his huge three-horned-head that prohibited raindrops from reaching the surface of the water. He quickly realised why they were ensnared and kept still while he himself looked upon the reflection of his bright dark-red scales that sparkled in the water. His thick-scaled skin protected the dragon from the most vicious attacks of fellow Drakhahouls or any human weapon, therefore this cold weather really stood no chance in making his bulk muscles flutter. Actually he preferred it when it was raining as other creatures were compelled to withdraw from the gardens, leaving him to enjoy the cleansing and relaxing experience by himself.

Alas it was not the case anymore; his enhanced senses allowed him to hear something approaching long before there was anyone in sight.

"Stop right there, creature!" His deep voice thundered across the pond, scattering the multi-coloured fish to safety.

He felt the creature try to stop but slip on the wet grass and fall with a hefty thud, only to instantly regain his standing, and almost freeze where he stood. He caught his breath, his tiny heart racing in his thin chest.

"Mh! What did I sense? Quick tiny bare-feet that don't mind wet grass, a thudding-heart as big as a potato, and…" the dragon let out a chuckle, "…a tightly closed mouth after this blast? You might want to start breathing through your mouth, imp, the nose is barely enough for the effort!"

The imp exhaled a mouthful, gasping for air to recover from the effort. It was only when his not-so-pleasant-to-see purple-red face turned more towards his natural pale-shade, that he was ready to reply.

"It was too easy, master Ghaeloden! I'm the only barefoot

creature at the castle, the humans prefer to wear dead animal's skin as shoes!" he replied. "I'm sorry to bother your tranquillity, but the splendiferous king's assistant and wise-wizard Felduror has asked for you! You shall meet with him now on –"

"Creature how many times do I have to say that firstly, I am not your master, you can simply call me Ghaeloden, and secondly, and most importantly, in my presence you shall not refer to the old wizard in such an appreciative fashion, unless he's among us!" He felt his nostrils widen and puff a wave of smoke.

He also realised his huge mouth remained opened. A frightful sight for the little one to stare at such rows of imposing fangs. He chewed some air and recomposed himself.

"I ap-apologise! It's that, I always feel him standing right behind me," said the frightened imp.

"You are coming from a long line of Iprorims, the wisest race amongst the imps, is it not?" asked Ghaeloden.

The imp swallowed hesitantly.

"Yes maste –, yes, your dangerousness Ghaeloden!" The little creature quickly corrected himself.

"Then how is it that you cannot gain control over your own thoughts? Has the wizard put a spell on your mind as well? Are you prevented from reasoning? You might not be a pretty sight, I must admit, yet you have definitely been blessed with many skills, and you too are capable of magic. Throughout time, your race had accomplished many deeds worth of praise. So I want you to compose yourself and…" The dragon stopped as he noted fresh marks on the creature's neck and shoulders.

Again, the wizard's doing!

Inside his own mind, he went to confront the cunning wizard for such a weak gesture of unprovoked violence, but the helpless creature's face, frozen in the same position, made him reconsider. He felt compassion for the tiny imp, and wondered how many more like him had been subjected to the endless powers of this old man. How many had to suffer his treatments? The consideration was bitter; even he himself was bound to serving him, through the sworn loyalty to Belrug-the-Black and he knew there was no easy way to recover from such a dire predicament. He would have to outsmart the astute wizard if he were to regain his freedom. Reaching the dragon king was far more arduous than one could imagine – the wizard never allowed anyone to gain a consultation with the king without his presence.

The fumes of rage passed and he regained some tranquillity, wondering what the wizard wanted of him this time. Couldn't he use one of the other dragons? His mother, Sereri for instance, she always seemed so keen to obey every command. Alas, he knew he had no choice.

"And?" the imp asked, seemingly curious to know his thought.

"Never mind, imp! Tell the wizard I will meet him as he pleases. And, as always, mention nothing of what we discussed!" He left no space for misunderstandings.

There would be consequences if his harsh tone and voice were not understood. Yet, he realised he had been a tad too harsh on the helpless creature, which already started back on its way.

"And whenever you can," he made the imp stop on his steps, "come see me again, imp!" His voice acquired a softer and less commanding tone and he could almost feel the joy pouring out of the imp's skin.

"It would be a pleasure, kind Ghaeloden." There was an honest smile on the imp's face.

The dragon watched the little creature run off, his soaked shirt a dirty rag fit for disposal. Spreading his monumental wings and flapping them vigorously, a myriad of drops splattered across the pond's surface. He flipped his tail in the wet air and with a suffused roar and a leap, he took to the grey sky.

Felduror was waiting with discomfort under one of the arches of the tower's topmost-structures. The special place, designed for the taking off and landing of all flying creatures, dragons most importantly, allowed him not to get wet from the sideways showers of the rain. But its insistency was dragging him towards a very bad mood, adding to the irascibility caused by the dragon's tardiness.

Although in past times the tower had seen the greatest of the mighty beasts consult with their king, for many years it had seldom been used by anyone but Sereri-the-White and the King Belrug himself. The younglings never interacted directly with their king, nor did they take part in any decisions, so they were as estranged to the structure as most of the empire's subjects.

On this occasion, the Drakhahoul king accompanied the wizard, motionless as a statue. With each, slow breath, his chest made the Blight-Stone move up and down and shine against the dullness of the sky. A priceless sight for his old eyes, considered the wizard. Yet, the king appeared indifferent to the powerful token. Perhaps he had become so. His eyes were a testimony, if one knew what it meant. Like the result of a sultry disease, a foggy thin layer of murk obfuscated what had once been deep-brown irises. Felduror knew what the realisation of entrapment must have been for such a beast, perhaps constantly unsettled in mind and soul, though his body did not reflect any of it. He could not. He was standing still like a waiting, old dog, careless at the rain which bounced spiritedly all over his massive body.

A sound issued somewhere far and travelled across the entire sky with a muffled thundering feel. When the wizard shifted his gaze, a black spot high above the tower was dropping towards the ground with preposterous speed. For an instant he hesitated and considered moving away, but before he acted, young Ghaeloden had already opened his wings revealing wormlike veins across his thick membranes. He circled the roofs a couple of times and then landed with a heavy thud.

"Your majesty!" Ghaeloden bowed his head in front of Belrug.

The body of the king stood thrice taller over the younger, red dragon.

"Young Ghaeloden, you're late again!" echoed the king's voice after a weak, welcoming nod.

"I thought I had time to see the sunset before coming here, my lord! It's been a couple of gloomy days with all this rain and I wanted a little comfort from the last sun's rays!"

"Your insolence precedes you!" called Felduror while approaching the young dragon.

He knew very well that the young Drakhahoul had a predisposition towards challenging him, he had showed his nerve too many times. It would only be a matter of time until this dragon too would get what he deserved.

With gratification, he then forced him to meet his face. "We're not here to talk about your character, that in itself would require too much effort. No. We want you to go somewhere beyond the walls!"

"Am I to be allowed?" Ghaeloden did not appear at all bothered.

"These are dire times, and as such we have to act accordingly. We knew it would eventually happen. There's only so much one can do to keep an entire city concealed, me and our righteous king are strained by the efforts that you, younglings, have been spared to experience," Felduror said.

"But, why me? Why cannot a human servant aid in such endeavour? Why not any of the regiments from Liarhï, Iriath, Hulverion or Doradhur? Or why not the Gholaks?" Ghaeloden argued.

"It might come as a surprise to you, however, neither Hulverion nor Doradhur are as solidly in our control as before. They're growing bolder. Too much idleness. And the fear of the Drakhahouls and Gholaks alone will not be enough to keep them at bay. At this rate, we'll have to fend for ourselves and most likely go to war. And that's why we need you for this task," Felduror said, appreciating how the light in the young dragon's eyes sparkled brighter the more he seduced him with his words.

"You can fly high, be swift and invisible to most! Even if you were to use magic few would be able to sense it," Belrug added.

"I understand. Where shall I travel and what shall I do?" Ghaeloden asked.

"You shall go to Sallncoln! Though, magic should be not used light-heartedly, as a matter of fact, if possible, do not use it at all! The very success of your assignment will depend on it. There's someone I need you to bring back to the citadel. Her knowledge is…" and he hesitated, looking for better words, "… her skills are required for deciphering some ancient scrolls and maps. We're afraid that without her knowledge the whole damn papers are useless and we could lose another hundred years trying to understand it with meagre prospect of success."

Ghaeloden listened attentively.

"Once there, you should look for a witch, by the name of Naghnatë, whom I have no doubts that you'll sense long before finding the small village. She reeks of magic!" Felduror's words were tainted with a trail of hate, though he regained self-control quickly, before his anger clouded his judgement. "Words travelled of a curious event, the kind the old witch cannot ignore and won't waste an opportunity to come out of hiding. I want you to find her and bring her here! Yet I warn you, Drakhahoul, do not underestimate her as she is far smarter than what she likes showing."

The young dragon looked towards his king, their gazes locked for a long moment. A vain attempt in whatever he was trying to do, thought the wizard as he cleared his throat.

"And what if she refuses to come? What do I do then?" Ghaeloden demanded.

"You tell her I've sent you to summon her, her past is forgiven, her assistance is required. She will not give away the chance of regaining access to Arkhanthï, I promise you that!" Felduror let out a small sound of contentment.

"Understood. Though, will I be able to find this place? I've never ventured outside and –"

"You will, you will," started Felduror reassuringly, "it's a surprisingly insignificant place somewhere south-west from here. I shall provide you with all the necessary to find it. Besides you won't be travelling alone!"

"I beg your pardon?" Ghaeloden's surprise could not be restrained.

"The imp that summoned you here. He could come in quite handy since humans are not accustomed to the Drakhahouls anymore. There will be a time to show them our might, soon enough, but for the time being we should proceed with caution," Felduror replied.

"I see."

"He can easily be mistaken for a human child, and if need be, I'll allow him to use some spells to assume human-shape while making enquiries. You do not need to reveal yourself and, once again, no use of spells. Me and your king are keen to see how you fare without the need of such thing. Are we not, my enlightened king?"

"I am very keen indeed," replied Belrug.

"Then it shall be my mission to please you, my king." Ghaeloden bowed.

Felduror was pleased to see the young dragon accept his task without being too quizzical. "Good! I will send the creature with directions and further instructions! You are to leave at first light!"

CHAPTER VII

THE ARMOURY

Ghaeloden / Nuuk

The quiet dawn was promising a cloudless sky, even if a salted, sharp breeze picked up from the seas of the east. It would carry autumn's piercing cold pretty soon; the type of cold that made the sun appear distant and weak and turned vegetation yellow, orange and then dead-brown in a matter of days.

Ghaeloden was waking after a restless night; the wizard's request to venture beyond the walls had troubled his sleep aplenty, even though it was enticing to say the least.

What could he possibly want with a witch?

He remembered how hard he had tried to keep his curiosity at bay when the wizard had revealed his plan the previous evening. He recalled the wizard's wicked smile, tinged with trails of disgust and even envy, at the mention of her name. And he could also recollect the desperation and urgency in his voice as he told him to find her.

Only one thing had been more distressing; his own unanswered attempts at reaching Belrug's mind. Without any words, Ghaeloden had tried to reach deep within his king's mind. He had dug beyond the foggy irises and deadly flesh, somewhere

where only dragons could reach. He had hoped to find him somewhere in there, alas all he had found was emptiness; a desolate darkness he had been unable to pierce. In vain he had whispered, all he had received was silence. Whenever his king had spoken, his words had been cold and hollow. And that hadn't been the case for the previous evening alone, no, it had happened every single time he had been summoned.

It was as if the king was absent-minded.

With a jaw snap at empty air, he delivered himself to the present, thinking that the opportunity to leave those forsaken walls and lands was sweeter than any other foul instinct the cold morning could deliver from the previous, restless night.

He stretched his wings and body and displayed his potent stature upon the dark waters of the pond. A yawn that could encompass an oxen cart exposed a crowd of sparkling, sharp fangs and a long and pointy tongue that undulated up and down. His briefly glimpsed the reflection of his big eyes, like burning embers, glowing brightly against the morning's dull light. The cracks that issued along his long neck, spine and tail dimmed the noisy footsteps that were rushing towards him.

He could hear the imp panting hastily towards the pond. The rhythm of his bare feet appeared to be disturbed by something he was carrying. The consideration of that peculiar thought carried another frustration from the previous night; he was supposed to carry an imp on his back.

A mighty Drakhahoul reduced to being a beast of burden?

The rekindled desperation of his mind, made him wish he had let his instinct run and bit the old man's head like a rotten twig.

He swallowed his ire and let it wane with another brief stretch. This was not how he liked commencing his day.

The imp was almost there. A tall and loose shoulder-bag hampered his steps and made him run awkwardly. Obviously, the bag was not made for him, nor had the wizard bothered to find a more appropriate one. It fell and he picked it up a couple of times and when his arms gave in from the effort, the bag touched the ground and slowed his stride – it was about time that he stopped and made a knot in the lengthy straps.

"Are you ready for this venture, imp?" Ghaeloden asked

when the little creature arrived at the pond.

He dropped the bag at his feet and stooped with his hands on his knees, heaving for air. There was something funny about his reddened face, yet the dragon's attention was captured by a piece of paper that the imp kept in his right hand.

"Yes, mast –" the imp took a deep breath, "yes, your mightiness, in a moment."

"Is there any particular reason for the bag?" continued the dragon, curious to know if there was anything inside.

"Well of course, clothes and my food! I cannot eat what a dragon eats. I wouldn't try to consume meat, not if I was being starved to death," the imp replied.

"Have you ever had to suffer hunger? Really suffer it, as you say, 'starved'? I think you'd reconsider if that were the case and someone offered you a piece of meat."

"I have not. I've suffered many other mistreatments; however, I consider it wrong to consume someone's or something's flesh. I mean it with no disrespect, your might –"

"I am not your mightiness, creature!" growled Ghaeloden.

"I apologise," the imp replied, chin low on his chest.

It took a moment before the dragon continued. "Never mind. I know you are, or used to be, a very capable flyer over short distances, still, I hope you are not too scared of dreadful heights and astounding speeds!" he asked with an air of superiority.

"I was afraid of mentioning it, most kind Ghaeloden. I could not sleep a wink last night thinking about it. Not only am I not scared, but I would be honoured! It would make me the happiest of the Iprorims, the only imp to have been granted such an opportunity." There were honest sparks of tears in the imp's big eyes, and his voice was shaking.

Imagine the joy! An imp-rider on the back of a dragon.

The idea of being a beast of burden was hard to shake off. If it wasn't for his own plans, he would have rebelled at such a preposterous proposition.

Saddened by the sight of his indolent king, an idea had formed in his mind with suspicions of the wizard, a long while ago. He had to be right – what other possible reason could be there to explain why his king had become so dim-witted? And if he was right, and he succeeded, he would become the redeemer, the one that freed his king. Who knows what favours he would be granted then? He had vowed to keep things to himself, disliking ardently the idea of sharing his plans with other Drakhahouls. Most likely they only considered Belrug to be afflicted by some illness, or worse, believed what the old wizard told them, that he had been poisoned with the help of some old stones.

He kept the need to growl in the back of his throat and managed somehow to mask his annoyance. "To that extent, I hope this will stay between us. There's no need for others to know what we are doing."

"Surely!" A big smile formed on the ignorant imp's pale face.

"And that in your hand should be the instructions?" The dragon changed the subject.

"Yes." The imp flapped the papers in the air.

"Good! While you read them to me, we shall check for a saddle wide enough to fit my neck, that is if you still want to be able to walk after three days on my scaled-back. Unless, you'd want to ask the wizard to lend you his." Ghaeloden let out a mocking snort.

"No, that would not be wise. Better to check with the horse master, he surely can be of help," the imp suggested.

"Why not the armoury? There surely must be a dragon saddle unused sitting there about, otherwise why would they still keep that old structure?"

"That is an excellent idea, mighty Ghaeloden. I've always had a passion and fascination for human weapons. I find their nature to excel in deadly tools curious."

"Isn't that the most peculiar thing to learn today?" The dragon was truly surprised. "An imp with a passion for human-weapons, ha!"

The imp wrongly interpreted the dragon's remark and started tittering.

Ghaeloden interrupted him with a muffled throat-growl, which wasn't entirely intentional, still, he was pleased the amusing moment quickly passed. Skies forbid someone saw an imp laughing alongside a dragon.

They exchanged no other words until they reached the

armoury.

The edifice was fenced and squared by a thick set of fortifications and the entrance guarded day and night by shifts of Gholaks that blindly and unquestionably served Felduror. Few, if none, were ever permitted in this structure as it preserved many armaments of long-lost empires. Personal weapons of kings and queens, their armours and jewels, thrones and chariots and beloved works of art, some of which were considered to be imbued with magical powers. But, the wizard had little taste for works of art and never cared to inspect or arrange them inside his castle. He preferred to amass them and let the dust and insects of the dark eat them instead.

On this occasion the two brutes guarding the entrance of the fence that surrounded the building, were taller than the dragon expected. Their leather armours were stretched and cracked at the tiniest of movements, accentuating the bulk of their muscled bodies. They both had helmets partially covering their heads. The tallest of the two had a round wooden shield on his back and two curved swords showing dazzling-sharp edges. The other Gholak had a big spear, with a very thick shaft and a long spiked-blade, which at the tip was decorated by a silken-ribbon of red and black.

As they approached, the orcs did not even flinch, which was remarkable, considered Ghaeloden. He was accustomed to any orc, small or big, being scared and shiver at the sight of a mighty Drakhahoul such as himself. Some ran, some squeaked and some became as still as statues with eyes wide open; it comforted him and fed his ego every time, yet now he had already decided he despised these two orcs.

They actually proved bold enough and keen to put on their best war-faces, while lifting their palms in mid-air.

"Hold'eet there! What'z yaur businez 'ere dragon?" The smaller orc spoke while the other grimaced, showing his two oversized fangs.

"We came here for a dragon saddle, on special orders from our master, the wizard. Let us through!" the dragon replied authoritatively, avoiding the surprised look on the imp's face.

"Got paperz?" the taller orc asked, stepping in front of his smaller mate.

"Of course we do. Show them, imp!"

Ghaeloden could see the imp trying to gain his attention, and he let out a snort to make him do as bidden.

"Here, here!" The imp took the list with the directions, the wizard had drawn and written for him, and extended his hand.

The two brutes moved simultaneously to grab it and started to quarrel in guttural, incomprehensive and low-pitched noises. Their bickering was brief; the taller one had managed to make the smaller recede with a sharp spin of the other's wrist. He took his time to check the instructions and then handed the paper back to the imp.

"'Ere, all's order!" he said and when the other orc tried to reach and check the papers himself the taller one stopped him with a hand on his chest and continued, "I sayz, all's order!"

The smaller orc did not insist, instead he barked his own command, "Once ee're done, be sure you lock'et back whiz thiz key. And bring'et back!"

The imp grabbed the key and paper and thanked the beasts. He folded them together and waited for the gates to open. He stood silent and only when they were far enough from the orcs' prying ears, did Ghaeloden hear him heave a sigh of relief.

"How did you know they would let us pass?" the imp asked.

The dragon chuckled. "None of them were able to read, imp. How could you not know that?"

"I was very scared, even with your mightiness alongside me. Whenever I am scared, I cannot think clearly. I should've known that two brutes like those had never seen parchments before."

"You must learn to control your emotions, creature. Many bad situations can be avoided if one thinks clear enough and doesn't fall prey to distress." The dragon spoke softly, brushing purposely and gently his knee on the tiny creature's shoulder.

"Apologies," said the imp moving slightly to one side, clearly thinking he had stepped in the dragon's way.

"No need for it." Ghaeloden smiled.

"Acknowledging the problem is the very first step towards its resolution!" Ghaeloden exclaimed and decided it was time to play a little trick on the imp.

Well I most certainly cannot fit inside the armoury nor can I watch through the thick walls of this windowless building, so you'll have to be my eyes and ears while I wait outside! The dragon's mind issued his thoughts to the imp without the need of spoken words.

"Surely, we —" the imp suddenly stopped, mouth ajar, eyes fixed on the dragon's.

Clearly he hadn't experienced such a thing before, thought the dragon and smiled.

You didn't think my eyes and years simply meant that you'd be left alone in there now, did you? The Drakhahoul's ironic tone echoed in the imp's mind.

The little creature took a long while to realise what was happening, and when he did, he almost shouted, "Your mightiness can speak inside my mind?"

Yes, and there is no need to give voice to your words either, once you hear me! continued the dragon. *When I am speaking in your mind you can think of an answer and that is what I will perceive. This way we will can communicate and nobody will be able to listen to us. Think of me as if I lived inside your own little head.*

There was something strangely humorous about the confused visage of the imp. He looked like a human child, overwhelmed by things he could not completely grasp.

"So you can hear all my thoughts?" There was a certain trail of doubt and fear, mingling upon his face when he spoke. "And what if my own thoughts offend your mightiness?"

It is not as simple as that, Ghaeloden continued in the imp's mind. *I cannot hear that which is not directly linked to me and you! First there has to be an initial contact between us in order for me to gain admittance to your thoughts, hence my knee touching your shoulder just a moment ago. And not everything in your mind can be read or understood, even by our minds. Many thoughts lay obscured and blurred, woven in one's mind and are very hard to deduce and comprehend their true meaning. Your thoughts are still your own, only what is related to the temporary bind between me and you can be perceived by my mind!* The dragon's explanation seemed to placate the frown on the imp's forehead.

"I see!"

I know it is hard to fully comprehend, but you need not to worry. Besides, almost nothing of this world is of concern to a dragon. Why would I care if you consider me ugly, dangerous or a hideous meat-eater? Most of the time I am considered far worse things by the orcs, and boldly so with spoken words. Most of us dragons have learned to ignore and not actually care about these petty things. The dragon's voice was less harsh, and he began to fear he had revealed a little too much of his own thoughts. *Why don't you give it a try?*

To the imp, it appeared that the Drakhahoul was rather entertained by his difficulty in comprehending what he just said. Was he amused by the faces he made? Did the dragon, too, find him hideous? Was he to be mocked and ridiculed by this being as well?

Nuuk could not say for sure, nor could he comprehend how he found himself on such endeavour? Nothing made sense anymore; since being freed from the basements, he had hardly been allowed to leave the floors where he was serving Felduror, and now he was about to leave the empire's lands entirely. Accompanied by a Drakhahoul, and better, on the back of one. It was beyond his wildest imagination, yet, opposed to the excitement the endeavour provided, he was scared of what it might bare.

He wondered if the dragon had *heard* any of his concerns, but it did not appear so since his expression remained unchanged.

Then I shall apologise now for things you might learn about me that may upset you, kind Ghaeloden! Nuuk's thought found its way in Ghaeloden's mind.

That won't be necessary, now go on then! The dragon's tone confirmed that none of his worries had been sensed, or maybe ignored, which was good either way.

The imp unlocked and cracked open the double wooden-door of the armoury, only to be hit by a stale smell which filled their noses and lungs.

An uncontrollable cough took over him, one the dragon had been smart to avoid with his tall neck.

When he was ready, he moved inside. It was too dark to see so he started looking for a torch, which he knew well enough where to find; to the left-hand side, where every single structure or room he was allowed to visit, kept one.

"Ghaeloden? I need some help lighting this torch, there's nothing in here I can use," he whispered, still unsure that his own thoughts would suffice to be heard by the dragon.

So if you were in mortal threat, you'd obey your master and not use a spell that could save your life? The dragon's voice sounded cynical. *Either way, come here!*

Nuuk kept up the torch for the dragon to be able to light. With what was more like a cough to him, the torch set ablaze and he could now return into the darkness of the armoury.

If only I were allowed to use spells! thought the imp and no reply came back from the dragon.

Spells had been banned by the wizard throughout the castle and the empire's lands. There were severe punishments for those caught using them, and his acolytes, the foreign creatures, had proved the most talented on sensing their practise and provenance.

The light of the torch sufficed only to appreciate how much dust his tiny feet could lift up from the old space. He could make out shapes up to a few feet in front of him, the rest of the vast and occupied armoury was not to be penetrated by such a dull light. Nothing inside seemed disturbed by daylight in years.

He quickly gained some distance from the entrance, the pace of his bare feet shifting to a more sliding stride so as to lift less dust on his way. Though, very few objects still revealed their true nature as the dust was piled in thick layers on every horizontal surface and where it failed to settle, dense spider webs took on decorating them. In such fashion, numerous tall statues stood like spectres lurking in the blackness; frozen warriors of defunct kings and queens that now, one could not tell which was what. Piles of sharp swords, spears, glaives, shields and axes, carelessly amassed, seemed blunted by time and dust, and only on a very few spots did his torch glimmer with reflected light from their metal sheen.

"Mice!" he whispered the thought that has shadowed him since the entrance.

If the smell had not convinced him, their sound was

everywhere, their small steps drawn erratically on the dusted floor disturbed by his intrusion. They ran and hid between the mountains of abandoned objects and there they squeaked until they felt safe.

Further ahead, a carriage that he could tell was festooned with golden ornaments, made an eerie spectacle immersed in thousands of spider webs thick as straws while deep in their cores the spiders were gleaming in his orange light, creeping deeper still on their bouncing surfaces. Undisturbed, he moved closer and with a hand brushed the dust off one door only to realise that the carriage was made in the purest of gold. The heavy golden doors and panels were bolted with small golden rivets and stood on four big and heavy golden wheels all held together by a square golden frame.

He must've have failed to keep at bay his awe as the dragon intruded in his mind. *What do you see?*

A carriage made entirely of gold! answered the imp, still mesmerised by the sight.

Oh my, a golden carriage? I would very much like to see that! said the dragon. *Have you found the saddle yet?* he continued.

It's hard to see anything in here. Unless I knock into one it will take me a while to find it, if there are any. And there are many spiders and rats! I think I can even hear one breathe, the imp replied spotting one that just dashed from under the carriage.

Keep looking then! replied the dragon.

The imp circled the carriage and went straight for the pulling harness which he could just about see under a blanket of web. He was confident that it might be of some use, though there was barely any space to move around the carriage and here the spider webs seemed even thicker. He had to carefully place each foot to avoid getting hurt or trapped between the countless objects he could not see, and felt underneath.

Moving sideways around the back of the bulky wagon, his foot slipped and rolled over a round object of some sort and he fell to his knees. He saved himself thanks to his free hand that clutched at one of the two golden steps. His torch flickered worryingly almost losing its strength, and when he thought its flame would die, it recovered its full brightness. In that moment he thought he had spotted something; a different light that reflected brighter on the carriage as soon as his torch appeared to lose its strength. He turned his head while lowering his torch behind a shield. He was right; on the far-left corner, between protrusions, something was glowing a bright purple-orange. The imp abandoned the harness in its place and started moving towards the beam.

Considering how hard it had been to make the few steps to reach the harness, he gave up the idea of walking on the floor and started climbing on top of the chairs, crates and coffers that he thought were probably filled with silver, gold and foreign coins.

From up there he could see better towards the beam of pulsing purple-orange light. It appeared to call him. He felt compelled to reach it, the faster the better. Still, he had to pay attention to the wobbling pieces of furniture, tools and items he was crawling on. He did not mind the dust and colourless crawlers anymore and he was moving as fast as his senses allowed. Whenever something trembled and felt unstable under his knees and free hand, he shifted and tried a different route. He slowly made good progress, feeling satisfied to burn the sticky webs in his way. It was not exactly a stroll in the gardens, more like a slow and arduous task to reach that corner.

He finally made it. He was standing few feet away from the gorgeous beam of light, it's purple haze clearly overwhelming the orange one. It emanated from behind a pile of things on top of which sat a sanguine-red imperial chair covered partially by a blanket.

Taken by excitement he lifted the blanket too quickly and the flimsy wardrobe he was on shook for an instant before it quickly dropped to the floor taking the imp violently all the way down the pile. The chain reaction he caused, brought a havoc of sounds in the dark space that echoed through the room like brief thunder. Except a small knock against his lower back, he did not hurt himself, nor did he get stuck, yet the cloth he carelessly lifted was now burning, having fallen right over his torch. He picked it up fast from a corner and climbed hastily to the very top on the flipped wardrobe that lay over a pile of broken pieces of furniture. Once free to move his hand, he slammed the linen piece against the flat wall heartily. The cloth sparkled brightly for an instant and sizzled with many sparks, though the flames soon started to die down. With a deep breath of dust, burnt webs and fabric, he relaxed his body and looked around to see if there was still risk of fire, but there wasn't.

Dust fluttered and billowed in the air filling the back of his throat and his lungs. Falling prey to the thick grime, he started a convulsing dry-cough until his stomach hurt and big tears started falling down his cheeks. He closed his eyes gasping for air and pulled the neck of his shirt higher to cover his mouth. There was not much else he could do so he crawled back on the wardrobe and buried his face in his elbow while propping his back against the wall.

And there he stood for a long moment until the thick wave of dust settled enough and he did not find breathing quite so harsh. Alas, the hand that kept the torch started to hurt. He had to hurry.

With caution he advanced towards the light that had tumbled somewhere on his left side, deeper under the rest of the objects. Descending from the wardrobe, he found it on the floor, between broken pieces of rotten wood, metal bowls and cups and a chainmail. He had to squint his eyes as soon as he lifted a curled chainmail that partially covered it, the strong beam of light forcing his eyes to slits.

It was an odd fashioned sceptre, rather short and with intricate vine shapes deftly sculpted on the stick, which was of a very peculiar matter, neither wood nor stone – more like bone. The tip, from which the light emanated, was even more peculiar, fashioning a head of a beaked-beast, that resembled a hawk of some sort, in the imp's opinion. The source of the light were the beast's eyes that had been replaced by two glowing, ember stones.

Any luck yet? The irritated voice of the dragon disturbed his examination.

Unexpectedly the imp felt rather impatient, *I found some cords that might help, still, not a single saddle!* though he was keen on examining the marvellous object on the floor, *'I'm sure we can do with a horse's one. We could try from the stables instead…*

With a bit of effort, he elongated his hand and carefully took the sceptre in his hand. A rush of energy issued from it and spread through his fingers all the way down to his toes and up to his big ears.

The light of the hawk-figure's eyes completely faded as he issued his thought towards the dragon, *…the horse master might be able to help. I am certain he would not dare going against your mightiness' wish.*

There was no reply.

A long time passed and he started thinking he had said something he shouldn't have.

Master Ghaeloden, I am sorry I did not mean to offend. He tried thinking of what he might have said wrong.

Nothing still. All quiet. He must have really offended the dragon. Fear and anxiety lifted from within and he knew he had to convince the dragon of his innocence; he could not compromise his journey on the back of the Drakhahoul, not like this.

With reinvigorated strength he climbed back up the pile of objects, and reached the path he had previously found. He increased his speed, feeling confident of his trail, alas, he fell hard when his knee hit a protrusion he had missed.

"Youch!" he screamed, trying to claim first the torch he had lost again and then the sceptre.

At last creature, what happened? I could not sense your presence anymore! The dragon's tone was harsh.

Master Ghaeloden? Nuuk was surprised to see that the stones inside the creature's eyes started gleaming with the same purple-orange light, while the sceptre lay on the floor.

What happened? repeated the impatient dragon.

I fell. The pain was still acute, yet he was more intrigued by the object. *I found something particularly strange. I think it's because of it that you could not sense me anymore. It's a bright sceptre that was buried by piles of other objects in a corner.*

What is it with you and shiny objects? Ghaeloden grew even more annoyed.

I apologise, it caught my attention and once I finally found it and touched it you could not sense me anymore, apparently! He preferred to keep for himself how he failed to resist the wild and seductive force of the sceptre's call.

Find that harness and let's be on our way! the dragon commanded. *Promptly!*

The imp took his time to carefully retrace his steps and avoid another rough up with the dust and spider webs.

Once back at the golden chariot, he took all the leather harnesses and wrapped them once, twice and thrice over his shoulders and returned to the entrance, the loose ends of the bridle still trailing on the dusty floor.

Master Ghaeloden… oh! He realised that the sceptre was still in his hand.

With care, he placed it on the floor and tried again, *Master Ghaeloden, I am at the door!*

What took you so long, imp? Open the door but do not come out, put off that torch and leave the sceptre on the floor. I'll peek inside!

Although his voice sounded rough, there was a certain trace of unease as well as lust in the dragon's voice.

He did as bid and the dragon bent his long neck, touching the ground. His head was bigger than the massive double-gate of the armoury.

"My, my!" The dragon allowed the words to break free out of his mouth as he peeked at the glowing sceptre at the imp's feet.

That is a really nice object, and it is glowing all right! Now let me see what you were jabbering about. Try picking it and speak to me, I want to see what… He did not finish his sentence as the imp disappeared entirely as soon as his fingers clutched the sceptre.

The dragon blinked persistently, while moving his head sideways and trying to take a better look. "What sort of trickery is this?"

"Ha-ha! You should see your face, master Ghaeloden!" said the imp as he dropped the glowing object on the ground.

"Imp, you do realise what happened, do you? That sceptre made you completely vanish from my sight? There aren't any items I know of that could accomplish that, and not in more experience and magic accustomed-hands than yours!"

The imp stopped laughing and the dragon continued to talk.

"Now I start to understand why the wizard keeps the armoury guarded. I wonder what other wonders might be concealed inside. This thing must've been here gathering dust for a long time. I think we should keep it!" Ghaeloden suggested.

"But, what if the wizard finds out? He will not hesitate and turn me into ashes," said the frightened imp. "No, you take it! I do not want to have anything to do with it. You keep it, master Ghaeloden!"

"Imp, just put it inside your bag and let's get moving. We are already late! There is no need to fret. Moreover, I do not think that the wizard will come looking for it any time soon. You've been well acquainted with the dust, that much of it only means years. And make sure you lock the doors!"

The argument did not fully convince the imp but he knew that against the dragon there were no odds of winning the argument. He had recognised too well the lust in his voice when he had mentioned the golden carriage and had seen the sparkles in his eyes at the sight of the glowing sceptre. Yet, he could not blame him, he felt equally attracted to this object.

So he took the sceptre, disappeared for a moment, and reappeared once he had placed it inside his bag. He checked once more to make sure there were no fire risks remaining, then lifted the harnesses from the floor. He locked the door as requested and returned the key.

As they walked away from the armoury gates, leaving the brutes still arguing about in their guttural tongue, the dragon looked at the imp and said, "See, imp? I told you there was no reason for concern! And by the way, do you have a name?"

The imp smiled, pleased greatly that a mighty Drakhahoul had asked. "My name is Nuuk!"

CHAPTER VIII

AMONGST THE CLOUDS

Nuuk / Ghaeloden

Up in the sky above the citadel, the air was cooler even as the sun rose higher. Strong currents carried sporadic drops of rain from far along the coastline, which darted like dulled arrows against their skins and tasted salty on their lips. At this time of year, and this far north, the weather could shift frequently and brusquely. Luckily, Nuuk and Ghaeloden were already well on their way, soon to reach warmer lands.

The morning events left them to gather their thoughts in silence, while enjoying the comfort of the fresh air caressing their bodies. The visit to the stables had provided them with the needed and improvised saddle and the imp couldn't have been more grateful to the skilful services of the horse master – had he ridden the dragon on his sharp and stone-hard scales he would have seriously injured his bony legs.

A long time had passed since Nuuk had flown, having been forbidden and impeded to do so since the very first moment of his capture and enrolment in the service of the wizard. Although the speed and elevation of the dragon's flight was something he was not familiar with, it consoled him like nothing else to be up in the air again. He had never reached such heights and was fascinated with how soft and moist the clouds they encountered felt. The feeling made him smile, a smile that lingered on his wrinkled face at length.

Overwhelmed by a strong desire to close his eyes, he freed one of his hands and raised it up while imaging it was him flying, not the dragon. With eyes still shut, he tightened his legs around Ghaeloden's neck and freed his other hand as well, allowing the pleasant sensation to become more thrilling. Resentment, nostalgia, joy and fear, all mingled in his mind and body with vigour. Maybe that was the cause, not the powerful gusts of wind, that allowed bitter and happy tears to free themselves from his tightly shut eyes. Yet, he was smiling nonetheless. This was by far the happiest moment of his entire life. If only he could share it with his fellow Iprorims; Zula, Zilpha, Firk. But soon he realised he was not in Grora anymore and hadn't been for a long while. The sad feeling overcame the joy in his mind and soon, too soon, the pure moment of happiness vanished. He was now tightly holding the harness, the smile upon his lips gone.

What is the matter Nuuk? The dragon's voice invaded the imp's mind, as if aware of his inner turbulence.

It is funny how fate mocks us, master Ghaeloden, said the imp. *One moment we are happy and the very next instant we are sad!*

It is the rule of the living! We are not immortals and, even if one lived as long as the Drakhahouls live, this would not change. As a matter of fact, it could only get worse if one did not learn to cope with life's measures, replied the dragon.

The imp lost in his own observance, barely made sense of what the dragon said, and allowed his thoughts to leave his mind, *I have been kept against my will for far too long. I have lost my youth alongside a path that was not mine to travel. I wish to be free again!*

Ghaeloden took some time to respond. *We should always cherish what we have in the moment and never regret our own choices, be them wrong or good. Alas, I've made many wrong ones myself, I consider that what mattered more, was the success in amending them.*

True, though the reason I am here was not my choice! replied the imp, awoken with interest from his own demeanour.

How is it that you came into Felduror's service, if I may ask?

It was a long time ago, started the imp, *and I barely remember how it had happened. I was a youngling then. All I remember is that I had never seen such an unfamiliar creature like the humans. Inside the northern forests of Grora, we had never felt fear before; Iprorims grow up learning that all creatures are not harmful to our race. The wolves and bears were not interested in our flesh but actually scared of our magical knowledge. We lived peacefully in our colony and never dreamed of leaving those lands. We felt protected, we felt safe. How could I have known how different mankind was? Greed for power and wealth made man a vicious creature that would go to any lengths in achieving its own petty goals.*

A growl issued from the dragon's throat, dulling the strong current and the powerful flapping of his muscled wings. Was that disgruntlement, the imp considered briefly?

The imp continued, *When the wizard's fellowship arrived, all of us gathered around, and no one knew what the odd creatures were, nor what their purpose was. Our curiosity and genuine lack of fear was our doom on that day. I remember staring at their clothes; a curious decoration that served, as I later came to understand, against the cold weather and also as a sign towards their rank and gender; pointed hats, sparkling gloves and robes, boots and bags fashioned from animal skins. What a horrid scheme, I thought, when many years later I learned how these were made.* Nuuk paused, sickened by his own words. *That is all I remember before waking up, being carried through the narrow corridors of the castle's prisons and thrown into a small cell unable to use magic anymore. It was as if I never had the power to do so!*

That and, of course, the string around your wings, added Ghaeloden with some curiosity, and continued without allowing the imp's reply. *I never understood why the wizard needed the imps. Our mother and the king haven't had much to impart of old times to us younglings. I only know from others that Iprorims were of utmost importance to his cause, and never understood why. It is not that you see imps all over the citadel of late. Honestly, I think you are the only one around the castle now!*

"Neither do I, Ghaeloden!" Nuuk whispered with faint intensity before resuming to their inner conversation. *Many were locked with me in the cells below the towers. I could not see them in the darkness, I could only hear them. We often told tales of our beautiful home in Grora. Some of them were from far distant lands I hadn't heard of. They spoke a different tongue than mine and only occasionally did we manage to comprehend each other.*

Nuuk allowed himself a weak smile, given the circumstances. He did miss conversation with a fellow imp, and one behind bars would still count.

Though, too soon I was the only one left while others were being freed one by one. Many days of solitude passed before I was taken to meet the wizard. And when I did, I was forced to swear my allegiance to him and bend to his powers for as long as he deemed necessary to use my service in the empire's cause.

The wind against which they were flying now whistled harder and colder. It made them pause their flow of thoughts for a moment and Ghaeloden had to glide lower where the air was warmer and its currents less intense, so they could hear each other's words.

The imp noticed his intention as he started talking rather than using his mind. "Once sworn into his service, life became a little easier for me and days started to pass faster. I became so enthralled by my ordinary tasks that I subdued the hatred towards the man that enslaved me. At one time I thought I could forgive him for his deeds, if only I managed to use my wings and not lose them for good. And many a time he had promised to do good by me if I did good by him, so I obeyed to my best of my ability."

No immediate reply came from Ghaeloden, but clearly he was keen on knowing more.

The opportunity was his to take, the imp considered as with closed eyes, and gently embraced by the warm air, he continued, "He taught me how to write and read and I was just as surprised as him to know I was capable of such things. And not the common tongues only. No, kind sir. To his gratification I was able to learn all the dialects of the past centuries with little effort and that gave me the function I hold now, as his assistant and interpreter of foreign manuscripts with all this wretched stones' research. Mostly, I only scribble his notes and mutterings."

"Nuuk, what I know of these stones is what accidently reached my ears, and I trust almost none of it! But, if he is so keen for your skills, why do you have all those marks and bruises?" asked Ghaeloden.

"His behaviour is unrecognisable at times," Nuuk explained. "One moment he is serene and peacefully reading through his books and the next he is very angry and upset. I often blame that brew he likes to drink." The imp's hand was softly moving around his neck caressing the fresh bruises. "I'm sure he never means to hit me willingly, at least I hope so. Maybe blinded by rage he cannot see who's standing in front of him as the throws whatever he chances upon with his hands. Had I been allowed to use magic I could've protected myself most of the times. Without it, I'm just as defenceless as a goat surrounded by a pack of hungry wolves."

The dragon scoffed, clearly disturbed by the imp's revelations.

Nuuk recollected with dread Felduror's expression from the day before, when he had been instructed to fetch the dragon. Whenever his wraths started, they had always been preceded by an ominous moment just like that one, his unreadable face would shift into a raging fever.

It was Ghaeloden's voice that returned him to the present. "I never knew that the wizard had these moments of lunacy. Has he ever apologised or said anything at all after these flashes of anger?"

"Never, though once he stopped in the middle of his furious bout and acknowledged I was there, while carefully lifting the heavy tome he was about to toss at me. He looked straight into my eyes that day. I could see the dumbfounded expression on his contorted and reddened face and I'm almost convinced he was crying. I'd like to think that he saw me that day, me Nuuk, his humble servant, and that's why he stopped. Yet we may never know. He never had the desire to speak of this with me," concluded the imp.

"The wizard must be a curious and interesting being, behind those guarded doors, Nuuk. I must confess I do not envy you but I do think I see why the wizard has chosen you," the dragon said, surprising and intriguing the imp.

"And why would you think so, Ghaeloden?"

"I think he never expected you to become accustomed and learned in human ways. And most likely amongst all others of your own kind, you were the only one capable of such. That's why you are still…" the dragon paused as if he was trying to rephrase his words, "the most respected imp in all the citadel."

Nuuk was sure there was something else the dragon had wanted to say, yet his words cheered him up nonetheless. "Thank you, master Ghaeloden! It means munch to have someone to talk with and be understood."

"Again, Nuuk, Ghaeloden is more than enough, no need for master or mightiness or anything else." His voice was gentler as he continued, "Besides we are friends now!"

"You and me, friends? I never had a friend outside of Grora." The delight in the imp's heart found its way in his frivolous voice. "I promise you, Ghaeloden, you'll be just as glad to be my friend as I am to be yours!" Nuuk added candidly.

A suffused growl vibrated inside Ghaeloden's long neck.

Dear me! An imp that thinks to have a dragon as a friend? A creature that likes eating beeswax? How low am I willing to go with this farce? The dragon was bothered by his own words, and kept silent for a long time.

Though, he had to carefully measure if he was to trust the imp with his own ideas or not. He had even told the insignificant creature not to call him appropriate names, when he hankered to be called in ways worthy of such a mighty presence and appearance. But again, it would be a shame to imperil his own devices by not carefully planning his every move. The imp let it known there was desire in his heart to be free, similar to him. That had been a fortuitous revelation and, since the imp knew more about the wizard than any other being in Arkhanthï, far more than he hoped to find out on his own, his dream of being the one to free his king suddenly rejuvenated his soul. If he wanted to rid the empire from the wizard's influence, he would have to learn as much as he could about him by any means available, and that meant including the insignificant, imp creature.

He had decided to scrutinise and befriend him, if he wanted

to get to the truth.

They had covered many miles from the citadel and reached outside the second row of walls, thanks to the cold currents that pushed towards the south. The Drakhahoul felt almost no strain on his wings' muscles, curiously so after the sleepless night, and was confident he could continue for much longer. Yet, he was concerned of what might lie ahead; he had never ventured outside the walls and could not hide a feeble sense of dread.

Like any of the mighty winged-creatures, he enjoyed flying almost as much as eating, and cherished every moment up in the air like it was the last one, even if he had to carry the imp on his neck. Besides Sereri-the-White, his mother, who had become Felduror's ride, there weren't others who allowed to be ridden. And for good reason; dragons were supposed to be free creatures and if such an occasion ever arose to allow someone to ride them, it would definitely be because of the dragon's desire and not the opposite. Alas, times were different and Drakhahouls were not the free creatures that they liked to believe. Perhaps those that had forsaken the empire many years ago were, perhaps they had found their true freedom.

To push such thinking away, he half closed his wings against his body and dove for a short couple of heartbeats, and when he opened them again he undulated his body upwards to regain altitude. The motion lifted his spirit. It appeared to have done the same to the imp, as he let out a loud chuckle which came to a sudden stop when a rancid stench saturated the air they found themselves in. A reaction of equal revulsion was shared between them.

"What is this stench?" asked Nuuk, leaning on the dragon's neck to inspect on each side the lands below.

"It must be the cattle lands!" said the dragon, understanding now why they had been placed that far from the citadel.

The reek saturated the current patch of land and air. It made the dragon shake and snort, his head darting about. He glimpsed the imp covering his mouth and nose.

"I never thought it would be that ghastly up close!" Ghaeloden continued. "I often hunt the beasts on the meadows between the walls, and rarely sensed it. And certainly not as strong. These are the farms from which we get the meat to support our dragons, the Gholaks as well as the humans and probably the imps too!"

"No, no! We don't eat meat, Ghaeloden!" The curt reply of the imp made it clear there was some displeasure towards meat-eaters. "Though, what use is there for an army when there is no war or conflict?"

The silence Nuuk's question raised, showed that neither of them had an answer.

With a tail swipe, Ghaeloden turned to the left and descended to a level where they could see more clearly.

Vast patches of land were compactly occupied by little black, white and brown marks far beneath them. Like a bleeding bruise on a living body, the land showed its scars only to those able to see it from high above. The dragon gasped in awe and abhorrence. He had never seen such a thing. A thread of fear lifted from within; could this compromise the way he thought of his prey?

Vast squared patches of forests had been eradicated to build the shelters and the milking parlours for the myriad of cows, goats and sheep. Now that he saw it closer, Ghaeloden was not pleased to acknowledge how the common beasts had to live; amassed in tight places and exploited throughout their lives. He briefly considered how displeased the imp might be, though he understood its purpose and, awkwardly, one of the smells stimulated his appetite. No, perhaps nothing would change for him.

What he felt utterly angered about, was the radical transformation of the landscape; the endless covers of green in this side of the realm were gone, replaced by black, foul-smelling pools of sludge and mud that wafted their nauseating fumes for many miles around. Thick rivulets of the same dark-brown matter of dirt trailed like sharp cuts from underneath each big building. They joined into a vast pond which glistened in the sun's light, while the fetor released into the air. Those were the places where the beasts were being kept for shelter overnight. The clusters of wide buildings made the shepherds' village the main source for meat, milk, cheese and skins to the citadel and perhaps the entire empire. Ghaeloden marvelled and wondered if such amount of meat was solely being raised for the few dragons that lived at the castle. Definitely most of it would find the orcs' tables. A shiver ran across his neck, back and tail; it hadn't been long since they passed the throng of Gholak's armies, idling within the walls. Luckily, their fetor wasn't as strong, definitely the imp hadn't perceived it and he had no desire to talk of such brutes.

Following the single road that directed southwards, they left behind the reeking air and reached another circular-shaped village. Perpetual wafting smokes puffed their way out from too many houses. The road cut the entire village in half and led to a market, much bigger than the one inside the walls. There was a myriad of humans, the size of ants from where the dragon and the imp looked. They darted from side to side, among the dozens of carts, shacks and stalls.

Busy about their tasks, the humans did not realise that above them a dragon was darting with great speed. As high as they were, most likely the dragon appeared like a hawk.

Miles down, Ghaeloden broke the silence. "I don't know about you, Nuuk, but I am starving. We've made good progress and, if you were right, we should be on the right path. The currents are already pleasantly warmer now and I think we could rest for a couple of moments while we eat. What do you say?"

"As you wish, Ghaeloden. I'm not that hungry, though I'd appreciate a moment's rest while you eat."

They crossed a thick forest and landed deep inside, on a clear patch surrounded by tall trees, quite high on a mountain top. The dragon stopped only for a brief moment, so Nuuk could get off, then he went hunting.

Once in the air, Ghaeloden perceived the pleasure the little creature took on laying himself on the warm ground. He could even feel the solace offered by the tall, soft blades of sun-warmed grass, lulling his body to a sweet drowsiness. Clearly Nuuk did not know how to unbind himself from the connection, and every thought was almost entirely felt, as long as the dragon remained in proximity.

Alas, hunger had the priority and so he dedicated proper time on chasing a few wild goats.

The little beasts gave little, if no trouble at all.

Satiated, the Drakhahoul contemplated how to make the imp do his bidding. If he wanted to gain access to the wizard's secrets and use them to stop him and his greed for power, he'd have to get closer to him. The tiny creature seemed foolish enough to be beguiled into small talk, but he could not let overconfidence jeopardise his plans. He had to be certain of the imp's loyalty. It was a sign of the stars that they had met; it was the Drakhahoul's spirit himself that had brought the atoning creature to him, of that the dragon was convinced. The imp was the perfect candidate; he had already gained Felduror's trust and, with the sceptre, he could also be invisible to the cunning wizard, unless of course, his powerful spells protected him.

It would be a risk worth taking, thought the dragon, if the imp managed to provide enough secrets from the wizard's chambers and libraries in the main tower. Tainting the imp's mind with his own thoughts would be rather simple, though it could also reveal his true plans to the creature and this was not the way he wanted to proceed. He'd have to keep delving with his words and let the imp reveal whatever information he was keeping safe.

Just as he was thinking of Nuuk, an unexpected shiver of compassion tainted his mind.

No creature should be bent to any malicious minds, be it for greater goods or not! His own thought was strong and took his mind to his king.

Belrug-the-Black, the only one that needed rescuing, the only meaningful victim of the realm. Nuuk and perhaps all his kin had been doomed already and beyond salvation. Alas, having a dragon completely in the wizard's hands, and a powerful king nonetheless, was unacceptable.

Rage reached Ghaeloden's mouth and he let out an instinctive, furious roar which issued and mingled with a wave of bright-orange flames that echoed through the valley. He did not care that he could be seen or heard. The anger filling his core rejuvenated his desire of ridding the whole empire of Felduror's influence, even if he had to burn the old man himself.

He dove back towards land and saw Nuuk jump onto his feet from the comfort of the soft grass, as if burnt by fire. It would have been too late if Ghaeloden was a foe, as before the imp recovered and reacted, the dragon was already upon him.

"It is time, Nuuk! We should be on our way," the dragon said as he landed.

"Was that you, the sound?" The imp tried to compose himself.

"Yes, I had to clear my throat."

"That was scarier than our king's roar!"

His honest compliment beguiled the dragon, and he preferred not to reply.

"One thing I forgot to mention," said the imp, "as you might well know, Ghaeloden, the wizard specifically asked us not to be seen by anyone outside the valley and to avoid travel during the day far south!"

"I imagined he might ask that. I think he'd like everyone to believe we've been long extinct. Either way, it will be hard not to be seen if we travel by day. I'll try and keep as high as we can comfortably fly," replied Ghaeloden.

"From what he said," the imp started, "people have always been afraid to venture beyond the valley of the Whispering Peaks. As a matter of fact, southerners often tell tales and fables to scare their younglings into travelling this far. They believe that Arkhanthï is a doomed place from where no one returns!"

"Well, that isn't far from the truth. The wizard has his way of treating his guests, as you might well know. Do you recall the dwarf that came to the wizard, not so long ago, asking for shelter and work in the citadel? I think you might agree that nobody has seen him since that day, and I doubt he was sent away!" Ghaeloden could almost remember his strong, musky scent.

The dwarf had stood motionless after the gates opened before him. His eyes met the young dragon's, by coincidence around the entrance at the time. He remembered well that amusing expression of disbelief ornamented by the long wispy hair and beard. A minute creature, shorter even than the imp, yet stronger and bulkier, almost as wide as a wine barrel.

"I do remember that day," replied the imp with sorrow. "I was with the wizard and he was not particularly cheerful about their conversation. I wonder what happened to the poor soul?"

The dragon almost perceived the unguarded thoughts of the imp making him hopeful about his undertaking. If the annihilation of the wizard scared the imp away, maybe his salvation might sound more acceptable. Not wanting to give away the fact that he understood the imp's thoughts, the dragon decided to guide him into voicing them out.

"There must be a reason why he is behaving like this! Greed alone can't account for everything as a greedy person would not spend time surrounded by books in those ragged robes he's always wearing. I wonder if his mind has been poisoned by those stones he's meddling with?" The dragon's words surprised himself; he had never seriously considered the possibility.

"That is most interesting, Ghaeloden, and could very well be the case! Yet, who in their right mind would try and find out how many he has, or if he has any? To me he has always failed in his endeavours." The imp appeared intrigued.

"It would take a very brave creature indeed!" lured the dragon.

"I reckon it would become a hero, praised in song for days to come," added in the imp, climbing slowly into his saddle.

I reckon indeed! The dragon allowed his thought to be heard by the imp, hoping that the intriguing seed had been deeply planted in his little mind.

In silence they carried on at length, Nuuk still trying to unravel the meaning of everything he had been told by the dragon. It appeared that he was keen on finding more about the stones, but to what extent? Would he try and use them for himself? Could he do such a thing?

After an almost taciturn consideration of the map, they concluded they were crossing the moderate plains between Doradhur and Aranthul. Below them, life was silent. The sun had set, its last rays almost completely unnoticeable at their altitude. A few orange sparks could already be seen inside the forests, far on the horizon. Though, underneath them, pitch black reigned.

Small drips of rain pattered over their bodies, portending an imminent heavier rain even if they were carried by softer currents and a pleasant warm air permeated the sky.

"I think we should take cover for the night!" the dragon broke the long bolstering silence, gliding effortlessly in circles to approach the ground.

Sheltered by the lack of light, they landed in a clearing in the heart of a dense forest. It was surprisingly colder than in the sky, and the air they filled their lungs with was a rich mixture of sweet, delicate wildflowers and fresh pinewood. The tall trees that surrounded the grassy patch provided perfect shelter for the night, protecting them from winds in the high mountain and prying eyes.

"I will sleep in that tree!" said the imp, pointing at a crooked-shaped pine, convinced it could provide a comfortable, hoisted bed.

"I will sit here. At first light, we leave!" Ghaeloden replied sternly.

The imp nodded. Once up the tree, he tested a couple of forked branches and as he had anticipated, the tree contained a perfect bed-branch.

He wrapped the bag with the clothes, sceptre, his food and the scrolls around a twig, and used one side of it as a pillow.

"It's been a really long day!" he sighed, feeling his back and arms wearing him down.

He then started wondering if the dragon might still be able to read his mind. "Good night master Ghaeloden!

When nothing came back, he knew he'd be alone for the night. He had plenty to think about, and it would be better if he was left alone to do it.

The day reminded him, in part, how it felt to be free again, to do as one wished and soar the skies and venture with no aim. He smiled while he stared at the dark-clouded sky above, thinking with pride that the dreadful heights hadn't bothered him. In fact, he was keen to continue again in the morning.

Though, the day had also tangled his mind and his smile faded. The dragon had slowly started to show his true purpose and hatred towards the wizard, which he could only understand. Probably, he would have felt the same if he had to see his own kin and king driven mad by the will of Felduror. Yet, he was not sure that the wizard was that powerful. He had seen and observed the man at length, almost daily, and it was hard to believe him capable of overwhelming a Drakhahoul king.

He lingered on the thought. He considered how, to some extent, they shared the same destiny; bound by an old man's will. He realised just now that the string that bound his wings was almost insignificant, compared to the weight the time with his severe master had bestowed on him. Perhaps he could not abandon his master that easily.

He yawned wildly.

If only there was a way in freeing the wizard's mind without endangering everyone's wellbeing by unleashing a madman's fury. If only... he fell asleep.

The dawn arrived with a chill wind. Certainly it would have been worse to sleep on the wet grass, considered the imp as he stretched and looked towards the opening.

Ghaeloden was already up, inspecting the surroundings.

"Good morning, Nuuk," he said, seemingly in a good mood. "I had a slumbering, dreamless night. I remember closing my eyes and opening them at first light. This place is so quiet! I haven't had a calm night such as this in a very long time."

Nuuk jumped onto the ground from his tree-bed.

"We should do it more often!" Ghaeloden's genuine suggestion surprised him.

Nuuk smiled at the dragon. "We should certainly do it," he said, preparing the harness over the dragon's neck.

Once ready, the dragon pounced in the air and soon gained altitude with powerful wing strokes.

Unlike the evening that had brought some rain, the sky on the horizon was clear. The early sun's rays encouraged a warm, rainless day and it felt as if outside Arkhanthi's territory, the air itself was less sharp and cold.

Soft shadows gradually advanced from the tip of the tallest trees unveiling like a muddling blanket a remarkable display of autumnal colours. From the darkest evergreen to the multiple variations of red, orange and yellow of the oaks, maple trees and larch, they all proudly took their place in the vivid canvas of the forest. Flocks of birds gathered near river beds vociferously preparing for the long journey they would soon have to undertake. Sporadic smoke puffs found their way up from the dense forest, revealing human presence in the nearby lands and forcing the dragon to raise higher in the sky.

We should be careful now! Ghaeloden resounded in Nuuk's mind.

You are right, replied the imp. *We are passing into unknown human territories and it would not be wise for us to be seen.* Just as the imp finished his sentence a thought occurred to him. *I do wonder, master Ghaeloden…*

Yes?

… If I were to hold the sceptre and ride on your back, will it make us both completely vanish?

That is a most valid question! the Drakhahoul replied. *I guess however, there'd be only one way to find out! But, who could we ask to take a look at an imp and a dragon without having them disappear first?*

They both started to laugh.

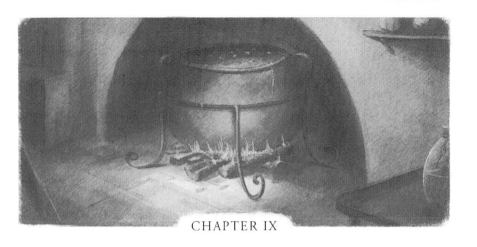

CHAPTER IX

SHIFTING

Naghnatë

Hot, murky water was boiling loudly inside a big, charred cauldron. The voracious fire underneath made it jolt freely sideways on the craggy spit it was locked on, making its thick liquid vigorously spill over the edges with sweltering sounds. The bubbling popped in dozens of muddy, greenish drops that landed all over the place. Yet, it wouldn't matter the mess it caused. It never did as long as it worked.

This time Naghnatë has decided to use more of her ingredients and give it one more try. Last time, she had felt the marrow powder hadn't been enough, and now she procured herself a whole lot more, as a precaution. A bunch of dry leaves made of yellow rattles, linden, lime and hickory was shredded into a pestle with the aid of deer and rabbit fat to help blend the scents. If fur fell inside by mistake, it would not matter at all either; the flavour only improved.

The witch scratched at her head, causing wispy white hair to poke out from underneath her stretched, dusty-black scarf into what resembled more a twig broom than an old woman's hairdo. Her wrinkled and weathered face was peculiarly deforming upon and through the jars' reflection, as she strolled back and forth. She needed to collect everything from the shelves and drawers of the centuries-old, wooden furnishings. Every step caused many creaks and cracks on the old floor where the nails had long rotted inside their holes. That did not matter either, it wasn't that she would linger longer than necessary in this atrocious place.

As she paced inside the small hut, made entirely of one big kitchen, she mumbled something between her thin lips. She stopped and grimaced as the waft of vapours interrupted her with a refreshed liveliness of bad smells and she decided it was time to amend that. Reaching the trunk that served as table bench, as well as storage case, she took out a small box. The fruits within had been judiciously wrapped and kept dry. They weren't as fresh as a few days ago, but were still emanating their vital trails of flavour. Bright yellow lemons, which made one squint the eyes by puncturing the thick skin, and reddish oranges as big as fists. They were not common fruit for such desolate and cold lands, she had specifically requested her trusted traders to bring them to her from far-away southern lands, and at a good expense too. Though, they had become a necessity of late.

She grabbed one of each, the freshest ones, and then closed the trunk, making sure to cover and protect the remaining fruit with the same care. With a sharp knife she then started chopping the fruit. The gesture caused the thin wrinkles on her veined hands to move animatedly up and down above her protruding hand's ligaments. She squeezed the last drops of lemons and oranges and, before she threw their peels into the cauldron, she filled her lungs and nose with the pleasant scent their thick skin released. With vigour she stirred the cauldron one last time.

This will help to gulp it down! she thought as she took the burned-metal pot from the spit and placed it on the floor, where it steamed and stained a dark, round mark.

Although she had drunk the potion countless times, she still could not get accustomed to its heavy stench and bitter taste. Though it always worked its magic. Maybe she was getting a bit slower with age, after all she was three hundred and sixty-one years of age today. The realisation made her linger as she stared at the murky brew at her feet.

Once the concoction had cooled and was ready to be consumed, she considered what she needed to do next. In order for it to fully work it was fundamental to consume it on the first night of the full moon after her birthday. What was important was that her solar year had to be completed, even by a few minutes, for drinking it sooner and the potion would not work and she would have to wait another year. And a year without it could be a little too much, too dangerous at her age. Coincidentally this year, the first day of full moon in the month occurred on her birthday and this pleased her very much. Although she had made a cauldron full of it, what she'd use was one single vial; the first one. It also had to be taken outside and left for a couple of hours in the moonlight, that was the trick, she believed, that made it all possible.

So many times had she practiced the same routine, that she had almost forgotten how she learned it in first place. The same process, repeated for at least two hundred and thirty years, had become as natural as drinking water or eating; one doesn't have to remind himself how it's done as long as it was done.

Yet of late, she felt less in favour of her elements. She gathered the signs from the air, the sky and the movement of everything around her, and knew that something was about to change.

"Has the time arrived to finally meet my fate?" she murmured.

She wrapped the vial in a clean linen-cloth and placed it carefully inside a round wicker-basket, amongst a wool blanket, some cheese and a slice of bread.

This far north, there was only one season and that was winter. The snow remained throughout the year with the exception of a very brief thaw which lasted barely a month or two. Few were those that ever set foot upon these lands, be they human or beast. But, she did not mind the gelid air or the plainness and the stillness of the frozen trees. She did not mind that she was the only soul for many miles around; she had spent a few lifetimes of solitude. This place was by far her favourite place to shift and she never had to clear her traces as no one ever found the spot.

With all ready at hand, she paced towards the river, aided by a crooked cane made of hazelnut wood. One might mistakenly think this was an accidental choice. She always feared, as well as disliked, slippery snakes and lizards, and never understood why they could only die after the sun had set, even if one smashed or cut their heads off. Only by chance had she learned, a long time ago, that the only way they could be killed without them hissing and bending endlessly before the last sun's rays, was by slapping them with a hazelnut twig. It was nature's magic she thought when she had first found out, and she never again parted herself from the magic tree. Since then, she had started to make all sorts of potions to cure skin sicknesses and various other maladies out of the plant's leaves and bark and they had worked just as well. Of course, the snow sufficed to keep the cold-blooded creatures away, but she still felt more secure holding onto her special stick.

She now stood by the river and stopped to lay the basket on the blanket. She might be a witch, but she could still feel the snow-covered ground's sharp bites.

The clouds, like many times before, were unwilling to reveal the light of the moon, though this had never been a problem for her and her skills. She sat beside the basket and closed her eyes. It was cold, a cold she did not mind for the moment, and measured that, with any luck, it will be all over soon. With one hand half-lifted in the air, she murmured something from her throat that made the buried, frozen grass quiver and the surface of the water ripple. A recite she had learned long ago from her mother and which she had mastered in the service of the mad wizard. A simple and effective spell, which made the clouds around the moon vanish and scatter in every direction as if wafted away by an invisible force. Even the meanest and darkest of fast-moving clouds stood no chance and faded before blackening the moon.

She sneered at her fulfilment, weakened, dizzy and out of breath by its demanding strength; a full year had passed again and she needed to recover aplenty. She crawled towards the almost-frozen river and cupped her face with a handful of fresh water, splashing twice her pale skin. She did not feel its coolness and luckily the gesture provided some ease of mind.

Magic always drained her of her strength, and of late a bit too much for her liking. Was it time to stop using it? Could this be the end of her road? She knew that magic wasn't something one could give up easily, nor one could rid oneself of. It took as much energy into renouncing it as it did to learn it, so that was not the case.

She walked back on her knees and lay on the blanket staring at the moonlit sky. The river bathed in the pure white light of the bright moon and she could see clearly now. Some free patches of grass not trapped under the snow glistened with a horde of sparkling flecks caused by the dew. Everything was calm, everything was silent. Only the soft whisper of the slow flowing water could be heard accompanied by a sporadic night owl's calls and her reviving breaths.

Satisfied with her work and a little restored, she unwrapped the vial from the cloth and placed it on her side, on the blanket facing the rays of the moon. She then decided to enjoy the slice of bread and cheese and lay her old body on the thick blanket in an attempt to fully recover from the magic's strain.

When she was sure the hour had passed, she opened the vial and drank it all. Knowing what would follow, she changed her position and dug her fingers deep inside the snow; one hand dug through the cold ground and one clutched around at a frozen tussock.

She had to be fast, she had to be ready, and the long breathless moment that passed made sure she would be. When the coughing started, the pain came sharper than before. Little veins of blue, purple and red fractured the white of her eyes and tears gushed down her furrowed cheeks. The cough was unbearable. She gasped for air with raucous sounds, convulsing on her knees on the rumpled blanket while her hands still held her steady; she had learned to lock herself in one place as the long frenzy of coughs would often put her in harm's ways.

She struggled to breathe. Against her body's fight to push the brew out, she forced herself not to regurgitate. It was never a pleasant business, yet she wouldn't give up now. She freed a hand from the tussock and covered her mouth, aiding her sealed lips from losing any more of the precious bile. Her ears started to whistle and her forearms' muscles started to pull with pain.

When the coughing subsided, it was replaced by a dreadful sensation of nausea. Her eyes continued to wet her wrinkled face and inside her mouth was the bitterest of tastes; a harsh, sharp flavour that made her throat pulse up and down energetically in the attempt to free itself from the revolting ingestion. She breathed through her nose and gradually released the tension on her tight fingers around her lips. Another long moment was gone.

The tearing stopped. The worst was over, her body had accepted it and she lifted her hand from the frozen ground and relaxed. Slowly, she opened her mouth; once, twice and then with the third inhale she succeeded in breathing clearly. She kept still and lingered on the blanket clearing her eyes from the dazzling indistinctness her tears have caused. The whistling in her ears retreated and she started to hear water run again. She collected herself and glanced at her veiny hands. As her sight cleared, her wrinkles seemed to soften, retreating into the depth of her skin. She rushed towards the river and carefully inspected her reflection upon the stillness of the water. The potion started showing its effect; the face had mended, tempering those age marks that towards the end of the year always seemed to worsen and reveal her true age. The white hair slowly faded into a darker shade of grey and as she stood, her back was straighter. She now looked like a common old woman of around eighty.

So young and strong. She smiled happily as she fell back on the soft blanket thinking it would be a full year before she had to endure the wretched feeling once more.

"It worked again," she shouted as she tossed the vial into the river, using a tiny spell to make the vial disperse before touching the surface of the water.

She liked her surroundings clean, that's only appropriate, she considered, her gladness ending with a hiccup.

She had forgotten about those too, and they would last a while. Yet, she smiled nonetheless. Everything was welcomed now.

From where she lay, she released the clouds from under her spell with a finger, bringing everything to darkness again. The clouds that faded just around the moon resumed about and over it like starved dogs over a piece of meat. The night was brought to a moonless sky again, just like a curtain upon a play's end-scene and she felt revitalised.

She woke up really late, not really recollecting how she had returned to her hut. The dry straw-bed was a welcomed sensation, thinking back at the alternative cold grass of the night.

A reviving emotion traversed her body in its entirety. She cheered, feeling the vivacity of her own core. Lots had to be done and little time to do it. Now that she was strong again, she could continue her research and, if she was right, this was the year. All the signs had spoken of the same event as clear as day, and as it hadn't been her end, she was determined to resolve her life's conundrums.

She raised from the bed and started stimulating the embers that were slowly puffing under a big pile of ash, aiding them with a handful of chaff. Filled with new energy she mustered a very long blow and swiftly the almost-dead cinders sparked back to life lighting the dry straws. She grimaced, as she would have liked to use a spell to light the fire. She then arranged a trestle of dry spruce wood around the cinders and placed the metal pot filled with fresh water on the spit, where the concoction had been boiling animatedly the day before. Traces of that ghastly cooking could still be seen around the fireplace; on the box of dry wood she kept nearby, on the wooden floor as well as on the pale white walls and she knew she'd have to clean at some point. Perhaps next year.

First things first. Her consideration came in the shape of a strong sage and earl grey tea this morning; a daily habit that was hard to break.

Her stock of dried herbs was always packed; every shelf inside her huts had at least one prudently sealed jar with various dry herbs inside.

The scented tea warmed her cold and sunburned hands as she stood by the fire contemplating her next move. If she was right, many things were about to change and she was resolute to be there when they did. Words travelled faster than the wind and rumours of the big fire in the southern lands had reached her ears on multiple accounts. It had to be true, she determined, and she knew it was only a matter of time until the history repeated itself.

Many years ago, she had witnessed in first person what dragon fire-breath could do to a village, when the white dragon had torn apart the elven citadel in the forests of Elmenor and stole the Lux stone under the spells of its master, Felduror. Loreeia and her elven kin had always suspected him – knowing his lust for the tokens – but for the sake of her own people and many other races, the wise queen had decided it was better to wait and find solid proof of his involvement before taking action.

Naghnatë sighed, thinking how she had missed her only chance to expose the evil wizard when, during that day's attack, she hadn't been able to confront him. She had reached Elmenor on that day, many, many years ago. Having learned the whereabouts of the elven queen, she had ventured far to see for herself the magic token and learn as much as she could about its powers. She was still confident the wise queen would not hesitate to spread the good tales of those peaceful times when humans, elves, dwarfs and dragons were friends and not foes.

Yet, as she had entered the citadel, buried in the depths of the green forest, she had seen from a distance the wizard imparting his last instructions to the long headed white Drakhahoul. As the dragon had taken off and left the wizard alone in that clearing, she had known that Felduror had sensed her. They had exchanged the longest, wordless glance before Naghnatë had decided it was best to vanish with a single effective spell, rather than try and obliterate him to dust – she had never felt ready to harm another being, and now she regretted it dearly. Luckily, she had judged well, as the old wizard hadn't spared his flame-spells and had directed them towards her with the intent to kill.

"Argh!" Naghnatë exclaimed, jumping from her comfortable position on the chair.

The memory of being so close to death startled her, and she spilled a bit of the tea on her neck and bodice which she was now trying to clean and dry with her hand.

"I will get you back for this as well, mark my words!" She stood up from the chair and went to place the hot mug on the battered table.

She took the bodice off and placed it near the fireplace, letting its warmth do the drying for her. She then dressed up and refilled her mug with the scented tea and took her time to consume it, this time without any distractions or bad memories.

"Good!" she exclaimed as she placed the clean mug and tea pot on the table and inspected the dark-blue bodice which was now dry, but stained.

She moaned something with her throat and placed it on her small hay bed. With clicking lips, she knelt and took from under the bed a small and dark painted wooden box.

Click!

She opened it and after quickly delving, she found what she was looking for; a dark leather pouch tied with a string.

Click!

"Ah, there you are!" She untied it and took a long peek.

An emerald-blue powder, fine as river sands, was glowing and saturating the pouch, sparkling in her eyes. She poured a small amount in her left hand, dropped the pouch on her lap and rubbed her hands thoroughly with the dust until it seeped inside her palms.

She took her coat from the bent nail behind the hut's door and went towards the fireplace. A quick mumble of her lips put the fire out as if it was never there. With another glance, she determined the cleaning would have to wait for another time.

Click!

And she vanished from the hut.

"Ahaa!" she exclaimed as she landed perfectly with both feet on the wooden floor of a bigger and newer cabin.

"I still can manage well, shifting myself!" she added coughing and waving away the dust cloud that had lifted upon her arrival.

She inspected the place attentively to see if it was as she had left it many months before. Strictness defined her when it came to choosing her hiding places, she'd make sure they were stable and most importantly, secluded from prying eyes.

A handful? Dozens? Tens of dozens? She had lost count of how many she had, they were as varied as the colours in the forest. From doomed castles and hunted citadels to abandoned huts, mines, caves, mills and cottages. She had tried them all. Many of them had acquired the haunted characteristic specifically because of her errant comings and goings and her odd practices of guttural chanting and spell performing. It was something that made her proud.

Someone had been inside the cabin she could tell. Perhaps a shepherd, forced to take shelter from perilous weather or a hunter that ventured too far and took lodging for the night. But she was sure nobody had stayed here for long as her magic wards would have prevented it. Not once had they failed in startling unwanted visitors. Frightening sounds outside the house, banging doors or footsteps approaching in the middle of the night, howling beasts and confounding noises, were all things she liked experimenting with and to her amusement, she felt accomplished by. In this case she had probably overdone it, as the cabin was situated far from reach, on the eternally-white peaks of the Wicked Ridge.

A low chanting filled the cabin and as she lifted her right hand a chair, a table, a big cupboard and a secret door in the wooden floor appeared all of a sudden. She had concealed the items that she could not carry and were necessary for decent living when she had to stay here for long spans of time. The secret door led to a storage room, which she was now inspecting. To her surprise the plants had thrived in the dark and she was looking at big wooden crates filled with rhubarb, lettuce and potatoes.

While every gardener had told her that light was the principal source of energy for a plant to grow, she had discovered that it was not actually true. Of course the sun was important, though it is not solely because of the light, but because of its heat. Seeds lay dormant many months a year in the dark soil before sprouting, so the sun's light cannot be the cause for this happening. Surely it wouldn't have been possible without a little help-spell or two to keep the cabin walls dry and the plants moist and warm, but that was her little secret. All that mattered now was that she had vegetables for a much-needed soup – shifting from place to place left her ravenous.

Inside the cupboard she found everything she needed for the

stew; spices, oils, dry bay leaves, dry lovage and dill, cutlery, a piece of dried-smoke meat, plenty of onions and a braid of garlic.

A big ball of snow, taken from outside, was melting into a chipped-pot, heating on the old stove made of sturdy, mountain black-stone. She finished chopping the vegetables and went searching for the flour sack, realising to her dismay, that there wasn't enough left.

Just as she started reproaching herself for having forgotten to refill, a faint, distant sound caught her attention. A shudder made her back tickle as if a soft gust of wind blew against one's wet skin on a chill day. A thud echoed in the air from no apparent direction.

Thud. Another one, growing stronger as it closed the distance.

"Could it be…?" she whispered, making haste for the small window, opposite the hut's door.

She glanced about but could not see a thing in the dim light so she went outside instead. Grey clouds billowed on the top of the mountain and the last faint rays of sun were still visible on their western sides.

Thud. This time it felt like it was coming from behind her, high in the sky.

She looked up but the fast-moving clouds didn't allow her eyes to make out anything besides moving puffs of moist.

Thud. She heard it right above her now.

And, as she glanced high in the sky above, she saw it. Blurred and obscured by the moving clouds, lit by a dying light of day and not entirely concealed, its monstrous bat-like wings spread like a ship's sails; a mighty Drakhahoul in flight.

CHAPTER X

SALLNCOLN

Ghaeloden / Nuuk

Ghaeloden and Nuuk flew without disruption for the entire night, hoping to make up for a slow portion of their journey, after Aranthul. Some unexpected, strong currents pushing against them, had sent them wandering off their path by many miles, stripping the dragon of much of his strength. Exhaustion and hunger were beginning to take their toll on them when they reached the Lament Valley at first light.

The warmth of the southern region was the finest greeting the dragon had hoped for as his gliding was now made easier by the rising columns of hot and dense air. As he let himself be guided by the currents, he realised how much the landscape had changed. Trees and plants, with their still-strong sweet and variegated aromas, covered the horizon all around and the forests displayed a wide diversity of greens. Flocks of multi-coloured birds were waking up, unconcerned for the moment about the travels that the change of season would necessitate. Most likely the very same birds they previously saw gathering in the northern region were travelling to these green lands to linger for a month more before venturing deeper to the south. Far in the east, the rising sun slowly revealed itself engulfing the surrounding valleys and mountains in a warm and bright shimmer, reminding the dragon they could be clearly seen.

Ghaeloden flipped his tail and stirred slightly to one side in a quick movement, disturbing the imp's sleep and forcing him to grab at the harness he had tied around his wrists.

"We are here," he announced, "and we need to land quickly!"

"Surely, master Ghaeloden," replied the imp drowsily, as if trying to hide the fact he had been sleeping.

They started gliding faster towards the foot of the mountain, between cliffs where it was safe and hidden from humans, that populated in great numbers these temperate lands. Once landed, the dragon stretched his long spine, tail and neck trying to be as quiet as possible although his back was making loud, cracking noises. Meanwhile, the imp took out the map and followed an imaginary line with the longest of his small fingers.

"I think we are here." He pointed his finger and showed it to the dragon. "The closest village is further that way," he indicated with his other hand not taking his eyes off the map, "and it is called Irenthir. From here to Sallncoln should be less than a day's walk crossing the mountains, in that direction."

"Good!" exclaimed the dragon, "I've done my part, I've taken us this far, in only two and a half days. Now I am starving. This will have to be your part, Nuuk!"

Nuuk nodded.

"You shall go and inspect Sallncoln and I will follow above in the cover of the night. Are you clear what you need to do?" The dragon quickly continued, "Although I must say, I have not sensed any magic wielders in this area, nor all along our exhausting journey. If the witch were around, according to Felduror, we would have sensed her."

"I agree! Even if I do not possess your mighty knowledge and capabilities, I could sense it, if it's wielded in close proximity. Nevertheless, I will go and enquire in the village, as the wizard instructed me," replied Nuuk.

"Surely, but first you need to show me how good your disguise is!" demanded Ghaeloden with a twinkle in his eye.

The imp nodded and dropped his bag, kneeling beside it.

From inside he took a ragged shirt and a pair of trousers and some small boots with a wooden sole. He then took a cloth strap which he used to bind his small wings tighter on his back. The shirt covered his wings entirely and he made sure they were flat enough against his body. He then pulled up the trousers and popped inside the boots.

"Happy?" he asked, seemingly content.

The dragon looked at the imp for a moment, stretching his long neck to see him from all angles. "I must say, you could pass for a human youngling, almost from up close too, were it not for those big eyes and the flappy ears."

"Oh that. I think I need more cloth to wrap them with."

"Nonsense!" replied Ghaeloden, "you'd not make them disappear, it would only make you look more awkward. No, you need to use magic, or I will!"

"My master –" the imp began.

"Your master is not here!" Although the dragon knew that Felduror had allowed using small spells, he wanted to see what the imp was about. "The success of our task may depend on your ability to pass as human."

Nuuk was still reluctant, his big eyes and small, still mouth almost begging him to reconsider. Though he did not, he allowed a small growl to funnel in his long throat.

That convinced him.

The imp lifted a hand in the air, gulped nervously and looked pleadingly once more into the dragon's eyes. When nothing was said, he murmured a soft spell.

Ghaeloden knew the little creature had longed for such a moment. It couldn't have been otherwise, judging by the imp's closed eyes and the smile of happiness stamped on his face.

The spell worked its magic. Nuuk's skin slowly started to stretch in places where it was loose, becoming smoother and warmer in tone. His eyes shrunk to a third of their original size and his ears lost their elongated shape. In just a moment, the imp's face acquired a typical human look. Nothing betrayed his impish face, he looked like a child. A quite handsome one, considered the dragon.

"Marvellous," exclaimed Ghaeloden, pleased to see how well

the imp's spell had worked, "though, why is it that you have to say words when you wield magic?"

"It assures me of my intention, master Ghaeloden, words are very important!"

"Yes of course," the dragon replied. "Words are always important, for all inferior races that is, yet you are not one of those. For us Drakhahouls, the mind does not need to express out loud what it thinks as long as body and mind are in accordance. I think you should try and exercise your mind. Your spells will only benefit from it; words are slower than thoughts so your spells would become more effective and definitely quicker to release."

"It has been long time since I've used magic. Felduror did not allow it and I thought I had forgotten how to use my powers. I do remember however that, very rarely, some of the easiest and most practiced spells would need no word to be wielded, but I have never considered why that was. Perhaps I should," the imp reflected. "Thank you, master Ghaeloden, for encouraging me! I'll go now. As soon as I approach the village, I'll let you know."

"Good! I'll hunt and rest. We'll meet here at sunset, and not a moment later!" With a pounce he leapt into the air while the imp set off towards the steep mountain.

More than by hunger, Ghaeloden was driven by curiosity. The imp had used a spell and soon any wizard around would be drawn here. If Naghnatë was around she would most certainly find the imp and then he could easily entrap her with a prevailing Drakhahoul spell.

The powerful strokes of Ghaeloden's wings pushed the little creature sideways and lifted pebbles and dust in an uncontrollable swirl of air. Yet Nuuk giggled, his happiness overwhelming whatever shadow of doubt and fear he might have had about this journey. He had finally used magic after a long, long time. It was hard to shake off this sort of happiness; it made everything appeared easier.

The morning light was still too dull on this side of the

mountain to see clearly, and inside the dense pine forest the air was wet and chill. Silence prevailed as the imp slowly moved between the trees, with no noticeable path to follow. Among the multitude of bird song that resounded from all directions, two sparrows distracted him, loudly complaining at each other in the brushes straight ahead.

He passed a bramble and noticed with pleasure that a couple of berry shrubs were enclosed within. Delighted by the opportunity, he used the chance to fill his belly, grasping fistfuls of the ripe, juicy, sweet fruit. Happy with his misdeed, he cleaned his red lips on the back of his hand and proceeded.

The forest uphill became denser and it was harder to advance at a decent pace. Having to skirt and duck dead pine branches and the variety of bushes he encountered, he decided to make himself a stick with which he could bend and clear the path ahead.

This will do! he thought, as he stooped to pick up a sturdy grey branch, which, with a couple of twists and kicks, he cleaned from smaller twigs.

All well? the dragon asked.

Yes, master Ghaeloden, all is well! It's only that I am not that accustomed anymore to walking through dense brushwood like before. I haven't seen or smelled the forest this close in a very long time. Nuuk was surprised that they could still communicate, yet he found more staggering the scent of the forest and the freedom of strolling about.

To his surprise, the branch helped him move more easily even when there was nothing to clean or hit. Now he understood why some of the mountaineers favoured the use of canes to help climb the steeps.

As he slowly advanced towards the highest peaks, the woods cleared and he was now standing closer to the ridge. He wondered where he had ended up, having to find his own way without the aid of any battered paths. Of one thing he was sure; he had not turned or changed directions drastically, and always kept on the right-hand-side of the forest as he had initially decided by checking the map.

Once on top of the ridge, he climbed a tree and started to

scrutinise the land around, hoping to see the clearing of the village. And just as he expected, towards his left, he could see the Sallncoln lay in the valley just before the sparkling lake. Crossing the valley from this side of the ridge would certainly spare some hours, he considered, though he did not feel safe nor confident enough to do it just yet. So he decided to continue along the peak of the mountain through the forest where he felt safer.

Master Ghaeloden? his mind's voice was soft, *I see the village and I shall be there in the next few hours, maybe two or three, give or take.*

Take your time, Nuuk! I am back where we landed this morning. I am confident nobody will notice me here as long as I don't fall! the dragon replied, seemingly gratified he'd get a chance to bask in the sun.

The imp continued on his way until he felt confident enough to descend from the peak and into the valley. The brisk pace of his determination allowed him to traverse it in a shorter time than anticipated.

He passed a few houses that were seated at the edge of the village. Luckily, there was nobody around that he could see and he hoped it would stay that way. A narrow path among the tall grass indicated where the village's centre would be found, alas, he had yet to find a human on whom he could test his disguise. And just as he was about to pass another small house, the door of a wide hut, with bent walls and thatched roof, banged open.

A plump man with an axe on his shoulder came out. "Good'ay to you, young master!" he called with a quick greeting of his left hand, lazily lifted.

"Good day to you, kind sir!" replied the imp, exchanging the friendly greeting, spreading all four fingers in the air.

The chubby man's face shook swiftly, bouncing his fat cheeks from left to right. He twisted his face and squinted his eyes with effort.

Yet, Nuuk was faster. A rapid murmur and another finger popped into view, making the chubby man blink restlessly.

"Gargulhia, young sir. For a moment I thought I saw four fingers, hah," he said. "I must stop meddling with that brew of mine." The man let out a long chortle as he patted Nuuk on his head and continued on his way.

That was close! The imp exhaled with much relief.

What happened? he heard the dragon ask.

Why didn't you tell me about the fingers? I've got four of them and humans have five! said the imp, frustrated.

Oh. I considered you knew it already, isn't it obvious? Did anyone approach you? Is all in order?

I believe it is. The imp turned around to check and, once assured he was alone, he let out the tension with a deep exhale. *But at least he did not notice anything else. That makes my human disguise pretty decent, I should say.*

I had no doubt! the dragon said reassuringly.

After some time, Nuuk found more houses set on either side of the pathway, and the people he encountered confirmed that there was nothing wrong with his disguise. They all smiled and greeted him with a wave of a hand, a nod or a 'Good day to you, young sir!'

A gathering of young girls in white aprons and combed hair, under coloured scarves, were vivaciously and cheerfully exchanging the latest rumours of the village while cleaning long white soapy-sheets. They all smiled at Nuuk making him merry by witnessing the joys of their humble lives. It reminded him of Grora with its simplicity and cordiality of its inhabitants, each bringing its own contribution to the community and its prosperity. But the happy feeling was short-lived, when the air he walked within became permeated with a raw scent of burnt wood and death. The houses he approached were those that had been spared most of the wrath of the fire, yet they still bore the scars of its rage. A smoky trail persisted in the air and from here onwards the ground was tinted darker with a gradient of dull tones. Grey smudges crawled from the outside area and advanced towards a tar-black at its core.

The flame appeared to be so violent that even the earth had been deformed and moved. He searched and failed to find any signs that men had been the culprit for such a ravenous upsurge of force. Though he knew little about fires. Muddy ruts and ditches, filled with turbid waters, were spreading outwards along the direction of the fire, decreasing in intensity as they reached the outer edge. Remnants of the wreckage pushed by the impact's energy were still visible everywhere; shattered pieces of stone, wood, bone and metal, stuck in the trees and walls of the houses, made Nuuk shiver with distress.

He dared not think of how he would have felt, had he been in Sallncoln at that moment. Surely the Felduror he knew was not capable of such loathsome deeds. Besides he had mentioned this to be a mere rumour. His insanity would often make him violent, angry and greedy, though, certainly, he could not be the responsible for these cold-blooded murders. Because to Nuuk, that was what they felt like; cold-blooded murders.

If the people he passed on the edges of the village had been cheerful, content to have been spared, the people here were sad and heartbroken. There were no more greetings, many of the villagers didn't even lift their gaze from their tasks and very few acknowledged his presence.

Absorbed in his inspection of the wrecked houses, Nuuk almost bumped into a little girl. She was standing by the edge of the muddy path and was amused by two men committed to fixing the wheels of a broken cart. Her eyes were just like his, a warm jade green colour, and her long and golden hair was dusty and uncombed. Held between her tiny fingers, she was slowly swinging a little straw-doll with black-buttons eyes, slung about her tiny hand.

The imp smiled at her and she smiled back, yet her smile appeared wounded. With some delay he came to realise why; her left forearm was broken. A row of thin, wool threads was aiding in keeping her little arm suspended halfway across her small chest. Wrapped against her bone there were two flat pieces of wood to keep the bone as straight as possible while mending.

"What happened to you, little girl?" he asked gently.

"I fell and hurt my arm."

"Can I see?" He extended his hand to look at her wound.

The little girl nodded and pushed, ever so slightly, her arm towards the imp. By the look of the fingers it didn't seem a simple bone fracture. Swollen and dark-purple, most certainly there had been some vein and sinew damage. He fleetingly considered he had to be careful in using magic if he didn't want to be exposed or drained of strength, but he could not leave her like this. Not today. Her life could be forever shaped for the worse, if she lost her forearm entirely at such a young age. He gave a compassionate little smile and placed his other hand on her shoulder. With his eyes closed and chin propped on his chest, he whispered a healing spell. He felt her little shoulder twitch under his palm and he knew then that the magic had worked. Though, just as he was about to ask her how she felt, a hoarse voice erupted.

"Oi, what're ya doing over there?" asked a bulky man, coming towards him.

"I- I meant…" the imp stuttered.

Did you just use magic, Nuuk? The dragon's voice carried both concern as well as worry.

"Yes, not a good time now, Ghaeloden!" replied the imp not realising he was speaking out loud.

"Who're ya calling, Ghaylordan?" The man took a menacing step towards Nuuk while the little girl walked towards her father.

"Papa, he's a friend! He looked at my arm and now the fingers don't fizzle anymore." The little girl had reached the bulky man, hugging his right leg.

All well. Explain later! Nuuk managed to direct a reassuring thought towards the dragon, before speaking to the angry father.

"I only wanted to help her hand, kind sir. My brother had a similar wound," added the imp, thankful that the girl managed to calm her father's temper. "I will be on my way now. I bid you a good day!" He waved at the little girl and bowed to the two men who were wordlessly inspecting his every move.

The girl waved back at Nuuk as he moved away, and with pleasure he noticed the colour in her fingers turning more pink than purple. He smiled and winked at her, a gesture he had seen do one of the young human guards at the citadel.

Seeing her try to mimic his gesture, made his heart swell with happiness and joy. Her smile was brighter than before.

I had to mend a little girl's arm, master Ghaeloden. Nothing to worry but her father thought I meant her harm and I had to extricate myself from that challenge. All is well now. I am on my way. The imp's thought could not hide the sense of accomplishment and delight he felt at his action.

Imp, I understand. Though, don't be getting us into trouble, not for anyone! Try to avoid interacting with humans, unless it's about the witch!"

I apologise. No more magic, thought the imp, a little disappointed at the dragon's reaction.

Yet, as he continued on his way, he could not contain how happy he felt. The effort had only required a bit of his strength. He felt a little dizzy, though nothing a few moments' rest wouldn't fix.

And thinking that the wizard did not agree or allow anyone to use spells. How much good could be done if only those like him were permitted to practice healing spells? With dread, he then imagined the various ways the wizard might punish him if ever learned that he had used magic, but determined that the joy of the gesture felt like it was worth tenfold the risk of the madman's wrath.

What else could he try and do with magic before draining his strengths completely? Certainly the place was in desperate need of mending. Alas, material things could easily be fixed, houses rebuilt, trees planted again and in time they'd grow to their full splendour. The immaterial things could not. The souls of those departed were lost forever.

With such a consideration, he reached the village's market and stared at the hall. It seemed that a meeting was about to take place. Many people were gathered in front of a tall building, clearly those were the market's streets. They were debating in small groups how they'd proceed and if they should rebuild Sallncoln. Frustration ruled their words and figures. Fear persisted, buried in their flesh and bones.

Among the people, Nuuk noticed that there were two distinct types of behaviours. The first one was of those that had lost material things; they were the noisiest and most verbal – driven by anger at having lost their houses, their animals or other goods. The second one was those that had lost someone dear. They were the most taciturn, deprived of any joy or fear and with absent will of life. Husbands, wives, fathers, mothers, daughters and sons were silently mourned by eyes that had no more tears to cry. In their presence the talkative ones quietened themselves and tried their best to console the less fortunate. Where words failed, compassion was accepted with a touch of a hand, a pat on a shoulder or a voiceless hug or nod of a head.

Struggling to endure the laments of the silent and their palpable horror, the imp left the crowds and decided to explore the village. If Naghnatë had been still here, he would have been able to feel her presence. After all, that was what the wizard had said and, if that was true, such powers would be hard to hide even with her experience. But Nuuk felt nothing. And he hadn't felt a single spark of magic while crossing the mountain that led to the village. Likewise, in here, at its core, surrounded by what must be all the occupants of Sallncoln.

I am here at the centre of the village, master Ghaeloden! he said feeling near a dead end.

I was wondering what were you waiting for to apprise me! replied the dragon, almost yawning away his reply. *Have you found her?*

I am sorry; I am surrounded by a throng of people. They are holding a meeting. The condition of this village is dreadful! Some big fire has befallen it. I fear many have been lost, by the sight of these sad people's faces. Nuuk replied.

I shall need to see this with my own eyes, Ghaeloden said. *I will wait for your expedition to come to an end and upon your return, I'll survey the village from the sky.*

As you wish. I am on my way to the other parts of the village I still have to see. The imp was keen to leave the gathering behind him.

It took him good hours to scout the entire village. Although small compared to the citadel, he did not want to ignore any of the shattered huts, nor fuming stables. He meticulously inspected the surroundings checking inside every place he could gain access to and asked everyone that seemed willing to reply. Not one of those people knew to whom he was referring.

He was sure that if the witch was drawn to the place, as his master said, he would've felt her.

There was not much else he could to but to return to the landing area where, together with the dragon, he would spend the night and decide what to do the following day.

It was late afternoon and the light was starting to weaken. The water that filled the ruts reflected the crimson light of the red-dying sun, deflecting wafts of vapours from the heated ground into the chill of dusk. From up in the half-burned trees, birds lifted louder and sharper calls, uncharacteristic of an evening song. The people had disbanded from the market streets and the hall and centre of the village was almost deserted. The hammering and cutting noises that had accompanied him during the day carried into the evening.

Tired and confused, Nuuk could not rid himself of the sadness and anguish that had accompanied him since entering Sallncoln. He wanted to do more, but felt powerless and disheartened.

I'm coming back, master Ghaeloden! I am afraid I didn't find the witch nor have a clue where she could be. The only thing I am sure of is that I haven't felt the smallest tingle of magic today. What about you? Nuuk felt abashed.

Well, we haven't felt anything because there's nothing to be felt. I sensed your spell as easily as hearing your thoughts right now, but nothing else! answered the dragon with the same tone of frustration. *I will wait for your return before departing for my airborne inspection.*

I will be there in a couple of hours, if I don't indulge in those sweet berries on the crest! chuckled the imp, quickening his pace and thinking how thirsty and hungry he had been the entire day.

A short while after, he reached the house where he had healed the little girl's hand. He could see that both of the cart's wheels had been fixed and re-attached to the cart. Everyone was inside, happily chattering. He could see their gestures of joy and happiness depicted by candlelit shadows cast on a small curtained window. An inviting smell swelled from the bent chimney and wafted into the evening sky, invading his nostrils and making his stomach growl. He gulped a mouthful of wet air and reluctantly took his eyes from the window. He intimately hoped that he had aided to be a happier home today.

Though, as he turned his head towards the pathway that led outside the village, he was startled by a presence.

Few meters away a silhouetted figure was grimly staring at him. In the chill air of the evening, the mist springing from the warm ground cloaked the figure rather well. He could not make out any features of the face, even if he was almost certain that it was an old woman. She started walking towards him, aiding her slow steps with a crooked wooden stick.

"Are you lost, child?" Her voice was soft when she spoke; she was now close enough for him see her face.

"Oh not at all, I just came from the market and I am on my way home," Nuuk replied, trying to diminish a trail of fear that unsettled him.

Yet, he felt she was an outsider to the village just as he was. Her clothes seemed from a different place; her robe must've been at least a century old. Her wrinkled skin, burned by the sun's light, didn't give away her age and there was something odd about her face; her eyes. Her eyes were too sharp and vivacious for someone of her age, sparkling with almost unnatural light and blue in colour. He dared not hint at his suspicions, though he could not take his eyes away.

The desire to ask her something was strong, but his tongue felt numb. Something was embracing and tightening its grip around him, an invisible clinch he could not overcome. In vain he tried to look about him, he was still as a tree. He could not move; he could not speak. He only managed to think of the Drakhahoul and issue a soft, crying thought.

Help!

CHAPTER XI

BILBERITH'S SCEPTRE

Nuuk / Naghnatë

Nuuk woke up on the dusty wooden-floor of a place he did not recognise. Half-spent candles, spread about the place, lit the interior with their yellow flares. Yet, their light was barely enough to identify any particular feature. The dew on a small, square window revealed how moist and warm the air inside was and how much colder it was outside. Somewhere behind him, he could hear water boiling on an angry fire. Most likely there was soup cooking inside a cauldron – the pleasant smell of herbs and spices accompanied the wet waft every time droplets of water spilled on the ardent pot.

He propped himself on his elbows but his spinning head prevented him from rising further. He tried to voice a word, failing when his throat burned with thirst. What came out instead, was a hoarse noise between a cough and a hiccup. His aching, feverish head forced him to rest motionless for a few moments, before feeling assertive enough to start rolling to one side and inspect the place. As he moved his head to the left, the front wooden door opened briskly.

"Oh, you're up!" A gruff old-woman's voice broke the silence as she entered the hut, a snow-filled container tight in her hands.

Nuuk tried to speak and instantly stopped to gulp down a painful, dry breath that made his tongue stick to his palate.

"Here, here. Drink this!" The old woman knelt beside him and handed him a mug of water.

She held his head up and helped him drink slowly. There was no desire in fighting the need to quench his thirst.

The cold liquid burned his sand-dried throat, though after a few moments he calmed himself and felt reinvigorated. Her gesture made him consider she couldn't want him dead, not if she had offered him water. His mind was slow in remembering why he was there, but he could finally breathe properly without a burn in his nose or neck. Staring at the old woman, he felt that he had seen her somewhere, failing to remember where and when. His mind was hazy.

"Who are you?" his dried-out voice scorched his throat.

"Uhm, I've almost forgotten," she exclaimed, and with her knuckles, pressed on the imp's forehead, she closed her eyes and mumbled a long word. "Feel any better now?" she continued.

All of a sudden, Nuuk felt refreshed. The inbound energy allowed him to slowly lift himself on his elbows and then raise to a sitting position on the floor. The spinning and headache were gone. Memories flooded his mind and he remembered the silhouette of the old woman staring at him outside that house, hours ago.

"Are you Naghnatë?" he asked.

Her head tilted to one side, one hand gently brushing her chin.

Seemingly lost in her own reminiscences, she quickly added, "Oh yes, that indeed is what I responded to." She looked at Nuuk and smiled. "It's been so long since I heard that name, I'd almost forgotten it was mine. Now up, you need to drink hot tea to recover from that spell."

"What spell? Have you used magic to restrain me?" The imp thought that must be the cause of his horrid headache and lack of memory.

He followed her to the fireplace where a vegetable broth was cooking.

"I had to make sure you were no foe of mine. I sensed your healing spell and I came to see who was wielding magic in this valley, even though my purpose was not solely that." She paused her effort of lifting the boiling cauldron from the fire and then placed it on the floor, on a flat, square piece of stone.

"How could you know what kind of spell I used or if indeed it was me?" Nuuk was astonished.

"Heh, I think I might know a thing or two about magic," she replied sarcastically, "the question is, however, what was a magical creature doing here? I surely did not expect to meet an imp anytime soon."

"How –" the imp stopped himself.

He realised he was trying to hide behind a finger from the all-knowing witch, and feared what she might do to him.

"I cannot tell you!" he said with an unconvincing voice.

She smiled at him, "That might've just given me the answer I was looking for!" and turned her attention to the cauldron.

There was certainly no fooling her. As he tried to put an order to his thoughts, a shiver ran down his spine; the sceptre. He quickly glanced about inside the room alarmed he could not spot his bag.

"Don't worry, imp! Your things are in the cupboard. Now, I don't know about you, but all this magic-wielding and talking has made me hungry. Be a sport and bring me the ladle and the bowls I left on the table."

He was truly hungry; of that he was certain. So much in fact, that he totally ignored every instinct of not trusting the witch and did as bid.

"This soup is delicious, Naghnatë." He found his words after the third bowl of the delicious broth. He couldn't recall the last time he had had such a delightful treat.

"Very kind of you, I enjoyed it myself too," she replied.

"Now can I have my things back?"

She nodded and indicated towards the cupboard where he was able to find his property. Inside everything was intact; the map, in which were folded the notes from Felduror, and the glowing sceptre, which in the scuffle, had squashed part of his adored beeswax almost flat. He returned to the table where she was still, slowly, sipping from her bowl. There was no doubt she had rummaged through his things and there was no point in trying to pretend she hadn't.

"Do you know what this is?" the imp asked placing the opened bag with the sceptre clear in sight.

"I didn't at first. Now I am certain of it. That cannot be anything else than the sceptre of Bilberith, the lunatic. I saw his marking etched on one side of the shaft; the goose head." She looked at him as if expecting him to know to whom she was referring.

The imp did not.

"Well, this powerful object has a very peculiar and amusing story, which I'll spare you right now. Suffice to say, it is a very dangerous item to meddle with, lightly. It can sap your strength and leave you in terrible pain if you misuse it. I can't but wonder, where you found it and, mostly, why do you carry such a thing with you?"

"I…" The imp hesitated.

There were not many directions he could take the conversation while still earning her trust. If he decided to lie, she might do the same with him. Or he could try to escape. That would not be acceptable. Cleary Felduror had known all along that she could easily surpass him and his use of spells, and perhaps the Drakhahoul too, and he wondered why he had been so foolish to believe he could achieve what his master asked of him. He doubted that his safety had been of any concern to the wizard and probably their failure and demise would be interpreted as a successful mission, having revealed that, indeed, the witch was still alive. There was no other way to know what he was up against, other than to be honest with the witch.

"I come from Arkhanthï —"

"I knew that," the witch interrupted excitedly and waved at him to continue.

"I found the sceptre in the armoury of the citadel, and I only know that when I touch it, I become invisible and unheard by those around me."

"Invisible, unheard?" She plunged into another reflective state and after a while added, "Can you hold it briefly for me?"

The imp took it in his hand and saw the face of the witch change into an expression of awe. Was that a smile?

"By the blades of Balathul, that is a real treat you've got there! Remarkable Bilberith, nothing I thought even possible. I thought it was supposed to provide wealth and riches to those that handled it, that being the main purpose of its existence, though you seem not to be attached to any material things, eh."

The imp dropped the sceptre with a thud on the table. "What I truly want has a higher price." He sighed but continued, "Since you know I'm an imp, what do you know about my people, the Iprorims of Grora?"

"Know about you? Don't you remember me, Nuuk?" asked the witch, moving her chewing face closer to the him, "I'm the one that took you away from Grora!"

All of a sudden, the room seemed too small and Nuuk found he could not breathe properly. Scared and confused by her confession, he did not know what to say or if there was any point in saying anything. He grabbed the sceptre with one hand, pushed aside the chair with the other, and made for the door.

Unfortunately, the witch was quicker and moved a cupboard with a flick of her fingers, smashing it against the door and barring his way. Although he was invisible, she seemed to know where he stood. Yet, he did not ease his clenched fist from the sceptre's handle. Nor did he breathe, for a while. He held it tight to his chest, feeling his heart beating rapidly. His eyes fixed on hers.

No, she did not know precisely where he was. She started to look elsewhere.

"There is no point in running away, Nuuk. Where would you run to? To those that ordered me to take you? To the same master that tied your wings and kept you locked in a tower only to show you the disguised gesture of gratitude by sending you to your certain death?"

In the rage of the moment, he could not think or hear anything of her words. He could only try to recall a spell that would aid him escape, but his mind was clouded and his brain thumped inside his skull. The more he tried the more he failed. As soon as a word seemed to form in his mind, it blended with another and nothing of use could come out.

"Would you return to Felduror who trained you like a dog and forbade you to use magic? Denied you your freedom?" She continued to search the room.

He was trapped, Naghnatë was too strong for him. He dreaded the feeling of having to submit to another powerful mind. Alas, she was right; Felduror hadn't been any kinder. The thought gave him courage to move towards her, sceptre still tight in his hands.

She did not seem aware of his movements, nor did she hear him approach. "What would I gain by killing you, imp? Think about it, had I wanted you dead, would I have shared my soup with you?"

There was no other choice than to see what she wanted and why had she kept him alive so far. Now that he was back at the table he could scrutinise her face and look for any signs of evil. He could find none. Her wrinkled face was serene and her eyes were not bursting with the rage he, too often, witnessed in Felduror's moments of lunacy. She had prevented him from escaping, yet she hadn't hurt him. It only meant that she wanted something.

He wondered what that was.

"I am still hungry," he said, revealing himself at the same side of the table, sceptre rolling on the wooden chair beside him.

"Splendid, I would like another bowl myself, too!" Naghnatë moved the cupboard back from the door with another gesture of her hand.

When she finally placed two bowls on the table, the imp found the courage to ask, "What is it you want from me? Why did you take the Iprorims?"

"I was merely an apprentice then and knew nothing of what I know now. Elder wizards had mastered a way of extracting the strength from magical creatures and had used it for their benefit. Unfortunately for you, the Iprorims represent one of the most abundant sources of magical wisdom. Abnormally so."

That was a very unexpected thing to learn about his own race, thought the imp.

"That is what Felduror has always needed from you and your

kin. What I want from you, instead, is far simpler and more generous," she added, handing him another chunk of dark bread. "I want for this abomination to come to an end! I want to destroy all the tokens of benevolence and I need help in finding them. You know what I am talking about, don't you?"

Nuuk's thoughts were disordered. He considered at length what she just said and could not think of one good reason why he should help her and go against the wizard. He had learned how to deal with his moments of madness and felt, somehow, that Felduror would one day free him from his wards. He was torn; could he risk what he considered to know, for something that sounded better but he completely mistrusted? Even if he wanted to deny her request, what if she went as mad as Felduror and constricted him with her own kind of magic wards?

He could not go against the witch, not alone. Maybe if the dragon was here it would be easier to leave this place unhurt.

"I know what you mean," he said after a while, "Felduror has been looking for them for a long time. It's what drives him crazy, although I don't believe he has been able to find any, as far as I know." He quickly glanced at the sceptre. "Is this such a one?"

Naghnatë chuckled, "No, no. Bilberith was a fine magician and he managed to imbue some personal items with magical powers, though not always succeeding. I believe this sceptre to be his greatest success and am not surprised you found it in the wizard's armoury. But I doubt the real artefacts are in the same place. If you managed to find it and easily extract it, I wouldn't count on finding anything more valuable than this!"

"I do not know where they are, if that's what you are asking," the imp said.

"I trust you don't," she quickly replied. "If anything is true about the Iprorims, it is that they have a tendency to be honest and loyal – too much if you'd ask me. No, what I want from you is help in understanding where they are being kept. Since your wings are still bound, I believe you are supposed to return to your master?" she added a bit scornfully.

The imp hesitated. She was right, again. "That is true, I've been sent to get you, and I shouldn't return empty-handed," he finally admitted.

"Ha-ha! You were –" Naghnatë started laughing, dropping her spoon on the table.

She appeared unable to subdue the hideous giggle. Only when she realised the imp was serious did she manage to force some seriousness into her expression.

"You must not think ill of me, Nuuk. I find it very amusing that he made you believe such things were possible." Her laughter faded. "I mean no offence. We both know I could escape the magic of one imp if I were forced to, don't you think? Your master must know this surely. Unless," and she paused, her face sterner still, "of course! Unless, that Drakhahoul was sent here with you as well. It can't just be a coincidence!" She fixed his eyes with a serious gaze, half rising from her chair.

He had a doubt that she had known it all along and was only testing his character. She might be old, but there was no tricking the witch. There was no point in denying the obvious. She could easily force the truth out of him if she so wanted.

"His name is Ghaeloden –"

"Ghaeloden-Three-Horns," she interrupted. "I know him very well, since he was a pup no bigger than a lamb." She giggled. "And where is he now? He is very well trained for a young dragon. I lost his trace last evening."

"I haven't spoken to him since I met you. And from what I gather, your presence prevents me from thinking straight and I cannot sense him anymore," Nuuk said.

"Well it is not my presence. It's the protective wards I placed around this place that impede anyone from staying too long or sensing its existence at all. Try outside!" she waved at him.

The imp sprinted outside, and instantly dismissed the thought of escape when he realised how high up the mountain he was. The chill air made him shiver and, as soon as he stepped foot on the plain rock, he could think clearer. She was right, it was the inside of the hut. He took a deep breath and exhaled lengthily.

Master Ghaeloden, I am well!

Nuuk? What in the skies' names? came the deep voice of the dragon. *I thought you had died, imp. Again! I am still flying above Sallncoln trying to see you. Where are you? Why couldn't I sense you? Have you been using the sceptre all this time?* His voice was filled with concern and liberation and that in itself was a relief to Nuuk's heart.

He seemed genuinely worried about his wellbeing and he could not help a sudden smile.

I found Naghnatë. Erhm, well, she found me. I was not able to talk to you. More so, she knew I was not human and she knows we came together, but she means no harm. I think it is safe for you to come. Only I will have to ask her where we are.

After providing the dragon with directions, it took Ghaeloden less than half an hour to reach the peaks across the valley. It wasn't that far from where they had previously landed, though easy to miss, if one didn't know what to look for. Especially in the evening, the small hut was almost invisible, concealed by the white snowy cliffs and the lack of sun's light. Yet, Naghnatë was sure the young dragon would be capable of finding the place.

She had gone outside to await the dragon's arrival. She was keen to see a Drakhahoul again, especially one she had known as a pup. Dragons were intelligent creatures and she hoped he would still recognise her.

He landed with a loud thump, thrusting snowflakes about. A huge lump of snow, which had gathered on the small roof, collapsed noisily. None of them were distracted, the tension was too high.

He let out a low, guttural growl loud enough to make the snow and small rocks tremor under their feet.

With a stamped smile on her face, Naghnatë approached fearlessly, her hand extended to reach the tall snout of his head. He darted his head to the side, just slightly.

She could see him clearly enough. "Brave, bright Ghaeloden, I knew it would be you!"

The dragon winced and blew a puff of hot smoke from his nostrils, following her movements with keen eyes. "Do I know you?" His full, deep voice resonated through the air and made her shiver.

"Dragons have a good memory, even when they are very

young," she said craning her arm to touch his big nostrils with her thin fingers.

Her confidence appeared to discomfort him, though as she moved her hands about his scales, she was sure he picked up her scent and recognised it; he quivered and opened his eyes wider, his big irises pulsing with light.

Nuuk let out a gasp, the Drakhahoul's expression of disbelief, joy and curiosity was plain on his face.

Ghaeloden growled more softly and lowered his head on the ground so that Naghnatë could reach his brows. She gently caressed the thick scales above his eyes as if he was a fragile piece of glass.

"When Felduror brought you to the citadel you were very little. Now look at you, all grown and strong! I wouldn't have guessed you'd turn this tone of crimson; you were way darker then." Naghnatë marvelled at how big he had become.

A really long time had passed since she had laid eyes so closely on such a magnificent Drakhahoul. The last being Belrug-the-Black, the new king, who to her discontent, had left a mark on her soul and threatened to taint her opinion of all mighty dragons. It hadn't been her fault he had been so easily corrupted. How could she think otherwise? How could she hope that all of them weren't the same?

Yet, as she glanced at Ghaeloden, moving her fingers upon his thick, red scales, she knew there was hope. She had felt it for many years, dreaming of this moment and now she was standing in front of him.

"Where am I coming from?" the dragon's powerful voice was tame.

"If my memory does not fail me, I believe you are from Myrth," the witch replied. "Oh yes, Myrthen Valley sounds about right. I had only arrived in Arkhanthï and that was the first time I met Felduror, having travelled from my village to be instructed in the magic arts. That was…" she paused, afraid she'd reveal too much, "many years ago. In dragon years, only a blink of an eye, alas for me it is a very long time. And speaking of age, it only makes me shiver. I am freezing!" She rubbed her hands together looking at the evening's sky and realised it had just started to snow.

"We should get inside, Nuuk. And leave the door open so Ghaeloden can see us while we talk. That is, if you are interested in hearing more, of course!" She hurried inside the hut knowing too well how curious dragons were.

Once inside, Naghnatë put the kettle on the stove and started looking in various jars, attentively searching for herbs appropriate for such a gathering.

"I hope you won't mind if I indulge myself in a hot cup of tea?" she asked. "The wind's got into my bones and I can't shake it off. Would you like to try it, Nuuk?"

"Me? I have never tried tea. Will I like it?"

"I don't think you'd mind it," she replied, "otherwise I can melt a candle, if the tea is not to your liking." She winked at the dragon and they all shared an honest laugh.

As soon as the tea was ready, and their bodies warm enough, Naghnatë started talking again. "You have every right to doubt my intentions, but we can all agree that Felduror in power is a problem for everyone. And he will soon become unmatched if no one stops him." She started moving her hands on the table restlessly. "You might know or have heard about, what he has done to the dwarfs of the north, or to the Iprorims of Grora. Not to mention to the elves of Elmenor!"

"Yes, master Ghaeloden, Naghnatë told me I was taken to be drained of my magical knowledge, together with others from Grora," added Nuuk, with some enthusiasm.

"How so?" the dragon asked.

"Haven't you been living in the citadel?" The witch was confused; she had thought that at least the dragon would have known about it.

"Felduror has used every single Iprorim to expand his knowledge. He found ancient texts where the wizards of ancient times, unable to wield magic, had learned a way to draw powers from pure creatures of magic, such as wild elves, faeries and imps. Unfortunately, at the cost of the poor creatures' lives themselves." She paused for a moment and reached for Nuuk's hand. "I am afraid none survived his greed. That is the reason I left in the first place. I could not and would not learn magic at the cost of another's living soul. You clearly must've served him in other ways, to still be alive."

She realised that the more she said, the more the imp's face turned paler and disordered. He was speechless and only rotated his head to look at the door where the dragon's eye was following their reactions – his big, bright-orange irises fully dilated on the little creature.

He swallowed a mouthful of the dry candle-scented air and took away his hand from Naghnatë's, "I- Iprorims? It can't be!" He let out a weak squeal and tried to wet his dry lips. "There must be a mistake. They were freed before Felduror took me into his service. He told me so."

"I must admit, it is rather odd that I've never seen any other imp at the castle these past years besides you, Nuuk." There was a tint of sorrow in Ghaeloden's voice.

"Yes, because they have been freed," the imp added unconvincingly, seeking sympathetic confirmation from one of the two.

"Or they have been slain." Naghnatë measured that her brutal words would make him at least consider such a possibility.

He winced and she grabbed his forearm, firmly this time. Tears started falling on his human-looking face and he gulped uncontrollably. His aimless stare went through the wooden floor when neither the witch nor the dragon knew what else to say. Hand in hand, his fingers were hesitantly moving without a purpose and it took the dragon multiple calls to get his attention.

"Nuuk, look at me!" Ghaeloden's words were loud. "We will make that rotten wizard pay! I have always had my suspicions about his behaviour and I cannot understand why the other Drakhahouls have turned a blind eye for so long. It is beyond my comprehension."

With excitement and hope, Naghnatë measured the dragon's words to be honest. She had dreamed for a moment like this and had almost given up hoping for an opportunity to make things right. The signs were right; the time was near.

"Most fail to see what lies in front of them! You are an exception, Ghaeloden," she said. "Perhaps your rebellious young spirit and your stubbornness enabled you to see how things really are, alas I doubt you'd succeed to convince any of the older dragons on your own. Especially that cold, blue-eyed and black-hearted Sereri-the-White, your mother."

The dragon's throat vibrated with distress.

"Felduror had learned to wield the power of the stones just as he had been about to destroy the first one he had found," Naghnatë continued. "He probably thought that by ridding himself of such a threat he might stand a chance to claim the reins of the empire, only to discover that his chances improved if he collected them. Do you suppose the clans of the northern dwarfs had a better fate? Or the elves in Elmenor? Felduror and his Gholaks massacred them all, and those that survived cowered under the ground or deep in the forests. With these two powers kept under control, he cannot be stopped, not by the feeble attempts that sporadically break within his empire. And the humans? Bah," she let out her discontent, "they don't stand a chance; they'll never join arms and even if they did, they're not strong enough." She felt sickened by the weak nature of humans that never agreed on anything and always wanted everything.

"What about the other Drakhahouls, those that have fled?" Ghaeloden asked eagerly.

"That is something only you might be able to tell us. I cannot sense a dragon and I haven't been at the citadel in a long time. I haven't the faintest clue of how many of you still live there or what their inclination is."

The dragon let out another suppressed sound of angst, and appeared as if he wanted to avoid a direct account. "If only I knew," he replied.

Naghnatë did not fully comprehend his comment, yet she knew there were things that the young dragon would have to understand himself first, before imparting what he knew to others, or trusting her.

"Why do you think he sent us after you? And why did he say you would not give up an opportunity to return to the citadel?" the imp asked.

"Heh," Naghnatë sighed, "the citadel was the only place that felt like home. I have lived my most vibrant years behind those walls, and he knows how much I liked it there. As for what he wants from me, well, I suppose he thinks I found his wretched stones. But I haven't!" Naghnatë was almost angry; the recollection of how she had left the place was something still inexplicably disquieting, even after so many years.

"He is a liar," Ghaeloden added as if he just now realised something. "I reckon he's lied to my mother as well, about the stones. Yet, I fail to comprehend how could she believe such things and aid him in his plans. How could she not know he's corrupt?"

"It wouldn't be the first putrid lie to come out of his mouth." The witch struggled to stay calm and started grinding her teeth.

Neither the stunned face of the imp, nor the loud exhale of the dragon distracted her or soothed her nerves, as she turned and grabbed a chair to sit on.

"I suppose, then, that it is a good thing he is still looking for you. As long as we're the ones looking for you, and not the orcs, it is a good sign." Ghaeloden's voice made her turn to face the two again.

"For now that is. Still, I wonder how much we still have," she replied in a low tone.

"How many stones are there?" asked the imp.

"No one can tell for sure. I've only learned about six powerful stones!" She counted on her fingers.

"Six of them?" The voices of the dragon and the imp resonated in chorus.

"Well, there must be countless more. I reckon he's mainly after the most powerful ones, which coincidentally are the most ancient ones. There is the Blight-Stone and the Lux, which I know already the wizard has. There is Lifir's Feather which I destroyed, that makes three…"

"What? You have already found and destroyed one?" Ghaeloden sounded amazed.

"Yes, Lifir's feather, the only proof that a feathered dragon existed." She was proud to recount such a deed, knowing how hard it had been to find the rare artefact.

"I'm beyond disappointed, Naghnatë." The dragon's words were something she expected, and even if she tried to explain, he would not understand.

"Well, I didn't kill the dragon, I only found out that he or she existed, if that was your concern, master Ghaeloden. Would you rather Felduror had kept it?"

The dragon did not reply and the imp did not intervene.

She closed the argument listing the rest of the tokens she knew of, "Then we have the Armuren's Scale and Ulrenmyr's Tusk. So that's five of them. And there is the Blood-Stone, which I strongly believe he hasn't found yet."

"Why so?" The dragon seemed still upset.

"Because," she failed to hide her irritation, "the Blood-Stone was the first artefact ever made, and therefore has acquired much more power during the millennia. This makes it the most precious for those that seek them, especially for the crazed wizard. You really don't know anything you two, do you? Have you lived in a cage your whole lives?"

"None of the dragons in Arkhanthï ever mentioned the stones and the artefacts you humans seem so keen to obtain. And I, like all the other Drakhahoul younglings, are not allowed to venture far way. This is my sole journey outside the Aranthian realm!" Ghaeloden snorted and shook away the snow that had started piling on his head.

The witch reconsidered her outburst. Perhaps she underestimated Felduror's intelligence. He had indeed succeeded in keeping everyone in his realm unaware of his intentions as well as prevented his subjects knowing or spreading the true significance of the artefacts. All those long years since she had decided to spread the truth, with the exhausting, long journeys that covered every major village and town from east, west, north and south, seemed to have yielded no positive results at all. Was it possible that human race wanted nothing to do with this? Was it possible that nobody saw the real threat Felduror posed to the entire land?

She rubbed her hands and poured herself a second mug of tea, adding a spoon-full of bee's honey, ignoring the following gaze of Nuuk and the ever shape-shifting iris of the Drakhahoul. She slowly stirred the spoon in the warm, scented tea until the honey melted and she then cupped the mug with her palms.

"I apologise for my irascibility." Her voice was weak, more

because she was ashamed of having to excuse herself, than anything else. "Arkhanthï must be a fortress of late. The days where everyone could visit its endless libraries are long gone," she said. "Felduror is far more cunning and clever than I thought and there is one thing alone we have advantage of…" She let her words linger purposely, waiting to see if either one would show an interest.

"What advantage do we have?" it was Nuuk who asked, while the dragon kept silent.

"For a start, nobody knows I am alive, except you two!" Once again, she paused to ensure they understood what she implied. "Then, besides my powers, which might not be enough, we have this!" She pointed at the glowing sceptre.

"Oh that," added the dragon with rejuvenated interest, "speaking of which, we were wondering if, given that Nuuk disappears whenever he holds it, does it make us both disappear when we fly together?"

She hadn't considered such a thing. "I wonder if that might be the case? We should find out!" She was keen to see what could be achieved.

She lifted herself up and took few steps to sit in the middle of the little room. Nuuk followed her attentively.

"If you will, grab the sceptre and take my hand!" she said extending her hand towards him.

As soon as Nuuk placed his hand upon the glowing object, he vanished entirely. A couple of long instants passed before anything else happened. Both the dragon and the witch were impatiently waiting for the imp to touch her hand. And just at the summit of their waiting, when hope was almost gone, Naghnatë disappeared as well.

At first, she did not know what had happened. The light was paler, as was the shade of the candles' beam. She recognised the same room, even if it seemed different now, as if she were looking through a piece of clouded glass. Were it not for the strong grip of Nuuk's hand, she wouldn't have known that it had worked. They were both invisible.

"I think it worked!" she exclaimed admiring the bright-blue glow that surrounded them.

Nuuk nodded and confirmed by indicating towards the dragon's eye that was scrutinising the room with more velocity. As soon as he dropped the sceptre back on the table and released Naghnatë's hand, they could see themselves appear in the reflection of Ghaeloden's eye.

"It worked!" they exclaimed in unison.

Nuuk tried a second test, this time touching the dragon's brow while holding the sceptre. She never expected it to work, yet it did; the Drakhahoul disappeared as if his own might weighed nothing.

Naghnatë was dumbfounded and had to change her mind on Bilberith's capabilities. After all, he had exceeded his skills and accomplished his lifetime's dream; forging a magical item 'worthy of a tale' as he had used to brag to everyone in the seminary.

She had met him long time ago when she had started her apprenticeship as a young student in the citadel of Arkhanthï. She was but a child with no magical experience, who soon surpassed his skills, making what could have been a real friendship die out before it even started. Although they never had a real argument or quarrel, they had grown distant and took different paths; Bilberith had to continue with his speciality, the practicalities of magical inventions, while she took a more natural approach to magic; the herbal method. She had soon understood there were ways to extend one's life. Unfortunately, when Bilberith had fallen ill, years after her arrival, she had barely started the study of the ageless-potion and her knowledge of herbs had been insufficient to treat the gravity of his illness. She could do nothing to help and the wizard passed away.

Tremors ran along her spine and she came back with a shiver from the sad recollection. The others hadn't noticed her absence; Nuuk was eager to share what he had learned about the sceptre to the dragon. She took the opportunity to top-up her tea once more; it was starting to get cold.

She cleared her throat before starting to speak. "So now that we have established that this sceptre can indeed come in handy, we should plan our next move!"

If either had ever wished to free themselves from the wizard's grasp, she knew they'd have to speak now or continue to succumb to their already-decided fate. She was sure that, to some extent, both of them had plausible reasons to want it, though neither of them spoke.

Only when the silence lingered to a resounding point she continued. "The key to free your king, as much as your kin Drakhahouls," she continued, "is to understand how many artefacts the wizard has found. Possibly get them and destroy them, although that is a wild desire for now. If that happens, however, he would be deprived of their powers and easier to defeat."

"On this we all agree," the imp acknowledged.

"But, how are we supposed to look for the artefacts when Felduror never leaves the tower?" the dragon asked, seemingly interested in joining her cause.

"And what should we tell him that happened in Sallncoln?" added the imp.

"Do not fret, my dears!" Her voice picked up some excitement at their interest. "You shall take me with you and bring me to him!"

"Nonsense!" shouted the imp. "He will most likely lock you in a cell or bind you with magic and you will never free yourself! Look at what I am forced to wear?" He lifted his shirt and pointed at his restricted wings. "And I am neither foe nor a real threat. Imagine what he'd do to you?"

"Don't worry, Nuuk!" she replied angered by the sight. "He needs me! There is no other way for him other than to treat me with respect and keep me alive and well fed, otherwise he will get nothing from me!"

Surely her knowledge and her magical expertise would prevent her from getting into harm's ways, she considered.

Many times she had imagined the moment when she'd have to confront the wizard. And it had always been an alternation between a civilized encounter and a duel to the death, yet there was not a single scenario in her head that ended with her being harmed or jailed in the wizard's towers. Not with her shifting technique! The practice of moving from place to place unseen she had perfected during her long years of hiding. It had always proved to be the right asset against the many spies in the service of the old wizard.

"He will ask me what I know about the stones and if I managed to find any in my long absence from the citadel. I will delay him as much as possible as well as keep him busy and concentrated on me alone. During this time, I want you, Nuuk, to put to good use the sceptre and search inside each tower… by the way, does he still live in the main tower of the citadel?"

"Has he ever lived in any other place?" returned Ghaeloden, followed by a quick nod of confirmation from the imp.

"Well, that's that, then! Though we'll might find it harder to explore since he spends so much time inside those walls and is unlikely to leave its premises. Who knows what wards has he placed to guard his beloved treasures?" continued Naghnatë. "Either way, we do not have any other choice. We'd first need to know how many artefacts has he found and, most important of all, which ones. This will give us a clue on where he has already travelled to and where he will venture next. And, with some luck, maybe we can anticipate him."

"And what should I do? I am unable to go inside the towers." Ghaeloden's concern could be understood.

"You shall continue with your routine at the citadel and be of service for the wizard. That way, we won't arouse suspicion…" Naghnatë interrupted her sentence, lifting her hand in mid-air as if demanding a moment of silence.

A feeble, but palpable flicker of energy was gaining in intensity in the air. By the attentive look on the dragon's and the immobilised gaze of the imp, she realised they had sensed it too. "Someone else has wielded magic!"

CHAPTER XII

THE CALLING

Lorian

The rain stopped completely when I decided to return to Sallncoln. Clouds scattered towards the east, taking their menacing presence and allowing a weak early-autumn sun to be glimpsed in the sky.

I was content with what I'd learned, though still confused about many aspects and only too keen to ask the elder's opinion. As much as I enjoyed Alaric's company and his tales, I was eager to return home. Heaven alone knew how worried my grandmother was. Though, I knew she'd be delighted to offer her opinion on my findings and perhaps she'd have better news to impart about Elmira's.

When time arrived, I bade the old man farewell, understanding that Alaric, more than the artefacts and stones, was looking for someone who he could talk with, a friend, a companion. That could explain the reasons for his many diversions and his slow way of talking. He had offered me some food in a clean cloth that smelled of lilies; apples, bread, cheese, and a jar of jam of his own making. I had been reluctant to accept it, yet I could not offend his kindness by declining and instead I had promised to return the favour one day.

Reading the map that he had sketched for me, was easy and I could already see the mistake I made in attempting to find his place. How could I have been so wrong? What Nana had mentioned to be a simple path inside the forest ended up being a miles-long detour for me. Now with the underlined path he indicated, I would cut the mountain range straight down the middle, and emerge near the south-eastern valley of the village. From there, I could reach Sallncoln in only a matter of hours, having had abundant rest and food for the past day and a half.

The bulk of my voyage was crossing the mountain range that expanded in front of me.

Firebreath was as keen as me to be on the move again, and I was confident we could do it before nightfall.

Autumn seemed closer than a few days ago and hastened its drastic mutations of the landscape. There was something about the sky that made the air feel intense and rich with a tinge of cold portending the unkinder season. The clouds moved faster and their shapes evolved more drastically, billowing in a display of sharp shadows in the midday sun. The moist air near the foothills, rather cold and rich with a pine and oak scent, made me lose myself in a couple of long, deep breaths that inundated my entire body and made my eyes tear. Being quite high on the mountain and still close to the many rivulets, I perceived the enhanced fragrances that the air dispersed abundantly.

Firebreath had carried me along the forest at a brisk pace, though after some hours we had entered a brushwood and the mountain had become too steep for continuing on horseback. I had to descend and walk alongside him at a slower pace. The mountain eventually took on a precipitous nature and it was clear we'd have some difficulty cutting straight ahead on this section of the peak. Sharp rocks with tips like spears were dangerously protruding from underneath the wet black soil and I decided it was safer to go around the left side of the slope.

"Better late and safe!" I said while gently pulling Firebreath after me on a small path of dead leaves and twigs, most likely formed by the deer and boars that, obviously, had been taking the same route.

Judging by the amount of moisture in the air and on the ground, I could tell that the sun rarely reached this side of the mountain. The perennial shadow made the air feel sharper and every plant and rock was filled with a multitude of sparkling, perennial dew drops.

I took my time and looked for a sturdy cane that I could use to aid my walk as well as to move aside the tall and wet vegetation. A day in this dank air would certainly result in a sleepless, feverish night at the very least, even without drenched clothing. Once I was happy with the pine twig I found, I started bending the waist-tall ferns and giant butterbur leaves that were in my way. Nana would have something to say about this, as they were one of the most wanted plants I was forced to gather with her during the year. The tender roots of the freshly sprung plant in the early months after the taw, were a priceless remedy for fevers, head and stomach aches and we'd have to collect enough to last the whole year round. When their harvest in spring would not be as productive, we'd venture to collect in places just like this where summer's heat could not affect the vegetation so drastically and humidity persisted throughout the warm weeks. A task I never liked carrying out, but I could only appreciate the fast and quick effects of the concoctions she achieved, never once failing to cure the illnesses that afflicted us – even if the cost was having to deal with its bitter flavour.

The exercise of bending the various impediments, left and right, did well to my body and I did not mind the cold air anymore. More than a half an hour passed before we reached a dry patch of tall pines with a floor made entirely of brown needles and sporadic tussocks of herbs and mushrooms. Nearby was a big shrub of blackberries, the perfect supply to refresh my stamina.

I approached the massive shrub salivating over the dark-purple, round fruit perched on the very top of the bush, the bottom part of which seemed to have hosted something else.

I tethered Firebreath to a nearby pine and took out my knife, which easily aided me to snap a couple of long branches. Consuming the delicious fruit in a more comfortable position was key to savouring and enjoying such a moment, rather than standing on tip toes to reach them. My crane came in handy once more as with its crooked tip I bent a twig that I couldn't have otherwise reached. It was loaded with a row of fat and juicy berries. I cut the twig as far as I could reach it and let go of the remaining bit, shaking off to the ground some of the ripe berries.

"Nothing goes to waste" with calm, I recollected the fallen fruits which I then brushed from the dust and ate.

My horse was quietly gnawing at a small twig and I went to sit near him. The pine-needles bed was drier here and I was enjoying the fruit's sweet juices. I couldn't wait to reach Sallncoln and tell my grandmother and Kuno about my findings. Far too many times, when we went gathering forest berries for our winter preserves, we found the shrubs already stripped bare. The brushwood near the village was a common place not able to sustain the growth of our population. Everyone in Sallncoln knew about the best areas, where to look for berries, and everyone made their own jams and preserves. Though I had a feeling that this place would soon become our new favourite location, regardless that it meant travelling a bit further out. I indulged myself in another long branch of ripe berries and I opened the map to make sure I marked and remembered the precise spot.

All of a sudden Firebreath became unsettled; he neighed and violently pulled the harness in an attempt to free himself. Before I lifted myself up to try and calm him, the branch on which he was bound snapped with a loud crack and he galloped away, breaking in half the bow I had tied at the back of the saddlebag.

I jumped to reach the leather bridle, which was brushing the forest floor with a part of the broken branch still attached to it, but I was too slow and only fell and hurt my ribs on something hard buried under the dead needles.

"Firebreath, you come back right now!" My angry voice soothed the sharp pain in my chest, even as my irritation persisted.

I lifted myself back up, yet I had to keep a hand pressed on the left side of my torso. In my desperate pounce, the knife and the map had dropped to the ground and, afraid of losing them, I rushed to retrieve them. I took the map and put it in my pocket and as soon as I placed my hand on Winterhorn's handle, I heard footsteps snapping the dried foliage behind the berries' shrub.

Wide and heavy footsteps – four of them.

A gruff breathing accompanied the stride and I could feel its loud, inquisitive sniffing pushing the leaves and pine-needles aside. Although I could not see it, I had a clear picture of what would soon emerge; a bear. There were no other beasts I knew of that moved so firmly and heavily.

I hoped I was wrong.

Each thudding step made the beat of my heart increase and I dared not flinch a muscle. With all my strength, I found myself squeezing the antler-handle of my knife in my right hand and with the help of my left I propped myself against a solid pine trunk. I bemoaned the cane which was too far from my reach. Even if it proved useless against the beast, there was something comforting thinking about the size of it compared to my short dagger.

Make it be a boar, please! I voicelessly implored the sky, hurting my back against the hard, coarse bark in the attempt to push myself further back.

The heavier breathing from my right-hand side soon revealed a wide, large paw adorned with five curved sanguine-brown claws, as big as my fingers. Its sight made my hurting ribs spike in pain again.

Then another paw.

When I braved myself and looked up, I knew my initial instincts had been right; that was a giant black head.

I froze.

A thick, blood-draining growl erupted from his wide-open maw as the beast locked its charcoal-eyes on mine.

For a strange reason, the only image that stuck in my mind were its dark-purple, slobbery, coarse tongue and the four sharp, long fangs at the tip of his mouth. His furious eyes pierced right through me and I could feel my heart beat in my throat.

The confidence of the bear grew as it sensed my frightened presence; it continuously moved on its front legs, from side to side, roaring its big mandible towards me. Though, it did not advance.

From where I stood there was no running away. I knew I only had a moment to react. If I had two healthy legs, I could have probably made a couple of yards before it reached me, though with my broken knee I was as good as dead. I considered climbing the tree, but being pressed with my back flat against it, there was no way I could climb it fast enough; the beast would tear at me before I even spun. The consideration of jumping, and reaching the branch that Firebreath had broken, was just as impracticable as running.

I was doomed.

This damn knee!

I swallowed nervously, overwhelmed by anger and raw fear, fighting to hold back tears of frustration and terror.

These were the last moments of my life.

My heart was uncontrollably pounding inside my chest and I felt like the fresh air was not getting in anymore.

Closer to my end, I took another glance at the bread-knife I was holding, knowing too well it wouldn't penetrate the bear's thick fur. Fear got the better of me and I allowed uncontrollable tears to wet my cheeks and blur my vision. Frustrated by my helplessness, my hand squeezed harder around the handle, so hard I felt my fist's knuckles detach noisily from their sockets.

The brief moment the bear had taken to study me was gone. Acknowledging me as prey, it then bent his forelegs and pounced towards me.

As I swallowed my sorrow, I looked the beast right in the eyes thinking I was about to die, eaten alive.

And then something beyond my comprehension happened; the tears that started falling uncontrollably on my cheeks, the fear that I would not see my family ever again, the fast beating heart and the desire to live, were gone.

It was all gone.

I could feel only the salted tears that reached my lips.

I was stunned.

A warm, bright light encompassed me and I could remember memories I did not know I held. Brief and intense chapters of past, joyful moments flashed in my mind and before my blurry sight. One memory in particular lingered more than the others; I was very small and I could hear the laughter at my own cooing and giggling, as two adult faces looked at me.

How could I remember the faces of those I had seen as an infant? Are these the faces of my parents?

I wondered and thought for a moment that I was being devoured by the shock, that I was already dead.

Two pairs of vivid eyes, one blue, one green, were smiling down at me. I flinched and instinctively moved my free hand upon my chest in an attempt to touch and feel the imaginary, yet awkwardly-real, bright-red hair of the woman tickling my skin.

Mother? Father?

The words did not reach the air, they were only inside my head. My face was numb.

And just as fast as the images appeared in my mind, they vanished. All I could see now was the slobbery and fetid mouth of the ravenous beast, a few inches away from my face. Stuck in the air, as if a gelid gust of wind had frozen the bear in its pounce. Right in front of my nose the bear's enormous maw emanated a rancid smell of digested meat and warm entrails.

My right hand's fist, firmly clutched around the handle of Winterhorn, was visibly and painfully pulsating with blood pressure. What moments ago was a loud and animated forest-life scenery, had altered in a muted scene of quiet sounds and faded echoes.

A sweet and gentle voice gained in intensity inside my mind, isolated from the dimness of the others. It grew until I could make out a half word.

Ardar...

I could perceive the incomprehensible whisper coming from behind, somewhere to my left, yet when I turned there was no one.

Ardarah... the woman's voice grew more commanding, compelling me to say the word aloud.

I took a breath and swallowed to moisten my dried throat; I knew the word now.

"Ardarahia!" I shouted in a clear voice, not knowing what it meant.

As soon as the sound left my mouth, my body involuntarily and uncontrollably carried me to the right side of the tree, just clear of the beast's powerful jaws. With a sharp movement, still out of my control, my right arm arched backwards in an attempt to gain the strength needed for a powerful blow. And just as it did, it returned restored with reinvigorated power and thrust Winterhorn right through the bear's neck, plunging the blade deep inside its throat.

Astonished and confused, I was incapable of making my body respond to my commands. I only felt the grip on the knife being released and my hand pulled out, bloodied and shaking.

Silence subdued. The confounded state I was in suddenly died and all sounds came back to life from the momentary reverie, bolstered with vivacity.

Charged by the force of its own leap, the bear's roar resonated in the forest and died as it crashed its massive head against the pine trunk, shattering a portion of the thick bark. It made a havoc of cracking sounds, scattering birds away from nearby trees.

Where I had been standing, a fraction of a moment ago, the lifeless body of the beast was convulsing for one last time. It twitched and quailed with brief movements until its innards started steaming in the moist air through the wound I made.

I could not comprehend what had happened, but I was heavily gasping for air, feeling weak and wavering as never before. Tears of joy and fear mingled together and clouded my face again. I tugged at my eyes with my heavily shaking sleeves, clearing the unfathomable vision in front of me. It felt like I had run for an entire day, my feet could barely endure my weight.

I took a few steps back. Instinctively, and without purpose, I lifted my backpack and propped myself against a tree where I could still see the heavy body of the collapsed bear. Between gasps, I felt heat lifting itself in my muscles with delayed adrenaline.

Water!

The urge to drink finally reached my brain and I found the courage to interrupt my gaze from the bear for a moment, in search of my waterskin.

I gulped down almost half of what was left and returned to

the tree.

I knew I had to calm myself and recover from the strain and I forced myself to breathe slowly and deeply through my nose and spurn the sense of nausea that was making its way from my stomach. It took me a really long time before I managed to calm myself and stand again. But I could not stay still anymore. I started pacing around in circles, never for once abandoning the beast from my sight, and after many long moments I regained some of my lost strengths and clarity. I closed in on the beast and stopped, palms on my knees, scrutinising the enormous dead mass of meat, bones and fur.

"Did I do this?" My voice sounded surprisingly loud in my pounding ears.

With the tip of my boot I poked at the bear's paws to make sure it was completely dead, prepared to try and run in case it moved. When it didn't, I encouraged myself to advance closer and have a better look at the big gash that my fist and knife had created.

Blood still spewed abundantly out of the wide wound, creating small and dense wafts of steam in the cold air and a puddle on the needles-floor. I knelt beside its head and pressed my chin on the ground so I could see inside. Winterhorn was buried deep. It had lacerated skin, muscle, sinews and arteries in its devastating way, almost to the other side. The smell of blood was inebriating and it hinted of raw metal being worked.

Reluctantly, I extended my arm to pull the knife out of his throat; I had to push way past my elbow before I finally touched the handle and extracted Winterhorn. Being buried deep inside bone, I had to put some serious effort to succeed in my attempt. As soon as I freed it, I stepped aside and cleaned out the blood, gore and stray fur fibres from my hand and knife on the back of the bear's skin.

The realisation of what transpired only made me more agitated and I knew I was stuck with a moronic smile on my face. A black bear this big would be worth a fortune and certainly be of much support for me, my family and Elmira's. Its skin alone could earn at least half a year's worth of Henek and Kuno's wages in the wood trade.

Although I had seen skinning done many times before, I wanted to avoid damaging the bear with my untrained hands and started thinking of the most practical and convenient way to carry the beast back to Sallncoln. A sturdy cot would do, if only I could retrieve Firebreath.

"Where did you run, you coward?" I barked, standing up and looking around for the horse.

I had no choice; I needed to go looking for him, otherwise the imminent lack of light would make things way more difficult for me; I certainly could not afford to lose my way in a forest again and was not particularly keen on spending another night in the open.

Luckily, it sufficed to return to where we had arrived previously, the same direction he went in his rampant flight. I found him among the giant butterbur leaves, nibbling as usually, which he happily interrupted to come towards me. I stroked his neck and patted his big head, feeling guilty for having called him a coward. It would have been a big problem back home, explaining the loss of our horse.

Once I retrieved the body of the bear, I started building the cot I would use to lug it back home. I used the saddle straps and the bridle to tie sturdy branches together and make a foliage bed on which I'd roll the body of the bear. I knew it was going to be a challenge to move such a dead weight but with the help of Firebreath and a big pile of logs I managed to trundle over the fore part of the bear; its head, neck and front legs. The rest followed with exhaustive attempts on both my part and Firebreath's. In the end the bear was secured by the paws on a cot made out of thick branches and twined twigs.

"And it's not even that late!" I exclaimed satisfied at the task we had accomplished even though daylight was gone inside the forest.

I picked up my bag and checked its contents. When everything was in order, I quickly rummaged inside for the food that Alaric had given me. I took few bites of the bread and cheese and a generously-sized apple and ate it in four bites, giving its core to the horse, only then realising how thirsty I was. I took another one and counted two more that I decided to keep for later. Scared that anything could happen in this forest, I decided not to leave the knife out of my reach and so I tucked it under my belt. I decided the bow was not worth the trouble of repairing, so I left it there and placed my bag on my back. With a quick glance at the map, I stirred Firebreath to start pulling.

At first it seemed as if a piece of the mountain was tied around his back. Only after a couple more attempts, the bear and its foliage-bed started moving, leaving deep marks in the black soil. I rewarded my horse with half of the apple I was eating, glad to be on my way home.

After around six breaks and three hours of arduous pulling toil on behalf of my horse, we finally passed the summit and were slowly descending the other side of the mountain. The pine trees were sparser here and from where I stood in the clearing, I could make out the yellow beams of fire-lights being lit inside the houses of the village.

Sallncoln was in sight and a sense of joy and deliverance filled my being which reduced the fatigue I felt. I couldn't remember when was the last time, or if it there ever had been one, when I have been away for more than two days. I was desperately eager to reach home and have my grandmother's hot soup over which I could recount all my achievements.

At least a couple of bowls!

I giggled. The brief and intense moment of excitement made me rejoice. I made sure to share my feelings with Firebreath, offering prolonged caresses and bolstering, flattering words; he certainly deserved plenty of treats and rest once we reached home.

Yet, before I was able to take another step, a silhouetted shape caught my eye. It was standing still at the bottom of the gentle descent on what seemed like a pathway towards the village. I held the horse in place and squinted my eyes.

The shape appeared clearer and it resembled a child, a young boy whose face I could not distinguish in the dull light of dusk.

"Hey, you there!" I yelled, making sure he would hear me.

But no reply came as he seemed to glance in the opposite direction. I decided to leave Firebreath to enjoy a longer and much deserved break and started walking towards the boy. He did not move a muscle and only when I came within a few feet of him, did he turn and look at me.

"Hello there! Are you lost?" I wondered where he could be from, clearly not from Sallncoln.

He didn't reply. He only wore an immobile odd smile until I caught a brief flinch in his big, round eyes, almost as if looking at something behind my back.

And when I turned around, the face of an old woman was the last thing I saw before exhaustion caught up with me and I fell prey to a long and dreamless sleep.

CHAPTER XIII

THE DRAKONIL ORDER

Lorian

Echoes of distorted voices slowly carried my sleeping mind towards consciousness. Unfortunately, I didn't have the energy to open my eyes yet. The invisible hands of an illness were keeping my body locked in the same position, making me feel like I had been battling a week-long fever. And still was.

"I think I used too much juniper on this young lad!" The hoarse voice of a woman, came from far away.

"Oh, so that was what you used on me as well!" A second, younger voice hopped in from the same direction.

"No I didn't! I knew you were different the moment I laid eyes on you. Everyone knows that chanting does the trick for Iprorims!"

Another failed attempt to open my eyes.

A warm waft of mint and marigold brew made its way inside my nose, persuading me to swallow thirstily, and try once again to open my eyes. It did not come easy with the numbness I was fighting against. My neck felt stiff and all over my back I could feel my muscles sore with pain. The intense aching was comparable to the one when I had to carry potatoes sacks for a day, after my grandmother had decided to plant the tubers instead of autumnal cabbage.

I slowly succeeded in opening my eyes, but was unable to see clearly. Everything was blurred. Through my fogged vision, two faces perched over my body were preoccupied in an animated conversation and did not notice my awakening. I instantly thought that I was using Winterhorn again; the same blurry vision and confused state, one where I couldn't make out anything from distorted and mingled sounds. Yet there was no handle and no knife when I clenched my hands with revived effort.

"He's waking up!" A potent and deep voice resounded, giving shape to the small space I was in and covering the chatter of the other two.

It must be one of the voices I heard before! I considered.

I gave up thinking what was real and what wasn't and slowly pushed my head upwards in the effort to lift myself up.

"Here, take my hand!" An old woman offered me a thin and veiny hand. "Slowly now! You'll still need a while to recover!"

The young boy's, surprisingly, strong hand came in aid, supporting my left shoulder and I finally secured a seated position.

With a sequence of slow breaths and repetitive blinks, I felt more restored. Likewise, my sight improved somewhat and from the position I was in, I could see the pair of hands clearer. The wrinkles and the veins on the woman's skin reminded me of Nana; hands of a hard-working woman, strained, marked and battered by sun, rain, snow and time itself. The realisation made me think with distress how concerned she must be, not knowing anything that had happened. My worry added to the physical discomfort I was in.

In her old age, especially during the last few years, she had often fallen ill with what the village healers called the sadness illness – she needed to avoid excessive efforts and worry. Especially petty concerns and preoccupations. I was certain that she'd be fretting at home, asking one of my two brothers to come and look for me.

The thought gave me no peace and dismay forced words from

my mouth, "I have to go to home, soon!"

"Are you sure it was him?" The boy's face appeared in my vision as he asked the old woman.

"Where am I?" I managed to let out in a dry voice, for the first time able to see the boy's face.

"You are close to where we found you, young..." the old woman paused, enquiring about my name.

"Lorian, my name is Lorian. Why did you bring me here?"

"Lorian, I hope you are feeling better already, but just in case, let me get you a hot cup of tea!" She lifted herself up avoiding my question.

As soon as she left, the boy approached me and whispered, "This was not of my doing, nor my friend's. We never agreed to such a deed, though I am pleased to see you are not hurt."

What was he trying to say? I understood less than half of his rushed words. The idea of a warm tea was more alluring than his mumble.

"Here drink this! It will cure you in no time!" I was offered a mug of scented tea made with spicy herbs I could not distinguish.

My thirst was too fierce to decline and I was too weak to consider if it had been poisoned.

I took small sips and burned the tip of my tongue with each of them. Providentially, as soon as the liquid reached my stomach, the ache and back-stiffness melted away.

The old woman smiled at me and nodded comfortably in what I considered to be more a gesture towards her own satisfaction, rather than the expectations she must've had of her own brew.

I keenly finished the entire mug and then asked, "Who are you and why am I here?"

The boy shot an odd look at the old woman and she moved an inch closer to me.

"Have you heard of the Drakonil Order?" she asked with a restrained voice.

A veil of confusion clouded my mind briefly and I struggled to pick up her reference at first.

"Only what my grandmother had read to me and my brothers," I lied, thinking of the lovely blue book that Elmira and I had read at least three times each.

Apparently, she wanted to know more of what I knew, as she said nothing else. I continued, "I believe it was the order that went against this evil wizard, called Fellodour or something similar, because he had stolen an artefact and poisoned all the dragons. He wanted to rule over an empire that once was at peace and lived in harmony. The Order was made of a group of people that did not subdue to his —"

"It is Felduror, not Fellodour!" the old woman snapped. "And it's quite as you said. Only that from the twenty-three members of the Order only one survived, while the wizard found almost all the stones that could prevent anyone from stopping him achieving his dreams. The Order represented hope and once its members vanished, so did the courage they bore. And most importantly, no one here means you harm!"

The boy nodded at me, his lips curled.

"We found you because of this!" Flat on her palms, my knife was sparkling in the candlelight.

"Winterhorn!" I exclaimed. "What of it? It's the knife my grandmother gave to me and she has been —"

"Do not fret, young Lorian." The woman lifted her calloused-hand in the air reassuringly. "Nobody wants to take it from you. What use can we possibly have of a knife that in our hands would merely be cutlery?"

Her face betrayed no emotion, her words however, awoke my curiosity with fervour.

"So you know about the tokens?" I asked, knowing her choice of words implied nothing less.

"All of us here do!" replied the boy.

The suspicious exchange of glances between the two, forced the old woman to say, "You are safe here with us. And honestly, it is only thanks to a fortuitous sequence of events, a happy one I might add, that all of us happened to meet here and now!"

"Yet, I am here against my will on a dusty, rotten-floor heavens know where." Her warm smile allowed me to find some courage and state my discomfort.

"And I apologise if this has offended you, it was not my intention. If you consider it wise to leave, you are free to do so.

Although, if I were you, I'd wait just for a moment longer."

As much as I wished it, my strength did not allow me to leap to my feet and run. I could only haul myself onto the chair behind me, encouraging them in doing just the same.

We sat at the small table, as distant from each other as it allowed, and for a short moment; all of a sudden I felt I could not breathe properly. The hut was warm but categorically too small for the three of us. The rich, candle scent permeating the air did not help either and I was in desperate need of fresh air.

I stood up with some effort and went towards the door experiencing annoying dizziness. Once at the door, I opened it and propped my shoulder against the jamb, taking a deep breath. With eyes shut I welcomed the cold air scented with fresh snow, and instantly felt refreshed. A few flakes made their way over the threshold as well as on to my face.

The dull sense of sickness vanished away only to leave space for more questions that I had no answers to. The more I tried to focus the more I became confused.

"Feeling refreshed?" The deep voice that I heard before came from closer this time.

I looked at the old woman and the boy. "Did you hear that?" I asked, troubled that it could be a voice inside my head.

"Up here, young master!" the preposterous, deep voice came from above the house.

Propped against the door and with the flickering candle light bouncing in my face, I could not make out anything more than a few inches away from me. So I took few steps, scrutinising the darkness above. I screwed my head around, yet all I could see were patches of symmetrically-arranged stars; patterns of bright specks of light, dancing against a curiously dark-red sky. Though the more I advanced, the redder it became and more lights danced against it, seemingly moving with my steps.

What is this trickery? I thought as I swirled my head around in search of some celestial formation I could recognise.

Though, as I completed a full spin, I hit my forehead against an invisible boulder that knocked me to the ground.

"Ouch!" I patted a hand against my throbbing forehead.

As I looked up, the boulder started moving in an undulating

and awkward way that made me feel dizzy. A hissing noise of rubbing and crackling arose from where I stood. I fretfully started dragging myself back towards the hut, heedless of what was happening. It was like the whole world started spinning. The stars were moving in a row now and I was afraid I would return to that delirious state where I could not distinguish what was real and what wasn't.

"Do not fear, young boy!" The unexpected voice made me emit a broken yelp.

Ten feet from where I was, a pair of burning, snake orange-eyes revealed themselves in the cold of night. For the second time in the same day, unlike never before, I could feel my heart throbbing in my throat. Loud thuds resounded in my ears as I heard blood travelling towards and away from my head through the swollen veins on my temples. Its menacing stance with those burning eyes fixed onto mine, penetrated into my soul and mind and made me completely stop from moving.

A profound, guttural growl compelled me to listen and did not allow space for fretting or distraction. As I stood, the fear subdued and I knew such thing was possible only because it was not real.

Yet, everything seems so real!

The cold of the snow that chilled my being to the very core of my bones and sinews was real enough for me. And definitely real was the raw smell of iron mingled with raw meat that emanated from the vision and invaded around the hut.

The candlelight was not enough and the night was faultlessly allowing *it* to disguise itself. It forbade me to get a rough estimate about dimension and shape and only allowed me to understand that what I previously perceived to be stars, were actually the being's hard and shiny scales that sparkled with the light emerging from inside.

Unexpectedly, *it* coiled towards me, aware it could be seen and inspected. From the mere imagination that I had formed in the darkness, I could see how wrong I had been. Its colour was not dark-blue, it was red; a vivid blood-red colour which once on the move emphasised the ridiculous size of the beast, four times or more than I had initially and misguidedly imagined.

I gulped nervously, but miraculously I was not afraid. The scales that appeared liked fingernails a moment ago were now as big as my palms. His spiked head was almost as wide as our stable back in Sallncoln, and it fashioned three coarse, jagged-horns grown outwards from his skull in an asymmetrical fashion. I gathered they were long enough to hang my long coats on and they would still not touch the ground. A beautiful range of terrifying fangs, protruded sideways from his shut mouth and from where I was, I could swear they were at least as big as my fingers.

"What are you?" Convinced I was in a dream I found the courage to ask.

Hearing the approaching steps of the old woman and the boy encouraged me momentarily.

"Is this thing real, or am I dreaming?" I did not move my eyes from the beast.

They did not answer.

It must be a dream, then.

"Young master!" the creature spoke to me, revealing the crimson red and mauve inside its massive maw and a coarse tongue that moved like a snake.

"They call me Ghaeloden-Three-Horns, and I am not a thing. I am a Drakhahoul." The beast concluded *its* sentence with a too-real authoritative growl that shook off the little snow that had settled on my shoulders.

And that was the moment I passed out.

I was woken the next morning by flickers of light dancing on my sleepy face. In the early hours the sun was passing right in front of the small window of the hut and cast its low, tepid rays over the floor, where I happened to find myself lay about. An old, itchy, rough blanket was wrapped around myself and as I moved my head, I realised how bad it smelled. I tried to extricate myself, though realising how cold it was as a result, only made me change my mind, wrapping the dusty blanket around myself even tighter.

My night had been tormented by images of bat-like-winged beasts. Enormous creatures with sharp fangs and flashing eyes had surrounded me; Drakhahouls. They came in various sizes and shapes; some with horns and some without, some with longer tails and some with spiked backs. Their multi coloured, plated skins sparkled on a burnt and dusty barren landscape where heat distorted the perception of the horizon. I was only too happy when morning arrived and I could wipe the frightful images from my mind.

Though I needed time to get up.

On the opposite side of the door, by the stove, the old woman was crouched, fighting the overnight dead-embers in an attempt to rekindle the fire. When it seemed like her lungs would fail, the fire sprung back to life. She then placed a pot filled with fresh snow on top of the stove, which would most certainly become a hot morning brew.

"Good morning!" she whispered without looking at me, "I am almost done making us breakfast. It won't be much, but it's enough to get us started!"

The cornmeal she was browning on the reawakened stove and the boiled eggs, which were dancing between bubbles inside another small pot, made me feel ravenous.

"Good morning!" I replied not clearly remembering why I had slept on the floor.

I cupped my face with both of my hands and started rubbing the sleep away. A shiver made me jolt when the heat escaped my blanket but at least it enabled me to regain some clarity. Everything that adorned the interior of the hut resumed to a square table, two chairs and a small bed, tucked near the stove. Inside of it, hid between multiple blankets of various colours, a boy's foot was poking out.

A rather long foot for such a short body.

As if disturbed by my thought, the boy lifted himself from under the blankets and yawned widely. In an attempt to cast away the tiredness and remnants of what I hoped had been a restful night, he stretched and twisted his head, massaging his face with his big hands. Tired as I was, I thought I saw four fingers on his hands, though I could not be sure. Yet, as his hands completed his morning routine of face rubbing and eye scratching, two big ears, similar to those of a pig, popped out from under his palms, revealing the wrinkled face of a creature I had never seen before.

"What?" he asked not knowing why I was staring agape.

"Oh dear," exclaimed the woman as she looked at him, "did you forget that magic doesn't keep when one's asleep?"

"My face?" The boy fretted with concern as he felt for his nose and ears with the tips of his fingers.

"Nuuk, no need to play the fool!" the old woman reassured him as he pulled a corner of the blanket to cover his face.

He calmed from his agitated state and looked at me. "I am Nuuk!" he said waving his hand at me.

This time I could count, clear as day, his four fingers.

"I'm an Iprorim of Grora. You might know my kind by a different name; the imps."

"And something tells me you already know who I am." The woman lifted her brows with a quirky expression not giving me time to make much sense. "Whoever owns a token must have heard about me at some point in their life, am I right?" She winked.

I had convinced myself that the dragon was part of a dream but at this point I was not so sure. Now, an imp was waving his four-fingered hand at me and a fictional witch was winking with joyfulness.

"Naghnatë?" I dimly asked, holding off the excitement that was building inside my stomach.

She nodded and smiled. "That I am and have always been."

I jumped to my feet and took a better look at her and then at the imp. I did not know what to ask first.

Foolishly, the most irrelevant question came out before I reflected on it, "Are you really three hundred years old?"

"Hehha," She let out a wicked laugh. "I am indeed!"

I was astounded and disordered by such an encounter, yet delighted beyond words.

"I was looking for you! My grandmother told me you lived in Velkeri, that would have been my very next place to visit –"

"Hold your horses, master Lorian!" she interrupted. "All in due time. Velkeri you say? I haven't lived there for ages and I doubt you would have been able to find me, were it not for fate itself and these two brave souls!" She pointed her wrinkled hand at Nuuk.

"Two?" I asked bemused. "The dragon was real then? Is it at

your service?"

"Firstly, and most importantly, *he* not *it*. Don't ever let any of the mighty creatures hear you say it!" Her gaze turned serious. "And secondly, no; Drakhahouls are free creatures, they do not follow anyone nor go anywhere, unless they decide so. Alas, you aren't completely wrong; there is one dragon at the service of a human, and that is because that human happens to be a very powerful wizard. The dragon is trapped, against his will and we are going to free him!"

"And where is the dragon now? Is he gone?" I totally ignored her revelation, impatient to see the Drakhahoul in the daylight.

"He went hunting, master Lorian, and is probably on his way back. He departed early to avoid being seen by people. It's always better to keep things as they were, for obvious reasons!" the imp explained.

It now came to me why he had been so eager to whisper his apology, the previous night.

"According to Felduror that is!" added Naghnatë with a stinging tone, "however, we do not want to keep things as they are, do we now? We want every human to be able to see things as they really are, not to remain as ignorant as goats. Yet I agree, for the time being it's better to be patient."

There was a trace of anger upon her face she could not hide. Subtly, and nervously, she was clawing her thin fingers, opening and closing them into a knotted fist.

A sudden realisation disrupted my absorbed examination; I had forgotten about Firebreath and the bear. With a leap I jumped to my feet hurting my knee in the process.

"Where's my horse? Where's the bear?" I clasped my knee trying to rub the pain away.

"He's well taken care of! Nuuk would have been very sad, had we left your horse unprotected for the night," she replied.

"I've tethered him at the foot of the mountain and made sure he had food and water aplenty." The imp appeared satisfied.

"Now, let me see that knee of yours!" the old woman demanded as she dried her hands on her ragged apron.

She took a chair and told me to sit on it while she knelt to take a better look. With a gentle hand-patting, she started feeling my left knee's deformity. After few moments, she lifted the leg of my trousers and inspected all around the knee cap. With short and determined movements, she gently twisted my leg from side to side mumbling something. It felt like a soft chanting of her thin lips, which lulled me into lessening the tension of my body.

"Auww!" I bellowed as she twisted my leg with a snap.

The violent and sudden screw brought tears to my eyes and I pushed her cold hands away, trying to massage my knee in consolation. While stroking it, I could feel with the inside of my palms less protuberant than before. But the pain did not cease. I lowered the trouser leg back and blinked away my tears.

"I cannot do much more I am afraid, young Lorian! That is a foul misshapenness. What birth had given I cannot mend easily without magic. And I do not use magic to heal anyone," she said, lifting herself up.

I could tell something was bothering her, yet the pain in my knee distracted me. Only when it lessened in intensity did I retrieve my courage and lift myself up.

I was impressed. The difference in my posture was obvious and immediate; I was standing straighter than ever before and I felt I could lean more to the affected side. Not able to contain my surprise I let out a loud exultation of joy. I started taking steps in the small space and realised my improved stability and strength. I could even balance my entire body-weight on the left leg.

"What did you do to make it heal?" I asked, smiling.

"Do not get your hopes too high, lad!" she replied. "It can return as it was with the smallest sprain. The knee did not fully grow properly in young age and it will be hard for it to mend now. This fix can last a while, though if you injure it most certainly it will return as it was."

"Thank you! Thank you! Thank you! I feel I can walk properly now." I glanced at my knees and compared them.

The deformation was still there, but the much-improved stride made me happier beyond words, and grateful for what she had done.

"I can't wait to tell Nana!" I exclaimed pacing back and forth vigorously, enlivened with new confidence.

The imp and the witch exchanged an odd look and I found myself staring at his curious face.

"I suppose you would like to return to your village, Lorian, but I do not think it's wise." Her words crushed my enthusiasm and inspection. "We must depart as soon as this afternoon, there is no time to waste!"

"We?" I exclaimed. "What has any of this to do with me?"

"I hoped you'd like to become part of the Order, master Lorian!" she added with a serious stare. "We need all the help we can muster, especially if that help happens to come from one who has wielded magic before."

"What? Me, magic?" I almost started laughing, were it not for the flashes of memory that unfolded before my eyes.

Unwillingly, I found myself again in the same foggy vision. My voice rang slow, my arms moved slower yet with deadly precision; a black bear was leaping towards me, towards its end.

"Can't you see?" Naghnatë came closer, "there is no escaping fate. It was because of *it* that we all met, I am certain of this. Magic wielders are supposed to gather again."

The imp craned his head to see my face better.

"I can think of no token-holder this young, who can perform that well without proper training! Some fail with years of practice, though you have your grandfather's blood running through your veins and that is important." Her voice was gentler now.

"How do you know about my grandfather? How do you know anything about my family?" I avidly pushed away the thoughts of the family I barely knew.

"I said I haven't lived in Velkeri in a long time, not that I cannot remember its people! I knew everything about Dhereki and the stag and prayed to the skies that he was the one to bring hope to our long-lost cause. Yet, fate didn't provide that. And I, myself, wasn't probably ready either. So I've waited, keen to see if your father was supposed to take on his path. Inauspiciously, fate had a say in that too." She paused, almost waiting for my tears to start falling.

But I didn't want to cry, not for this. For a moment I thought I hated her; her words cut sharp and deep. I considered I had made my peace a long time ago with my unknown past, though her words reawakened the pain just as easily as cleaning a dusty blade with a single swipe of a hand. I only hoped my face did not betray the sorrow that was swollen in my neck and chest.

"I apologise, child. It was not my intention to bring back sad memories."

"It's all fine, I am well!" I lied and cleared my throat with a fake cough, a good opportunity to blink the surfacing tears from my eyes.

"There must be a reason why everything has happened the way it has," Naghnatë tried to offer consolation, "and sooner or later you'll realise that things go always as they should, and seldom as we want them."

With an improved smile I nodded my agreement. She was right, after all, none of this was her fault.

"I could see now what I could have done better, what I should have done, yet nothing can change how things went. What we can change instead, is what lies ahead!"

"Indeed." Nuuk seemed equally convinced by her words.

"How did you know about me? Did you know anything about the fire in Sallncoln?" I asked flatly.

"I only sensed it when it had occurred. That is the reason I ventured this way. But I have been waiting for such an opportunity to meet you, for many months now." She placed a hand on my shoulder.

I looked at her hand and even if my instinct was to jerk away, I did not do it.

"Less than two years ago, everything started to move in the right direction for me. Things you could not comprehend, neither of you could," she glanced at the imp for a moment, "and ever since, I have stopped searching for the stones and dedicated myself to finding magic-wielders. You'd be surprise to know there weren't any, not in the free lands at least, and not until now, when I have met you and Nuuk. A happy, fortuitous event allowed us to finally be joined; were it not for the fire, as wrong as it was, I wouldn't have sensed your spell, nor the imp's, and we wouldn't be here!"

The imp appeared as marvelled and confused as me, perhaps

a bit more restored with an optimistic sparkle in his eyes.

We stood in silence for a moment, contemplating and digesting what Naghnatë said when a thudding started gaining in intensity.

"Ghaeloden is back!" Before I said a thing, the imp darted through the door barefoot.

A tremor started picking up in my legs and they felt less stable. I was certain that my knee was not to blame this time.

The Drakhahoul was coming from the mountain side, following the ridge to avoid being seen. His powerful wings moved the snow from the tip of the mountain in swirling clouds of mist making him look magnificent. Dangerous yet astonishingly beautiful, I could not take my eyes off him. His red scales sparkled brighter with the sun rays, that on the top of the mountain crests, was at its highest intensity in the cold morning.

With a couple of strong strokes of his long wings Ghaeloden tripled in size. The sun was eclipsed by his massive body, his elongated shape darkened and distorted against the sky. For a moment we found ourselves in complete shadow where we could appreciate the light that filtered through his transparent membranes, revealing a throng of scarlet veins. My eyes teared in the powerful gust of cold air and I felt blinded by the sunlight when he alighted his wings.

Once on the ground, the dragon concluded his strain with a long exhale that turned into a suffused growl. Its vibrant potency made small rocks tremor under the layer of snow.

I was startled, awestruck; my mouth wide opened and my heartbeat almost non-existent. What I failed to see at night, during the day surpassed all my wildest dreams and nightmares. The beast was astoundingly marvellous and big. His long, spiked-tail moved unceasingly, vibrating through the air like a whip. His entire body was covered in hard and glistening scales that ranged from dark blood-red to bright red and orange fire-flames. Against the blue of the sky, a mere reflection bounced on and about his body making his sheen appear like polished metal. Last night, in the lack of daylight I had the impression that his eyes were rather big, but now I could see that they were relatively small for the disproportionate size of his horned-head. They were buried deep inside his thick scaled brows.

The need to swallow and breathe made me temporarily blink and return my posture to normal, only to regain my daft look of reverence. Such was the state of admiration in which I found myself, that I briefly considered that being eaten alive, or burnt to ashes by such a mighty creature, could be one of the most honourable ends one could meet.

Could it be that the creature was imperceptibly using its glamour on my feverish and weak mind? My question instantly drew my attention to his sharp fangs, some of which were covered with blood stains, fur and small chunks of gore. The vision made me shiver and I nervously swallowed again, shifting my view from the peculiar sight.

"Good morning, young Lorian. I do hope you won't faint this time!" The dragon's voice sounded surreal to me as the tip of his long tail slowly brushed against my leg.

I felt I could not move; a dragon had spoken to me.

"I hope you had a peaceful night. We have a long journey ahead of us!" he said.

"I…" I quivered, slowly stepping aside afraid and at a loss for words. "… I cannot come. My family needs me, I must return to Sallncoln, master Ghaeloden-Three-Horns. Elmira needs me." I bowed my head, my words trailing to whispers.

"Ghaeloden will suffice," he corrected me, "and, what will you do if the wizard decides to send one of his dragons again?" He now watched the witch and the imp. "I've seen the fire from the air and I can confirm it is not manmade; I can almost scent a faint dragon-trail. Do you think your people will be able to fight a full-grown Drakhahoul?"

Unexpectedly, his affirmation felt like a splinter removed from under the skin. It relieved me to know at least what had happened to my village. Even if many had seen the signs, who would have had the courage to try and convince others of what had truly occurred?

Yet, another matter concerned me; I could not believe there could be bigger beasts than the one that was standing in front of me. "Aren't you a full-grown dragon?"

Ghaeloden seemed amused by my words. "I'm way short of

completing half a full cycle, master Lorian. And a cycle is made by a full hundred years in human days. There are Drakhahouls that reached ten cycles and they never stopped growing during that time. I am just a youngling compared to our true king!" A measure of pride poured from his face.

"Master Ghaeloden, Belrug-The-Black is merely two hundred and sixty years of age," the imp added with some confusion, "surely he is bigger, but I reckon –"

"I meant our true king, Nuuk, Yrsidir-Two-Tails!" the dragon interrupted with a thundering voice, tilting his big head to have a better view of the tiny creature.

"Let's not lose the point of our mission here!" intervened the witch, perceiving just like me the wrath in the dragon's eyes. "We all agree that things are not as they should be and there is only one thing to do about it! The question is," and she turned her attention towards me, "if our new friend agrees to come with us. Or perhaps he considers it is better to waste his talent on tending sheep and cultivating crops?"

Her question brought to mind my two brothers and my grandmother, and the poor state my absence had probably delivered them to. I was really keen to tell them what I had found out and accomplished on my own, even if I suspected no one would believe me except, perhaps, Nana. Being able to walk straighter now was almost as important as having defeated the bear or having seen and spoken to a dragon and an imp.

"What help could I be? I know nothing and my slaughter of the bear I cannot even recall properly!"

Oh, Elmira. Where are you? If you could only be here to see what I am seeing and hear what I am hearing.

Everything was happening so fast. I had seen a dragon and had met the oldest woman alive, a witch nonetheless. The odd-looking creature alone, the Iprorim, must be worth a thousand songs and praises back in Sallncoln. And still, I could not tell what it all had to do with me.

I believed I knew a way to extricate myself from the situation. "I really need to take Firebreath back to them and at least let them have the bear's fur, which will be of big support for the coming winter. Coin has never sufficed of late, especially now with that bloody fire which destroyed our stable and ruined part of our house. It would be a shame for that much meat and fur to go to waste!"

"Would you dare hope that you're safe if you just return home? Would you rather wait for another fire to break out or a maddened beast to unleash its wrath? What if this time you don't escape? You don't strike me as someone who lost someone dear in that fire. If you had you'd definitely think more clearly," the witch insisted in a harsh voice.

Her brazenness and disdainful tone made me angry to a point I wanted to scream. Instead, I only clenched my jaw, hard. Elmira was still gone, and I knew nothing of her or her mother. The same vivid emotion of anger and frustration suffused my body. Tears were closer and it took me an iron will of determination to turn them away, clasping my fists until my palms hurt with my buried fingernails.

"If that's the case then I'd rather be with them than alone when that moment comes, if it ever does come!" I let out my frustration with less the tone I had intended to use.

You will not be alone! The calm and deep voice of the dragon resounded in my mind.

"What?" I was startled to see nobody move their lips.

It is I, Ghaeloden. I alone am talking to you now!

"How can I hear you so clearly and yet you are not talking?" I turned toward the dragon, making the others realise where my confusion came from.

We, Drakhahouls, are magical creatures, are we not? he gurgled. *And you need only think of an answer and I shall hear it as loud as your voice!*

I was awestruck.

And to correct you, you will not be alone, and it will be I who brings you back to your family once all this is over, I give you my word! Could anyone else in Sallncoln say they have ever had such honour? His big head was now turned sideways towards me and I could see my own reflection in his lustrous eye.

There was a constant, feeble flicker on his big, colourful iris and the red, yellow and orange seemed to pulse brighter with life the more I stared inside. I was mesmerised by its beauty.

I am afraid master Ghaeloden, and not only for myself. I thought.

I can feel your distress, but it is only natural to feel afraid of the unknown! It is the same for every creature that breathes air or water. Drakhahouls too, are afraid, but we are very good at hiding it. But the question remains, are you brave enough to secure your own future? Or do you prefer that the future should find you instead? There is no shame in any choice, there is only the choice. And nobody here will dare go against it! You have my word! he concluded.

An unusual sense of peace and hope spread inside me with each wise word the mighty dragon delivered to my mind. I felt calm and reassured to be in his presence.

Refreshed in attitude by his promise, I started to realise it was not such a bad idea to join them. What harm could possibly come to me if I had the promised protection of a mighty Drakhahoul, who, in turn, had some help from a witch? After all, wasn't I the one who wanted to know the truth? Could I back out now when I was so close to it? With surprise, another consideration came to mind; poor Alaric would probably give his legs to be in my place even as old as he was now. The memory of his bearded face reinforced my motivation.

Noticing that I was silent for too long the witch insisted, "Besides we could help you do that and way faster than you ever could!"

"Do what?" I asked, completely lost.

She replied with a mocking smile. "Take your horse and the carcass of that bear to your family, what else?"

"Would you?" I rejoiced.

"If that is what it takes to convince you, then let's be done with it. But I warn you, do not change your mind once there!" She seemed awfully serious all of a sudden.

"There will be no need, I only want to see them and reassure them I will be fine!" I said, knowing well I'd take the chance to make sure someone would look for Elmira and her mother in my absence.

Then here is what we need to do!" Naghnatë started imparting her instructions. "Lorian, you shall come with me and Firebreath! Ghaeloden, Nuuk, you shall take that carcass and drop it at the edge of the village, somewhere where you cannot be seen nor heard. A good place might be near where I found you, Nuuk! And make sure you use the sceptre!" She winked at the imp.

The sceptre? I wondered what she meant.

"Nuuk, once arrived make sure the bear is tightly secured back on the cot Lorian made, so we can take it from there." She placed her wrinkled hand on the small shoulder of the imp.

"I shall do just that then," he promised.

"Splendid! Then we should all get ready. Master Ghaeloden, Nuuk will show you where we left the bear's body. It's not far from where the horse is tethered."

The imp took a long-bag over his shoulder and mounted on the lowered neck of the dragon holding a harness I had previously failed to notice.

With a leap high as the tallest trees, the dragon took to the air and after a couple of wings strokes dropped to the valley below.

The witch called me inside the hut and shut the door behind us. She did not say much afterwards and instead dedicated her attention to some herbal and chanting errands. She mixed and squashed dried leaves and powders from jars hidden in her small wooden cases, spread across the tiny room. At one point I was sure I saw a wooden crate appear out of nowhere, yet what was there to be marvelled at anymore?

"We're ready! Let's get Firebreath!" She led me out of the hut.

After a slow descent of the snowy slopes, we found ourselves by the forest's edge where Firebreath was tied. I ran towards him and embraced his big head, stroking his face until he had enough and neighed me away. My excitement always lasted longer than his but I knew he was happy to see me.

Naghnatë approached the horse and patted his forehead as well, whispering something. She extended her hand towards his mouth and I could see inside her palm the same, dark concoction she had prepared earlier. Before I could argue, Firebreath had consumed it all and seemed to be looking for more. He suddenly became agitated and shifted from hoof to hoof.

"Steady now, boy," Naghnatë said, stroking him on his forehead. "We're ready, up you go!"

With enhanced ease, thanks to her mending, I lifted myself on the saddle and gave her a hand to climb on the horse too, which she attained with the same grace and ease as mine.

"You'd better hold tightly on those reins!" she giggled as she wrapped her hands around my stomach with a strong hold.

I stirred Firebreath with the softest little-kick of my heels, and he darted from the brushwood with a tremendous push. I almost fell from the saddle and strained all my muscles on my stomach and legs in the effort to recover from the knockback. Even though we were at the edge of the forest, there were still many dangerous scrubs and branches lowering almost to our height from the pine and birch trees. Firebreath darted left and right and only increased his speed as if possessed or chased by a famished wolf pack. The horse neighed and crushed everything in his way, running like a bat out of hell. The cold air of the morning and the maddened haste of my horse, made my eyes water to a point I could not see ahead. How was it possible a horse could run that fast? Such was his speediness that I had to lower my body and wrap my fists around the bridle with another tight-loop.

Firebreath was galloping at twice the full speed I have ever seen him run, or any other horse for that matter. Definitely faster than Charcoal, the fastest mare in our village was not a match anymore, and that horse had won every summer sprint-game in Sallncoln for the past five years – every year we'd celebrate the longest three days of the year with a feast where the villagers would bring their own delicacies and special brews; there was always plenty of food, drinks, dance and games for the whole duration of the event, which often resulted in disputes and grudges that lasted a whole year-round, until on the next occasion the bravest men and bravest horses would have the chance to compete again in the muscle and speed competitions.

We finally cleared the dangerous edge of the forest and ended up running alongside a small river – the river Irhe. Its green, clear waters could not be mistaken and I joyfully remembered the many times I had fished the stream with my two brothers. It felt good to have a sense of orientation finally. From here we'd end up just few miles outside the western edge of the village where, curiously enough, the river bends and goes underneath the Ridge; the mountain that divides Sallncoln and Irenthir. Few were those that dared venture inside the big cave that draws the river underneath the rocky mountain for a good and dark mile.

My eyes stopped tearing and I could make out the feature of the landscape better, but speed did not allow me to loosen my grip for one moment. Firebreath was tireless and the rapid beat of his hoofs crated a constant cloud of yellow dust that seemed to chase after us. Naghnatë appeared unaffected by the perilous situation in which she had placed us. She laughed and cheered like an unmindful child carried on someone's shoulders.

"What did you give him?" I had to scream to make myself heard with the air battering in my face.

"Oh, a bit of this, a bit of that." She continued laughing. "Do not tell me you are not enjoying this?"

She was right. The fear of being hurt, soon turned to exhilaration. In the open valley I was itching with excitement and started enjoying the astonishing speed we achieved. I let out shouts of joy as my confidence and sense of security grew and joined the witch in her silly, crazy laughter.

We reached the village in a short time, and I was determined to ask Naghnatë about the ingredients to make the horse-speed potion. Maybe, given the momentum of the joyful ride we'd just shared, I could persuade her into giving me a tip so I could have it ready for the sprint games, next year. Though, as we stopped at a safe distance between a patch of trees, Naghnatë dashed away and I lost the opportunity.

I was puzzled to see her return with the imp, dragging the cot with ease. It was like they were only lugging a sack of potatoes, and not even the biggest one.

"Magic!" I babbled.

They harnessed the cot to Firebreath.

"Nuuk, you still hold the sceptre, it's better they think it's only me and Lorian! Which way," the witch asked, turning to me.

While I indicated the direction, the imp took out his sceptre and vanished, to my utter disbelief. Before I could say a thing, his voice resonated in my head.

Master Lorian, I am still here, near you!

You too can talk with your mind? This time I made sure not to voice my question.

Ghaeloden taught me on our way here, he replied proudly. *We found the sceptre in the armoury at the citadel. There are so many beautiful things left to rot in that place!*

"Curious thing that sceptre, isn't it?" The witch seemed to know exactly what me and the imp were talking about.

"Magic is truly amazing!" I replied.

"And perilous!" she swiftly added. "It can eat at your soul as the rot eats through wet wood, don't ever forget that!" She sprung Firebreath's reins to move a bit faster, allowing me and the imp to continue our muted conversation.

He couldn't have waited for a better opportunity to recount all the exciting things he had accomplished during the past days; his illicit rummaging through the armoury and the discovery of the sceptre as well as a golden chariot; the mocking of the two tall and ignorant Gholak guards; and especially riding on the back of a dragon which, judging by the excitement in his voice, was by far his greatest accomplishment. He also told me everything the witch had told them about Bilberith and his sceptre and the powers it bestowed. Though, when it came to recounting further back in his past, he became vague in his choice of words. I did not insist on knowing more as I had my own trail of thoughts to disentangle.

I walked mystified and without words for a long time, contemplating the marvels that heroes of old, wizards and witches had been able to accomplish with magic. Unquestionably, every story I had read must have contained a small amount of truth and, as was the case of the sceptre, their magical weapons might still be within grasp. Weapons from ancient times, wielded with masterful skill in the hands of their heroes. Heroes that accomplished great deeds and secured their place in timeless pages of history.

Absent in my thinking, I lost track of time and place, and when the witch elbowed me back to reality, we were standing in front of my cottage.

I was nervous.

There was nobody outside and we slowly approached the door, the imp still concealed by the power of his sceptre. Before I could open the door, quick steps approached from inside. I instantly recognised Kuno's pacing before he even opened the door.

"May I help…" he froze for the briefest moments, "Lorian! Where the hell have you been?" He embraced me in a hug.

How much I missed his voice, I thought as I responded to him with the same intensity.

"Nana, Henek, come! Lorian is back, he's back!"

Nana's quick and stiff steps could be heard approaching and I almost shivered while waiting to see her face. There was another door loudly banging somewhere inside and I supposed that was Henek, still reluctant to leave a task unfinished.

When she came outside and went to hug me I could see her eyes were red and swollen with freshly wiped tears. It was a powerful and attentive hug neither of us wanted to break.

"What took you so long, son? Are you hurt? Are you hungry? Look at you, you thin thing!" She managed to detach herself from me only to clasp her hands on my shoulders and closely inspect me.

"Nana, I am well and sound and I'm not hungry!" I replied holding her hands.

"Is this…" almost as if not hearing my reply she looked past me and asked, "… Naghnatë?" She sounded befuddled.

"I take you do recognise me then!" Naghnatë tersely replied. "No need to concern yourself, he is well and he is following in his grandfather's footsteps."

"What is wrong, Nana? Who's this?" asked Henek as he came outside, his rushed breathing giving away his alerted state. "Lorian, you rascal!" He clasped me in a brief hug, as always, afraid that someone might judge he had grown soft.

I knew he had missed me and worried about me just as much, even if he preferred not to show it. It was nice to see my brothers together.

The witch did not reply, nor did she take her glance away from Nana. She only extended an inviting hand towards Firebreath, who was hidden by the corner of the cottage. "Maybe this will help you trust my words, I dare hope!" she then said.

"Firebreath!" Kuno exclaimed as he rushed towards him.

Grandmother and Henek followed behind, pleased to see our

beloved horse.

"And what is this?" I could hear Henek as he spotted the bear's corpse. "What on devil's name is this?" he kept asking dazzled and amused.

"Henek!" Nana rebuked.

"That is…" I started to talk but thought no words would make them actually believe me.

"That is the proof he'll be just fine, Allarea!" Naghnatë's soft words made my grandmother return the attention to her.

Remembering her name appeared not to distress my grandmother as much as what those terse words implied. I could read it in her face. If she was impressed about the big, black bear, I could not tell. She left my two brothers to marvel at the beast and returned her eyes to me.

"Lorian!" she whispered.

Her words stuck in the air and prepared me for a typical reprimand. A reprimand which did not come.

"I am so proud of you! And I am sure your mother, your father as well as my beloved Dhereki would be just so!" She swallowed dryly and allowed a feeble smile to break the flatness of her expression. "I will not stand in your way if this is what you want! I only want you to be sure of what you are doing! The choice is yours!"

My mind cleared as the noon's sun clears away the morning's fog. I did not see until then how much hearing her say that I was free, mattered to me and made my choice simple.

"Nana, I need to see this through for all our sakes. Everything you said about grandfather is true, all of it!" My enthusiasm made her smile more. I saw no doubt on her face.

"Promise me you will look after yourself!" she demanded.

"Promise me you will not worry, I mean it!" I replied.

"You are every bit like your grandfather. I know you will be well." She grabbed me by my shoulders and pulled me towards her.

My check squeezed against hers I whispered, "Nana, any words of Elmira?"

"Kuno has just returned from there. Some neighbours said they left the day before the fire. It's got to be that; all the victims have been accounted for. I will have your brothers keep an eye out and two ears on the ground. Do not worry!"

"Thank you, it means a lot to me."

My two brothers returned with dozens of silly question and remarks, clearly not understanding it had been me who had killed the bear. And who could blame them or make them change their mind?

"Boys," Nana directed at them, "Lorian will be departing for a while. There are some things he needs to take care of!" Against the discomfort I knew she felt, her voice sounded reassuring and authoritative.

"Where are you going, little brother?" Kuno was the first to come salute me when he realised I wasn't going to step inside.

"There are some things I need to find; it will be quick."

"Elmira then!" He smiled.

That would have been a better excuse, I considered.

"You're a big lad now, almost a man!" Henek joined with a chuckle and patted me on my forehead.

I knew he meant well, despite his condescending gesture.

"I will miss you!" I kept the tears at bay while I tightened my hands around theirs. "I will be back soon!" I promised.

There was no point in lingering. Troubled emotions were making me more anxious. Nana was showing signs of weakness as well, even if she was genuinely happy for me and my new venture. She understood it was time to go but didn't let me leave before she had wrapped me some food and some clean clothes.

"Still here?" she almost barked at my brothers. "Before that meat gets spoiled would you start the fires and sharpen the knives? We'll have a long night ahead if we want to prepare it all? Lorian's game should not go to waste!" She was hushing them inside like chickens towards the bear's carcass.

"Lorian's?" Kuno asked sharply.

"You're kidding, Nana?" Henek added.

"Do you mean he…?" Kuno, with a marvelled look upon his face, turned to face me, as he got pushed towards the horse by our grandmother.

"Who else you think? I'll tell you all about it later, once you've cleaned and fed the horse. Fast now, the both of you!" Nana avoided turning to face me.

I knew then that she was crying again.

CHAPTER XIV

THE CAVE

Lorian

After leaving Sallncoln, I felt torn and empty and dreaded even turning my head to take one last look. When I finally found the courage to do it, it was way too late; it was out of sight. What had been a pleasant and fast ride on Firebreath's back to get there, was now a slow stroll where my thoughts wore me down more than the exhaustion of the lengthy plains.

Inside my head, a constant battle raged between wanting to return home and continuing towards the unknown. Its distressing power was wavering from one side to the other in a never-ending cycle, causing an annoying headache. When one seemed to prevail over the other, new questions emerged restoring the balance. One of the most pressing concerns I found myself facing was the unusual company I was travelling with – a dragon, a witch and an imp. Creatures that until a few days ago I thought were only imaginary characters, invented for the delight of young children, were now to be my companions on a mysterious venture.

How did I get here? Could it be that all this is a dream?

As a matter of fact, ever since I used Winterhorn and killed the bear, everything felt as if I was not in control of myself. The mist of glowing light, that engulfed me at the height of my action, had disappeared and the dulled sounds around me felt as vibrant and sharp as ever, but I couldn't tell for sure if I was still in the same state or not. There was also something else persisting, a feeling I could not see nor distinguish. Something that I picked up from that moment and lingered about me, making me wonder if it would ever go away.

Aren't dreams supposed to feel like this?

It was no coincidence that everything started to happen after my tussle with the bear and, almost convinced of my theory, I started closing my eyes for long moments and opening them again. A silly sight, had anyone looked at me. Then I continued walking and tried to ignore any sort of thoughts whatsoever.

The air whistling above, sounded angrier and bore news of the summer's end, forewarning the arrival of a heavy autumn. Its sharp bite left deeper marks on the open skin of my hand's blisters and cuts that still had a long way to fully mend. In the coolness of the evening I could think of only one thing that would ease the tumult of my mind; my fondness for the night's light, or better the lack of it.

Since I was small, I felt attracted by the mystery that night provided with its dark veils. Common things turn to frightful and daunting monsters in the midst of night, at the pace of one's imagination. Yet when everyone else was scared, I only wanted to venture and explore. Often I loitered inside the forest and listened attentively to the curious laments and calls of the night's predators, that in the same fashion as objects, changed in the lack of light. Back then, I hadn't known what danger and fear meant. Only when I became big enough to be needed around the house and stopped doing childish things, had my fear begun to surface. I stopped venturing towards and fighting my demons. Nana always told me that if you are scared of something you should fight that fear and not let it delve within your core until it becomes a bigger monster than it actually is.

I am sure this will make for a decent demon to fight! The thought made me smile, and added motivation to my venture ahead.

Alas, for the very same reason, I had often been grounded for thoughtlessly putting myself in danger and scaring my family. Thinking back on it now, I knew their luck and my salvation had been because of my condition. Had I been able to run freely and easily, I would've most likely ventured too far for them to track me and ended up lost in the woods or eaten alive by the wolves.

I wondered if this was about to change as I was free and I venturing somewhere unknown, farther than they could come look for me.

After my mind's wandering, my body made my wits return with a spiked pain. My recently-mended knee was giving signs of fatigue. Still, we kept on.

We reached the snowy slopes in almost complete darkness, and if it weren't for the witch's sharp sight and her remarkable knowledge of the mountain, I could have been searching for the small hut the entire night without success.

The light that emanated from inside was not visible until we stood a few feet away, inexplicably so, until I understood it was magic that concealed the place.

"Welcome back!" The imp greeted us as we entered.

"It is so nice and warm here!" I shook the snow from my boots, and rubbed my palms together. "Where is Ghaeloden?"

When both the imp and the witch looked at me perplexed, I knew I shouldn't have asked. "He went hunting, obviously!"

I wondered how much a dragon of his size would need to gratify his appetite for a day.

"I am happy you have decided to join us, master Lorian! There are so many things I would like you to see once we reach the citadel." Nuuk found me by the stove.

Probably it was exhaustion that made his enthusiasm seem a little out of place, however I did appreciate his interest. If it weren't for the troubling thoughts of having left my brothers and my grandmother, I would probably have felt enthusiastic myself.

"The tea will be ready soon, and before we leave this cold hut, you should eat a chunk of bread at least," Naghnatë suggested.

"Leave now? But it's night and we just arrived. Getting to Arkhanthï will take us weeks to reach on foot. Isn't it very far north?" I was concerned at my ability to undertake such a long journey after having lost my strength and desire to walk.

"We're already late! We were supposed to leave this afternoon and we have delayed our departure to give you a chance to see your nana and your brothers." Naghnatë ignored my apprehension.

I sighed, too tired to argue.

"I know I may seem unkind and unfair, lad, yet we have more pressing matters to attend to. If you only realised how things really are, you'd understand what I mean," Naghnatë said with a softer voice, gently placing a hand my shoulder.

"I understand," I pretended I did, "I'm only tired and a bit miserable; I fear for my grandmother's wellbeing. She likes to show she's strong, though I know she worries."

"Be strong, master Lorian, if we succeed in our quest, things will change for the better, and for good this time. I promise you that! And if you behave, I might decide to divulge some of my little secrets." She winked at me with a smile. "How would you like to learn how to cook the haste-powder? Your horse appreciated it a great deal, don't you think?"

"Would you do that?"

"Sure, I don't see why not. And also, just so you know, we are not going to walk or fly to Arkhanthï. No, sir! It would be too perilous and would take us way too long as you've already pointed out." She laughed with excitement and exchanged a glance with the imp, who appeared more impatient than me. "We are going to shift ourselves closer to the citadel and from there, once ready, walk."

"Shift?" I was confounded.

"Yes, shift. It doesn't require a horse, only some magic. You'll see, it's plenty of fun!"

"I've heard Felduror mentioning something similar on occasion. Not sure it was 'shifting' he called it. It did, nonetheless, imply travelling without any known means," Nuuk added.

"Felduror? You personally know the evil wizard?" I was alarmed at how little I knew about my companions. "Can someone please tell me who you really are?" I asked curtly.

A moment passed.

"You're right, young master. I beg your forgiveness for not having properly introduced ourselves, and I blame it again on the urgency and lack of time. It is only proper to tell you a bit more about ourselves," replied Naghnatë.

She paused for a moment and the imp took a seat.

"Both me and Nuuk have known the wizard at some point in our lives. I was his apprentice and the imp and his kin, were taken against their will from Grora to be studied by the wizard, since Iprorims are, like dragons, creatures that are born bearing magical powers. Felduror, thanks to other wicked minds' scripts, has succeeded in extracting the knowledge of magic from within each creature, but at a dear cost. The weak creatures have been left to die or abandoned, who knows where, having lost their strengths and wits. Though, for unknown reasons, the wizard decided to keep Nuuk and, as far as I can tell, he doesn't seem to have lost any of his powers." She appeared curious herself. "Nuuk, does it seem that you are lacking any of your powers?" she asked.

He swallowed tersely and look at us both, "I could perform the healing spell quite easily –"

"I think there is a better way for us to see if you are still capable, although I wonder if that piece of magically-imbued thread would not alter your prowess," she interrupted him.

Nuuk looked concerned.

"You should try and test your magic skills!" Naghnatë said.

"Can I?" Nuuk seemed surprised, and pleasantly so, as a nod from the witch made him jump eagerly to his feet and stand in the centre of the small hut.

He lifted his right hand towards fireplace where the embers were dancing with the flames in a sparkling-noise whirl. He held his breath and moved his lips slightly for the briefest of moments.

Unexpectedly, and with nervous flickering, the fire escaped the metal stove and started moving in the direction his hand was pointing. The burning flames moved as if still powered by the embers, though the embers were dead black in the stove. The fire-ball was dancing now in mid-air animated by his fingers and as soon as he approached any candle, the smaller flame would join the biggest one leaving the black wick wafting with smoke. He giggled and moved the flame closer to my face, making me wobble on the rear legs of my chair.

"Do not fret, master Lorian. I would not hurt you, not ever!" His amused faced reassured me.

I lifted my hand and tried to reach closer to the sizzling, dancing fire-ball, and as I did, I could feel the comforting warmth grow into a dangerous raging fire.

"This is incredible!" I exclaimed, mindless of how foolish I must have looked.

"Very well, imp! Do you feel tired?" the witch asked.

"I am fine!" He could not contain a wild grin.

"Would you dare try something more?" Naghnatë asked.

"More?" I asked, but they did not even consider me.

What more could there be than wielding fire?

The imp apparently knew what she meant because he nodded his consent. Instantly, the flames were restored to each candle and the ball of fire to the stove. He then sat himself comfortably in the chair and took a moment, as if to recollect his strength. With both hands cupped on his knees and tight-shut eyes he appeared as still as a sculpture.

A long moment of cold silence followed and when he opened his eyes again, they were as black as charcoal. All the candles went out with a glimmer and a poof while the fire inside the stove started flickering with vigour and turn blue-white. As we stood dazzled, watching the motionless imp, a whirlwind of energy burst visibly around him, making his body tremble and shake with verve. Soon, everything around him started to shake. I fixed my eyes upon a noisy, shaking board on the floor, and noted with surprise the rusted nails were slowly being pulled upwards by the spinning mass of energy around his body. More boards followed, and the noise inside the hut became unbearable – as if a violent storm was tearing apart the loose shingles of a roof. I grasped my chair tightly, feeling it move in spite of my weight and as I lifted my eyes, I saw Nuuk's chair fluctuating steadily in the air. The shakiness of my chair increased and as I tried to hold it tighter, I became distracted by Naghnatë's laughter. She too was lifted in the air. Surprisingly she was not scared; she was dangling her feet like a child in awe, laughing crazily with her face upwards. The noise grew louder and all around us bigger objects were being lifted in the air, dangerously spinning with vigour in the same direction.

"Is this safe?" my shout reached nobody.

The crackling noise of the boards and the gusts of wind made it impossible to be heard. I almost couldn't hear myself think. Even Naghnatë's loud laughter faded to a faint, barely distinguishable turbulence to my left. My heart started beating faster and I vacillated heavily realising I was floating above the floor on my chair. I did not have time to react as the foundation of the small hut started to crackle with loud snaps, as if it was being unearthed from the mountain. I gulped nervously and clutched tighter onto my seat, prepared to be completely lifted into the air together with the hut and everything inside it.

Yet as I closed my eyes, the cacophony of noises ceased. The whirlwind recoiled, quickly losing in intensity and volume. All around inside the hut, every object that was fluctuating moments before, returned to its place.

Quick, short breaths helped me recover my normal heart beat and I watched astounded how every single nail was returned to its place by a magic, invisible force. A persistent scratching noise of metal against the wood distracted me and I looked towards Naghnatë. She was keeping the tip of her sole on a rusty nail, which was restlessly trying to escape. She appeared entertained by her petty deed and only too reluctant to free the vivacious piece of iron, which flew straight back across the room to its hole. As soon as it settled, every candle burst with tiny flames again and everything was as it was before. The ravaging whirlwind had left the room noiseless, making my ears whistle.

Nuuk recovered from his statue-like state and I witnessed his dark charcoal-eyes regaining their vivid green shade.

"What happened?" His first words were weak.

He tried to lift himself but landed back on the chair unable to stand. The witch hurried to assist him and gently settled him on the wooden chair, stroking his head with tenderness.

"That was a very fine demonstration, master Nuuk! If it weren't for that darn string, I think we would've witnessed the most beautiful and powerful display of pure magic!"

That was the first time I heard the witch speak with proud and trembling voice.

"Was it pleasant to the eye? I cannot remember much." Nuuk let out a faint and tired smile.

"I believe you performed a recall-spell," she continued.

"What does that mean?" I asked perplexed.

"It is one of the hardest spells to achieve. A recall-spell is a spell one can cast even if he or she doesn't remember learning it. It's a natural spell written in your core and blood and stays with you forever. Obviously if you are a magical creature, that is. You are not taught a recall-spell; you only earn it by your magical existence. Every magical being has one that reveals itself at some point during their lifetime and I think Nuuk has just found his."

I felt infected by her joy.

"I've seen only a few of them during my years and I can only say they all differ. This was just marvellous!" Naghnatë continued.

"And what does it perform?" I insisted.

"I am afraid that is not something we can know. Only the caster can understand its true significance, once completed. Though I am afraid our friend was interrupted just before the end." She raised herself from the wooden floor and collected some fresh water for him.

"Thank you!" Nuuk eagerly grabbed the mug from her hand. "I feel very tired. Ghaeloden will return any time now and I would not want to upset him by not being ready to depart. Do you mind helping me rest a moment on the bed?" He appeared worn.

The witch helped him to the bed and pulled the blanket on top of him. He fell asleep as fast as a stone hits the bottom of a river.

"We should let him recover his strength. He is not accustomed to wielding magic any more, and this here, was one of the big spells! Even I'd fall fast asleep after something like that." Naghnatë dashed outside the hut.

I followed her outside into the dark, cold evening.

"Will he be alright?" I asked.

"Magic takes its toll on every caster! Every spell, as small as it is, requires strength. Sleep, food and rest is the only remedy. You might have experienced something similar."

The astonishing, magical trial of the imp, made me forget how tired and stunned I had felt after my trial with the bear.

Magic is a strange thing! I thought.

Indeed, it is! Yet, it is also the most powerful force in the world! Ghaeloden's voice rang inside my head.

"Ghaeloden!" I looked up, searching the dark-blue sky.

When his powerful wings could be heard, Naghnatë told me to step inside and prepare something for us to eat, before our departure. She'd take care of explaining what transpired to the dragon, as most likely he had felt the surge of magic and would want to be advised.

While I busied myself on heating the broth, I heard Ghaeloden land. The witch welcomed him with a reassuring 'Let me tell you everything,' before he said a word.

It took me a couple of sneaky bites of the smoked cheese, wheat bread and red onions that I found under a piece of cloth in the storage crevice, before they settled their discussion and Naghnatë came joining me for the warm soup that was boiling on the stove.

We ate without words, cherishing the warm dinner in the cold of the night. The rich flavours of the soft vegetables reminded me of one of my favourite soups; the smoked-pork soup, that my grandmother liked finishing by adding a generous amount of fresh cream and a couple of spoons of vinegar, right before she'd take the pot off the stove. The only thing I loved more than a warm soup, was a warm soup accompanied by a good amount of pickled hot peppers.

"How did our new friend find the magic trial?" Ghaeloden's voice brought me back from my musings.

"It was the scariest and most exciting thing I have ever witnessed, master Ghaeloden! Second only to almost being killed by that bear, that is!" I replied, wiping my mouth.

"Magic has this effect on many, young master. Disastrous, treacherous, yet astonishingly beautiful!"

"I only pray I'll be there to witness your recall-spell when time comes!" the dragon added.

"My what? How is that –"

"Enough with this magic brandishing. I've had enough for one day!" Naghnatë's voice was angrier than before, as she interrupted me. "I think we are ready to leave this place! Have you had your fill of food?"

"I- I have!" I replied, wondering what caused her distress so abruptly. "I am ready for the journey!" I lied.

"Oh don't be silly, it's not proper to call it a journey, it will only take a moment." She looked around the small place with care. "Take your things and give me your hand!" she commanded.

I obeyed.

"Master Ghaeloden, I believe you know how to make this place secure and hide it from prying eyes. As soon as Nuuk is ready, we shall meet where we agreed." Without waiting for a reply, nor a warning to myself, her hand squeezed mine with mountain-like force and all I heard was an echo of her voice saying, 'Spectra!'

I have only once, in my sixteen years of existence, experienced the hallucinatory outcome of strong drink, and that had not been a pleasant affair. It had been during the grape harvest, some two or three years back, when me and my brothers had been asked to watch the giant oak-barrels that were to be transported to the cellars. The smoky-smelling, charred barrels had been filled to the very top with a sweet winemust that was later to be used for the strong wine in part and in part to be left to become vinegar. Driven by our keen curiosity and the very sweet smell of the red liquid, we had tried our luck with a mug or two. We soon had come to regret it. Its illusory, reeling effects had only arrived after the second mug, making our heads spin wildly and lasting until the very next day. We had promised then, amid persistent sickness, that we'd never drink again.

Compared to that day, the *shifting* Naghnatë performed made me feel tenfold worse. My head felt like it had spun for an entire day and I couldn't stop regurgitating the vegetable soup. The muscles in my belly ached from spasmodic contractions and it felt like a lifetime before the foul sensation loosened its grip on the back of my throat.

Slowly I let go of the floor and turned on my back; an undertaking in itself, and rested there, pleased that the spinning fleetingly diminished.

"Water!" I perceived the blurred figure of the witch somewhere on my left side.

She brought me a mug of fresh water and helped me gulp it down, only lifting my head slightly.

"Th- Thank you!" I let out, strained by the effort of keeping my neck tense.

I closed my eyes and only opened them when my body felt it could handle some movement. With the first blink, I could finally make some sense of where I was. The space was dark, the only source of light the firelight that bounced on the dark-grey stones that surrounded us. We were inside a cave of some sort. I could feel the damp air permeate the small space and the cold stone at the back of my head.

What is with the witch and suffocating spaces? I thought, realising the unusual aspect of her habitations.

A draught made the sweaty hair under my nape send cold tendrils across my body and as I turned my head to the right, I could see a big, irregular boulder blocking an entrance almost completely. The imperfect door allowed a small opening in one of the upper corners, from which the breeze was invading the cave. The small aperture allowed me to catch a glimpse of tiny sparkles up in the dark-blue sky and I could tell outside was ruled by a cold, cloudless night.

I gathered all my strength and, feeling less disoriented, I looked around and studied the small space. The uneven shape of the cavern was made in such a way that the left side was sharp-cornered and the right side was curved and more spacious, near the entrance. An irregular pear-shaped space where at the tip there was a fireplace and a bed, sculpted in the raw rock, with hay straw as a mattress. The fireplace where the witch was already boiling some water was less fanciful than the one in the snowy-slopes' hut, with a simple hole in the rock that allowed the smoke to escape. But the space was stocked with all the necessary for our stay; cooking pots, various tools and plenty of dry firewood that'd warm the space restlessly for an entire week. In the same corner, nails and small wooden wedges had been pushed inside the walls, between cracks and crevices, and were holding dried meat, herbs and other supplies I did not recognise. The one plant I could distinguish, was the dried, yellow-rattle that the witch decided to prepare a tea with and was slowly wafting its way inside the dank cave, invading my nostrils.

I slowly lifted myself to a sitting position, slipping one hand in my own vomit.

"Ewww," I cried out, hearing my echo bounce between the rock walls. "Yuck, that is disgusting!"

"Yes, it is, and it's all yours! The only thing that's mine there is the soup!" The witch started to laugh. "Be a sport and clean that up, will you?"

She tossed me a ragged cloth and kicked a twig broom towards me. I did my best to clean away the poorly-digested soup before washing myself and joining her by the fire.

The dancing orange light of the fire cast soft and dark shadows upon the cold stone, and her candid giggle caused by my mucky face appeared like an evil spectre elongating over the walls.

I blinked away the ghastly image and diverted my thoughts. "Had this ever happened to you?"

"Ha! I think I've had it worse, I'm afraid. I had to break many bones before I finally mastered this peculiar skill. Yet, I must be honest, you did rather well on the landing. It's the waking up that needs some practice!" She let out another chuckle.

I was starting to improve from my wooziness and her joke made me chuckle too.

"We have few days before Nuuk and Ghaeloden make it here and, when they arrive, you three will go to the citadel, while I'll try to force out that old crook from the safety of his stronghold. During the next few days I will get you ready for any unpleasant encounter in Arkhanthï. Also would be good to get to know more about you and Winterhorn, what do you say?" her expression was stern.

"I would like that, though I am afraid I've told you all I

know!"

"I would still like to hear it one more time." She extended her thin hand towards me. "If you do not mind, could I hold it for a moment?"

I grabbed it from my backpack and gave it to her. She examined it with care for a long time, my warming hands and body appreciating her slow inspection.

"Marvellous how pure magic works!" she stated. "Typically, magic is perceivable through the air especially if one comes in physical contact with the wielder or any magical object, yet these tokens emit nothing of the sort to be seen or felt in estranged hands. Marvellous indeed!" She handed it back to me and as soon as I touched it, the reviving tingle spread throughout my body with a refreshed intensity and vibrancy I hadn't felt before.

She must've have seen my fingers twitch, because she was surprised by my reaction. "It grows more accustomed to you! And the more it does, the more powerful it becomes as you'll fully understand its strengths and acquaint yourself with it." She picked two earthen-mugs from a wooden crate, which appeared out of thin air.

I did not have time to issue a word.

"Nothing is at is seems, child! Do you think I like to live in empty, rotten, bad-smelling huts or caves without all the necessary to live decently or enjoy a warm, delicious cup of tea? No, sir! I hide my places as well as my personal objects, so nobody knows where they. Often they are right in front of their noses." Her laughter was contagious.

The flowery scent that permeated the cave was now wafting under my face, between my hands in the hot mug of tea.

"Now, what do you recall from your encounter with the bear?"

I was silent for a moment, envisioning how the event unfolded.

As I proceeded forward in my memory, it felt like I was there again, living the same moments. Particulars that I hadn't recognised at first, came back with ease and clarity and my heart started beating faster as I finished talking. She remained silent for a moment with the thin fingers of her right hand tapping on the back of her left.

"I wonder why the voice?" she then said pensively. "Nevertheless, you found out, by mistake and under mortal threat, that you and the token are bound together. However, if that bear had been a wizard or even an acolyte, I am afraid you wouldn't have survived. That's why you need to be prepared. We do not have much time so I can't see any reason why we should delay your introduction into proper magic."

The suggestion tickled my curiosity.

"Up, up! There you go! Magic…" She was talking and moving with the same enthusiasm I witnessed in her, when Nuuk had performed his trial, "… is everything around us; the air, the water, the fire and the earth and therefore any living being. Magic can give you anything! Anything at all, with just one word, but it can also take everything you gained in your entire lifetime with a misspoken one." Her eyes fixed on mine, making me startle for a moment.

I picked up that her intentional pauses were meant for me to take a mental note of what she was saying, and I made sure to remember, *the importance of words.*

"Luckily for us, you don't know any, except the one you were told when slaying the bear. And since I do not know its true origins nor meaning, so far, I advise you to pay close attention to the few I will teach you!"

"Is really anyone able to learn magic?" I was unaware of any stories or books that mentioned common people being capable of learning magic.

"Well of course! If anyone had a magical item about them and with the proper education."

A subdued titter escaped me as I noticed the similarity between her and Nana – whenever I pestered her with my queries and she'd become annoyed.

"So, the most sensitive thing to do with you is to try and teach you four spells, which are mainly aimed at protecting oneself rather than attack. You will have to learn to avoid conflict, not create it!"

That brief pause was totally meant for another note; *defence, not attack.*

"You'll have to understand what your opponent's main element is; air, water, fire or earth. There are not many wizards around than can wield more than one element at a time, except perhaps Felduror. And I dare hope you'll not be unlucky enough to meet him face to face because there wouldn't be much you could do anyway."

"Hold on one moment! Do you mean that if I meet Felduror I die?"

"I doubt he would kill you for sport. You are not a real threat to him. What's important is, to make sure you aren't seen."

The nervous cough I gave was emphasised by the uneasiness on my face. I could tell by her worrying face and sudden change of tone.

"That's why you and Nuuk must carry the sceptre at all times. I wouldn't send you to meet your deaths if I didn't know it could actually work now, would I?" She tried to reassure me. "Besides, Felduror will be distracted by me and therefore the castle will be deprived of its most powerful wizard. It's going to be all fine, trust me!"

That was certainly something I hadn't accounted for and was undeniably alarming, yet curiously, not as threatening as it would have appeared to me a few days ago. Had it not been for what I'd witnessed Nuuk capable of, I would have run away immediately. If I still had my doubts about Naghnatë, I felt at least the imp was someone I could count on and trust. The moment I laid my eyes on the odd, friendly-faced creature, I knew there was something different about him.

The thought encouraged me to stay. Also, I did not have the strength nor the heart to cower at this point; it was easier to continue to listen to her and satisfy my voracious curiosity.

"So when Nuuk made the fire's flames escape the stove, that was his ability to wield the element of fire, is that correct?"

She seemed pleased by my evasion. "Indeed it was, but Nuuk is an Iprorim and his race can master any of the elements. You've seen what he did right afterwards, and there haven't been no flames as I recall!" she said. "If a wizard throws fireballs you are correct to assume he is mastering the fire element, though the air element wielders could gather wind to move the fire and that could be easily mistaken by an untrained eye such as yours," she pointed out.

"And how would I –"

A palm lifted in the air interrupted me. "Happily, there are spells to disclose one's core powers, and easy enough to master. Listen and carefully repeat after me!"

Shorter than me by a full head, Naghnatë fixed her glare on me and placed both hands on my chin saying, "Revherio!"

"Reverio!" I said imperfectly.

"Almost. Re-vhe-ri-o!" She emphasised each syllable with her mouth.

"Revherio!"

Her smile of agreement confirmed that this time I got it right.

"Important to know; you will have to be rather close to the one you are trying to scrutinise and the key to this spell is to make sure you keep eye contact at all times when casting it."

Keep eye contact at all times when casting spells. I made another mental note without interrupting.

"There is no need to speak the words loudly as long as the word is spoken correctly in your mind and meant with all your heart!" the witch continued.

"How would I know if it worked?" I asked, confused.

"Ooh, you'll know when a spell has worked. Never doubt the power of magic." She moved towards the entrance. "Now, I would like to show you a few examples of spells for different elements. Then, I will tell you the spells to defend yourself from each of them. Whenever you feel ready, we can put your learning to the test."

Although I appreciated what she was trying to do, I did not feel quite ready to cast any magic. A palpable pain rushed through my body and made me falter as memories of my tussle with the bear came to mind. They were as exciting as they were frightful and I dreaded to feel that sense of weakness again. Even my sore and blistered hands seemed to disagree with her plan. Still, I could not say no.

For a moment, she closed her eyes and brought her ten fingers up, tip to tip. When she opened her eyes again, they had lost the vivid-blue irises and turned completely black. A fearsome sight, I admitted.

Once she separated her fingers' tips, a small vortex of white-grey clouds started spinning between her palms, distorting and contorting everything behind the flow of energy.

"What element am I wielding?" Her voice sounded altered, deeper and sterner and it made her more frightening than the old, helpless woman she had appeared as before.

"Air!" I replied.

"Very well!" She spread out her hands in a circle around her figure, making the fast-spinning sphere of clouds expand until it completely died out.

I covered my eyes swiftly, feeling the squall of wind travelling inside the cave with haste. It made the fire jolt perilously inside the little stove and blew my hair wildly.

"And now?" Her voice drew my gaze back to her.

In the same posture, between her palms, a small spinning-sphere of water was waving and splashing ravenously as a sea in the middle of a storm.

This is easy! I thought and smiled.

"Water!" I replied with overconfidence.

"Wrong!" Suddenly the angry water turned to a burning sphere of fire, dripping loud-steaming drips of hot scorching lava on the rock floor.

"It is fire and you better be paying attention to every sign because if I were your enemy you would've melted by now!" Her angry words made her seem even more petrifying as she released the spell into nothingness.

"How could I tell the difference?" I was confused.

"If you had looked more closely at the very beginning you would've seen a small detail, an unmistakable sign. Remember? Eye contact at all times. Now try again!"

I fixed my eyes on her fingers and concentrated to see what I missed. Her fingers slowly touched together and she closed again her eyes.

I did not blink.

A small bend on her fingers gave away the moment at which she would separate her palms, so I strained my eyes harder. I was so tense and absorbed that I could not hear any sounds.

And then I saw it. Just before her last two fingers separated, a small spark of light pulsated to life between her palms. Then the same liquid sphere started growing, just like before, between her opened palms, floating freely in the middle.

It has to be that.

"I saw a tiny spark!" I said.

She let the liquid vanish in thin air and moved closer to me, her eyes turning blue again. "Yes, that was it! Sparks make fire in real life and so it is for magic. Magic only makes it quicker and without apparent effort. The liquid is what fuels the fire, yet it has to originate from fire itself in order to be concealed in something else. If that had been water, there would've been a drop at the very beginning. For earth it would be a small speck of rock or dirt whilst for air, it's air itself and therefore nothing to be seen and easy to recognise. Air is very difficult to hide which is why air spells are easier to master."

It started to make a bit of sense.

"Now, let's get you ready!" She took my hands in hers. "I will teach you four defensive spells, that are just as effective as the most complicated ones. All of them start with the same word; 'Arhea', an ancient term for protection." Her pause suggested she'd like me to repeat.

"Arhea!"

"Very good! The second part of the spell refers to the element it is trying to counter. So, we have '*tcha*' for earth, '*ulah*' for water, '*hia*' for air and '*ignat*' for fire.

"Tcha-Ulah-Hia-Ignat!" I said confidently.

"Heh," she giggled, "never thought of it that way. Perfect! So, therefore we have; *Arhea-tcha, Arhea-ulah, Arhea-hia, Arhea-ignat.*"

She made it sound easy and, after few times of repeating it and listening to her again, I memorised them all.

"Time to see how they work, shall we? It is important to remember that they'll last as long as your strength and concentration allow. Whenever you feel ready, I will release the spell. You better be prepared when that happens!" She made it clear there would be consequences if I became distracted, and thinking how reluctant she was on performing healing spells I knew I'd better pay attention.

The same routine applied; a few steps towards her wielding position and the change of her gaze to the emotionless stone-faced appearance with dark eyes and deep voice.

"We will start with the easiest one."

Air.

My heart started beating as fast as it could and I gulped nervously focusing on repeating the fours spells in my mind.

She moved her fingers close together and stared at me. Then, with one last, long breath, I nodded my readiness.

As soon as she released the spinning, wispy-ball of clouds that vibrated between the palms of her hands I yelled, "Arhea-hia!"

The ball travelled towards me with blinking speed, expanding to a bigger sphere, twice my size. An almost blinding light was produced at the impact, and all I could hear afterwards was the sound my body made when it bashed heavily against the hard walls of the dark-grey stone, and the whistling of my ears. The blow had compressed my rib cage making my lungs decompress with a nervous cough I could not govern. I had to give my body time to recover from the outburst and wondered if my head was bleeding from the blow.

Only when I could finally breathe normally was I able to check if I had any broken limbs, cuts or bruises. The ribs felt intact, everything did. There was no pain at all, except a curious feeling caused by a multitude of shivers, crawling like small spiders all over my arms and legs.

"Very well done, young master!" Naghnatë approached me.

"You call this well done?" I lifted myself straight, still feeling the urge to cough. "I almost coughed myself to death!"

"You are alive aren't you, master Lorian? This spell could have killed you just as easily!" she continued.

I decided to ignore the pang of anxiety her words delivered and replied quickly, "But, anyone would have got a second chance to attack and then I'd be dead surely."

"Would they? Do you think a spell like this is a small task?" She laughed loudly.

I hadn't the faintest clue what that meant and did not insist on knowing. Yet, I kept thinking of the same thing; could her spell have killed me if I hadn't been ready? With another brush of the dust on my knees, I distanced the negative thoughts and concentrated on the positive ones. I had used magic consciously for the first time! Me, the cripple of Sallncoln. The knockback inconvenience seemed a small price to pay for having been able to wield magic and I became happier and content with my first attempt at a defensive spell.

"If you feel ready, we can continue!" She briefly checked to make sure I was fine.

"I am ready!" The confidence in my voice surprised the both of us.

Same stances, same looks.

When she gathered the spell, I noticed a tiny pebble, the size of a fingernail, only darker, which slowly multiplied into many other rocks of various shapes and colours, becoming a very fast-spinning conglomerate of dirt, mud and dead brushwood. It looked more menacing than the previous sphere of clouds and I feared that I would really get hurt regardless if I countered it correctly and prepared myself. I was sure it was the earth element and so I started repeating the defensive spell before I nodded my readiness.

With the same flashing intensity, she released the spell and I shouted the counter spell 'Arhea-tcha', which echoed through the small room.

When it struck me, I was surprised to see the many rocks and twigs disperse right before they touched me. And even though I stood steadier than before, and I did not get pushed against the wall with the same intensity, I still lost my balance and fell on my bottom. A much more tolerable pain followed this time, even as the crawling sensation intensified and I had to brush my legs and hands with vigour to make it disperse.

"Excellent!" She checked for injuries and helped me up.

Her thoughtfulness, my achievement and the lack of serious pain made me calmer.

"How did it go?" I asked.

"It went better than I had anticipated. I was expecting you to get knocked back again." She chuckled. "Every spell strengthens your magical abilities and the more you use them the better it gets before you tire yourself. Though, there is no need to yell when you use magic. You can only whisper or think about it and it will be just as effective." She winked at me.

Her words bolstered my strength and determination and I was ready to continue, itching with curiosity and reluctant to let go the smile etched on my face. As soon as she regained her offensive stance and the tickling sensation was completely gone, I repeated the last two counter-spells for the two missing elements; water and fire.

With the same gesture and preamble, a tiny drop appeared between her palms.

Water.

The fast-spinning ball of angry water seemed bigger than the previous two as I set my mind on the counter spell. Determined to avoid yelling again I tried to calm myself, though it was hard to ignore the ever-growing sphere.

With my left foot in front of my right, I steadied myself and nodded my readiness. Her fingers split and with flashing speed a huge wave of water hit me, trapping me inside the salted-water sphere that had now reached the height of the cave's walls.

I was drowning.

Caught unprepared, I had allowed little air inside my lungs and it would not last much longer. Whenever I tried to touch the sphere's edges, something would pull me, spinning me back into the middle of it. The dreadful sensation of drowning was not new to me and it only made me more agitated, as opposed to what everyone else had told me; to keep calm. I was running out of time. A sip of the bitter salty-water signed the depletion of the air inside my body which twitched with uncontrollable spasms. Through the semi-transparent, murky cold-water, the witch approached with no apparent haste or intent to pull me out. Distorted by the thick waves, she was motionless and only tilted her head to watch me drown.

"Help!" My mind issued the soundless word, but she did not move a muscle.

My throat was pushing and pulling at my tongue, which was stuck on my palate in an utter void. I fought the urge to open my mouth and I thought I felt my eyes bulging out of their sockets. Only when I thought all was gone, the voracious sphere splashed to the floor, dropping me with force.

I gasped for air with raucous sounds as I embraced the cold stone and spat out salt water. My eyes burned.

"Water, I need water!" I spluttered weakly.

With no words, the witch went to one of the cavern's corners and returned with a mug of fresh water which I drank down eagerly. Cold started to make its way over my soaked body, shivering in my bones.

She must've noticed as she knelt beside me and started whispering with her eyes closed.

A warm draught of air crawled over me and slowly dried my body and clothes. I stopped shivering and felt warmer as all the water that impregnated my clothing, quickly spread outwards in a wide puddle around us, not touching any of the two. Oddly enough, the walking-spiders' sensation was missing this time.

She went to get another mug of water which I drank more slowly.

"Thank you!" I gasped. "For a moment I thought I would die."

"For a moment I thought that too!" Her cold reply took me by surprise and left me speechless.

I was expecting a totally different reaction, definitely a little more compassion for my tested body.

"Take your time to recuperate your strengths and once you feel ready, we will proceed with fire!" With swift pacing she dropped a log inside the stove and went towards the small cupboard, returning with a piece of dried meat flat on a piece of dark bread.

"Eat this and have another mug of water. You'll recover in no time." The food appealed me more than her plain words.

"Thank you!" I replied, sitting on a stool near the stove.

Even if I didn't feel cold, the firelight cleansed me from the afflictions I had lived through. Many thoughts and questions crossed my mind, but I knew better than to give in to weakening emotions. A languid sense of sorrow washed over me as I thought about Nuuk. I missed having the imp around. We barely ever talked or did anything together, and still there had always been something kind about him. I knew for sure that his presence would have comforted me. Probably he would have been able to explain some of these spells in a simpler way than the witch.

The meat, bread and cheese made me feel almost ready for the final counter-spell, though what really pushed me to see this through was the urge to finally be done with it and properly rest. I was exhausted and still famished.

"I am ready!" I regained my position with some timidity.

The witch went to her place. She appeared strangely more silent and pensive than before.

With the final fire element to defend from, I set my mind to the 'Arhea-ignat' counter-spell and gathered every remaining ounce of strength.

Her eyes turned black again and the unmistakeable spark between her palms turned into a raging spinning-fireball.

A quick twist of my front foot, settled my defensive stance and I nodded I was ready. If previously I had only whispered my spell, at this point I did not even move my lips. A strange sense of confidence kept my lips tight together as I locked the magic word in my mind. I felt my feet firmly pushing against the stone floor almost as if they were bonded together.

The fireball expanded from the witch to a deadly extent and I stopped blinking as the flash of light travelled towards me with head-spinning speed. In a fraction of a second the flames engulfed me, spinning and hissing like a tornado made of fire. I shut my eyes impulsively, expecting to be set ablaze.

Yet it did not happen.

When I opened my eyes I saw my feet securely on the ground, untouched by the flames only pleasantly warmed and lit by the red-yellow firelight. I quickly looked around astounded only to find myself instinctively pushing with my hands outwards. From where my palms were touching together, a shielding field of an almost invisible force, thrusted outwards, restricting the heat and fire to curve around me. The angry fire could only bounce back and forth on the glass-like surface, not able to penetrate and harm me. The distorted reflection of the witch was bouncing concomitantly with the flames that kept trying to penetrate the invisible, protective armour.

"Let go!" I more read her lips than heard her voice. "Let down your hands and it will cease!" she continued.

With some hesitation, I dropped my left hand alongside my body noticing how the protective shield slowly started to fade away. The flames gradually diminished their intensity, trailing in the direction that my hand had taken. I released my other hand as well and soon every flame vaporised with a clear-grey fume and a dying hiss. The howling of the fire subdued and every other sound became clearer. I could hear myself achingly breathe again as I relaxed my tensed body.

"And with that I think we've found your element!" Naghnatë exclaimed as she joined me.

"Fire?" I said between acute exhales. "How is it that I have a magical element when there have been no wizards or witches in my family. Not any that I know of anyway." I was equally excited and perplexed.

"Everyone has an inclination towards one of the elements, be it wizard, witch or common mortal. Think about your friends and family. I wager some of them prefer warm weather rather than cold, some of them like heights and others don't and some like to swim whilst others don't. That is all related to one's propensity for one of the natural elements." She seemed a little distracted about which herbs to use for hot tea. "And I wouldn't be so sure that you don't have magical kinsfolks in your family. That knife of yours didn't get to you by sheer coincidence!"

Could that be true? From all I knew, or have been told, grandfather Dhereki only had received the token quite late in his days and that was the only event that had anything to do with magic. There were no other magical occurrences previous to that event and I was sure my grandmother would have mentioned it.

However, it was also true that few weeks ago I did not even believe in magic nor had I ever dreamed to see a Drakhahoul in the flesh, so I put aside my incredulity and dedicated my attention to her.

"And are there counter elements?" I asked, thinking with dread at the intense, life-threatening situation of few moments' past.

"Obviously, and water is yours," she replied. "I'm afraid water will always be your weakest element and you should pay additional attention to that whenever you have to learn a new spell. I had a hunch that fire was your element when you said what word you used inside the forest. And had it confirmed moments ago when you almost drowned fighting the water spell." She concluded with a long sigh.

"Why isn't there a spell that protects us from any element?" I continued.

"Well there is, but it's more complicated than that! Magic comes from the wiser magical-creatures; the Iprorims, the Drakhahouls, the eldest elves and many other creatures born within magic. None of them had ever used magic to harm others. It was only a part of their lives and not a tool to conquer or inflict pain. A very different way of thinking to us. It was because of the weak minds of mankind that magic has become dangerous. In time, humankind learned to use magic for own benefits and tried to master whatever element allowed them to become impossible to defeat, yet never achieving the ultimate goal. Luckily, magic has a will of its own and does not allow anyone to bend it that easily. You will always face your opponent, one cannot sneak up behind you and kill you with magic. Momentarily stun you, yes, but not end your life. A wizard will have to duel another standing in front of him and only his ability to think clearer and the sharpness of his reflexes can better the other. Obviously, the more you know the more powerful you get, and in your state, you'll be no match for any of those you'll meet. We're only aiming for no encounters here and trying to acquaint yourself with magic." She placed a hand on my shoulder.

Her words were bitter but true, though I was keen to hear Nuuk's opinion on my conduct.

The elements that had so strongly marked the cave before, did not leave a single trace or trail except what was left inside my mind. Everything appeared as before.

A scented herbal-tea invaded the small cavern with a strong, pungent waft that billowed towards the stone ceiling. Thick embers inside the fireplace, crackled noisily and vivaciously spiriting flickers of firelight all over the space and we both appreciated the unexpected moment of silence and effortless inactivity as we stood by the hot stove.

She gave a small wince of pain as she settled in her chair and appeared more tired than before. From her new position, she lifted through the air the two painted, red mugs and flew them towards her hands. Her gesture made me smile and think how nice it would be to learn that trick as well. Stirred by my awed expression, she let out a chuckle, that with exhaustion suddenly turned into a wild laughter.

For the first time since I had left Sallncoln, I felt serene.

The second day had passed even quicker than the first. We had practiced the same four counter spells until exhaustion, dedicating greater attention to the water element, which after a handful of dramatic outcomes, where I had almost drowned again, I had started to progress – probably because I was becoming accustomed to the disturbed conditions and managed to relax my mind as well as my body. One thing had definitely improved; my capability of lasting longer while holding my breath. Having to recover for longer strains and harsher outcomes, we had taken several tea-reviving breaks.

Around midday, during the longest break and upon my annoying insistence, we had taken a singular and rather disheartening exploration of the outside surroundings of the cavern. As I had already suspected, during my brief-escapades for necessities, the cave was in the middle of a featureless, snow-covered nowhere with nothing of any more interest than a desolate, endless, flat lowland, broken only by one or two, rather peculiar, ruthless brushes that apparently were able to survive in the cold climate. The bitter wind that had accompanied the leaden landscape had cut short our jaunt and forced us back inside.

The evening had arrived in the best possible way; mending my bruises and strains and celebrating my achievements with one of the best soups the witch had managed to cook that far. When it came to soups, I had always thought Nana was the best, though Naghnatë could really put up a real *duel*. I wondered if she ever used magic to improve her ingredients, or if her cooking skills were entirely natural.

Comforted by the heat of the small stove and by the quiet, windless evening, the old witch complimented me for how well the day had passed and how my body had managed to adapt to the raised intensity of her spells. The thought had only lifted my spirits and allowed me to think less of the daunting, unknown near-future that I would soon encounter. The fears that lay ahead were soothed by her warm words and the prospect of visiting the citadel was becoming a rather exciting undertaking.

We went to bed quite early, thinking that the next day Nuuk and Ghaeloden would be back, and we definitely needed all our concentration and strength if we were to succeed with our plan.

There was still plenty to do.

CHAPTER XV

A CHANGE OF PLANS

Lorian / Nuuk

A muffled voice could be heard from behind the massive boulder-door. "Anybody home?"

"They're here!" I exclaimed half asleep as I jumped to my feet from my warm, straw-mattress bed.

In my rush I lost the wool-blanket to the floor and was not bothered about it; the excitement to meet the imp and the dragon was overwhelming.

I reached the entrance and pressed my hands and one ear on the cold rock, shuddering upon the contact. "Nuuk is that you?"

"Yes, master Lorian. Open up, we're famished!" His blunted voice did not hide the exhaustion their journey had brought upon them.

The fire in the stove had almost died and the light that emanated from the fading embers was merely enough to make out vague shapes. Luckily, her bed and my improvised cot were sited both near enough to the stove to be still perceived. I felt the coldness of the stone-floor as I ran to wake Naghnatë and couldn't help wondering why she was taking so long to wake up.

"Naghnatë, they're here. Wake up!" I almost yelled when I sat on her bed, at her feet.

She did not reply and I could hear her fatigued breathing from where her head lay on the small pillow. I panicked and rushed to open the stove door, to allow more light, but still it was not enough. All I could make out was a faint line of her prominent cheekbones, her nose and a dull outline on her wide opened eyes.

"Naghnatë?" I moved myself closer to her head as I realised how poorly she was.

With apprehension, I took her hands in mine and felt with distress how cold they were. She gasped with much effort and tried to move her chapped-lips, unable to sustain a word.

Water, I need some water. I thought and leaped away to the far corner, moving by recollection in the dark.

With some luck I managed to find the jar with water and a mug which she drank avidly from my hands. The panting slowed a bit, though she was still unable to speak.

"Lorian, Naghnatë, why aren't you opening the door? It's bloody freezing out here!" Nuuk raised his voice with concern.

"Coming!" I yelled, wincing at my own pitched voice that bounced on the cavern's walls.

If at first, the water seemed to sooth her pain, after a short while she became more agitated and her hands started to shake vigorously. And if that wasn't enough, a nervous blinking on her face added to my concern. I desperately tightened my hands around hers trying to still the tremors. Scared as I was, I only hoped she wasn't able to see my face much as it would most certainly betray the broad shock and fear I was feeling.

"Hold on, Naghnatë, I'll ask them for help." I leaped towards the entrance.

Having to wake up prey to such clashing emotions, from excitement to pure fear and anxiety, definitely did not help my concentration and I soon found myself imprecating with a sudden, acute pain.

"Damnation, this darn blackness!" in my race towards the door, I knee-kicked one of the small stools with as much strength as my hasty stride carried.

Tears of frustration spurred instantly in the corners of my eyes and I had to sit and cup my left knee with both hands.

Magic my boot. Where is it when you need it? I asked myself through my discomfort.

I was not even capable of creating a simple flicker of flame to see in that dark cave, let alone protect myself from magic wielders.

"Nuuk, Ghaeloden! Naghnatë is really sick. I don't know what's happened and I cannot open the door. I need help!" I yelled as I crawled behind the boulder-door.

"Master Lorian, what is the matter?" Ghaeloden's voice made my skin crawl. Experiencing a sense of relief, I wondered why he didn't communicate with his mind already.

"I don't know! Naghnatë cannot breathe properly and I cannot move the rock that is blocking the entrance! It requires a magic word I don't know." I managed to gulp down the tears against the sharp pain.

"Move aside!" he commanded.

I scarcely moved few feet towards the safer corner of the cave when the massive boulder blasted inwards with such force that it scattered into thousands of pieces. The impact almost made me fall, were it not for the same stool that I had carelessly kicked to the side moments ago. The early, blue dawn-light sliced inside with equal violence of the sound the door had made upon destruction. It made my eyes squint in anguish. It also revealed thick dust that was smoothly floating around and allowed the fresh and bulky snowflakes to trail through the wide entrance, pushed by the gentle after-trace of the delivered force. I checked to see if any of the shattered pieces reached Naghnatë's bed, and soon realised the blow had been magically constricted to a very narrow range.

"Lorian!" Nuuk entered the cave, waving his hands to clear his path through the dust.

"I'm here!" I replied from the corner, "I am well, but Naghnatë needs help."

Luckily the imp's sight was better than mine and he came straight towards me. "Let me see!"

Once he made sure I was not bleeding, he went to check on the witch. I attentively followed his moves.

"Naghnatë!" his voice was soft as he clasped her hands.

I could clearly make out her face now. She appeared relieved at the sight of him and he became distressed by the sight of her haggard face.

"I need warm water," he said without looking at me.

With a quick glance at the stove and a pointed finger, he revived the black embers that brightened the cave with vivacious heat and firelight.

The wooden pail where we stored water was almost empty and I went out to collect some fresh snow to melt – during one of our evenings inside the cave, Naghnatë had told me that snow was the only water source for miles.

A shiver engulfed me as soon as I left the entrance; I had left without my coat. Still, I dared not waste more time.

"Master, Lorian!" From behind me, Ghaeloden's voice made me jolt.

"Master Ghaeloden, I'm glad you made it back so fast!" I replied, his majestic sight momentarily annulling my pains.

The extensive red-tones of his massive body was pleasantly enhanced by the whiteness of the snow-covered ground and the mass of white and grey clouds that covered the sky. A small hint of pale orange could be distinguished in the desolate surroundings as the low rays of the sun briefly and alternately penetrated the thick blanket of frozen-moist. Against the featureless background his scales sparkled with their own light and I wanted to stay there and watch for as long as I could, though the urge to see Naghnatë got the best of me.

I piled generous chunks of the freshest snow into the pail and ran inside where I found a large enough cauldron in which to melt it. With the fervent magical fire inside the stove it took me less than few minutes to have some tepid water for Nuuk that, in ways known only to him, managed to appease Naghnatë's pain.

"How is she feeling?" I asked, worryingly.

"She is better now." His short reply confirmed to me there was more to it than he was willing to disclose. "Just some weakness, that's all," he continued as he gently wiped her forehead with a sodden cloth.

His tender gesture made me smile.

Her hands reduced their trembling to, what I reckoned, was a normal condition for her age, and she was able to breathe more steadily, even if her face was still pale. When my eyes met hers, she was already staring at me, cautiously inspecting my moves. Her agitated blinking had relented too and Nuuk's relaxed composure promised she was on the mend.

I could finally feel a bit less worried, though the prospect only made me aware of my own aches and pains.

With the adrenaline gone, a bone-deep pain lifted itself from my left knee and shadowed the optimism the witch's wellbeing had provided – she had warned me it could easily return to the broken state in which I was born with. It was only that I had easily grown accustomed to my enhanced walking and hoped my improved walking-stride would last. I sat myself on the same, cursed stool, which I would have loved to smash to splinters and toothpicks, and lifted my trouser leg to have a better look. At the sight of the purple, swollen bulge that was supposed to be my kneecap I hissed in pain and remorse. Its trails of pain were accentuated by its mere sight.

"This must be the unluckiest knee from here to Rontra Valley!" I remarked to myself bitterly.

With a finger pressed on it, I felt the malformation underneath. The skin turned from purple to yellow and then white. I knew I had to use some snow; I had to do whatever I could to avoid going back to how it was. This was not a time to give up hope. With Naghnatë ill, there were few chances that I'd ameliorate anytime soon. The pain was growing more intense and I couldn't prop my body's weight on my left leg anymore.

Will I ever learn to pay attention and be of some help?

I struggled to keep at bay the rage that suffused my entire being.

Master Lorian, there is no reason to be so hard on yourself! Ghaeloden's voice startled me but also assured me with all his mighty influence.

Ghaeloden, I replied feeling dejected, *if I had been better prepared all would've sorted itself quicker and without so much damage. What if Nuuk couldn't save the witch? What if you hadn't been here and she died because of me?*

From where I stood, I could see his shadow moving closer to the entrance and I decided to go out to get some more fresh snow.

"How could all this have been your fault? There is no one to be blamed! You have done all that was in your power and you did it very well. Besides, it will take much more to rid ourselves of the witch than a mere weakness of the soul!" Ghaeloden spoken words succeeded in comforting me.

With my slow, aching steps, I reached outside. I was willing to spend more time with the Drakhahoul and let my eyes bask in that marvellous vision for as long as I could, being the sole distraction of mind that could aid my sorrow.

Alas, a blizzard was on its way over the plains around the cavern. The power of the wind escalated as the sun rose, deeply hidden behind the thick layer of clouds, making the fresh snow drift, curl and whistle around the desolate plains with hurting vigour. A quick glance upon the red dragon's face had to suffice, rushed between a quick hand-dab of snow and another. He was comfortably standing with his head propped on his forelegs, as if lulled by the angry wind into a quiet sleep, careless of the snow that started nesting over his body.

When I had a satisfactorily, big enough snowball I returned inside as quick as my legs allowed and gained my most comfortable position on the corner of my bed.

Please work! I let out the obstinate thought as I gently passed the cold ball over my bruised knee.

In the warm, orange light of the fireplace, the swollen, glistening kneecap throbbed. The delicate snow melted creating small streams of water and bringing goose bumps to my skin. Despite the brief shivers of cold, my leg radiated with an unnatural warmth from deep within my muscles. I knew it wasn't a good sign and grew more anxious. I kept at it until the snow had completely melted.

Although his attention was still dedicated to looking after Naghnatë, Nuuk spared some time to place a quick spell and parry the wide entrance. The invisible magic wall prevented wind from making its way inside the cavern, while allowing light and sound in. Thanks to his gesture, the warmth of the fire quickly filled the space. He then felt the need to rummage for some ingredients and start cooking.

The hours passed and the witch seemed to recover herself. Her skin turned to a healthier tone and she could properly move her arms and fingers without too much trembling.

"And how is it that you know how to cook for humans, imp? Don't tell me Felduror taught you because I won't have it!" Naghnatë broke the silence.

"It's –" the imp tried to reply.

"Naghnatë!" I interrupted him, lifting myself up and aggravating my knee again. "How do you feel?" I rejoiced to hear her mocking tone, even as I grimaced in pain.

"I feel much better, Lorian. And that is because of our friend over there," she pointed towards Nuuk, who exchanged a friendly glance from the stool where he was diligently cooking, "but I'm starving!"

"It won't take much longer for my *masterpiece*," replied Nuuk as he sipped the warm potage with a wooden spoon.

The smell was intriguing and I decided that I'd have to find which of the two was a better cook.

He then served us in wooden bowls right where we stood, impatiently waiting for our judgement on his skills before he joined us.

Delicious and rich. There couldn't have been a better reward for his efforts than us asking for another round.

With our bellies filled, we had plenty of time to re-consider what transpired. The witch's eyes still betrayed a feeble trail of faintness and I was sure that the imp had seen it too.

"There's no need for you to worry! I am well now!" the witch said out loud, anticipating my undisclosed thought. "I am only a bit out of practice and tired. It's been a long time since I had to use any of those spells and the past days' exercises had taken their toll on me."

It came to me, that it must've been true what she had said; that the spells she had used with me, hadn't been mere words for beginners, and had required a good amount of magical verve.

Nuuk was silently waiting for her to continue and I was

wondering why my body was not as shattered as hers, since we both had used magic with almost the same intensity; or was it something else?

Or perhaps, attacking demands more stamina than defending? I considered.

That is a correct assumption, master Lorian! The dragon's voice startled me again. *Magic is not a human art nor was it ever intended to be!*

Master Ghaeloden, I wavered, hearing his unexpected voice ring in my head, though I was more curious than concerned, *why so?*

There's a very simple explanation, at least to us it's simple! He let out a gurgle before continuing. *In human nature, releasing spells intent on harming others, requires the largest amount of energy because the purpose of magic has never been to harm. Body, mind and soul would ache even with the smallest of the offensive spells let alone with those that could bring death to one's opponent. The magical creatures that had deliberately shared their knowledge in the art of magic – and let me remind you that the first to do so was a Drakhahoul, Algudrin-the-Bold – had done so with the purest of intentions, not knowing that a human mind could be so malevolent to alter the use which was second nature to them. For these creatures, and I mean us, magic is an unbroken and inalienable way to live by, that acts like a binder between all beings and not a mean to reach a purpose...* he paused briefly, obviously trying to look for an equivalent example, *... just like the instincts in the tiniest of animals, that are awoken and inspired to survive by the unexplainable nothing that comes at birth, just the same, magical creatures are guided by an unperceivable force, the magic, that does not dictate to do neither harm nor good, it simply exists within our beings. For a magical creature, harming someone, is as mysterious as magic is, for a human mind. And with this I do not mean eating a cow or a sheep, that is a whole different story as harming implies hate! The two, magical and non-magical beings, were conceived of a different breed, the first of which, us, lives in serenity with magic and the second one, you, sees it as a mere weapon and means to wealth and enrichment.*

I wouldn't do that! I just want to be safe, and live a normal life with my family! I felt disquieted by his assumption.

You can fool yourself, but you cannot fool me, master Lorian! he replied sharply. *Don't try and deny that being able to walk straight again, stronger than ever, is something that you would easily dismiss.*

Of course I would love that! Yet, I always wanted this before knowing about magic! I tried to argue my case.

Exactly so, young master! You have always desired it and now magic is your sole mean of achieving it! Don't you see? It will always start with the most innocent desire and will expand to wanting more and more until that much can only be achieved by harming the others! His voice lingered in my mind as I made sense of what he was saying.

I knew he was both right and wrong and I partly understood his point of view.

You have just begun your magical journey and still have to understand its true significance. What is it to stop you from desiring more? After all, desiring is a natural thing. Do you think that once you will have healed your leg you will stop there?

Surely he had a reason to be so adamant in believing that everyone was alike, though I restrained myself from interrupting.

It's not about what you want, master Lorian. It's the fact that you do want! This, together with knowing you can have anything through magic, well almost anything, puts you automatically in the pool with other humans that have wielded magic before. I still have to find one that proves me wrong, and until that happens, please allow me to think you are just the same. Make no mistake, I am not blaming you; just like I was born on this side you were equally born on the other. Nobody's fault.

I decided not to insist nor try to prove something that, as a matter of fact, could still go either way.

I understand and I do hope that one day I will be the first to prove you wrong!

And I'm looking forward to that day!

The Drakhahoul retreated into a silent tranquillity after our conversation. Their long journey had undeniably drawn a precious amount of strength from his body as well as mind. His need to rest was emphasised by the carelessness he offered to the wretched weather outside.

"And how did the practice go then?" asked Nuuk, maybe trying to make Naghnatë feel less stressed.

"I think not that great. I'm starting to get accustomed to the nauseating effect of drowning!" I chuckled but not that much, thinking back to the dreadful feeling.

"So you were about to drown?" he asked.

"Indeed he was!" replied Naghnatë. "At least we found out that water is his counter-element. Therefore, master Nuuk, we have ourselves a fire-wielder amongst us!"

"A fire-wielder? How marvellous!" He jumped off his stool.

The exhilaration in his glistening eyes reminded me with pleasure why I took a liking for the awkward-looking creature.

"Apparently so, yet I cannot even fashion a flicker of light when most needed!" I lowered my face ashamed of my failure and the possibilities it could have born.

"Oh, stop it!" Naghnatë picked my allusion. "You should've seen him, Nuuk, wielding that fireball as if it were a ball of hay in his bare hands." She shifted her glance at him while pointing at me, her eyes wide open and rich with contentment. "And you want to know something else? I really used way more verve than I was supposed to, that's the reason for my poorly condition! I was certain you could do more when I used the first spell and I increased the strength of each following one until I could feel there was not much more left. When I reached *water* I thought I had exaggerated and I felt a bit reluctant to continue. Surprisingly, you managed very well. I knew instantly that with *fire* it would've been a spectacle to watch so I used all I had left, to test you!"

"Goblins' tails!" Nuuk let out his bewilderment.

"A spectacle indeed. That was a vision I really did not expect to see anytime soon, I tell you that!" the witch concluded, visibly revived by her own recount.

I remained silent, surprised by her revelations.

"Oh, I really wish I'd been there!" said the imp with some disappointment. "I do wonder, however, why neither me nor master Ghaeloden were able to sense it?"

"Do you think I chose this cave for its beauty, master Nuuk?" The witch chuckled causing the imp's frown to soothe.

"So you can sense magic with ease?" I asked.

"Of course we can, how do you think we found you?" said the witch and they both started to laugh louder.

My unamused face made Nuuk temper his delighted feeling.

"Do not worry, master Lorian, it will all be easier once you become accustomed to magic. It takes lots of practise and time," he tried to clarify.

If only it were that easy.

If he had spoken in a foreign tongue, I would have learned just as much.

I knew they weren't laughing at me purposely yet I felt that my ignorance was the reason for such mockery.

"Young master, if you will, may I have a look at your leg?" Naghnatë changed the subject.

"Sure!" I replied.

Having been motionless for quite a long time, my leg did not appreciate the effort. Tendrils of warm pain originated from the swollen knee cap upwards and downwards. With difficulty I reached the bed, fearing to balance my entire weight on that side. Once there, I sat near her and lifted my leg with my hands onto the bed.

Another day was coming to its conclusion. The brightness of the cloudy sky dramatically dwindled as sunset was closing in and what filtered through the magic veil, that Nuuk had used as temporary door, was barely enough to avoid any unfortunate stumbling mishaps.

Eager to see what she would do, Nuuk joined on the other side of the bed, bringing with him a candle which he lit through magic.

"Dear heaven! What did you do to this leg again?" the witch cried out as she placed her palms on my knee.

"I stumbled upon a stool while trying to reach the door. You were sick and I didn't know what to do, there was barely any light from the stove." I was ashamed of my clumsiness.

She whistled her compunction while looking around my leg with further care.

"This is pure misfortune, master Lorian! You've hit it pretty hard! It'll need at least a good week to mend. And as of how normal you'll be able to walk after that I cannot tell!"

Damnation!

The knot of disappointment that had built up in my stomach found its way and stopped in my throat, instantly altering my expression. Even though I had had plenty of time to get accustomed to the possibility of being crippled again, I was not prepared to hear it, not from her and not so soon. I had entertained more the idea of being able to recover quickly rather than the idea that I would have return as before. It felt like I was cursed with living brief moments of joy and happiness only to have them taken back by fate or some inexplicable force that worked against me. From the pettiest of things to those of the utmost significance I felt like I was being mocked. First my friendship and love, Elmira, whose fate I could not grasp, and now, after being briefly deluded of a brighter future, I was back to the starting point of struggling to walk.

Considering all the facts, it was hard to believe that *fire* was my element, or at very least it was a bit ironic.

"Why can't you use magic? You said it yourself we need to hurry and, in my current state, we couldn't even practice," I permitted myself to ask.

"I stand by my own rules, Lorian! And I shall not repeat it again, I am not using magic for healing! Not ever again!" She crushed her fist on the hay mattress, appearing heavily disturbed by my renewed suggestion.

"Aren't there any other, non-magical ways?" asked the imp.

"There could be. I've considered that myself, Nuuk." She said.

"My special herbs," she continued with reinvigorated drive. "Alas, I cannot shift in this condition. The plant I need is stored in some of my hiding places. I need time to recover before being able to *travel*, in that time you might recover on your own as well."

"Unless," Nuuk distracted the both of us, an intriguing smirk on his face, "you teach me how to shift to where the herbs are and I can go and get them. After all I fared pretty well, if I might say, in finding this cave in the middle of nowhere with only few directions; master Ghaeloden had entrusted me to be the guide for our journey." His puffed out chest suggested renewed confidence.

"That's why I gave you only a few directions! Iprorims should know how to find their way," Naghnatë replied.

Please teach him and let him go, I pleaded in my mind.

"Well, I suppose there isn't other choice here, is there? And you also know the place you'll have to shift to. If we want to make haste for the citadel, then we must do with all we've got!" she allowed a small leer of happiness.

"Thaaaank youuu!" Nuuk's amiable voice was pitched to its highest, surprising us with a burst of unexpected echoes of enthusiasm.

Naghnatë didn't seem to share the imp's reaction, and I thought it best not to give her reason to change her mind by appearing too excited.

"Thank you, Naghnatë, I really appreciate it!" I said calmly.

"You are welcome, Lorian!" she replied courteously.

Unluckily for the imp, that wasn't the treatment he received. "Well, don't just smile at me! Bring the other stool here and help me get out of this bed!"

The imp rushed to gratify her wishes, unchanged by her barked order.

Maybe it was because of the anticipation that I would soon receive a proper, herbal mending, but my leg already felt like it hurt less.

With eagerness I left the witch's bed and sat myself comfortably on mine, making sure I had a clear vision of both of them; I was curious to witness another magical demonstration of unconceivable dexterity.

Yet as I focused my gaze and squinted my eyes, nothing happened. And that quiet nothing was taking a really long time. Naghnatë and Nuuk were holding each other's hands. They did not move; they did not talk. They only sat with their eyes closed almost as if frozen in front of me.

I hoped for a while that something might happen, and only when I realised that I would not be included in whatever the witch was imparting to the imp, and neither they nor the dragon would care to consider me, I let myself fall on my tiny, hard bed with its thin hay-pillow.

"And that's how it's done, my dear!" The witch's voice pierced my sleep and scattered off the sparkling Drakhahouls I was dreaming about, again.

I must've fallen asleep comforted by the warmth of my itchy-blanket and the pleasant sparkling sounds of the flames inside the stove. With both hands cupped on my face I tried to rub away the sleep and forced my mind to remember what I was doing before falling prey to the nap. My mind played tricks on me; I couldn't recall anything except the shiny dragons of my sleep. But soon they faded completely from my mind and I remembered what Nuuk was supposed to learn from Naghnatë. My curiosity then woke me up more.

"How did it go? Are you able to shift now, Nuuk?" I brushed at my eyes as I uncovered my legs from the blanket.

"You would not believe how hard it is and how long it takes!" he replied, an air of fatigue about his face.

"It couldn't be that hard if you've only been gone for a moment. Maybe..." and I tried to peek outside through the magical veil-door only to see it was pitch black, "... you must've been idle for half an hour, perhaps?" I continued still unsure of how late it was.

"You must've slept like a log," Naghnatë's voice came in a mocking tone, "and a very tired one, at that."

"It's almost morning, master Lorian. I'm knackered!" said the imp as he crashed on Naghnatë's bed.

"That late?" I lifted myself up infuriated that I slept for so long and irked because I had missed dinner.

The witch saw my agitation and, even though she looked tired, tried to comfort me with a smile. "Not to worry, lad. Wielding magic takes its toll, and a proper rest is rejuvenating."

"That and proper food!" I saw she was headed for where the dry food was stored inside the cave.

"Very true, very true indeed!" she replied. "And speaking of which," she gave me a quick look, "I have a surprise for you!"

From inside another magically unveiled, wooden box she took out a big bundle wrapped around in a clean, white cloth. After carefully unwrapping it she took outside an unnaturally big, green leaf of which colour and shape I had never seen before. It reminded me a little of the giant butterburs, only thicker, greener and wider.

"What is that?" I asked, craning my neck to see better.

"This, Lorian," she lifted with a wide smile the contents of the giant leaf, "this is a wild duck!"

How does she keep them so fresh? I was astonished and ravenous.

The fresh, fat duck had already been plucked and was glistening in the orange light of the fire. I couldn't recall the last time I ate proper meat. My stomach gurgled in concord with my mind's thoughts.

"A duck?" I was almost slobbering.

"Shhh! Don't wake him up!" She gestured towards Nuuk. "We shouldn't let him know about it. You know, he has his own ideas about eating other animals or hurting them. Honestly, I've had my fill of potatoes and leeks and I feel like I'm always starving. I think you and I both deserve this and we should both savour it, on a stake! The only vegetables I'm going to ingurgitate tonight are the spices on the sizzling skin of this fat bird!"

I hummed in accordance.

"Give me a hand and go grab some more snow, we'll need a bit of cornmeal for this. I'll mind the spit!"

I did not wonder where and how she got the meat. Nor did I wonder if the magic veil would allow me to pass but I found myself outside collecting the freshest snow at the mouth of the cave before darting back inside. As expected, Ghaeloden was not there.

When I returned, everything was ready and the delicious, crispy skin had already started to sputter vigorously on a spit inside the stove. It permeated the entire space with dozens wafts of greasy and seasoned aromas. The garlic bulbs that the witch had inserted underneath the skin, into small pockets made with the tip of her knife, was an extra touch of skilfulness that made my mouth drool before she even placed the meat on our plates.

Nuuk appeared to sleep like the dead and, apparently, his tongue was longer than we could have imagined, always rolling outside of his relaxed mouth and reaching under his chin. The funny expression his face pulled, made me and the witch laugh quietly while we consumed our delicious dinner.

We talked about nothing of any importance during the slow, reinvigorating meal and both pretended that everything was well; only some random spikes of pain in my knee reminded me what reality felt like.

Hours idled by before Nuuk finally woke up. The dawn was almost upon us and through the veiled door, a glimmer of pale blue light found its way inside the cave. The brightness of the clear, dying-night's sky was promising another day of cold, though from what I could see, there were no signs of the irate blizzard anymore.

"What is this smell?" Nuuk's first words came out faster than his eyes could open.

"That?" The witch seemed to have just woken up. "Just some smoked cheese Lorian and I had for dinner. A tiny piece slipped onto the fiery stove and caused quite a bit of smoke. Never mind it, you should eat something and go, it is very late!"

"I should, I am very hungry now." The imp went to the water bucket and splashed his face with the cold liquid.

The slow, dejected walk towards the bucket was suddenly replaced by a brisk, reinvigorated pace as the water completely revived him.

"Good, good," he started, stepping from one leg to the other, exercising his limbs in a circle and shaking his head as if getting ready for a chase. "I know where I'm going, I know what I need to take, the only thing, if you will," and he stopped his jerkiness to turn his head towards the witch. "How am I going to do this again?"

The look on Naghnatë's face vanquished any sign that she had ever been capable of smiling in her entire life, "Are you serious?" Naghnatë asked dismayed.

"Naahhhh! I was just joking!" replied the imp with a laugh, restarting to bounce around with augmented liveliness and laughter.

Still hopping around he continued talking, "Of course I do know, I'm an Iprorim. I have a big memory and remember everything! I first have to find my inner peace, stop listening to any other noise around me and then I must think about the place —"

"Nuuk!" The tone of Naghnatë's echoing voice sent a cold shiver through my body.

He gulped an instant apology and dulled his enthusiasm,

realising his mistake of having spoken out loud.

What was that about?

It appeared clear to me that the witch would not allow the imp to divulge what he had been taught. Clearly, she did not want me to learn how to shift, and that brought an end to my good mood.

Why wouldn't she want me to learn it?

Even if I seriously disbelieved I was capable of such a deed, and actually didn't consider for a moment to do magic again anytime soon, shifting seemed the most appealing thing that magic had been unveiled to me. Of course wielding fire, water, air and earth would be something else, if one was capable of doing it. Yet, that seemed lessened too compared to being able to travel incredibly fast, unseen, unheard and relatively unhurt.

"Either way," Naghnatë's voice turned softer, "you should go. If you manage to return in the next few hours there's still time for you three to depart towards Arkhanthï this very day!"

"Then I shall be on my way! It will take but a blink." The Iprorim winked at me with the same kind smile upon his face, and completely vanished from sight.

Too bad the witch did not make it in time to shout her last words, "Mind the wards! Ah, never mind," she continued her phrase to me, "he'll see them when he gets there."

I did not know what she meant and I felt even less inclined to ask her for an explanation. I was disheartened to voice any of my questions and pretended I was tired. I told her I would lay on the bed until Nuuk was back.

A loud, clattering of metallic sounds burst in the air without warning, tearing the calmness that reigned at the break of dawn. If anyone had been around, they would have definitely turned towards the small and abandoned wooden cabin that lay hidden between the snowy slopes, barely noticeable in the low haze of the cloudless, morning sky. Luckily, there was nobody around. This high in the mountains nobody ventured, not this late in the year anyway, when snow covered everything around for miles, blocking all pathways and the cold made the smoothest breath of wind feel like a hard punch on one's frozen face. A perfect hideout for one of Naghnatë's stashes, the one Nuuk had previously visited and had now shifted to.

"What in heavens' name?" The imp emerged from a huge pile of used pots, pans and cutlery of various sorts and sizes that were stuck to his body as if he were completely covered in honey.

Every move he made, the tools noisily followed. With much difficulty he hobbled his way through the dreadful mound, hurting his limbs as he tried to avoid another fall. Inevitably, he dropped to the floor again as the tip of his right foot got stuck inside a very tight sauce-pot. Another loud clattering exploded inside the small hut and another nameless curse issued from his mouth. Weary, he stood where he fell for a moment, slimy drops of grease dripping on his forehead from one of the messiest pans. He sighed but did not lose spirit and with one hand, after many attempts, he fared to free his boot from the pot. Fuming, he took it and chucked it away, causing it to rattle around, countless times between the wooden walls and floor. The effort had allowed him to free his hands for a brief moment, which he took advantage of to lift himself up.

Alas, as if alive, the pans returned to spin and slide to cover the only bit of him that was not still covered. He realised his undertaking was far from done and he completely stilled himself; the cluttering stopped too. Now his biggest problem was the smaller items filling every hole or pocket of his clothes; spoons, forks and blunt knives popped out of his boots as if they were cutlery containers.

In one last attempt, he shook his body vigorously with all the energy he had left. The futile effort depleted his strengths completely. He knelt gasping for air through a very small gap between two pots and finally it came to him. He had forgotten that he was free to use magic.

He closed his eyes, mind resolute upon the proper spell, and when he opened them again, without a struggle, all the objects dropped to the floor, piling around him as dead leaves around a tree in autumn. He was finally free, though he looked like a wild beast; chunks of slimy, green grease dropping on the floor from all over his body. He was left with black chalk-smudges and red and purple bruises.

He hadn't remembered the hut being that small, nor did he remember it being filled with pots.

"I shall have a word with Naghnatë about this!" he said as he collected the biggest and cleanest pot from the pile and kicked nervously at another, before going outside to fill it with snow.

He lit a magical fire inside the stove and made himself some warm water which he'd use to clean himself and wash his greasy clothes. Though, when he took off his ragged shirt, he felt the presence of his long forgotten, suppressed-wings. With a stretched arm alongside his neck, he gently passed his fingers over them, caressing the wasting muscles and dry skin. He felt the soreness of his bones after being bound in the same position for so long. When his fingers passed over the thin, entwined, magic-thread, he shuddered and withdrew them instantly, burnt by its power.

"That cursed man!" he hissed while blowing air onto his red-marked forefinger.

He was not convinced anymore of the possibility that some good was buried deep inside the old wizard and he wanted now, more than ever before, to free himself from his grasp. Spending time away from his influence had allowed his mind to remember the good moments when he had been a free imp and had friends and, even though it couldn't be as it had been in the past, he felt that maybe there was still a chance for him to make new friends and live a normal life without fear, without a master.

He knew that only the wizard could undo the spell to release his wings and that was not going to happen willingly, not anymore since clearly too much time had passed since his and the dragon's expected return. He'd have to take whatever was his from the wizard.

With a look of gratification at the sceptre on the floor he refilled his spirit with energy. All of a sudden, he had a plan.

A smile formed on his face as he realised how easy it would be to reach the citadel and how easy it would be to move unseen once there; shifting for a magic creature such as himself only demanded a small measure of energy. He decided he'd travel to the citadel before returning to the cave.

As per Naghnatë's instructions, he found the stash of herbs that she had placed inside clothed bundles and hid underneath the wooden floor and carefully placed them in his bag, while his eyes lingered on the glowing sceptre. Since its discovery, he had become possessive over the sparkling relic and found it hard to part from. He felt it was his.

"Perhaps you'll come in handy if things go amiss!" he whispered.

There was a certain trace of fear in his low voice as he squeezed his fingers around the bone-like handle. But it soon disappeared with the transitory tingle of energy that sprouted through his arm, knowing he had vanished from sight. The feeling empowered his determination of what he was about to do and he dropped the sceptre inside the bag to get ready to depart.

A final check around the messy hut, patterned with lots of dirty, kitchen utensils, allowed him to compose himself and shift again; which he did with a cunning smile on his face.

"I shall see you soon, Felduror!"

CHAPTER XVI

QUICK

Felduror

The towers' bells struck midnight and Felduror was still in the
eastern library of the thirtieth floor. Similar to countless nights
of the past years, he'd spent the quiet hours of the dark eyeing
through his scrolls and tomes. The search had become obsession
centuries ago, though of late his desperation had ascended to
such a state that he started contemplating the idea of concocting
a potion that would negate his need for sleep.

"If only it were that simple," he mumbled hoarse words while
passing his thin fingers over endless rows of foreign scribbles
and markings.

Even the Golden Edel, or *eideilamirë* as the elves called it, the
rarest and most potent of herbs rumoured to give eternal life and
eternal vitality, hadn't been able to provide what tales claimed it
would – he had ventured further east than any living man, elf or
dwarf had ever been; at the edge of the earth, in the heart of the
remote eastern islands where Drakhahouls grew wild with no
master and no wish to be seen or heard of. Yet, for his failure he
hadn't blamed the plant itself as much as his lack of aptitude
when it came to matters of herbs and their preparation. As a

celebration of the sacrifices it had taken him to claim the feeble plant, he had conserved the blooming flower between the pages of his favourite book, long past dried as a bone. But that had been many years ago, so many, he had almost forgotten how it felt to be young and strong and ignorant, which was how he described the few young, human guards in his service whenever he deigned to observe them.

His shadow danced upon the layered scrolls in the yellow light of the candles and his long grey-beard brushed the old, waxed-parchment as he moved his head over the scripts of the one at hand. During his long years, he had mastered every element of nature and had invented hundreds of potions that ranged from healing to killing, none of which had been able to be imitated by his enthusiastic acolytes. However, there were still things he could not attain, nor understand, like these ancient scrolls that deceived him every time. They kept their secrets well-hidden and allowed only one correct interpretation of their meaning at the cost of many injurious misinterpretations. Regrettably, he had to learn the hard way about the many ways in which a transcript could deceive an inexperienced reader.

It had happened the first time, many years before, when as a young wizard he had let his enthusiasm and naivety get the best of him. Convinced of his knowledge, he had ventured into a hidden cave of a dead volcano that was supposed to be bursting with treasures. Instead he had almost marched towards his own death, when an unknown, ancient beast had lured him and his followers inside and killed nearly all of them. His magical superiority alone had allowed him to survive that day and, after the unfortunate event, he had planned his next moves very carefully – he'd decided that mercenaries and exiles would take risks first, with the promise of gold, though even that hadn't managed to achieve anything besides a new name for himself; 'Felduror, the cruel', for any that ventured in his name met a cruel and sudden end.

Many years had to pass before he had felt prepared to undertake a quest on his own; a new attempt of another scroll's interpretation. Fortunately, this time his patience had been rewarded; Lux, the stone of light, had been the first token he had recovered, and the one to amplify his thirst for power a hundredfold. Lux had sealed his destiny and acclaimed his name as the enemy of all, having violated the sacred pact of peace that was held amongst races. It hadn't been a coincidence that success had come when he had decided to use a Drakhahoul instead of any of the other useless creatures. With that, there had been no turning back for him and the only way to complete control of all races, was by finding what he was looking for before others. The elves had sworn to kill him, only to realise that they couldn't declare any war against his realm as long as the ruler of the empire was a dragon king. And if the elves couldn't do it, no one could. The dwarves, well they had no other choice than to retreat. Their propensity to keep for themselves and interact as little as possible with other races had always been renowned. He hadn't minded at all, allowing them to believe they were in control and well protected deep under their mountains.

For now, so they can think.

Humans, on the other hand, had always been divided; almost all of them had writhed from the menace of his growing empire in the north, and not only around Arkhanthï. The northern lands had always been steered by the rules of the most important city, Arkhanthï, and its demand for food and resources and, on very few occasions, he had to use his magic or his orcs to silence a bold action of a feeble revolt. The southern land instead, had never been a threat; the lives of their inhabitants was of such simplicity that it required no major organisation to oversee the flourishment of its own people. The underdeveloped villages were at the state of nomadism and tribal status. There were no kings, no queens and no realms and their authorities were only too easy to be influenced by the recounts that travelled, methodically he'd say, from the north; tales that were aimed to control and keep the ignorant people afraid to venture outside the safety of their homes and lands. They favoured the simple life, where their only desire was to protect their families and nurture their children in a place where everyone had an equal say in the things that mattered. He knew far too well that such a thing was not the right way, a sole ruler is imperative for success and wealth, he'd argue, even more than the people.

Yet, if ignorant of things that went above their stations, they were a valuable resource for the good of the empire's prosperity. That's why he had agreed to the great markets in the plains of Aranthul, that took place every three months. It was the sole opportunity for his chosen men of the north to trade goods with the people of the south, an opportunity to assuage their troubled minds, in case distress and doubt ever found their way in the minds of gullible peasants. It was only for the safety and wellbeing of everyone involved, and it was better they were kept in the dark. And he had managed to do that very well for many decades since his ascent as personal consultant to the king.

In the night's silence, the wizard's past achievements failed to encourage him like they once had, but Felduror felt peaceful nonetheless. The previous night had been worse; the maddened rage had conquered his mind again and in his fury, he had hurt his forearms and fists. He never tolerated himself or another to use magic for healing the bruises caused by his blackout rage and preferred to allow his body to take care of healing itself. The countless scars were kept as a reminder of what his sickness could cause and they provided a good way of measurement to see how worse his derangement had got since he could never remember what transpired during his wraths.

He interrupted his reading abruptly. Fresh drips of blood stained the clean cotton he used as a gauze. Luckily, the redness of his blood compelled him to remove his hand in time from the scroll he was reading. The previous night's trophy, a rather deep cut on the side of his right hand, was still seeping blood whenever he tried to clutch a fist. It did not hurt as bad as it looked. Most likely he had procured it when he had hit the ancient earthen-urn which served as a lamp, placed next to the door. It was a very solid piece of painted artistry that he had found in one of the deepest caves of the earth and had become one of his few, favourite art forms. Too bad he hadn't find any time to remove it, as he often had told himself. Now it lay scattered across the room's cold flagstones in dozens of smaller shards, which he did not know what to do with. He could easily state that the previous night had been the worse so far, and quickly dismissed that thought as his glance lingered on the shattered urn.

Oddly enough, his troubled mind carried him to Nuuk. Many a time the Iprorim had known how to soothe his soul and allow him to regain full possession of his haunted mind, often at a cost of getting hurt himself. Though the alienated feeling soon faded, allowing space for the eagerness of wanting to return to his scrolls; often a good excuse to interrupt unpleasant thoughts and every time sufficient to lessen the guilt.

What is this? Am I to grow caring the older I get?

A vigorous spin of his mantle made all the candles flicker in his wake. The brief interruption only caused more concern as he questioned his capabilities. A long time had passed since his motivation was enhanced by a new discovery and he was afraid he was getting too old, too lackadaisical. He had spent more than a third of his existence looking for the Drakhahoul stones, with very little success since he had only managed to find two of them; the Lux and the Blight-Stone; the latter being given to him, almost willingly, by the dragon king. If he wanted to be the undisputed ruler over the Aranthian empire he'd have to find them all before anyone else, especially those other few that had pledged their lives to searching for the tokens. Luckily, there weren't many beings devoted to such things. Only five he knew of, three of which had already been taken care of, and two still on the loose – he had paid a fair amount of gold and silver to recruit and send on their tracks his most skilled Gholaks, whose latest reports had been confirmation of the whereabouts of the fugitives. 'Alive preferably, but dead will do!' had been the order that he imparted to the hounds that had started the chase. If the confidence and devotion of the orcs had put his mind at ease, their inability and improbability of success had prevented him from concentrating on more important matters; the deciphering of the maps that led to the elusive stones.

Blinded by self-esteem and confidence, he had initially deployed entire armies in all the four corners of the earth, inside and outside of his empire, only harvesting failure upon failure. It did not matter that more than a third of the regiments sent never returned, having perished by brutal deaths caused by his misinterpretations of the ancient scrolls. He only blamed the incompetence of their chieftains, springing a fierce competition among the entire race when new leaders had to be recruited. Enraged, he had persisted for many years, sending his devastating Gholak warriors and acolytes at the smallest hint of success, only to allow them to pillage and destroy whatever stood in their way with the excuse of bringing back a Drakhahoul stone. Yet failure kept returning at the same pace. His sole consolation being that nobody else knew where they were either, and chances were nobody could ever find them. Where he had failed for so long and with the amount of resources at his disposal no one else stood a chance, except by mere coincidence and luck – though luck seemed to have abandoned the empire's lands.

In time, failure had shaped how he distributed his time and resources and a few years back, he had renounced the chase for the dragon stones and devoted himself to finding every other token of benevolence, from the most useless to the most powerful. If the dragon artefacts eluded him, perhaps with the smaller tokens it would become easier. His plan was to find them all and bind them into one single artefact that could become as powerful as a true token. He had also decided to change his approach, having failed with the same method for too long. Instead of the loud and hungry armies, he decided to hire individual expert hunters, exiles with years of expertise in the arts of war and a peculiar ability to track down people. Their races were as varied as their wages and they only bowed to one god alone; gold, which luckily Felduror had plenty of. Word had travelled fast and, around the northern hemisphere, every important town had rumours spreading hastily that King Belrug-the-Black was willing to pay good coin for real information about the tokens.

He had struck gold! The first promising results, had arrived right after hiring Rukmirek Anvilhead, a dwarf exile from the colonies of mount Nrom. He and his brother, Nakhuluk, had abandoned his kin after disagreeing with the ways of their king, Hegor Strongfist, and swore never to return as long as he was ruler. Upon their employment, and for a pretty hefty bag of gold, they had revealed precious evidence about the Rose of Ice and its owner, Takahok of Dolbatir; a token that the wizard himself knew nothing about. It had taken them merely a few months to track Takahok down, kill him and take his token to Felduror, even though one of the two brothers, Nakhuluk, had lost an arm in the process. Holding the Rose of Ice in his hands had only amplified his thirst for power and increased his efforts towards the smaller stones. Since then, he had found out about the existence of another seventeen items but was not sure if they still existed or if there were others.

Luck favours the bold, had been his thinking when in a relatively short space of time he had found himself to be in the possession of five of them. They were hidden in a room he alone knew of, buried below the dungeons and protected by deadly, magic wards. They were; Thenedril, the golden feather, Seh'tari, a ram's horn, Cinereus, the grey eye of a giant wolf, Iquit, a rabbit's foot and of course, the Rose of Ice. They were all adorned with the most delicate and exquisite details, and conferred the righteous dexterity to the artists of the regions in which they had been crafted. True art forms of varied kinds, precious objects even to the most ignorant of peasants. Among the five, dearest to the wizard was Cinereus. The wolf eye that had been fashioned into a big ring, far too large for his thin bony-fingers, and that was because its late owner, Ghorimm, had been a dwarf whose hands were almost as big as human shovels – a hard task it had been that day to rid him of his treasure by raw strength as none of the six orcs that accompanied the wizard managed to better the dwarf with either bare hands nor weapons, and he himself had to take pleasure in compelling his enemy to renounce his most precious possession. The ring had the hoop made from the darkest of irons, most likely forged by his kin as no other race engraved with such precision the thin intricacies of the thin loop. Yet the peculiarity stood in the stone itself where a coat of clearest amber surrounded and protected the grey eye making it sparkle as if lit from inside. Many times he had inspected the token with awe, moving with great attention his fingers about the shiny, smooth stone. And every time he found it more beautiful.

Alas, he knew well that none of the stones had any powers in his hands, or any others' for that matter. They would solely be useless, striking pieces of jewellery unless he unravelled the magical powers enticed within. Then and then alone, when the spell had been broken, could he bind them all together and take advantage of the powers they'd unleash. Though he still felt unprepared; five was a small number for what he was hoping to achieve and for the moment, the small measures of peace that each visit to the hidden room procured, had to suffice.

The thought of touching once more the little tokens elevated his spirit, revivifying his pale-skinned face. Underneath the scroll he was studying, a corner of a much darker parchment caught the old wizard's attention. With a fingernail he lifted the corners of the ones sitting on top and bent his head sideways so could take a peek. It was a map; one he had seen many times before. He pulled it out and gathered it was the same one he had scribbled from, when Nuuk and the dragon Ghaeloden had left for Sallncoln, only that this one had a much more patient stroke of ink and elaborate particulars. The realization brought concern upon his brows and his eyes squinted with bitterness when he recalled that they should have been returned by now. He dropped the dark map on the pile again with a quick gesture and brushed one finger over the word 'Sallncoln' one more time. Without even looking, he picked up a hefty, bronze bell from an aperture inside his desk and rang it with drive.

Only a breath's moment passed before a minute, thin creature with his head and ears bent revealed itself from behind the accosted door. He was an old Iprorim from north of Grora, one of the very first to be captured by the wizard and his acolytes, and the only one allowed this high inside the tower.

Many creatures had been brought to the citadel over the years; guards, servants, healers, and very few were allowed to serve inside the main tower. And those that did, were not entirely allowed to move freely to certain floors; they had to earn their trust to reach the highest levels. In the main tower, five old Iprorims had to maintain and serve upon the floors starting the fifteenth upwards, and below the task was given to one alone; Nuuk. None of them knew of the existence of the others and he preferred it that way. The eldest, having been granted permission to the secret rooms of the higher floors, were not allowed to venture neither up nor down from the floors they were appointed to; everything they needed for survival could be found on those three floors or brought upon request by the wizard's personal guards. Nuuk, on the other hand, was not allowed to use the stairs upwards, but he was freer than the rest and could serve his master for tasks that required him to leave the premises of the tower.

Although the oldest of the imps had been allowed into the most private rooms, the wizard learned that he had no interest in the secrets that lay within, which is why the imp gained Felduror's trust. Yet, that was not all he liked about him.

Felduror briefly listened to the creature's careful stepping between the broken shards and instantly comprehended that something troubled him.

It has never been easy with this one, perhaps he's the most stubborn of all the imps in my service, thought the wizard.

Abnormally, he had had no need to constrict his wings like he did with the others; apparently the beast was numb in his muscles, even if to the common eye, they appeared well-formed and decently muscled. He could never fly properly and certainly could not escape by use of his wings. Fortuitously, that hadn't been the case with his wealth of magical capacities. On the contrary, this imp had proved to be far more capable than the rest, abounding in magical strength and resourcefulness. It had been an immensurable pleasure for the wizard to deprive him of such a burden, collecting his wealth and leaving him as plain as whatever creature he resembled nowadays. Because this was not an imp anymore. If anything was left to him, then it was hatred, hatred towards him, his master. He could feel it in his silence and his fake humble eyes, every time he looked upon his withered wrinkled face. At times he was almost certain that it was disgust that he could perceive in his big, round eyes. Disgust for forcing him to obey and having reduced him to such a state. Still, there was nothing he could do about it, some creatures were meant to serve, some to rule.

The imp tried to make him acknowledge his presence with a low hum.

Oh yes, that was it. The thought was clearer now than before.

The creature could not speak. How was it that he had forgotten already? Especially since he himself had chopped clean his tong in half.

Or was it more than half?

It had been few months after his powers had been unwillingly taken out of him. In what Felduror still considered to be an act of good faith, he had offered the mutilated imp a different life; a life of servitude as a keeper at one of his libraries, a life nonetheless considering the alternative was permanent unconsciousness. He had known then, as he remembered now, that the imp would not give away such opportunity, but only because of the hatred he had accrued inside. A hatred that had made him wish to live when there was nothing else to live for anymore. The weight of his magical strengths had been erased, only to allow space for rancour against his master. And that Felduror had to learn at his own expense. The wizard had seen what the insolent creature was capable of when offered a chance to live again; the imp had tried to poison him. The weak attempt of poisoning the wizard's chalice had ended very badly for the imp and as punishment he had lost the very thing that had stung Felduror the most that day – his tongue. He had considered a painful death, perhaps meat for his orc chieftains, who preferred their preys alive. But somehow, it hadn't felt right at the time, and now he was only too content of having taken such decision. One would only expect that such a severe and painful retribution to have sufficed on placating his anger and resentment, yet the imp had surprised again his master on multiple other occasions, which had followed during the long years of servitude. At each one of these wretched affairs, he had received a suitable punishment, less intense perhaps, since his inventiveness was starting to become a reason of amusement and entertainment to Felduror.

The creature let out another hum.

"One moment creature!" Felduror replied with anger.

Being more than three times taller, the wizard turned towards the imp and did not bother to look downwards. He brushed his long white-beard, totally lost in his recent recollection, which he realised had distracted him from more important matters.

What was I supposed to do?

Even if he was not, Felduror must have appeared very lost in thought, because the imp did not lose the chance to squat furtively over the shards-rich floor and leap at his side with a *lethal* blow.

"Ahhh!" the wizard screamed in pain, pushing the creature away.

The imp rowdily rolled over the rubble and lifted himself back on his feet almost instantaneously, panting with a grin of repugnance and achievement on his face. The bloodied, pointy shard was still in his hand, his four small fingers clutched tightly around it. Miraculously, he had struck his master in the lower spine.

The wizard propped himself on the wall he was facing and pulled the very tip that was still buried under his skin.

A mad laughter escaped him, even if he was breathing heavily. "Ha-haa, that was a good one, Quick!"

It came to him right now the why of the peculiar name. Quick was the name he had given the imp, as on every occasion the creature attempted to harm him, he revealed himself to be rather swift.

"I was wondering when would your next attempt might be. It had taken you quite a while, I was starting to consider you had grown weak!" He threw the extracted piece of shard to the floor.

The imp's face was contorting with furious expressions. Could he contemplate another leap? His hand definitely suggested it, shaking visibly and firmly holding onto his shattered weapon.

How he regretted having his tongue cut. If the imp could've spoken, the wizard knew he'd have an ear-full of the most exquisite insults.

That had been a mistake, Felduror agreed subsequently as he stood silent and listened to the creature's throat-mumbles. There was some pain, he realised as he passed his finger through the aperture in his mantle. Had it been another of his servants, their heads would have stood next to their feet; his royal mantle was not some common rag. But, he appreciated the creature's ingenuity and effort.

He checked attentively about his wound and with surprise realised it had been the most successful so far. He decided to heal it through magic; he did not want the creature to know too much about the weakness of his flesh.

"You almost hit me properly this time, imp," Felduror said, pretending the shard hadn't penetrated as deep as it had. "Still, I have had enough of these games. I summoned you here for something else. Fetch me Guzheraak and be quick about it!"

The imp hesitated for a moment, as if incredulous of the punishment that did not arrive. His mumbling ceased.

"What are you still waiting for?" the wizard barked.

With a quick hop the creature dropped the broken chip to the floor and ran out of the door, careless of the debris he scattered.

The door opened with a squeaking noise when Quick returned. The wizard thought it hadn't taken him too long, or had he been utterly immersed in his damned manuscripts again?

"My master." Guzheraak, pushed the little imp heavily against the wall and knelt in front of the wizard, not the least disturbed by the sharp debris. "At your service!" His head fixed at his master's feet, his breathing deep.

"That would be all, imp. Back to your chores!" With a gesture, Felduror indicated the door.

Quick dashed out silently.

Knelt as he was and with his thick spine bent, the orc was almost taller than the wizard, who himself was above average height.

Yet, no matter how tall orcs were, Felduror knew he had this one's utter respect and devotion. Not once had he gone against his word.

"How soon can your Gholaks be ready?"

"Ready?" There was confusion in the orc's guttural words.

"Ready for raiding!" Felduror spoke gleefully.

Guzheraak lifted his sight from the floor only to look with admiration upon his master's face.

The wizard knew what the word would mean for his servant. He saw his eyes gleaming with pride and honour, most likely feeling privileged to be summoned for such a triumphant command in the main tower.

"As soon as I have reached their halls and dragged them out of their beds, my liege!" Guzheraak replied, his chest swelling with excitement.

With a nod and a sign of the wizard's thin hand, the Gholak stood.

He shadowed him with his bulky size, and were it not for the stench of meat and leather the orc emanated every time he moved, the old man would have let his reverence linger.

"Very well. I want a full squadron of the best of your comrades ready at dawn in the main square! You are to depart for Sallncoln in the company of a few acolytes!"

"As you wish, my lord!" The orc appeared resolute but strangely reluctant to keep the same eye-contact as before.

"Is everything well?" asked the wizard.

The beast's eyes scurried sideways, "Everything's well, master. Ahem," Guzheraak cleared his throat, "I only thought I remembered something. Maybe the sudden call made me imagine things, I beg forgiveness, I shall be on my way!"

Though as he turned and bent his head to pass through the small door, Felduror ordered him to stop in a peculiar voice, "Perhaps you were remembering me?"

As the orc champion turned, he stood utterly lost in astonishment.

The expected reaction for such a naïve brute, thought Felduror, who now was embodying someone else's body.

"Dharamir?" Surprisingly, the orc remembered the name.

"The very same," laughed Felduror in Dharamir's altered voice, "don't tell me you are surprised!"

Guzheraak stood speechless.

"You think you could ask about a potion or anything regarding magic in my realm and I wouldn't find out about it?" Felduror laughed sharply.

"Forgive me, master, for my rudeness, but why? Why would you hurt a Drakhahoul?"

"That is not a question for you to ask?" the wizard's voice returned to normal, to ensure there would be no further questions from his servant. "Even so, I confess that you and I want the same thing. And if I am to succeed with my plans, there will be a special place for such a special servant as yourself."

"I beg forgiveness, your highness, it was not my place. I'm at your service until I return to the pits of hell!" With a tight fist crossing his heart and his eyes fixed on the floor the orc pledged his allegiance once again, before taking his leave from the library.

Good, very good.

It was time to make a definite move, one that would bring his plan to a point of no return, crucial to the accomplishment of his quest.

When the orc's steps faded and the much desired silence had been restored, Felduror returned to his scrolls, determined to spend at least another good hour or two before returning to his chambers.

Though, as he placed his both hands on the reclined desk that supported the many scrolls, papers and parchments, an external field of energy disturbed his peace; someone has used magic at the citadel, and he knew none of his acolytes would dare.

CHAPTER XVII

A LAPSE IN JUDGEMENT

Nuuk

An unexpected thud broke inside the vast and unlit space of the armoury, causing a havoc that could've alerted even the drunkest of the Gholaks guards, had they been present – the two that were on duty at the time were warming themselves in the cabins further down the path that led towards the walls, convinced that nothing would occur during their absence.

I really need to get better at this! Nuuk's thought was almost a whisper.

He stretched his back with a row of cracks as he lifted himself from the dusty floor. If he had failed miserably with his landing, at least he had not hurt himself this time. Except that now, he had to fight to free his feet out of a meticulously-fashioned, royal chair's frame which he just landed in.

Once free, he cautiously listened for any noise and soon realised there were no guards outside the door. He fashioned himself a torch out of a broken stick he found lying around, using the very weakest of spells he knew. Then he briefly tried to mend the cushion over the hollow frame he had broken, but gave up as soon as he realised there was nothing he could do to fix it in a short time.

With one hand placed on the bag, a reassuring pat to *his* sceptre, he slowly started the laborious walk among the many objects, scattered erratically inside the armoury. He had forgotten the chill emotion the place had given him the first time he visited, yet he knew he would be safe as long he had a place locked in his mind to quickly shift to. Shifting, as the witch had instructed, required that the place be well known as none could possibly travel to places never seen. So with a safe place locked in mind, and the sceptre safe at hand, he felt confident his mission would be a success. Besides the loud, hasty patters of the mice and rats, he made good progress without any disturbing sounds or unfortunate happenings and soon he reached the golden carriage which he inspected incredulously one more time.

He heaved a sigh as he passed his hand gently on the heavily dusted door, leaving a long trace of his fingers where the gold shone at its brightest.

From there to the entrance was rather simpler than where he had landed to and he extinguished his torch before pressing his left ear against the solid wooden-door. No breathing, fighting, no growling and no farting. The only sounds were the small hissing songs of the drum fire-pit that was burning behind the doors and that was supposed to keep the guards warm. He knew it was safe to go out.

Still, he pulled out the sceptre from his bag and slowly opened the door. There was no one, but instead of being welcomed by the morning's light, he was befuddled to find out that full night ruled over the land. Momentarily, he lost concentration and failed to understand what had happened, almost blaming the sceptre for such a mysterious deed. He forced himself to think harder and nothing came. The conundrum made him lost precious time, time he could not comprehend anymore, and he closed the door and rushed out and away as lightly as he could, only stopping after a good forty steps to calm himself, realising that nobody could have possibly seen or heard him.

He sighed and closed his eyes. With a good, long breath, he released his tension and opened his eyes to look up towards the vault of heavens. An itching sense of marvel engulfed him as he realised he was standing under the clearest sky he had seen in a very long time. A denser knot of thousands of celestial sparks was cutting across the entire sky, from east to west; a gash on an otherwise seamless blanket of deep, dark blue. Like everything related to heaven and hell, its purpose was unknown to him and Iprorim lore. He could appreciate, nonetheless, its light which was aiding the cold, glowing, white of the full-moon. He felt ensnared by the marvellous sight. Right in the middle of the bright patch he could make out all sorts of colours; blue, orange, purple, red, yellow, a bit of green. To his pleasant surprise, he failed to spot any trails of cloud. No smudges of imperfection to blemish the vast, infinite canvas of the above. His allure increased when a star died out on the horizon, travelling at high speed across the sky, splitting the darkness of that area in two. It was a custom among Iprorims to think of lost, loved ones as the dying-star meant that someone else of his kin had left earthen form to ascend the unknown above. He whispered something in the ancient language to aid the wandering soul find true peace, once in the realm of the spirits.

It was time to go.

Cloaked by the magical powers inside the sceptre he picked up his pace and moved towards the main tower. He shuddered and almost screamed, as out of nowhere two Gholak guards almost bumped into him. They were returning to their duty of guarding the armoury, heavily reeking of ale. Once again he had forgotten that the sceptre kept him hidden from the external world, his fast-beating heart did not fully trust it. With another deep breath he cast away the brief moment of fear and regained his composure, waiting to calm before moving on.

Although during his short walk he had not seen any other living soul, he soon started perceiving the scent of a Drakhahoul, and not the characteristic dragon scent. No, this trail was of a different sort entirely. It stung the inside of his nose quite heavily and he knew it was not a good sign. Whenever the scent of a Drakhahoul was so pungent it meant that the dragon was infuriated. In his long years of servitude inside and outside the citadel, which was the only place he had had the opportunity to see the dragons, he had only once seen the maddened eyes of an infuriated dragon. The unfortunate day had been earlier in spring, when the young, green dragon, Jaro, had been punished for disobedience and his mother, Sereri-the-White had lost her self-possession and started behaving like a maddened dog. A mad-dog with wings, he had thought, completely unaware of what had caused her anger at that time. Her otherwise bright, blue eyes, had become black in the bitterness of her mind's frenzy and her body was out of control; she spat fire for the longest time towards the sky, clouding even the tallest of the five towers with her black smoke and white, burning flames, growling her sorrow to exhaustion. Some of the darkest smudges of smoke are still forged on the stone on that side of the tower, unable to be erased. It had been a frightful sight and one of the unhappiest moments too, when he understood the reason for her manic behaviour.

Though as he reminded himself of that ghastly moment, he was quite doubtful that something similar had occurred. It couldn't have been that another dragon had been punished. Perhaps Sereri, the dragoness, caught in the night's most intimate moments, had allowed herself to be reminded of the awful moment and had flung her rage and sorrow to the skies once more.

At the sight of the giant, double doors, Nuuk dismissed the thought of the dragon's scent and gave in to wisps of fear, emotion and cold. Awkwardly, there were no guards; the thought obliged him to wonder why he found the armoury's doors unlocked too, but he dismissed the thought. He approached the doors and made sure they were unlocked by pulling one of the lower knobs with the softest of touches.

He held his breath and widened the small crack of the door to allow his thin body through, without allowing in too much of the night's light to penetrate within. As soon as he stepped inside, he closed the door only to find himself surrounded by pitch black; just one of the many small windows, symmetrically arranged around the high walls of the entrance-chamber, had been left without the shutters closed. Unfortunately, its dull, bluish-white diffusion died a few feet from where it entered.

Luckily, he knew the tower's main corridors, entrances and

most of the rooms well enough to travel in the dark. A bit to the right-hand side from the entrance, were the main stairs that led upwards which could only be seen if one knew of their existence, since they were concealed behind a tall wall of brown and yellow stones, which bulged outwards.

Easily enough, he found his way and was carefully moving up the spiralling steps. After the first two floors, light increasingly penetrated the unobscured arched-windows. When he reached the sixth floor, he stopped to catch his breath while glimpsing outside.

Accustomed to the wild settings of his childhood in Grora, the imp had never considered Arkhanthï to be a beautiful place. Yet, in the silent, cold night, under the soft white-light of the moon, everything seemed different; there was a stillness of life and a sense of tranquillity that never before had occurred to him. He sighed and moved away from the window determined to reach the highest floor.

The citadel's main tower had been built with a tall, spiralling staircase. Unlike the other four smaller towers, the main one allowed access to every floor's rooms, the entrances to which were nested in a circle around its core. Between them and the outer walls was a narrow corridor big as two people's hands-span, that went round from end to end in a full loop. For the width of the tower one could say there weren't that many windows, but the light that penetrated from outside, if the shutters were opened, was more than enough to illuminate the floor in its entirety.

Nuuk reached the fifteenth floor without a break, rather swiftly. His lungs, strained by the effort, were taking in so much cold air that his throat started to ache. He stopped to recollect his strength, taking advantage to inspect the last of the floors he was allowed to serve on. There were no signs of any soul and the eerie silence of the outside seemed to have moved inside as well. He took a slow walk through the corridor that circled the tower's perimeter to check for any signs of activity. No candlelight could be seen under any of the seven doors. The wizard was not in any of these rooms.

He concluded the pathway and arrived back at the stairs, and just as he did, a faint sound came from above. He rushed to the stairs and started ascending to the next level, careless of his master's warning; never to venture onto the floors he was not allowed to.

I am clearly beyond a mere rebuke at this point, he considered.

As soon as he completed the steep steps with two-by-two leaps, he entered through the aperture that led to the sixteenth level and turned instinctively to the right. The sound was coming from that way.

Someone was there; dull, yellow candlelight was flickering behind the curve of the rooms that formed a corner, giving away the presence of another being.

Could Felduror be there? Nuuk was almost convinced it was not the case, as he leaned his head as close to the wall as possible in a failed attempt to see further ahead.

A moment of hesitancy distracted him; his hands were sweating and for the briefest of moments he considered to move the sceptre from his clutched tight-fist of his right hand to the left one, though he decided it was not the moment.

He moved ahead briskly instead.

The being ahead of him was mumbling something undistinguishable and Nuuk, sure it was not the wizard, was curious to understand who was allowed to walk that freely at the higher levels.

He soon recovered the distance that the blind-spot of the curvature of the rooms prevented him from seeing and found himself following in the footsteps of the whistling, whispering creature. Marvelled to say the least, Nuuk hastily covered his mouth with his free hand afraid he could not contain his astonishment.

Another Iprorim?

He was too scared to surpass the slow-walking imp and look him in the face, so he followed from a safe distance, confident he could not be seen nor heard.

The short imp in front of him was walking listlessly around the corridor, checking each door's knobs to see if they were locked for the night. At every stop he'd bang hard on the door's solid wooden-panels with his tiny fist and an enigmatic mumbling, and every once in a while a kick would take the place to his aching hand. All sorts of bruises and cuts could be seen across his neck, shoulders and hands, which were unprotected by the old shirt that he wore; a dirty rag worthless even as a pavement duster. Though his wings were not bound and looked rather healthy.

When he next stopped, Nuuk spurred himself forwards and stepped sideways so he could have a better look at the imp's face. The awkward muffled sounds he made, Nuuk now comprehended were not coming from his mouth but from his throat, as his wide opened mouth, agape as a chicken's beak in summer's heat, was displaying a tongue cut in half.

Nuuk almost lost his balance and fell, instinctively retreating at the sight of the smaller imp's mutilation. He hit his head on the corner of the wall, where the door's framing sat, and issued a moan while knocking the sceptre loudly against the door. He froze with pain in the awkward position he found himself into, afraid that he had been heard, but the older imp merely turned his head and blinked sadly at the nothingness he perceived.

A loud kick to the double-door followed and with another throat-mumble the imp toddled on, soon swallowed by the darkness of the corridor ahead.

Nuuk stood there considering what he had just seen. Another of his kin, an elder Iprorim, maybe from the same island of Grora where he had been born, was at the citadel and, like himself, had been tortured and forced into a miserable life, a life of servitude.

He pushed himself straight again, leaving the door on which his back was propped, and started chasing after the other imp. Inquisitiveness overwhelmed the many other sensations that were animatedly traversing through his mind and body. He was not sure about revealing himself to the helpless creature. Yet, the thought prevailed; he desired so much to be able to talk with one if his kinfolks, almost as if exchanging few compassionate words and glances could bring him back on his childhood's lands again, or remediate to his lost youthful years. Though he was afraid the other imp might run or ask for help.

What if he uses magic and vanishes? What if he's more scared of me than of our master?

Of the many thoughts, few had found their way to the forefront of his mind. He dismissed them quickly, the sight of the sad imp's eyes, tired and dejected, making him feel even worse. It was a face of raw sorrow, an old wrinkled face of sufferance, underlined by a dispirited dragging of his weight along to the next door – an arduous task Nuuk himself had to carry out regularly.

Nuuk had to think of something smarter than simply revealing himself out of thin air. And so he thought to use a bit of magic, after all the spell he had used in the armoury hadn't been perceived so far.

He went ahead of the old imp, in front of the next set of doors that he'd have to check, and with a murmured spell he stooped over the floor with an extended hand. As if his finger was soaked in a sparkling oil, letters started to form on the dusty surface of the pavement, magically dripping from his pointed finger. A few words, carefully and masterfully crafted in ancient Iprorim tongue; markings that for any human would look more like drawings, than anything meaningful, but to any imp would unmistakably remind of home.

When the old imp approached the doors where Nuuk was crouched and followed towards the candle-torch, he instantly stopped his mumbling. The split tongue moved disagreeably up and down as he hurried to crouch himself by the markings. He appeared incredulous of what he was seeing and moved his head disapprovingly, tossing the big key-chain he was carrying on the hard floor. With a brisk movement of his free hand, he rushed to clean the oily surface, smudging the markings with more dust in the attempt to cover it. He looked around afraid and shaking while continuing to brush the floor with his dirty hand of sludge. He looked everywhere in an attempt to see where the markings had come from.

Nuuk did not understand what was happening. He would have expected surprise yet, what the older imp revealed was more concerning. However, he did not give up.

Certain it was a misunderstanding, he continued scribbling with the oily substance crafted from his finger, *"I am Nuuk, an*

Iprorim of Grora!"

The other imp stopped from his frantic cleaning, his hum turning into a gasping gulp. His eyes were glistening as he looked straight ahead.

And for a brief moment, the two stared right into each other's eyes.

Nuuk shuddered, lost in the sadness that pair of dark irises exposed as he witnessed pure fear and sorrow. He knew what he had to do then, he decided to reveal himself.

The other imp appeared more distressed now, struggling to voice a word but impeded by the lack of a complete tongue. He appeared to be forcing himself to issue a word with his bulging eyes.

And just as Nuuk was about to place the sceptre on the floor, the older imp managed to force a whirr from his throat. His word come out as clear as it could under the circumstances. "Rrrun!"

Nuuk felt blood deserting his face, leaving him even paler than before. In that brief and confused moment, he understood the seriousness of the situation in which he found himself, and the mistake he had made. Without one moment's hesitation he readied himself by concentrating on the place he would shift to; back to the cave.

Alas, he failed. Stunned.

The sceptre dropped heavily to the floor, exposing him to the astounded old imp in front of him, who just like him, understood what had occurred.

From the dark shadows behind them, Felduror revealed himself. "Going somewhere?"

CHAPTER XVIII

CALL FOR ACTION

Lorian

"Something has befallen him!" Ghaeloden's surprisingly frayed voice put an end to the small row that had broken out between Naghnatë and myself.

It had been a day and a long and sleepless night since Nuuk was expected to return and we were really concerned about him. All of us had the nerves on an edge. While at first it has been a small delay of a couple of hours, reasoned to be caused by the imp's shifting inexperience, had soon transformed into a worrying sensation that expanded until it finally turned into a strong opinionated discussion. The witch was convinced that the imp had fled straight to his master while I, and clearly the Drakhahoul, were convinced that something had occurred that prevented him from returning.

"I have my own reasons to think as you do, Naghnatë," the dragon continued, "but I like to believe he'd cherish relative freedom here with us more than having his wings freed but still being under the wizard's service."

"I considered that myself. Still, you do not know how devious and cunning the wizard can be!" Naghnatë replied. "His lulling voice can make the most futile of things seem like a good bargain. Imagine what poor Nuuk has endured being unable to fly for so long? Do you think that flying on your back aided his spirit more than it hurt it? And I'm not really convinced he'd be able to fly ever again; those wings of his have suffered too much, his muscles are all torn and degenerated!"

"I have noticed! Still I'd like to think he would not betray me for just that. None of us has spent enough time with him to consider him a friend – heavens know I almost betrayed him myself. Yet I have seen his mind and soul and I have heard his fears and joys. If he did such a thing it would be under duress and I, for one, would consider helping him rather than accusing him," Ghaeloden insisted.

"I agree with you, master Ghaeloden," I added, not sure that my opinion held weight in the matter. "I do not know him. Actually, I don't know any of you as much as I'd like. What I do know is that Nuuk wouldn't hurt anyone. Are we forgetting that he does not even allow us to cook meet? Where would he find the strength to cause a human being or a Drakhahoul any harm? It's not in his nature."

A twitch at the corner of Naghnatë's mouth betrayed a faint smile. I felt she was in two minds herself which made me more determined to convince her that we were right.

"And what if indeed he's in serious trouble?" I continued.

"Where I've sent him there is no trouble..." the witch curtly paused for a moment, as if distracted by another concern, "... nothing of a serious nature that would be. Unless," she lifted herself from the chair which she had dragged near the stove, "he thought to shift to Grora or to the citadel, for whatever unfathomable reason he might want to do that." Her obvious disappointment caught us by surprise and we took a moment to deliberate on the possibility of her account.

Why would he want to go there alone? I wondered, gazing at the flicker of lights the moving flames projected on the grey surface.

Because he might think he'd be smarter and quicker than the wizard with Bilberith's sceptre, young master! Ghaeloden's voice took me by surprise, just like every single time when his voice had invaded my mind.

Why would he do such a thing, master Ghaeloden? Is there a way for you to talk to him from here? I asked worriedly.

I'm afraid we are a bit too far away, Lorian. And if that weren't the case, I'd still think twice before trying to use magic! Arkhanthï is not like these barren lands. There, even the walls have mouths to whisper and ears to listen to everything that is said! His reply reminded me of how little I knew about magic.

The idea of Nuuk being at the citadel appeared the only reasonable explanation for his delay.

"Would he go back to Grora?" I asked out loud.

"Would you go home to see your family if you could be there in a trice?" came Naghnatë's sharp reply. "Of course, you would. But I don't think he would have wasted all this time to check on his family. Not while the reason for his departure was something that would aid you!"

"I see only one solution to this," broke in the dragon. "I shall return to the citadel! If captured, Felduror won't wait for Nuuk to willingly tell him why we've been delayed and he'll want to know exactly what happened to the both of us. Most likely he will be very angry that Nuuk has stolen the sceptre from his armoury. I don't dare to think what he would do to the poor imp if he found out he used magic as freely. I can only try and lessen his penalty."

"Oh dear! I wouldn't want to be in his poor skin either!" added Naghnatë.

"With some luck, my arrival will distract him long enough to find out what happened to the imp and perhaps I can devise a way out of it and fly ourselves outside the walls. Although, I would not count on it; too many dragons are willing to prove their loyalty to the king and all hell would break loose if two of us fought in his name!" Ghaeloden said.

His head was propped on the ground at the entrance, making his words puff their way inside the cave with thick clouds of moisture. Outside the trails of a dying nocturnal blizzard were making the lands crack under its gelid winds.

"You are right to go, master Ghaeloden..." Naghnatë finally admitted, before pausing mid-sentence, "... as there is another, more urgent problem!"

She sighed. With a quick sequence of thuds against the pot, she cleaned the wooden-ladle she was stirring the broth with, and hooked it on one of the many nails arranged randomly in the wall near the stove.

"I only hope Felduror won't understand that Nuuk is capable of shifting as he'll demand to know where he learnt it from, as clearly the Iprorims do not use such spells. If that is the case, then I am afraid the poor imp is doomed," she concluded.

"So I say we make haste and stop wasting time!" I grabbed the coat that was hanging on my bedside while I jumped to my feet, forced to hold back the pain that the landing has caused in my still-swollen knee.

"And where do you think you're going with that leg of yours? Without Nuuk's help and the sceptre's, going to the citadel will have to wait!" Naghnatë almost barked at me, yet I was pleased about her consideration.

The reprimand added to my annoyance, and resonated with the acute pain in my knee, making everything worse.

Let me reason with her, young master. It's for our mutual benefit that we be in accordance, Ghaeloden directed his thought to me before I could reply, his tone soothing my anger.

"We appreciate your effort, Lorian," he then said out loud, "though, you are not in good enough shape to accompany us!"

"See!" The witch grabbed the ladle from its place while interrupting the dragon.

"Neither of you are! I'm afraid you aren't entirely fit to travel either, Naghnatë. And I'd rather go alone than with you lacking your full power." His words made her stop stirring. "I consider that the both of you should stay here while improving on your health. There is no need to endanger our goal so frivolously. I'll find my way out of there with or without him."

If at first his words have made her stop, now they seemed to have agitated the witch even more. She sat herself on the stool and dropped her head on her hand, apparently thinking about her options in silence.

I dared not say a word.

"Very well then! I shall prove I am fit!" Her reply came suddenly, and she vanished with a click of her tongue, her stool falling backwards with a dry clunk.

She left us confounded and speechless.

The sun timidly started casting intermittent rays of taciturn light in the dark of the cold morning. Its orange haze could be perceived here and there, between the fast-moving mass of clouds, fog and snow. There was less turmoil as the retreating blizzard trailed away, carried by the shrill gusts of wind.

Ghaeloden took advantage of the moment to stretch his limbs and go hunting while I remained in the cave with a soup I had yet to finish making.

Lost by rearranging adorable wooden-boxes that contained herbs and spices of various scents, shapes, consistency and colour, many of which I didn't recognise, I spent many minutes rummaging and deciding how my soup would be concluded. If I had some eggs, I would have done just as Nana often liked doing; beat two eggs in a bowl and mingle them with a couple of generous spoons of white vinegar and pepper then add it all to the soup in the last minutes of cooking; a perfect mix of flavour and colour, neither sweet nor sour, just perfect. But I had to settle for whatever I had at hand instead; it didn't turn that bad.

When I lifted myself for a refill, the witch's scornful voice surprised me, "What's this foul smell?"

I turned around to see her standing in the middle of the cave with a bundle in her left hand.

Surely the duck's burnt scent had faded by now, I thought.

"You mean the delicious soup I just finished with the aid of your spices?" I was a little scared by her sudden arrival, instinctively pointing towards the big box of pretty containers.

"Oh, damnation! I always said I'd get rid of that old box, it's been spoiled for years. Haven't you noticed the grubs thick as nails inside?" She moved to the box to check it one more time. "Look, this one has even made a moth out of it! And died, desiccated for months."

I dropped the bowl and the spoon I was licking and went closer to see.

"No, I didn't use that one! I saw it was off, I used these two and that one there. They looked good enough to be used!" I tried to argue.

"Well, I wouldn't count on it. Nevertheless, I'm famished."

It was only when our hunger was satisfied and we'd finished cleaning the table, that Ghaeloden returned.

"So you're back!" he said as he landed and positioned his snout at the entrance of the cave.

"You had any doubts?" Naghnatë replied mockingly, though she did not lift her sight from the bundle she was intent on unwrapping. "And I brought the herbs I needed to help Lorian walk again!"

The unwrapped cloth revealed a handful of wide, curious plants with furry stems and spiked-shaped leaves that permeated the cave with a metallic, stinging odour, similar to the dragon scent.

Although it was a dried bunch, I thought I glimpsed some of the spikes move up and down as if alive. And I was right. Just after they were unveiled, in the dim light of the fireplace, the pale-yellow dead-skin of the plant started turning a vivid shade of green. The mingled branches and leaves regained their strength from their flattened state and moved as if awoken by the morning's sun. Except there was no sun inside the cave and they had been clean cut from their roots for sky knew how long.

"Drakholia!" Ghaeloden sounded equally surprised.

"In the flesh and well alive, master Ghaeloden! I knew you might sense it!" the witch replied.

"What is a Drakholia?" I asked marvelled, while stepping a bit closer to see the moving leaves.

"It's a very rare plant, Lorian. And a very obstinate one to grow or collect. If I told you how much it took me to finally understand how I should gather it, you wouldn't believe me. This is what I sent Nuuk to collect and I can confirm he picked it. I had to shift to another, more distant place to get this one!"

"So he really is in trouble," I added, against all hope that he had shifted to his home in Grora.

"I knew it!" Ghaeloden let out a deep exhale.

"You were both right! I don't see any other reason for him not to come back once collecting the plant and I very much doubt he would take it to Felduror as a prize, as much as it might be worth, it is still a mere plant compared to his endless well of powers," Naghnatë admitted.

She appeared abashed. I thought it could have been because of a sense of guilt. She set some water to boil on the stove, and readied everything to make a mixture.

She placed two mugs on the table, one half filled with cold water and one empty. She then lifted one of the stems up and carefully plucked all of its moving-leaves and put them in the empty mug. She squeezed the leafless stem on the table with the blade of the knife and put it into the mug with cold water. Once the water was boiling, she poured it over the leaves inside the empty mug while whispering incomprehensible words.

The scent seemed to have faded a bit, or perhaps I was getting accustomed to it, though the water in both mugs had turned a dark crimson-red, similar to the coagulated thick blood that I often saw about the butcher's shop.

"This is for you, master Lorian." She took a third, empty mug in which poured the hot brew and the cold water, prudently making sure that the mix was equally balanced. "Bottoms up!"

I took it and looked at it for a quite some time. Its strong odour was starting to bother me less, even if the weird colour was not at all inviting. More so, as one of the leaves still moved its small spikes and spread trails of different shades of oily-reds. I tried to let Naghnatë see my uneasiness, yet her serious face only made me regret I tried to convince her. I spurred myself and took a long sigh before gulping it all down in a long draw.

At first it felt a bit like nettle tea, only much stronger. An instant reaction followed, my body strained. The bitterness of the concoction was making my throat feel swollen, compelling me to find my way to some fresh water as I put both of my hands around my neck.

"No you don't!" Naghnatë slapped my hand before I reached the empty mug, plainly reading my intention.

My eyes bulged. I could not draw as much air as I would've liked; not from the nose, not from the mouth. Once again, I tried to voice my concern, alas, the sour taste made my voice dwindle before it came out. It reminded me greatly of the unripe dogwood cherries, which made my tongue and cheeks feel dry and itchy while my face would fashion the most foolish of pouts. Only that now it was tenfold worse.

It felt like an endless moment before the mixture started to lose its bitter taste and take the swollen sensation from my throat to the stomach. Though, as it reached my belly the discomfort subdued. I stopped with my hands over my knees, finally able to take in the air that I craved.

"Now you can drink this!" The witch handed me a mug full of fresh water which I drank in a blink.

I asked if I could have more and when she nodded, I walked quickly towards the water-bucket. I drank a couple more mugsful and it was then I realised I walked with no pain in my knee.

"I told you it would work!" Naghnatë's laugh anticipated my reaction.

"Will it last?" I asked.

"Well if you hit it hard it will break again, obviously! It's a far better mending than the twist-fix I exercised previously on your kneecap. This herb will strengthen your weak ligaments and muscles and with care and exercise," she emphasised the last word as if telling me what my next steps should be, and I duly noted, "you should be able to recover."

"Magnificent! Thank you, Naghnatë!" I hugged her tightly.

My instinctive sign of gratitude was received with and awkward reaction on her end. She protectively dithered as if I had tried to stab her and gently pushed me away.

"I am glad it worked!" She dodged my glare and started chewing on a small moving-leaf, wrapping the remaining herbs.

"If ready, then shall we go?" the dragon asked impatiently.

"I do feel ready!" I shouted enthusiastically, dashing to check my things.

Pulling my coat over my shoulders I tried to tidy the bed in which I slept for far too long.

"Oh, don't bother with that," Naghnatë said when she noticed what I was trying to do, "step aside please!"

With a gesture of her hand and a whisper, the bed, table, stools, stove, mugs, cutlery and everything we had used vanished. Dirt and dust appeared out of nowhere and filled every crevice and corner of the cave, making it look like it had not been visited in a long time.

I found myself smiling childishly at the sight of magic happening and I convinced myself it would take me years to get accustomed to.

"So do we shift to the citadel or closer to it?" I asked, hoping that truly I was ready to face another weak landing and intestinal turmoil.

"I don't think that's a good idea. Besides, it's less than a day's walk from here. All we have to do is cross the snowy fields and find the green forest that surrounds the outer walls and we're there," she replied.

I did not know how to feel; upset for having slept that close to the threat for a few days already, or elated that we didn't have to shift.

"Do you think that Felduror would leave anything to chance and allow anyone approach his citadel?" Her comment was a direct response to the plain confusion on my face.

"And all this time we've been under his nose?" I was befuddled.

"There's no better place to hide than in plain sight!" The dragon sounded amused.

"It had taken me years to find my way back to the citadel. These routes are untravelled and can be treacherous for anyone that hasn't lived around these lands. If there's one thing I have to acknowledge about Felduror's skills, it is that he has managed to fool everyone. He protects his secrets as well as he protects the secrecy surrounding the citadel. There is a reason no one believes in Drakhahouls and magic anymore and that is because nobody is allowed in or out. The rest is just speculation, or my stories, which no one seems to believe." Naghnatë's voice had turned to a whisper.

"Imagine what he'd have King Belrug-the-Black do to me if he found out I've conspired with his arch-enemy!" Ghaeloden snarled, though not too displeased, as if mentioning his duplicity only hurt the wizard's pride.

"All done!" Naghnatë finished what she had started in making the cave secure, and moved to the entrance.

"Master Ghaeloden," she continued as we stepped outside,

"you will travel ahead of us. I assume you have your own plan and ways to convince the wizard of your ignorance of Nuuk's plans. I'm confident he will not put your loyalty in doubt when it comes to your word against the imp's. That shall give us some time to make it there, Lorian. We can only hope for the little creature's fate!"

Ghaeloden took to the skies and the witch, with another hand gesture and a whisper, made the boulder-door recompose from the many broken fragments. When her spell was done, the cave was freshly sealed and obscured.

We were ready to approach Arkhanthï.

After hours of arduous walking across the snow-covered plains, where we made no apparent progress and had to shield our eyes from the blinding whiteness, we reached an unexpected patch of thick fog. Its welcome, a thin layer of moisture that covered us from head to toe, a sensation, which after the cold we suffered in the plains, felt like a punch to the stomach.

My teeth were chattering noisily and if Naghnatë felt any cold she did not let it be perceived. Her attentive eyes were fixed straight ahead and her body seemed to have curved just a little more; similar to a stealthy cat before a lethal leap. The noisy wind, that accompanied us before the wall of fog, had subdued until it became a slender whistle.

We swiftly entered deeper into the thick blanket of fog, which swallowed us entirely after just a few steps. On a hand-span's distance nothing could be recognised. It felt like we were walking on a boundless cloud of a darker-grey shade, a cold cloud for that matter. I hurried my steps to reach Naghnatë, fretful that the few steps that divided us were still too many.

"Silence now!" She stopped and whispered.

I hate being lost! A far too-recent memory of a sensation that I wholly disliked claimed my attentiveness.

Moments later, after a series of slow, muted steps, the ground started to feel more solid. It definitely wasn't snow anymore. The realisation made my head turn towards my feet, which, to my utmost surprise, I could not see. A dizzying sensation, glancing at the fog that was reaching my stomach, the belt being the last thing I could make out.

Concentrating on looking down, I did not hear the witch stop, and I bumped into her shoulder, getting a mean, silent expression in reply. I apologised with my eyes, knowing that words would only add to her annoyance. Her posture denoted she was trying to listen for something to our right, yet I could not hear a thing. Nor could I see.

"We're not far!" The witch's whisper sounded muffled by the fog.

A few moments later I understood what she had been listening for; the subtle murmur of a river. Its pleasant sounds quickly started delineating its shape towards our right side not far from where we stood.

She turned to me and smiled and before I even asked where we were, tall, ghostly shapes of trees with their sinuous branches bursting with leaves and fruits came into view, surrounding us with their portentous presence. We had reached a forest, a far-stranger forest than the ones I knew.

More than us passing it, the blanket of fog seemed to quickly withdraw at our backs, leaving in its place a vibrant, rich scale of greens with just a few smudges of brown and orange. A sight for my sore eyes.

I found myself staring at a tall, thick canopy that almost completely blocked the sun's rays, except for a few cuts here and there. The white expanse of deep snow had vanished, faded somewhere in the dense blanket of fog, leaving the floor of the forest decorated with a variety of soft moss and lichens which dampened my legs up to my calves. Inch by inch and foot by foot, the hard, dark bark of the ancient giant-oaks became more visible. In some cases, the trees were as thick as houses and as tall as hills, a breath-taking revelation which made my head spin and my neck hurt as I tried to look around. Their body was transformed by the myriad of soft, dwarf plants.

On the floor, rocks could only be distinguished by their shapes and almost none brandished deadly sharp corners anymore, since the soft covering of moss rendered them innocuous, submerged green-sculptures. Sporadic roots of different dimensions would unearth themselves outwards, undulating in their turgid glory like frozen snakes, making the horizon seem like a place of battle where all the silent weapons had been carelessly abandoned and covered by the moist ground. The healthy layer of moss, that displayed the same variegated array of vibrant greens, felt pleasant to my sore and damp feet, and produced squelchy sounds as I stepped from root to rock and rock to root. The air in the thick woodland was not cold at all, feeling like an affectionate caress that escorted us with warm, fresh air. The thought made me wonder how such a green forest was able to survive so late in the year, and especially so close to the vast expanse of snow.

It has to be magic!

As I measured my theory, the witch stopped me with a hand on my chest and hushed me to be quiet with a finger on her lips. She then pointed at a thicket ahead of us, merely ten feet away from where we stood.

At first, I was perplexed until I saw small flickers of light appear all over the shrub. They were pairs of small eyes. Colourful dots that blinked arbitrarily in agreement and that could easily be mistaken as fireflies. Red, green, blue, purple and yellow pairs of blinking eyes were focusing on every movement that we made. I slowly lifted my hand around and that caught their attention, forcing them to chase my circular movements as if enchanted by my waving fingers.

"What are those?" I asked without taking my eyes from the scintillating dance.

"In our tongue, they are Dinkhali! A very distant relative of the Drakhahouls, and they can be quite annoying! So I suggest we better let them be and avoid getting too close."

"Are they dangerous?" They certainly didn't look menacing.

"They have often been mistaken for dragons by those that have never seen a real Drakhahoul. They are almost innocuous and very loud. Some of them produce a very strange type of venom, non-lethal, quite powerful for making healing powders for a peculiar type of wound. Sadly, they do not give it away freely. What they gladly give instead is a spitting welcome and a piercing hiss!"

Something told me that she had first-hand experience in

dealing with the curious creatures, but I was still reluctant to follow her as she started to move towards the left. It was only because I disliked her reprimands, that I removed myself from the spot. Careful not to hit my head on a big, contorted root that arched from the ground taller than ourselves, I lowered my head and, as I turned sideways, I caught a glimpse of one of the creature's tail out of the corner of my eye. It was of a turquoise shade with yellow-reddish dots speckled around. It was more like a stiff lizard's tail than the flexible tail of a snake, but I was unable to make out more, as it quickly returned inside the safety of its shrub.

So colourful!

Having avoided the Dinkhali, we ended up on a steep hill from which we could see the river underneath us, eating slowly into the foot of the hill. At that point its waters formed a fast bending knot, a hushing serpentine that continued to the right and then to the left and back to the right again in an accelerated fashion given the narrow passage the hills allowed. I prayed that the witch did not have the nerve to make us cross the fast moving water right there, it was perilously steep and friable. Luckily, she had only stopped to look around before continuing.

Unlike the warm, dry forests I was accustomed to, life here manifested differently and I could barely recognise any of the plants I saw. Plants with multi-coloured leaves that produced dots of every colour; yellow green, burning-crimson, teal and bright purple. Plants with leaves as wide as my arms could spread; plants that descended from the trees for feet in long, thick vines, sinuously plunging from tall branches to the ground like green snakes. Some of the trees had elongated-shaped fruits big as buckets. All around us, there were plants I couldn't have imagined, the most peculiar of which, a plant that displayed stamens as thick as my fingers and a giant bell-shaped flower. It was most vividly coloured in shades of yellow, orange and red, with a bit of purple and white to the top and blue dots, speckled all over.

There was not a square foot around that did not harbour an animal of some sort, and I was sure that many more were watching our every move, unseen. The most common and amusing were the odd coloured frogs. Their dimensions differed from the smallest ones, big as fingernails, to the largest and ugliest ones that would require serious strength to lift. They were blinking their bulged, colourful eyes and croaked at me if they were large, or jumped away if they were small, whenever I tried to take a closer look. Their prey, if prey that could be called, were the many different types of insects, harboured safely by the big flowers or awkward looking plants in exchange for a wide distribution of their pollen. Some of those insects were vicious and aggressive and in some cases their whirring was disturbingly and worrying loud. If those long needles, attached to fist-sized bodies, were the typical flies of the forest, I didn't dare think what a typical spider would look like.

Henek would hate this place. I smiled, thinking how much my brother hated spiders.

Though, I immediately had to smear my bemused expression from my face as a very long, red-eyed snake, coloured in sections of white, yellow and blue, hissed and crossed the path just in front of my legs. Its disgusting dark forked tongue flicked about his snout as it moved every foliage it slithered against vigorously, making me rush towards Naghnatë. Without giving it a second thought, nor taking my eyes from where the snake was headed, I found myself almost touching the witch's cloak. My fear made her snort at me, though I did not mind. For the rest of our march, I walked closer to her.

We had only taken a couple of small breaks to slake our thirst, since the slow progression through the dense brushwood was not as demanding for our legs as it was for our fears and worries. I could only imagine what she was afraid of, given her lack of words.

What at first had seemed an undistinguishable cacophony of noises, had gradually become a more distinguished pattern of chants and calls of the various birds and animals that were living inside the greenery. They echoed and bounced back from everywhere around us; some were gentle and soft, pleasant to the ears, whilst others were as threatening and piercing as whistles in the eardrums.

Having to circumvent the river on its uplifted left-side bank, we ended up in front of a more opened space. Here, the thick, tall, oak trees that darkened the forest behind, made way for denser patches of smaller shrubs and thick, plump-leafed plants. The sun was warming the terrain, making it the perfect spot to take another break.

"Here, drink!" Naghnatë passed me her waterskin.

Its rich scented plant brew was very bitter. I thanked her nonetheless, reminding myself to skip an upcoming invite.

"Where are we now?" I enquired, mimicking her attentive scrutiny of the horizon.

"We should be right next to the external walls, the southern edge," she replied, "and there should be a tall tower somewhere here."

"What happens when we get there? What should I do?" I was worried that without Nuuk's sceptre to protect me I'd be as good as dead in the hands of the wizard's disciples.

"I'll tell you when we get there, until then, all you can do is walk and be quiet."

It did not sound promising. Even if I acquiesced for the moment, I was still struggling to keep at bay the many questions that ran through my mind.

We kept inside the shade of the forest's edge, where the hushing waters of the river muffled our steps and the big trees and plants provided perfect cover from the wide opening on our left.

When I considered myself accustomed to the sight and noises of the awkward lizards, insects, birds and other unknown creatures, a thick shadow crossed the entire area of the forest. I knew I had to be still, but my heart pounded hard.

For a blink of an eye we were eclipsed by complete darkness as a giant dragon glided through the opening with a whistling sound that made the entire forest tremor. It was huge and very fast, making the smallest of efforts to travel through the tepid air. It had arrived from our right and crossed the forest towards the west. The white beast must've been three times, if not four, the bulk of Ghaeloden, and to me the red dragon was inexplicably big. I dared not move nor speak and coerced myself from thinking; an impossible endeavour for my distressed mind.

Bitterly, I considered how little Winterhorn would help around the citadel where Drakhahouls and Gholaks roamed freely and everywhere around us a wizard, a dragon, an acolyte or something else would be ready to give an unfriendly welcome to the trespassers or the wielders of magic. I slowly patted my bag and clutched my fingers when I found the bundle the wrapped cloth made of my dagger. It gave me a sense of acceptance and serenity.

These are no bears. I should've never agreed to this. The thought revived my memories of the dead people in Sallncoln, crudely piled in the market's buildings with their broken limbs and blood-smudged, livid bodies; a relentless thought I had to force away by blinking repeatedly until it let space for another, more sweltering memory; Elmira.

Where could she have possibly gone? Could she have fled back to her village with her mother? It did not make much sense as what little they had made for themselves in the long years in Sallncoln remained at their house.

There had never been a single occasion where either her or her mother had been gone for more than half a day. And I did not want to believe that she would have left without at least saying something to me. Not without a proper goodbye. The memory disturbed me and I had to force my way out of its tight grasp. Luckily, Naghnatë decided to talk again.

"That was Sereri-the-White! The oldest Drakhahoul in Arkhanthï and none other than Ghaeloden's mother. She is one of the most vicious and heartless of all dragons!" the witch whispered with a cold tone.

I had no time to voice my amazement.

"And that is the external wall!" The witch pointed far ahead to our right, where a tall, white stonewall, yellowed with age, was covering the horizon, maybe half a mile distant.

"Why the need for two rows of walls?" I asked marvelling at the size and spread of the tall structure.

"Wizard's insecurity I suppose. The first row, which was built during the construction of the castle itself, protects the citadel quite tightly and it is not as high as the one you see before you. This is the second row, and was only added some two hundred years ago. Once Felduror had freed the Gholaks from the pits of hell and they pledged their allegiance to him; they had to be kept at bay somehow. And this represents his solution of preventing such a devastating disease as the orcs from spreading and eating everything they get their hands on. It took a long time to get them to behave, far too long for the profit he's gained from their service. And if you ask me, I'd say it won't be too long before they revolt, given their idleness."

I could almost give weight to the hate in her voice when talking about Gholaks.

"Are there many behind the walls?" I asked trying to understand more.

"They were once as numerous as grass blades in the fields and grains of sand in a desert. Though, many years have passed and if their missions and raids have spared them, their own boredom and inclination for picking fights has more than halved their numbers. Yet, there are still too many. Even if there was only one left, that would still mean one too many!" She spat her disgust.

Before I put my next question she replied, almost anticipating it.

"We will not be seen by them, do not worry about Gholaks," she continued. "They're big and stupid and slow. With that said, I hope you won't try and wait for their blades to cross your flesh, they are still dangerous if allowed the opportunity. Either way, there are only four gates on the external walls and only one on the internal ones. But we won't go through a door, not today. We'll have to use a dirtier entrance."

"The sewers?" I instantly thought of the castle's draining arrangements and loathed envisioning a long and arduous crawl, on my knees and hands, through the dirt of the orcs, rainwater and mud.

"That would work as well, still, not that. Something else," the witch said weakly.

She continued talking, though suddenly her words lost clarity. I could not concentrate on what she was saying anymore, lost in my own thoughts and concerns. A dark sense of nervousness grew inside me, mingling with my own beliefs.

Every time I thought about the many ends that I could possibly meet, I had to find a good reason to keep going. And it worked; I felt like I was not being egged on by the dragon, the imp and the witch's opinions. I had my own reasons to continue on this journey and put myself in danger. Alas now, wanting to prove myself to the villagers and shed light on what had happened to us, with very little, if not any, chance of succeeding, seemed like a very silly and childish idea.

The pitiable cripple wanting to save a village?

The vision made me bitterly laugh at myself at how pathetic it felt to be me. I had no doubt it had been the sight of the white dragoness that triggered the sense of fear and muddled my thoughts, yet I could not escape it. Once it had reached inside my core, it clung to my bones and flesh, rending the reason that made me reach so far seem less ardent than before.

Finding myself in the shadows of a castle that secluded throngs of angry Gholaks and hosted the biggest dragoness alive, not to mention the many acolytes or the mad wizard, definitely did not help. My determination gave way to fear, making any attempt of retrieval seem absurd. I was inexplicably torn and felt uncertain of what was the right thing to do. If fear wasn't enough to make me run away, the memory of my family almost made my body instantly turn the way I have come. The sensation made me quiver and my eyes started collecting tears at each corner. Between sighs and gulps I let myself be lulled by images of the sunny landscape that led my way back to Sallncoln, shutting my eyes completely while tartly smiling as the sweet sensation stunned me. Even if I had to walk for weeks or maybe months from these unknown lands, I was sure the thought of being headed back would suffice to motivate and sustain the long and arduous journey. I would reach home, I would find Elmira, I would be with my family and I would make the most of my remaining years in peace, cherishing every moment together. Perhaps Felduror would not care to come that far from his castle. Perhaps I would be lucky enough to grow old and have a family of my own.

"This is not my fight! I have nothing to do with this," I kept repeating to myself.

I could feel Naghnatë's shadow moving closer towards me behind my closed eyes. Her cold, thin fingers softly grabbed my blistered hands and, with the gesture, she shook me from my reminiscences. She forced me to open my eyes, her expression sad yet her eyes were filled with unexpected kindness and compassion. I could tell she felt sorry for me. The feeling that I didn't think her capable of, only made me comprehend how little I knew about the old woman I was standing face to face with.

"I have no right to ask you to be part of any of this!" she spoke slowly and softly. "I can only imagine what you must be feeling right now as I have long forgotten what was like to have family or a friend. There were times when I thought I would go mad by the solitude and started talking with my own plants and dead animals." She smiled weakly and briefly and moved her eyes on the soft terrain underneath our feet, while squeezing my hands. "If you care about your friends and family, your loved ones, or those still have yet to come and find, even for just a moment, what true friendship and love means, then I say we should put an end to any doubt these lands can cast upon our unknown futures. I need you! I cannot do this alone, but I need you to believe in yourself like I do."

I had difficulty choosing from my many concerns and knew how stupid they would sound to her. A fouler idea insinuated itself in my mind like a cold draught of air finding its way between the smallest fissures of a door.

What if all the danger and threat that Felduror posed to mankind and other magical creatures was only Naghnatë's deception? What if she wanted the tokens for herself? The thought seemed so plausible that it made me flinch and pull my hands away from hers.

As if she had read my face, she took a step back and said, "I cannot ask you to come with me, only help me free Nuuk. I know he'll help me find the tokens. That's the only thing I ask of you and then I shall take you home." Her pleading eyes met mine.

My cheeks were drying out in the soft breeze, that picked up in the warm forest and I could feel my tears' trail pinching on them. I lingered before I carefully chose how to formulate my reply. Although I would disappoint her and the dragon, and especially the imp, I wanted to go back home; the dreadful sensation of homesickness was manifesting itself violently and I knew I had to go.

Though I did not have time to phrase my words.

"Pick up your knife!" she said curtly.

I did not expect her brusque demand to disturb me that much. Still, I obeyed. Her acrid, commanding tone permitted me to feel less guilty about abandoning her. So I dropped my bag and picked the bundled knife.

"There it is!" I lifted it up, still unseen behind its cloth.

"Take it out entirely and hold it as you would if you had to use it!"

I tensely flung the cloth on my bag and raised from my kneeling position, grabbing Winterhorn in my right hand, just as she asked.

A hint of dizziness accompanied me on my way up, though I blamed it on having lifted myself too fast. Determined it was the right moment to tell her about my parting, I took another deep breath.

Yet as the air entered my throat, it felt uncommonly colder than the warmth that pervaded the wet forest. My sight seemed to perceive brighter colours and my ears could hear more. I looked about me, trying to understand what was wrong, the blade of my knife sparkling sharply in the sunlight. It felt oddly cleansing to feel my hand perfectly match the soft, brown horn-handle, almost as if it had been made for the shape of my fingers. The blisters of my right hand that had bothered me for the entire journey, dulled their intensity to an almost imperceptible itch. I naively smiled at how the feeling had triggered my entire body to perceive the knife's vibrant existence; its glowing blade as if lit from within, its uncommon subtlety for the size it had and its peculiar odour of stag's hide and raw iron.

When I finally freed my eyes from Winterhorn, I turned towards Naghnatë.

"You were saying?" She looked at me, tilting her head to the left.

"I am not sure what I was saying, or doing!" I admitted, not without a good measure of confusion.

"Well, I can tell you what I felt like you were about to say if you want," she did not wait for my reply to continue her reprimand. "You were about to leave me, weren't you? I saw those little eyes skulking deep in your skull with shame, you cannot fool me."

"I was indeed." I was startled. "Why is my knife able to change my mind? I was sure I wanted to leave, and now, now I don't!"

"These lands are enchanted, there are many ways the wizard protects his secrecy. Luckily for me, I am a witch, and for you, well you can draw your strength and wits from your knife. It is a magical item, Lorian, your mind's lucidity can hardly falter once you're holding it! I hope you didn't think that the knife was only good for hunting?" She chuckled with relief as she approached.

I clutched my fingers around the handle as tight as I could.

"It must be the case. This warm air must be filled with poisonous magic, otherwise I cannot explain what got into me. All I wanted to do was to go home! I mean, I still miss home, but what about Nuuk? I'm sure he wouldn't have left me to rot in here." I tried to justify where my confusion came from, although I had a good idea that she had suspected it all along.

"It is indeed! I should've known better and told you to hold tight on the knife before." She turned and looked around. "This is a cursed place and I doubt Felduror will show anything less devious from now on!"

We both looked at the wall.

"Luckily, you were strong enough not to need any magical items about you, for otherwise we would've been doomed for good." I felt assured by her presence.

She turned towards me with a sly grin. Her hand was holding the left side of her long cloak as if she intended to reveal something beneath her countless layers of clothing. I thought I had glimpsed a bulge protruding from one of her inner pockets but then she stopped abruptly, letting the cloak flap back and cover her again.

She tightened the thin wool-strap she was using as cincture and looked at me. "Very true! We're lucky I'm more experienced than you, and much older."

"I'm good to go and I will be sure to keep the knife to hand in case I lose myself again!" I nodded my readiness and my forced laugh made her smile too.

"Remind me to find you a proper sheath. I can't stand you with that sharp, naked-blade on your belt!"

I knew she liked to have the last word, so I gladly bowed and picked up my step.

We were ready to move on.

CHAPTER XIX

DIVIDED

Lorian / Nuuk

That must've been the longest half mile I've ever had to walk!

What had seemed to be less than a mile had taken us more than an hour and half to cross before we arrived safely at the base of the walls. Not only did we have to stay very silent, but in some sections of our expedition, we had to crouch as the forest turned into a stout thicket of spiked-bushes with very little shelter. The small shrubs burst to life from a thick, foul-smelling bed of wet and dead leaves that wafted visibly into the air with a greenish hue. The horrible smell was so pungent and nauseating, that I barely kept my breakfast down, especially when I had to dip both of my hands in the murky blanket of rotten leaves in an attempt to hide, when the witch had thought she had heard a noise.

The racket of what ensued behind the walls had become clearer as we approached, dashing our hopes of finding no guards. Judging by the frightening and boisterous yells and howls, we arrived at the sad conclusion that there must be hundreds of Gholaks on the other side. Surprisingly, holding Winterhorn did not lessen my alarm.

We had long decided not to speak unless necessary and we were silently catching our breath and recovering our strength in the shade of a tall and broad oak, which had grown in solitude right against the wall. Its height almost reached a third of the way up the wall and I was astounded to see its massive scale suddenly appear tiny in comparison to the giant stonework.

It must've taken ages to build. I conveyed my astonishment as I let my back rest on a flat-shaped rock, which stood high enough for me to avoid laying on the malodourous ground.

If I had grown somewhat accustomed to the fetid smell of dead leaves that covered the ground, I was unpleasantly surprised at the fouler stench of the orcs. Between a stomach cramp and another I had only to admit to the witch's words when, on more than one occasions, she had defined the Gholaks as pigs. Yet pigs' odour seemed like dried summer-flowers in comparison.

I could not take it anymore, and from where I was perched on the flat rock, I rolled to one side and finally my breakfast made its escape.

"You have a very sensitive stomach; did you know that?" Naghnatë closed in to share her criticism.

I had only to admit it; since I have met her I have vomited more intensely than I have in the past.

"I'm sorry, I could not hold it in anymore." My weak reply came between long draws of air.

She came closer and before I knew it, she splashed water on my face. The cold sensation made me dart to a sitting position.

"You had something on your mouth!" She tossed me her waterskin.

As odd as it looked, it helped. I pampered myself in long gulps of the herb-scented water, loathing how weak and unprepared I felt. If I could not hold back irritable puking sensations and risk revealing our location, how could I dare hope that I could leave unscathed from a place where orcs and dragons roamed?

I corked the waterskin and took Winterhorn from my belt. The need to calm myself directed my every thought at the only thing that could aid soothe the revolting weakness; touching the knife. With my hand tight about its shaft, and another finger on the blade, it took me only the blink of an eye to start feeling better. The wretched air seemed not to affect me so much, though the most obvious change was the drop in intensity of the sounds around us.

As if something was covering my ears and allowed me to carefully listen for the noises that mattered, I became capable of identifying and isolating each sound with ease; the growling of the orcs was blunted; I could hear the wind move every tussock behind the witch, where she was sitting, just like I could hear every shrub shake, all the way up the path we had created when we arrived. The river, that we had long abandoned somewhere near the edge of the forest and the wet brambles, was sharply singing in my ears with its fast-moving waters, delineating every rock and dead tree trunk it hit as it travelled.

Feeling much revitalised by the clarity and calmness Winterhorn gave, I smiled at the sky, daring not to open my eyes. A small beam of sunlight, escaping through the dense leaves of the tree above, was warmly and amusingly caressing my face.

Though the blissful moment was soon shattered when, from the depths of the forest, the birds' chirping and chanting was silenced by a thick, guttural snarl.

I jumped straight from the rock on the ground, landing on my knees, assuming that both of us had heard the sound. I was mistaken; Naghnatë was startled by my gesture.

"There is a big something in the forest!" I whispered and pointed to where it came from.

Without a word, she lowered herself on her knees and joined me on the lookout.

A couple of nervous shrieks resonated in the forest, motivating all the birds in the vicinity to scatter away with haste. This time Naghnatë understood my concern and directed her face towards the same spot, where, at any moment, I was expecting to see a creature that lived in the foliage above. If that was the case, the beast must be really big, to be able to move thick trunks with such vigour.

We did not know what to expect and our anxiety was rising as more trees started to move and shake erratically. Our glances pounced from side to side with the same speed the beast was changing course and, before any of us could say anything else, a green and yellow spiked-tail came out from behind the branches, revealing itself in all its might, thick as a tree trunk.

"A Drakhahoul!" we said simultaneously.

Though the dragon soon disappeared behind the dense foliage, making our eyes strain with the effort of trying to find it again. A moment of silence followed, too long for my liking and when it passed, the beast leaped outside from behind the trees into the opening, revealing what his purpose had been all along.

A fat, colourful horned-deer of some sort was hanging lifelessly between his jaws. Still with the prey between his fangs the dragon checked his surroundings, making sure there was no one else to share his meal. Yet he appeared quite nervous, his body gave that away. He secured the tender deer in his powerful mouth and, with a leap and a couple of wing beats, he took to the air leaving a spiral of dead leaves and dirt in his wake. His bright green scales sparkled in the sun's light for a fleeting moment before he was completely out of sight.

"That was very strange." Naghnatë lifted herself from the wet ground, letting out a rich exhale of anxiety. "I don't know the youngling. He must've hatched somewhere in the past seventy years –" she interrupted herself. "Oh my! Has is really been that long?"

I only hummed, still following the speck that was the dragon.

"I just remembered, it's been around seventy years since my last *visit*." She smiled, though I could not share her elation.

If she hasn't been here for seventy years who knows what else has changed in the meantime?

"I wasn't able to sense him, and I'm most certain he wasn't able to identify us either, not even from that close. We would have known if he had. Previously, with the white dragoness I knew she was around. But, not him," she continued.

"I have no experience with dragons," my voice made her turn towards me, "still, to me he did look a bit scared."

"You did very well to hear it, I was quite oblivious." She ignored my remark and patted my shoulder.

"Thank you!" I appreciated her smile.

"I suggest we start moving. And, Lorian, if you will, please keep the knife with you at all times!" She took her robe and moved behind the boulder I had previously rested upon.

I was a bit slower to reach her and, as soon as I turned behind the rock, she was not there. I panicked, thinking she might have gone another way, even if I could still hear steps in the vicinity. When I had completely circled the big boulder that extended to almost touch the wall, I really started to think she was gone. There was no other way she could've gone unless she shifted.

"This way," her voice sounded a bit distorted as if from below, "circle the rock and bend where it almost reaches the wall. There's a small entrance, you'll have to kneel to see it."

I followed her direction and, when I knelt, I saw what I had previously failed to spot; a small entrance, a little wider than a fox's hole. It was also properly obfuscated by the rock's sharp corners, the wall and the shadow of the big oak tree.

"Watch your head once you get in! It's quite tight and dark in here…" her voice trailed from underneath.

Feeling her voice closer, only encouraged me to crawl through the small opening which, although it was quite narrow, still allowed in a good amount of light.

The cave's entrance brought back pleasant memories of the many times I had ventured into some of the caves of mount Velka, near Sallncoln, in the search of ancient tools; stone knives, arrow heads, pots. It made me smile now, how my two brothers would always wait outside, dreading to crawl in, awfully afraid of getting stuck. Luckily, I was smaller and braver for such things – though, on a couple of occasions, I got properly stuck and feared I'd bite the dust right there; only a mere miracle had made me wiggle my bones out.

What I was currently undertaking didn't seem that bad. The cave was actually quite wide and it appeared that further down it became even wider. The downside to it was that the sun's rays decreased rapidly, leaving a small hint of a blue haze to delineate some pointy shapes into its depths. What I minded more however, was the damp smell and soggy air that bit at my skin as I went deeper. I clenched my teeth and hoped it would improve further ahead. Maybe with some luck we wouldn't have to stay inside for too long.

I pushed harder to complete the few feet of crawling I still had to do before the wide opening. Once there, I realised it was tall enough for me to stand, and that I had to say goodbye to the last usable light from outside. With both hands cupped on my face, I turned my back to the entrance and took my time to accustom my eyes to the cold darkness before moving again. I could hear Naghnatë's steps closer and, once my sight familiarised with the lack of daylight, I crept inside the tunnel. When I finally found her, she was on one knee rummaging through the small bag she kept with her.

"What are you doing?" I asked her quietly.

"You'll see soon enough!"

She stood with a shiny, blue stone the size of an apple, tightly clutched in her right fist. Without a word nor a glance towards me, she placed her bag back on the shoulder and started to search the space we were in. From left to right and right to left, she moved her hands over the wall.

I followed at some distance, curious to see what she could possibly want to find in a tunnel that fashioned the same dull-coloured rocks all around. It was only after some slow minutes in the dark tunnel that her mumbling stopped.

"There you are!" she announced.

I rushed closer to where she had stopped.

In the dark-blue glare I could still make out shapes and appreciate the wideness of the tunnel, but I failed to properly identify the long shaft she had just pulled from a fissure in the wall.

"It's a stick you were locking for? I could've brought you a sturdier one from the forest if I knew you'd need one!" I could not mask the disappointment in my voice.

"This is not a stick, it's a bone!" She turned and softly hit my forehead with its end, making me scratch the itching it procured.

"A bone? Why would you need a bone in this tunnel?" Now that she faced me, I could see what she held.

"What is this, what is that? Why do this, why do that? Do you draw pleasure from pestering elder people with your endless questions? Eh?" She moved her face as close to mine as she could, her face neither too serious nor too amused.

"I'm sorry!" I said, though I wasn't.

I wanted to know her every move and intention and if I could, to offer my help. Yet she seemed to measure her words like pounds of gold as she seldom imparted her reasons for anything.

In the dim light her hand looked like a claw of a desiccated lizard as she took the stone and wedged it in an aperture at the very tip of the rod. With a twist, and her tongue out of her mouth moving against the upper lip, she pushed the rock inside even more. Once she made sure it would not fall, she turned her head towards me.

"Mind your eyes, will you?"

I hesitated not sure of her intentions, but it was too late. She swung and briskly struck the rod on the wall to her right.

A blinding glow emanated from the stone and lit the tunnel for as long as we could see before it curved ahead, leaving me temporarily stunned and blinded.

"I did tell you to mind your eyes." She giggled.

When I recovered, I was more impressed than upset about the stone that could create light.

"It is not of magic nature," she anticipated my question, "or better, not a magic that one wields. Here!" She handed me the bone-lantern to keep and indicated for me to step ahead.

I could only appreciate, having a chance to inspect the item.

"There are dormant items of magic as well, Lorian," she told me. "One has only to know how to use them to make the most of their hidden powers. This one's made of a rare stone that can be found in the depths of the mountains. Dwarves found them first and they are very jealous of their possessions. Luckily for me, I just happened to meet the right kind of dwarf at the right time to be able to get my hands on this one." She seemed happy and proud of her exploits.

"I see," my eyes were half on the way ahead, half on the shiny stone, "and why does it have to be bone?"

"Well, it doesn't! I just like it better on a bone." Another snicker followed.

She's certainly a witch, if I ever doubted it!

The tunnel seemed endless as it wound left and right with sharp corners. The only things that disturbed the same plain, brown rock formation were fleeting trails of water, that had been interrupted when the cave had been formed and had to descend to the floor. They were slowly and unceasingly eating at the hard rock as they drifted on the walls, only to hide beneath a crease or a crack in the rough ground.

There was no sign that tools had been used to create such a wide opening in the ground and I concluded it was a natural formation, one that hadn't seen many living beings nonetheless.

After many minutes of decent progress, the wide tunnel narrowed and became dangerously steep. The tricky, narrow part was also very slippery and often I had to stop and make sure the witch could manage. I gathered it was better to keep my eyes straight ahead when I saw her follow my steps just as swiftly.

Many minutes later, we were still descending. Although my bad knee hadn't disturbed me of late, the good one started cracking and snapping whenever I shifted my weight to the right. My muscles were sore and warm and I knew I couldn't continue much longer without a break, yet I did not want to be the first to ask for one.

I hoped that she would soon let out a whine of physical exhaustion, and when the feeblest of sighs arrived, I stopped and checked her again. "Are you well?"

"I'm not that young anymore, I need to catch my breath!" Naghnatë let herself down onto a protruding boulder.

I retraced my steps and joined her.

"It is quite steep!" I said as I took my waterskin and drank a long mouthful.

"We should be pretty close. Once there, it will become a bit better before we reach the citadel's shortcut," she said.

"How did you find this place?" I took her tiredness as a good omen for starting a conversation.

"Ha!" Her laughter bounced on the narrow tunnel. "Find it? I made it!"

"What?" I was dumbfounded. The tunnel would require an entire battalion of strong men years to make, how could she have done such a thing alone?

"How did you do it? It must've taken you years!"

"It did take me years but only because I had to do it bit by bit whenever magic was safe to use. It was only a rabbit hole when

I've found it, and it didn't go that deep. I had to ensure I had a safer way to travel outside and inside of the citadel!"

"Was it a long time ago?"

"A very, very long time ago! I was a young and foolish novice, new at finding my ways with magic. Still, it didn't take me long to realise it was not a safe place for those like me. I had to make do for a few years before starting to think about a safer way in and out. I even tried training a couple of Arpileè creatures big enough to carry me and fly me over the walls, alas with tragic ends for the poor beasts."

"Harpies?" I interrupted startled.

"They're merely misunderstood creatures, Lorian, don't believe everything that's told about them," she quickly replied.

My expression of awe allowed her to continue.

"When every other plan revealed itself a disappointment, I thought why not make a tunnel of my own where I could quickly escape at my convenience when things turned nasty? It wasn't until many years after I'd begun my apprenticeship that I felt prepared enough to start the actual digging. I also planted the giant oak."

A short exhalation of admiration escaped me.

"At first, I had to do very few steps at the time, and with very long breaks in between, afraid that someone might find out what I was up to. Little by little and stone by stone, whenever the use of magic was intense in the premises, I could advance my way deeper and more safely. In the meantime, I was doing my best to learn whatever it was given me to learn, and more – often I've renounced the things that those my age would do just to be able to read another book or try another spell." She paused, clearly hoping I was taking notice.

The mental note I made, was actually something similar to what Nana had once said.

Easy to remember, hard to put in practice.

"It's impressive to say the very least, Naghnatë. Does it lead to the citadel?"

"Yes, it leads right underneath." She then lifted herself and incited me to do the same.

She was right; we had already walked the hard part and it

didn't take us more than a quarter of an hour to reach the very bottom of the tunnel. The deepest point had a wide opening the size of the hall in Sallncoln, mysteriously lit by unseen sources of light. It felt disorientating after such a tight, narrow tunnel to reach the extensive aperture. Inside the space of the gallery, multiple drops fell from the high ceiling and landed in small puddles in a never-ending array of soft, pleasant, musical sounds.

I accidentally kicked a loose pebble, which made a disturbing sound as it bounced away. My clumsiness earned me a stern expression from the witch as a reminder to pay extra attention from there on.

When I directed my observation from the ceiling to the walls and to the floor, I found, to my complete bewilderment, what I missed at first and what made the entire place even more extraordinary. The pointy boulders and pillars, that sprouted upwards from the ground, were hiding something on the floor; holes of various dimensions, scattered all over the place revealing another level, deeper beneath the stony floor where the unnatural light seemed brighter.

I propped the bone-torch on the first boulder I considered safe, and leaned over a low rock of a flatter nature. It allowed me to safely insert my head inside one of the biggest apertures.

"Whoooaaaa!" I gasped in total awe, letting my sound of amazement bounce lengthily under us.

I could not believe what I was seeing. A deeper gallery than the one we were inside of, was laying beneath our feet. Its rock-walls had been partially and dexterously sculpted and chiselled into a tall building of some sort, similar to a tower with many pointy and curved apertures, which I soon gathered were windows. Some of them were fashioned into sculptures of unusual looking creatures with wings and beaks but no tails. The yellow tint of light that issued from below, gave the entire structure a dream-like quality. It made me long to see more. I could barely see the bottom and attempted to count all the levels by their windows. I estimated there were twenty-three levels.

"Did you make this as well?" I asked Naghnatë when I heard her moving closer to me.

"It was already here, and it has been for longer than even I have lived. It is the most ancient structure I know of and I believe it stretches before King Arkhan's time. I doubt many know of its existence since it's still intact!" She sat close to me.

"It's beyond words! I wish Elmira could see this place," I whispered to myself.

It certainly felt good to be able to witness the ancient, striking structure, and it definitely improved my spirits and determination to continue.

Who would believe me now? As if what I'd already witnessed hadn't been enough, I thought of the many things I deemed unfathomable just a week ago.

"It certainly has a special beauty! Ever since I found it, I meant to go down there and visit, but I never have. And now I'm not that sure I could still go. One thing's for certain; it'd surely make a great hiding place." The witch let out a quick laugh as she peeked through another hole.

I lifted myself, still overwhelmed, and vaguely cleaned my clothing of the yellow dust I had collected.

A long moment of silence followed while I mutely grabbed the stone-torch and sat in front of the witch. She was staring through the holes, seemingly without looking at anything in particular. I assumed she was lost in her memories.

"You ready?" she then asked, pushing herself briskly onto her feet.

"I am. Where to now?"

"Before we leave," a worrying exhale of air came out of her mouth, as if exhaustion had finally taken its toll on her old body, "I want you to keep this with you!" She took her own cloak off and gave it to me.

Its wool fibres were finely woven with prowess and, although it was of a pale green colour I did not like, it appeared clean.

"Why?" I asked as I took it from her extended hand.

"Just put it on!"

Beside feeling warm and nice to the touch, it also smelled pleasant – a subtle scent of flowers and dried herbs which names I thought I had on the tip of my tongue, yet I could not identify.

"It fits quite well!" I said, looking about my figure.

"It would be a first for this cloak not to fit the one who wears it!" she added.

"You mean –" I was quickly interrupted.

"I mean it's not a cloak to keep you warm, Lorian! Although it does that anyway. It may appear a bit plain but it's of a very distinct provenance and fashion. It occludes the sounds of the one that wears it and most of the times shades you from the most distracted eyes. You'll be as stealthy as a cat while you wear it and just as silent," she explained softly.

I could tell she was not done and there was a portent of bad news about her face.

"You will have to continue alone from here, lad!" Her cold words wrecked part of my recovered excitement. "I'll lead you to the stairs that'll take you almost underneath one of the citadel's towers. To the dungeons. Once there, you'll have to find Nuuk and get out the same way you got in. No matter what happens, do not release any of the other prisoners, take the imp and come here! If nobody follows you, you can take your time and wait for me, even for a few days. Inside this bag, if well rationed, there's plenty of bread, dry meat and cheese for the both of you. If he's fussy about eating any of this, I brought some stale wax for him, it's not that much. If I'm not here in two days' time, do not wait for me and return to the cave. To open the cave, you'll have to say 'Reverthua' as clear as you hear it. Now try and say it!" she commanded, denying me the opportunity to retort.

"Re-ver-thua!" I said it as clear as I could.

"Once again!" she insisted.

"Reverthua!" It sounded better now.

"Do not forget it! It's what will give you access to everything I hid and protected with wards when we left. Without this spell you won't be able to move the boulder that hid it, and even if you succeed in removing it, you'll walk into an empty, cold cave where you'd both perish if it snowed again."

"And what if I don't find Nuuk? What if Ghaeloden has freed Nuuk?" I wondered if indeed there was such chance.

"If Nuuk is still alive, he is in one of the cells in this citadel. Ghaeloden can only give us time to act, if that. He cannot compromise his standing among the rest of the Drakhahouls, not for Nuuk, not for any of us. I am sure he'll do whatever he can to delay an accursed fate for the imp, but it's you that has to find and save him."

I nodded at her words. They alluded to a dreadful possibility; that the imp was already dead.

"I will provide as much distraction as I can, though I rather hope you'll find him before all of us have to reveal ourselves. This way, we can still come back and start looking for the tokens."

"I understand." I was afraid I was not up to the task.

She had entrusted me with finding and rescuing Nuuk, and although I was proud, I was also concerned. So I made an effort to banish all negative thoughts and determined to take the opportunity to prove myself. If nothing else, I was eager to try my best to make them see I was not as bad as I looked, or at least I was more than willing to give my best.

"Have you had enough time to think about my offer?" Felduror's malice-filled voice rang sharply in Nuuk's ears.

As if he had been sorrowfully forced to return from a reviving deep-sleep, the imp panted with fright and effort for a much-needed mouthful of fresh air. He tried to lift himself up from the cold wall his body was propped against, but could not make it. His legs and arms were too weak and compelled him to return to his former position, realising that it was not sleep he was returning from. His ribs hurt badly, more than his hands, back and neck but less than his forehead. Especially the left temple. His vision was blurred and it was not because of the eyes that had been shut for a long time, it was his swollen-face's fault. He lifted his aching arms and checked softly over his forehead, cheekbones and lips. He hissed at each gentle touch and felt his dry throat whenever he tried to gulp down the slow realisation of his awakening. Through blurry vision he spotted wet, red stains on his fingers – blood.

Had he been caught by the wizard sneaking in the higher levels, those he was not allowed to venture into? Was that why he had been hurt? Was this his punishment? If that was the case, perhaps he deserved it, he thought. There had been many times in the past when he had been compensated in the same manner.

"I…" he achingly cleared his voice, forcing down a knot in the back of his throat, "… I am sorry, master! I shouldn't have ventured into the higher levels. I don't know what got into me!" He could not cope with the pain of keeping his eyes open so he shut them again.

"Pardon me?" The wizard's voice acquired a curious tone. "Oh, yes, that too! You should never go where you're not supposed to, you're only worth the fifteenth level. And now, I am afraid you've lost that privilege too. Yet, that was not what I wanted to know from you. What I want to know, and it becomes a bit annoying having to repeat myself again, is for you to tell me who taught you the spell?"

"What spell, master?"

"Nuuk, do not force me to do what I do not like doing! Do you like feeling weak and miserable and in pain? Don't you want it all to go away? Don't you want it to be as it was, between us? The spell that has brought you back from whoever-knows-where. Ghaeloden told me you had eluded him. You escaped from his sight thanks to this sceptre and I still cannot understand why. I doubt you'd be willing to go to such lengths on your own and I have a very clear idea of who it is that is helping you. Though I need you to say the name." His irritated voice became angry.

Nuuk did not say a word. Through his limited, one-eyed sight, he spotted a twinkling sceptre in the old man's hand and questioned why he was pointing it at him. Was that a weapon? He wondered what the wizard could do with it or if his bruises and cuts were not testaments of its already-provided services.

Of everything the wizard had said, only one word sounded pleasant to his ears; Ghaeloden. Even though it did not remind him of any face in particular he knew deep inside it meant something to him. A strong feeling of assurance and positivity sprung each time he repeated it in his head, and equally failed at each attempt to remind himself to whom it belonged. It briefly tingled against a cord in his heart and a vein in his brain before it slipped again into oblivion, clouding his mind as badly as his fogged vision. He gave up trying to put a face to it and settled with the thought that it must've been the name of his friend. That brought a small measure of peace upon his suffering figure. He tried to open his eyes again.

"Water!" he managed to beg.

"I'm growing impatient, imp. I'll have no choice than to let the Gholaks take the words out of your mouth. Do you want that?" Felduror bent over the imp, his breath touching his face.

"Master Felduror, I don't know what spell I've used, I barely remember why I am here and I definitely can't explain why am I being punished!" His shaking voice cast doubt upon the wizard's face.

This is the honest truth; I don't remember. The imp wondered at length what had he done to anger his master and, more to the point, why he was hurting so badly.

"Why did you steal the sceptre then, creature?"

"That," the imp tried to point at the object tightly held in Felduror's bony hand, "I can't recall, master." The shadow in his mind obscured every trail of memory.

The object was unknown to him, and maybe if his master said he had stolen it, maybe indeed he had.

"Don't make me hit you again, imp!" Felduror barked as he lifted the hefty object above his head.

"Master..." Nuuk forced himself in pain to lift his arm above his forehead and protect himself from the imminent blow, "... I don't know!"

The blow did not arrive; the wizard stopped himself in time with a long exhale of effort.

Nuuk did not know if his master believed him or he stopped out of compassion for his haggard state, yet now he was certain why he was hurting. It hadn't been the first time. That he remembered.

"Very well then, imp. If your memory has abandoned you, you won't mind some time alone to try and recover it," Felduror said with a harsh voice.

The wizard closed the metal door and nodded to the orc outside to lock it.

Before he removed himself, he added through the small, squared aperture of the cell, "And since you've failed in your task, as well as prevented Ghaeloden from fulfilling his mission, I give you time before my Gholaks return from Sallncoln to refresh your memory." He stepped away, leaving the imp in complete darkness.

Sallncoln? The imp repeated the word in his mind, trying to roll over. The numbness in his shoulder was unbearable.

Why did it sound so familiar to him? By the gravity in the old man's words it was clear his fate would be decided soon, and it appeared more inclined towards a dramatic end rather than anything else. He had to do something but he could barely move, wincing and hissing with each small change in his twisted body. He needed time. Time to recover his strength and time to find his lost memories. How was it that whenever he tried to picture his past days there was complete darkness in his mind? What he once knew with certainty, was now clouded and unclear.

Did he really try to use magic? If he did, he was not sure which spell he could have possibly wielded to upset his master so much. He propped his back flatter on the wall and forced himself to breathe more slowly. Although it hurt, he felt much better sitting in a straighter position and felt that his mind benefited from it. It was pitch black, though somehow, he knew exactly how the cell was made and where the door's handle stood even if he couldn't see it.

There's no escaping through that heavy thing! His consideration brought back resolute memories of his past incarceration, almost reliving the pain those many punches and kicks to the door had brought to his limbs.

Instead of wasting his remaining energy, he knew he had to put his efforts into remembering everything he could. Amongst the muddied visions, he remembered the tall tower and the cold rain that showered against the windows of the rooms he was serving in.

Was it raining?

There were endless moments of silence when he was with his master and, of late, he recalled being with him quite often in one of his libraries. He did not mind having to wait for him to dictate something, actually he preferred it that way. What he did mind was when he was required to impart his master's instructions to those few orc-commanders he seemed to favour.

Those nasty brutes! His mind's visions of the Gholaks brought back unpleasant moments; they wouldn't miss a single occasion to torment him for his small nature and his bound wings.

He had to quickly dismiss the new recollection as well and force himself back on track to remembering more recent events. The unpleasant thought, however, helped him recollect another event linked to his bound wings and he was thankful now that he had indulged for a brief moment in thinking about the orcs. His master, Felduror, had promised to free his wings; he could recollect that as if it happened a few moments ago.

"Of course! How silly of me to have forgotten that," he mumbled as it all became clearer.

He was supposed to watch a dragon up close, see what he was up to and report back to his master. If he had done everything correctly and his master's hunch was right, the dragon would prove to be one of those who dared to go against the realm and therefore, at the peril of said dragon, he would gain back his freedom of flight. The problem was; who was that dragon? Why couldn't he recollect his name? He recalled some of the Drakhahouls of the citadel; Yrsidir, Sereri, King Belrug, Jaro. Any of the others were unknown to him. Maybe Ghaeloden was one of them? It must've been since his master specifically said that he himself had prevented him from accomplishing some unknown assignment.

"Damnation! Why can't I remember anything?" He surprised himself with the loud and short-lived echo his voice created inside the cell.

It was becoming hard to maintain his wits about himself since it was not only the bodily pain that he had to deal with anymore. Now a wretched feeling of self-anger was raising from his stomach between his aching ribs. It made his teeth grind and his jaw clench. He shifted again his position with the intent of casting it away, though he interrupted himself brusquely as he thought he heard steps outside. He held still for a long moment and hissed an exhale of pain when he couldn't hold his position anymore. Certain he had imagined it, he lay flatly on his back again, on the dirty blanket and thirty, or so, straws he had between himself and the cold floor. Maybe a bit of rest would aid his sore mind and body and so, he decided to sleep for a while.

The meaningless dreams Nuuk experienced were interrupted when a hand briskly shook him. His neck ached when he twitched his head up and opened his eyes in pain, only to find another imp staring into his eyes. What astonished him more was his improved sight, a bit less blurred, and not the fact that another imp has brought him food. Somehow that felt normal to him.

He stared at the shorter creature who was holding a white candle in one hand, its yellow light bringing to vision the entire small cell. In his other hand there was a platter with a mug of water, a slice of bread, two boiled, small potatoes and one carrot. He could even spot the sprinkled grains of salt that were half way melted on the boiled vegetables, a sight that made his muscle burst with invigorated energy as he put his back against the wall.

"Thank you!" Nuuk said to the other imp, one hand already on the carrot.

Two bites and it was gone. It wasn't old. Same was true for the two potatoes that still had warmth at their cores. He gulped them down, peel and all, and afterwards he drank the whole mug of water.

"Thank you!" he said again, feeling cleansed in spirit by the cool liquid. "Who are you? I thought I was the only Iprorim at the castle. Are you only allowed to serve in these fetid cells?"

The other imp did not reply. Instead, he mutely sat himself cross-legged on the floor and rubbed the bottom of the candle to the abrasive rock until it was fixed in one position. Once done, he turned his head to his side and picked a featherless quill from inside his dirty, tattered shirt, which was secured by a dirty rope he used as belt.

Nuuk watched him with some suspicion, not really comprehending what he was trying to do.

The small imp lifted the quill, strongly clutched between his fingers, and smiled at Nuuk before he pointed the inkless and featherless feather on the floor, making sure that Nuuk's eyes followed his hand. He then started moving softly his clutched feather, just above the hard stone's surface, and, although there was no ink, words in Iprorims' tongue started forming in the light of the candle as if made of molten gold.

"My name is Quick, or so my master likes to call me. I have been here long before you arrived, master Nuuk!" Quick paused and opened his mouth while pointing towards his cut tongue for him to see.

"Oh," Nuuk instinctively placed a hand over his own mouth. "I didn't know, I'm sorry!" he then whispered, finally comprehending the old imp's deficiency. "It's a pleasure to finally meet another Iprorim, Quick!" He managed a small smile.

Before he even realised, the words on the floor started to fade away, making Nuuk shudder at the thought that Felduror would sense the magic quill being used.

"Do not use magic! Master could come at any time," he whispered fast.

"This is not any magic. This is a stolen pen from his desk. He boasted about it on countless occasions; a magic no one could trace, he said. But he never uses it!" Quick's smile became a grin. *"I never thought I'd find any use for such an item until now."*

Nuuk was amazed. He propped himself a bit higher against the wall so he could follow more closely.

"I must apologise and I do hope you understand," Quick fixed his eyes on Nuuk's face at each of his written sentence, *"I didn't know what you were up to, I only knew that Felduror was looking for someone and realised it was you when you revealed yourself to me, last night."*

"What? I don't recall seeing you, ever! I didn't even know there were other Iprorims in the castle." Nuuk slowly started to realise what this meeting could mean.

Quick lifted a finger on his mouth, a gesture that made Nuuk silence himself.

"Time is of essence, Nuuk…" the older imp paused with one hand on his chin in the attempt of rephrasing his words, *"…last night you shouldn't have used magic to talk to me. Felduror was already alerted that someone was around, and wielding magic was all he needed to find you."*

Could it be that what he was saying was the truth? Nuuk weighed his concerns, still failing to remember anything at all.

Quick let the magic, golden ink fade before he continued, "*I knew you'd be in grave danger and, since a spell has been wielded already, and your presence compromised, I've used a bit of spell myself too.*"

"What spell did you use?" asked Nuuk.

Quick gulped nervously, fixing the grey floor he was facing. "*I've put a muddle-spell on your mind so you won't be able to remember the past clearly. This way, at least, you have won yourself a couple of days. That's why you are still alive!*" he finished his sparkling sentence of words.

Nuuk could not believe what he read. He shifted with pain closer to the floor, re-checking the phrase. Although it was quite readable, he failed to grasp its meaning.

"So it's because of you that I can't remember anything?" His sharp voice surprised both of them.

The older imp flinched in fear, pushing slightly with his heels on the floor, lifting the elbow of his free hand in an instinctive gesture of protection.

The sight of the old imp's reaction made Nuuk feel bad for allowing himself to be senselessly so mean and tried to calm his ire.

Seemingly, Quick realised that Nuuk's reaction had been a natural and unwanted rush of anger, and he took his time to write on, "*It'll go away very soon. That's why I came here to visit you and not without taking any risks. I want to make sure that once you remember, you'll be ready to do whatever it takes to stay alive!*"

Nuuk sighed. He esteemed and appreciated the effort the old imp was taking in trying to convey what would have taken less than half the effort had he had a tongue to speak with. He was feeling even worse for his outburst now. Whatever he had done to be locked up, he knew for sure it couldn't have possibly been this creature's fault. Bent upon his thin and badly-fed body, the sight of the old imp only made his heart shrink and ache with unhappiness as it delivered fresh memories of his own youth in Grora.

"I am sorry! It is not your fault I'm here!" he admitted almost tearfully.

Quick smiled and wrote, "*I do need to leave before my master realises*

I'm missing. I will return if I get a chance."

Then he lifted himself briskly, hid the magic pen under his ragged cloth and picked the candle and the empty platter from the floor. With another look at Nuuk, and a wan smile in the corner of his mouth, he left.

The candid smile sparked hope in Nuuk's heart. And, perhaps because of the food or the sincerity in his fellow Iprorim's eyes, he soon started to remember.

CHAPTER XX

THE RESCUE

Lorian / Felduror

"I can do this!" I encouraged myself with some effort while I pushed my hand at a loose rock, that had probably once served as a step.

Once sure I would not fall down, I pulled my strengths about me and propped my weight on my right arm, preparing to attempt a vertical leap that would see me closer to a small opening in the ceiling. From there, I would only have to move a single flat rock and then I'd be on to the next level, through the ceiling. Being several feet above ground level, did make me quite nervous, especially when having to climb the ancient cave's walls barehanded, without any ladders, ropes or proper stones that could support my weight.

Naghnatë was attentively watching me from below. We both knew she was not concerned for my safety, not entirely – more than once she insisted I be as silent as possible and to make sure I left everything as I found it; it was of critical importance to keep my passage as undisturbed as possible.

And so, when the short break had replenished the strength I required to swoop at the ceiling, I looked at her and indicated my promptness. She saluted me with a brief wave of her hand and watched me move the rock-cover and enter through the small, secret aperture. To my surprise, that did not denote the hardest part of my climb.

She was already gone when I peeked back at the cavern floor from the other side and, with determination, I turned my entire concentration on fixing the slab into its initial position without too much noise.

Once concluded, I could inspect the different kind of darkness that surrounded me. I was above the cave now, inside a narrow passage between raw dark rock walls; a fissure in the heart of the mountain that slit it right across. There were small signs of tools being used to shape it, probably in an attempt to enlarge the passageway, yet even to me it seemed poorly executed. I blamed it on the nature of the rock which felt as hard as the iron under my palm's inspection. The slit allowed the mountain's sides to converge high above me, higher than I could see, and where they met, they did not completely connect. This allowed daylight to bounce all around with some intensity and made it possible for me to appreciate its size. I could tell it was quite long, however I could not tell if I stood in the middle of it or to its sides.

Right-side then, I recalled the witch's instruction, while slowly walking through the man-sized tunnel.

I kept brushing my right hand at the wall, palpating the surprisingly sharp and smooth texture – the gesture was more an encouragement to cast away the insecurity the dark space conveyed, rather than my desire to feel bare rock. If anyone or anything lived in such a place, or if it was used sporadically as a passageway, I could not tell. The wet, muddy floor seemed without a trace of footprints of any sort and the strong iron-scented air appeared undisturbed. Every sound was subdued by the enormous walls and few, if none, external noises could be perceived from inside. The only thing that visibly altered, was the daylight's brightness, flickering playfully and worryingly at the same time whenever a cloud shadowed the sun.

My steps echoed weakly in the small slit-passage and I continued more confidently ahead, thinking back to what the witch told me to look for. She insisted it would be straight-forward and easy and before the end of the narrow passage, I would find another aperture on my left which would lead me into the cellars of the castle.

And she was right; another hundred steps or so ahead, a sharp protuberance on the left side was hiding a smaller aperture that distanced me of no more than two feet from the cellars' manmade-wall. Through the two-feet thickness of the mountain's side, the light allowed me to count as many as four big square-rocks in their entirety and few smaller corners of those that continued behind the rock. Though the narrowness of the space forced me to crouch to reach my goal.

Just as she mentioned, the stone on the bottom-right was of a darker shade than the rest. I knelt and carefully knocked on it to confirm her theory, smiling broadly when I heard the odd, hollow sound in return.

The entry, she had called what I was pulling out now; a square block of fake rock that was easily removed.

The curious boulder was light as a pillow.

Had I been afraid of spiders, I would have easily let out a scream, as a furry-legged creature crawled hastily over the back of my left hand and jumped to safety into the darkness of another fissure. I was too slow to hiss about it and that was my luck; any noisy reaction could have been disastrous.

A foul smell exuded from within the walls, its stink making me move away from the course of the drift, which escaped the basements through the hole I had made. I propped myself against the other solid rocks, carefully listening for any unwanted sounds and calmed my breathing.

When my nose allowed my body to continue, I crawled inside halfway and checked where I was and what I could see. Having established that nobody was there, I crawled the rest of the way in and repositioned the sham rock in its place with as much attention as I could.

I was now in a wider room that had four tall, tarnished metal-cages with rusty chains and manacles of various sizes descending from the ceilings. All of a sudden, the damp smell acquired a different significance, its bitter taste compelling me once again to think of it as the reek of death. Tortured creatures of who-knows what kind had been kept there for the last moments of their miserable lives trying to escape the indissoluble grasp of their executioner.

The image of Nuuk's face fluttered in my mind and I dared not entertain the thought of him being tortured. More than a prison it seemed to be an abandoned execution room; luckily, one that hadn't been used in a long time. The place was brimming with cobwebs that garnished every corner of the room and every tool and instrument that had been forgotten inside the damp space. Even the rusty metal-bars that formed the walls of the cages were randomly patterned with dense webs that collected cocoons of dead insects.

Just like we use to hang the sausages back home, I thought as I slowly moved across between the cages. *And not only insects!* I noticed with repugnance that one of the biggest cobwebs, contained a dried-out bat.

After a quick walkthrough of the entire space, enough to memorise the precise location of my escape, I found my way out of the room with catlike steps. The fact that there was one single, broken door, made me realise I was possibly in the last room of the lowest levels.

I touched Winterhorn for reassurance as I moved ahead.

When I exited the almost-collapsed door, I found myself in another room, twice the size of the previous and with double the metal cages and torturing tools. There were all sorts of weapons on the floor, reclined to the walls or hanged on the metal cages as well as on the wall racks, their woods long rotten and darkened. It was clear that it was another abandoned place of torture. The reek on this side was less harsh and, after careful inspection, I continued as per the witch's instructions, through the middle of the room and to the door on my left.

Without a breath's noise, I pressed my ear to the dark metal door and listened at length for any sounds that might come from the other side. When all I could hear was the soft, cadenced dripping of a distant leakage, I knew I was alone. A bit too confident I opened the door which, old as it was, emitted a terribly loud squeak. I allowed a long moment to pass before I squeezed myself through the opening.

The door opened onto a narrow set of stairs that revolved to the left and ended somewhere around forty or so steps higher. At the very top, according to Naghnatë, I would find the door that led to the common cells, in which Felduror kept his prisoners.

Though, as I made my way to the top, I felt unsure as everything she knew about the basements was from many years ago. If the structure was still the same, would I still find prisoners? The two foul rooms I passed seemed to have been unused for a long time and perhaps it was just the same for the entire floor above.

Maybe this is not a place for prisoners, I thought as I climbed the final steps and approached another door.

Another moment of stillness passed with my ear flatly pressed on the metal door. The iron felt definitely warmer up here as indeed did the air in the back of my throat and inside my lungs. I gathered I was not underground anymore and the door would reveal what the first floor of this side of the building would look like.

With a couple more draws of the tepid air, I encouraged myself to try the door's handle, which to my surprise went all the way down, with a snapping sound. Something had broken inside the rusty casing of the lock, but luckily it was not the handle as the door slid open.

These things must be ancient!

The place appeared abandoned as if in a rush – perhaps even the prisoners themselves had escaped alive. It made sense, judging by the scattered objects and weapons that had filled the previous rooms.

I then opened the door wider and felt frustrated to see only a long corridor in front of me. On the upper right side of the wall, a couple of square windows allowed shattered-rays of daylight to penetrate the moist and dusty space. I made my way ahead with confidence, crossing the space almost entirely, before I understood that the left wall, fashioned a couple of thin, squared gaps in the stone. Had I been quicker I would have definitely missed them as they were actual doors, made of the same bricks as the walls. The sole thing that gave them away, the barely visible rectangular metal frame that delineated a fissure of their rectangular shapes. A mere coincidence that I had noticed them.

There were no handles nor knobs, only a central key hole big as my thumb. A bit higher, nestled in the middle on each of the two doors, were two small square-holes the size of half a brick. They were the cells' sole source of light and air, and sat a bit higher than my forehead.

I had to lift myself on my toes to be able reach them. "Anyone in there?" I softly whispered through the first door's aperture, averse to putting my fingers in the gap.

My voice died out fast on the other side; it really was a small cell.

I moved onto the other door and asked again, "Hey! Is anyone in there?"

Nothing still.

I pushed myself away from the door to glance outside from the opposite window to get some sense of orientation. I had to climb a bit higher to reach the metal bars. Once there, I pulled my entire body's weight and was able to see outside. Unfortunately, there was not much to be seen. The window looked out onto a shadowed side of the castle where there was another windowless curved-wall. Higher still, a sort of suspended bridge connected to another section and covered the entire skyline in that spot. To my disappointment, the reflected rays of light were not coming directly from the sun, they were just mere reflections of the bright, white stonework. The unawareness of where I was, together with the lack of perspective, made the citadel appear bulkier than ever.

I wondered how did it actually look from outside and how big it was. On the other hand, I did appreciate the fresh air with its highland aroma. It made me close my eyes and draw in as much of its cleansing freshness as I could, against the throbbing muscles of my forearms. I lingered until the burning sensation became overwhelming and then I let myself on the floor again.

The pleasant sensation was short-lived and, once my feet touched the floor, the dampness of the corridor brought back the disquieting sensation of the situation I was in. I wondered where to go next. The witch had been sure that if there was a chance of finding Nuuk alive and imprisoned, there would be no other place to look for him but these cells. She had mentioned the existence of other cells in the basements of each of the five towers, yet I questioned my ability to find them, not to mention that it would mean walking in broad daylight across the streets and pathways that separated each building. It was definitely not a good idea and definitely unlikely of success.

I decided to continue ahead. The short walk led me to another wide-opened door. It revealed a splintered section in the middle of its thick panels as it propped on the right wall out of its hinges. Dust, rust and decay had eaten through every fallen piece of it, be it metal or wood, and the cobwebs it accommodated had been rearranged multiple times. Even though the sight reassured me I would find no guards or wizard's servants in those rooms, it also lowered the chances of finding any prisoners alive.

Equipped with less optimism, I entered. The room instantly reminded me of a guards' chamber. On the left side, near the corner, there was a big chest-drawer with both of its doors spread open. Rusty and blackened cutlery, dirty pots and platters, both earthen and metal-made, littered the muddy-green floor in a wide area. A thick, oak table was still intact in the middle of the room, yet the two benches next to it were laying upside-down. The humidity in the room, aided by the small window, allowed foul-smelling lichens to grow between the cracks of the rocks on the floor. The pleasantness of my feet on the soft blanket of moss did not make up for the stink it produced and so I hurried towards the window, slipping and almost falling at my first step.

I calmed my alacrity, thinking how badly I could've hurt my knee had I landed on it and decided to inspect the small window, which was wider and lower than the previous ones; I could see more of the mountain top it faced upon.

Yet, before I leaped at the frame to pull myself up, a door at a higher level, opened and closed loudly and quickly.

Disconcerted, I intuitively lowered myself with the back on the wall. Crouched as I was, I strained myself to understand precisely where the noise was coming from; the only way to find out was through the aperture to my right, which opened onto yet another set of stairs.

I firmly clutched Winterhorn's handle. Unfortunately, the noise had died as soon as the door closed. It was a long moment before my ears caught another subtler sound; footsteps. Frail, bare footsteps crossed the raw stone of the floor, indicating the position and direction of the guest in the room over my head. The weight and pace sounded more human-sized, rather than an orc.

Would Felduror walk barefoot, and that swiftly? I stopped to consider.

With languorous movements, still crouched and helping my stride with my hands, I approached the threshold in front of me. My heartbeat picked up, but no external noises gave away my presence, thanks to the soft, malodorous blanket of moss. I passed the door's aperture, listening to what occurred above; thinking I heard the brief clang of something metal at one point. It reassured me as I noiselessly crawled on the narrow, curved set of stairs, until I ended up in front of a wrought-iron door.

The sounds died when I reached the top and I stooped even lower. The position allowed me to check the ante-chamber behind the iron bars, where there was a big double-panelled door on the right, which I gathered would lead outside, and one smaller door on the left, from behind which the footsteps had come.

With a quick, silent leap I moved behind what little corner was offered between the frame of the gate and the wall, and placed my ear on the cold bricks. There were no more footsteps I could pick up. Instead, there was a hollow voice, muffled and distant, and a dull metal sound. The mumble, belonging to a single voice, sounded weak and non-threatening, but I could not comprehend a word it said.

Countless moments passed before the voice stopped and the barefoot steps started dashing again on the stone floor. I decided to return below, descending the stairs with haste and care, taking cover in the moss-covered room. And it was lucky I did so, as when I reached the bottom, the small door and then the main double-panelled one, opened and closed swiftly. A quick succession of steps trailed faintly outside.

I issued a long exhale and, until I was certain there was nobody else upstairs, I lingered where I was.

Appeased and certain of my solitude, I returned to the top and, once through the unlocked iron gate, I pushed gently the door on the left. It opened without any unpleasant noise.

A waft of spoiled air, transporting a feeble trail of boiled potatoes, welcomed me. The place was certainly too neat and tidy to host Gholaks guards – a supposition also confirmed by the presence of scrolls-stuffed ledges.

My eyes came to rest on a stove that was in the left corner; it hadn't seen a fire in a long time, being devoured by a thick coat of dust and ash. As soon as I shifted my glance back to the right side, a sudden cough startled me, which I had to suppress with my hands on my face and a swift change of my position. My steps carried me across the room into the darkest corner of the space, afraid that I might be heard and by the time the moment was gone, I found myself standing in front of another tiny cell with a hidden door, with bricks nestled within a metal frame to conceal it.

"Quick is that you?" A rough, tired voice lifted through the small brick-sized aperture in the middle of the door.

"Nuuk?" I recognised his weary voice.

"Lorian?" he replied, pushing one hand through the aperture as he leaped at the door through whines of pain.

I took his four-fingered hand with a smile on my face, happy to find him alive and well, even if the dried blood on his fingers made me feel despairing.

"You wouldn't believe what happened to me!" he started. "I'm just recovering my memory. There was another Iprorim, just like me, only older, and to protect me he used a spell –"

"Nuuk, you can tell me everything once we get you out. Naghnatë is counting on me to release you before she reveals herself to Felduror. We must hurry!"

I was looking around for a way to open the door.

"Sure, sure," he replied a bit thwarted, "I should've asked Quick for the keys. He brought me food and just left. I did not think of asking him to free me, not that I can walk far anyways."

"Are you hurt?" I asked with increased urgency.

"The worse has passed, master Lorian, though I'll sit while I wait for the door to open." His breathing sounded alarmingly weary.

"I promise it will be all fine, just hold on in there until I find a way out!"

A quick search through the many broken and unused things inside the small space made it obvious I wouldn't find any keys; I had to try and break the door down.

Still reassured that there was no one in close proximity, I rushed downstairs and grabbed the healthiest axe I could find, and two metal spears that were not entirely eaten by rust – the spears fit nicely behind the main entrance, solidly stuck between the two rings that were used to pull the heavy panels open. With a quick push and pull, I tested them to see if they were as effective as they looked and then I grabbed the axe and returned to Nuuk.

"I'm going to try and hack it open. Stay away, Nuuk!" I said. "Do you recall which way the door opens?"

"I'm safely at a distance. I think…" his muffed voice broke briefly, "…I think it opens towards my right-hand side, your left. Yes, your left!"

"Good, keep back!" I was sure the heavy axe would not fail me.

I readied myself with a quick succession of breaths, I knew I had only a couple of attempts before drawing the attention.

No time to think!

The sturdy axe dashed above my head heavily, while descending with a shrill sound, guided by my stiffened hands. The strength I put into my blow, together with the hefty double-edge blade, acquired an unforeseen speed and precision and landed perfectly in the small crack between the wall and door, where the lower hinge was secluded. I closed my eyes instinctively and felt the multitude of tiny shards of broken bricks bounce dynamically around me. The blast reverberated and died in the room quickly, making my body vibrantly tremble, especially my forearms.

I exulted at the slash my blow had made; the axe had landed and remained stuck with quite a big gap. It would only require a secondary and definitive blow before the old, rusty hinge shattered. The warmth that lifted underneath my clothes was unbearable, I could feel sweat drips on my back. I blamed the lack of air and also the cloak Naghnatë had given me, which was starting to itch disturbingly on my damp skin. With a quick gesture I unlaced it and threw it on the squared table.

"Ready for another blow?" I asked as I hurried back in position and forced the axe out of the gap.

"Ready as ever!" Nuuk could not hide the excitement in his voice.

The fear that we'd soon have some company obliged me to make haste and, even if I feared for lack of precision, my second blow resulted twice as devastating. The hole that now took its place was big enough to insert the axe's tip and twist it outwards repeatedly. Swivelling between the top hinge and the opposite-side's lock, the door cracked with augmented intensity, bits of shattering brick falling like sand from the metal frame. With more back and forth pushing the door collapsed inside the small cell.

"Are you all right?" I ventured inside.

"I am well," Nuuk was sitting in the far corner.

He was not looking good at all; his face was swollen and there were cuts, bruises and wet bloodstains all over his upper body. The ragged shirt he wore had more holes in it than I remembered, and definitely one too many dried bloodstains. I would need to find him some clean clothing, sooner rather than later.

"Come!" I grabbed his arm around my shoulder and thrust mine around his back while walking towards the door; I was surprised how light he felt under my arms.

Just as we faced the small room's entrance, a loud horn exploded behind the main door which surprised us both and forced me to retreat a step. The battle-horn ended with a deep and threatening growl which made my skin prickle and Nuuk's body instinctively quiver. By the heavy hits that pounded forcefully against the door there was no mistaking what was outside; a Gholak.

I let out a miserable exhale. The small fissure between the

double panels allowed us to appreciate the full figure of the mighty creature that stood three or four times taller than a common man, shadowing the mighty door in front of us.

With a glance at the metal spears that bounced perilously between the door's ring handles, under the beast's pounding, I looked at Nuuk and started downstairs with haste.

"We have to reach the lower floors!" I said softly.

Behind us, the thick wood panels gave nerve-racking signs of failure, while from outside, rushing steps approached the entrance. Powerful kicks and fists on the door multiplied and, not after long, one of the spears bounced on the stone floor stridently.

I started panting with difficulty, the anxiety and Nuuk's weight started to add to my weary knee and make my arms' muscles burn. I feared we'd never make there in time; we still had to descend another set of stairs and pass other rooms before we approached the boulder of the secret passage.

The angry orcs had broken their way in and I could hear their heavy steps moving around the room above, smashing and crashing everything in their path.

Nuuk was contorting in pain, though I could not stop and only quickened my pace, trying my best to distract him with a silly recap of how close I had been to hurting myself on the mossy floor. His leg muscles failed to sustain him and his weight was pushing heavier on my already sore arms. Yet we were too close to give up. We had passed the long corridor, down the stairs and within reach of the last two rooms. My burning lungs implored a break, but the noise the iron gate made as it bounced on the stairs, made me reconsider.

"They're not so dumb after all!" I whispered between deep gasps, while guiding Nuuk's exhausted body through the narrow space that led to the fake rock.

Once there I let him slide to the floor with his back against the wall.

"What's this?" he managed to ask with eyes half-closed.

"It's our escape!"

The small break allowed me draw a long breath and shake the numbness from my limbs, recognising that he looked wearier than me. The sight did not bode well and I cast the thought aside, crouching near him.

The steps of the Gholaks approached. I counted three sets of boots. They reached the first room of the basement, their growls angry, filling the space with a dire predicament.

"Come on! Faster!" I told myself, my hands shaking on the stone with as much tiredness as nervousness.

A loud clattering sound and a deep thud made the group pause briefly, followed by two different mocking snorts, which I gathered were orcs' laughter. One of them had certainly slipped and broken something made of wood.

I took the fake rock out of its place, ignoring the questioning face of the imp. Eyes fixed on the room's entrance, I only pointed him with my head at the space I just created, demanding much silence with a finger on my lips.

The orcs were on the move again approaching the room next to the one we were in.

Nuuk did as I wordlessly told him to, his quick movements and slim body allowing him to reach the other side with ease, though not without pain, I could tell. I followed and just as I crawled backwards, with my legs all the way within the hole, while holding the light stone with both of my hands, I heard the small space of the room shatter with an orc's heavy breathing.

Flat on my stomach and still partially out of the gap, I froze, while glancing at the infuriated brute. Its angry stare was scrutinising the metal cages. The little I could make out, in the feeble light of the rancid air and behind the metalwork, was more than enough to make my blood chill. It was a frightening and imposing creature that almost brushed the tall ceiling with its head, which was protected by a metal helmet that gave way to a ponytail of the darkest hairs. Sparkling bloodshot eyes moved slowly guided by a solid neck while four thick, sharp tusks garnished his wide mouth. It had muscular, veiny arms, thick as a horse's hind-legs and his shoulders were as wide as a bull's. It was a fearful, blood-draining sight. The creature embodied the perfect deadly-opponent on a battlefield, one very few might dare to challenge. Even the pale, dead-green tone of his skin amplified the fear I felt.

Nuuk must've felt my astonishment as I could feel his arm grab on my calf and slowly pull me towards him. I slowly and quietly retreated with the help of my legs and elbows. The light stone slid back into its place with almost no noise – luckily covered by the loud stepping of the other two Gholaks that just ran into the room.

If I had lingered a moment longer, we would have been caught; one of two running orcs reached right behind the cage we just left from, his heavy steps and guttural breathing loudly penetrating the thick wall as he patrolled the narrow space.

"I sense human," he almost barked to the others in common tongue.

"Human use magic to escape! We summon the wizard," a thicker voice came in reply from the distant right side.

But they did not move.

In complete darkness, and behind the safety of the wall, the small crack of the dark mountain kept us sheltered as we lay flat on our stomachs for many, still moments. The heavy breathing of the orc close to me, pulled at his leathered body-armour, giving away his presence; they were still expecting to pick up on any little noise.

So long for dumb pigs. More like dog-sharp smelling senses and bat-like ears!

Yet we did not flinch, not until their steps had picked up again and faded into the distance. Then, we were safe to move again.

"What is with all this confusion?" Felduror's harsh response to the persistent knocking on his door came with plenty of justified irritation.

He knew there'd be only one reason that would excuse any of his servants being bold enough to bother him, when he specifically asked not to be disturbed. He now had to abandon unwillingly a trail of thought that promised much resolution, one for which he had sacrificed long hours, bent over a new scroll map. To his surprise the old maps of the southern regions, scrolls he had already scrutinised many years back and considered useless, seemed to reveal so much more than before in light of the most recent events.

With much displeasure and unwillingness, he lifted himself from the stool with a series of tiny cracks that issued from the back of his head and continued to his lower spine.

I am certainly not getting any younger! His thought accompanied a much-needed stretch of limbs and bones as he reached for the door's handle.

"I beg forgiveness, m'lord, there's a certain matter that requires your immediate attention!" The wizard's most trustful Gholak, Barakhuul, appeared troubled as he shadowed the small door of the library.

Responsible for the safety of the five towers, the orc was fairly clever for such a creature of the dark, and quite respectful; he kept his horned head bowed while he imparted his request with a deep, calm voice.

Felduror was comforted by his composure. He knew he had yet to use him for his true purpose and allow the warrior to prove his true calling, and he looked forward for such an opportunity to arise.

Lost in adulation, the wizard did not have time to reply, the orc has left just as swiftly as he has arrived, convinced his master understood the urgency of the situation.

Felduror followed him down the stairs to the ground level and the main entrance in front of which two subordinate Gholaks were waiting before the wide opened doors, daring not to step inside.

They both bowed lower at the sight of the old wizard, their master.

"What is it then?" asked Felduror, irritated that their gesture seemed purposely delayed.

"Our liege," the orc on the left started with some insecurity in his voice, "prisoner is escaped!"

They both lifted their heads up and stood straight with their hands behind their backs, seemingly readying for a burst of rage from their master.

One that did not arrive. Felduror passed his hand over his long beard, fixing the floor to his left.

None hissed a word nor dared to interrupt him.

"Mhm, just as I suspected. The imp was not alone. The problem is bigger than it first appeared." He lifted his gaze from the floor. "I want you to track them down, fail and I shall be very disappointed." His words were directed only to the Gholak that addressed him.

Then he turned towards the stairs that led to his residences, dismissing the two guards with a half-lifted hand. But he had to stop when the other orc had cleared his throat as if still having something to say, much to his annoyance.

"Forgiveness, your excellency! Inside cellars, we found this," the voice of the younger orc was softer than his comrade's. "A strong scent of human to it," he added, keeping a pale-green cloak plainly in sight.

"Human, in those abandoned cells?" Felduror stilled his face with the firmest of expressions, while rushing to grab the robe.

He knew it simply wasn't possible. Had he still human guards at his service so close to his lodgings? He was sure that, beside the empire's peasants, who lived far from the main walls and seldom sought a private interview with himself, there were none allowed here. He dared not think that one would be stupid enough to go against his wishes or try to trick the throng of orcs. Truth be told, he couldn't think of any capable of entering the cells and evading them with the imp right under their noses.

It simply could not be a human! he thought as his hands caressed and examined the soft, warm cloak.

It took him an instant to realise his mistake; it was not of human manufacture. The intricately-woven fibres were too detailed and of a pattern unlike anything he had seen. Even the fibres themselves were too thin to be produced by rough human hands. He briefly considered the elves and just as quickly discarded the idea, knowing elves had abandoned these lands many years ago; too many for any piece of cloth to be so perfectly preserved. He then thought of his own acolytes, that peculiar race that was neither human nor elf, but they could not have done it either. Not that there hadn't been conspirators and turncoats along the way, no, it was mainly because they were of a different breed, and weaving and embroidering was not something they were fond of, or proficient at.

He sighed and shifted his mind back to the humans. It was not possible for any to have aided the imp. He had stopped surrounding himself with the incompetent and avaricious individuals a long time ago; they were neither needed nor allowed in his inner circles. They served and progressed only through their manual and dirty-work. He had also decided to stop recruiting among them. It was simply too easy for them to lose track of their true purpose and concentration. Besides their ordinary, plain and physical incapability, curiosity was their most dangerous attribute when it came to serving him. And so, he had rid himself of them. He found other races were far better suited for his purposes and far more dexterous in wielding the elements. Although, thinking about it, he felt a certain bitterness in his own beliefs, since he almost missed having another special human-being such as himself around.

He cleared his throat noisily, willing to imply that it was a physical compulsion that delayed his reply rather than his brief redolent moment. With subtlety, he returned to the matter at hand, loathing himself for the incapacity of preventing such petty thoughts, which of late had become more common.

"You do as you've been told and be quick about it! I shall enquire about this rag." He watched them go and then turned away to the stairs.

"Actually!" he stopped himself after a couple of steps, "I want you to bring me their heads, my libraries are quite blank," he whispered without looking to Barakhuul, who stalked him like a mute shadow.

As he reached his little library, the one that latterly seemed to be more hospitable and familiar than his own sleeping quarters, he shut the door firmly behind him. He could now allow himself to relish in a noiseless space, where his mind could reach deeper into long-forgotten memories. A precious lesson, learned many years ago; one can hold much more information and memories than imagined, if one knew how to recall them. And to think that what aided his endeavour were just mere herbs; ones to act as powerful sedatives and bring the mind to the right point between total relaxation and rational function and allow it to delve through past times.

He decided he'd do it again.

He poured some water in a mug that served as dead-weight on a curly-scroll on his desk, and made it boil with a bit of magic. Although this library's stash of herbs was almost depleted, he found what he considered to be enough dried leaves for the current session and sprinkled them on top of the hot water.

Instantly, a strong scent evaded through the yellowish vapours and coloured the water a vivid dark-green. For a moment he closed his eyes and thought he could already feel the benefits of the soothing herb while deeply inhaling above the mug. He sat himself on a chair with a soft cushion for his back, one hand on the mug and one over the strange cloak, which he held on his lap. While placing his tired feet on a smaller chair, he let his head lay on the headrest and sipped from the scorching liquid.

He then closed his eyes and let his mind be transported back in time. If there was anything related to the cloak that his mind and eyes had ever perceived, and never actually acknowledged, he would be able to dig it out.

Shortly, faces of long-lost acquaintances appeared as brief birds' calls in the forest, that unexpectedly move from one side to the other with less and less intensity. They came and went swiftly from his mind, sometimes not giving him time to put a name to the figures. He liked to think of them as friends, although he knew categorically that he had not had one for a very long time. Perhaps since he was a young student himself and, eager to be learned in the art of magic, had forged alliances and friendships that would benefit his studies. Some would last and some wouldn't, and in the end they'd all be long forgotten memories. He had outlived them all and when their time had come, he had not shed a single tear nor a moment to recollect their memory.

He took another sip, eyes heavier than before. With some effort, he then accompanied the mug on the floor, almost dropping it as its weight felt unbearable for his drowsy muscles. The sensation was most welcomed and he allowed himself to be guided by his mind. He gave in completely to the desire of not moving and reposing his old bones as if caught by the sweetest of sleeps.

For anyone that looked upon his body, he would appear as a snoozing old man, yet his mind had never been so sharp and active as it was in this moment. He had ventured here before, but he could not recall when. The place reminded him of the same prevailing emotion each visit provided and with a slow smile he tried to whisper a lethargic word.

"The hereafter!" His elongated syllables brought serenity as he remembered just now, how much he liked to use that word to call his inebriated state of mind.

And if he tried to recount what the experience was like, he would probably have to use the same expression. An imaginary afterlife where light never ceased and warmth never dulled. It was like looking through a piece of glass straight into the sun, without fear of losing your sight because the sun was obscured by a billowing mass of clouds and fog. There, the memories formed out of nowhere. Like children that play at making shapes out of the clouds in the immense, blue sky, so he found himself serenely grabbing trails of missing memories.

But quite some time passed and nothing of worth was recalled. He thought to lift himself from his comfortable position and take another sip of tea, yet his relaxed body failed to accomplish less than a quarter of the action. The brief, small tension of his stomach and the quick twitch of his fingers caused one side of the cloak to fall on the ground. With the innocuous gesture, a reinvigorated waft, enriched with a flowery-scent made its way to his sensible nose, suddenly taking him back to when he was a young teacher himself.

A sequence of new faces made their way to his mind. As he glimpsed at each and every one, he felt with certainty that he was getting closer. Still, he could not tell what he was looking for, until from the multitude of figures, a pleasantly round and rosy-cheeked face of a girl stopped in front of him. She must have been eleven or twelve perhaps, and she had plenty to demonstrate how wrong he was in thinking that girls cannot make great wizards.

And how wrong I have been, he allowed his mind to observe as with shy joy he lingered on her honest, round eyes.

The new, dark-haired student, just months after her arrival at the citadel, had found a way to bind her true passion for plants with what he was teaching; the art of magic. She had been so convinced and bold to argue that the both can be fused into a more powerful knowledge. A claim that had stirred much mockery from the other students and a real argument with him, her tutor. But it was on that occasion that she had tried to prove her case with a powder she had extracted from some desiccated roots and a silken ribbon, untied from her hair. She had imbued the piece of cloth with her special concoction and defied anyone that did not believe her to unfasten the knot she had just made. To his surprise no one had been able to, not even himself. Not until he had used a demanding amount of magic, too powerful for the little girl's capabilities.

How could I have forgotten this? How could I have believed she was gone?

Felduror felt his face smile as widely as his drowsy lips could stretch, forcing his sleepy hands to try and grasp the cloak which now reeked strongly of the same essence of her concoction. Waiting for his numbness to recede, was not an annoyance anymore, not at all, not ever like before. Now, it was pure joy, accompanied by his realisation that Naghnatë was alive and closer to him than ever before.

CHAPTER XXI

THE CHOICE

Lorian

The difficult and gruelling descent that had seen us safe down the cavern's steep wall, had taken its toll. While Nuuk's aching body and drowsiness turned him into a dead weight, I had to ask of my own more than I knew it was capable of. The rope I used to tie his waist to mine and lower him to the floor had cut through my old wounds with ease. Against the bleeding of my palms, I had taken the time I required to avoid hurting his head or dropping him altogether; a spraining affair for my limbs to be carrying his dozy body, dangling almost lifelessly on the rope's end.

"What is this place?" Nuuk's coarse voice echoed buoyantly in the wide space of the cave once he had awakened from a lengthy, strain-induced sleep.

Plenty of minutes had passed since I propped him in the most comfortable position the rocky-floor allowed and tended to my bleeding wounds, somewhere in the middle of the big gallery. My throbbing muscles could only be thankful for the rest, and I lingered, sprawled over a rock until my breathing steadied and the pounding in my chest had eased.

"It's a secret passage that Naghnatë found. It extends right under the basements of one of the towers and leads somewhere near a forest, not that far from the smaller cave in the snow." His curiosity was a good omen of his improvement.

Though, he did not lift himself. He only turned his head as much as his torso allowed and gradually inspected the wide space in front of him. I approached and offered him a drink from the herb-scented waterskin, that the witch had insisted I carry. And I was happy I had taken it. The cold brew seemed to replenish some of his strength. His eyes sparkled with a more vivid light and his face regained some of its colour.

"Thank you!" He handed the waterskin back to me.

"You're welcome."

"No, Lorian. I mean thank you for coming after me!"

"You would've done just the same, Nuuk!" I smiled at him undecidedly, thinking back to my brief confusion of mind where I would have given anything just to return home.

Under the dim light of the cave, his face appeared less swollen and less purple, though the gash in his left brow had to be treated as soon as possible.

Without a second thought, I went for one of the wider puddles and washed my hands thoroughly. I then put a finger on the tip of my tongue and checked if the water was a fresh mountain-vein or just saline moist that was dripping from the ceiling. When I ascertained that it was fresh water, I soaked the sleeve of my shirt and cleaned the dry blood from his forehead and eyebrow. Luckily, the incision was not bleeding anymore.

He thanked me with a weak smile of empathy, one which I returned candidly with a soft pat on his shoulder, taking the chance to look for other wounds that might need immediate attention. It wasn't too hard to find one; my eyes fell on a big stain on the side of his shirt, which promised a couple of broken ribs. Unquestionably, my competency was surpassed by that sort of wound; I dared only to prod around it with the tips of my fingers.

"Is that hurting badly?" The sound of my silly voice made the question sound even more stupid.

He hissed as he shifted his shoulders. "If I stay like this it doesn't bother me too much. The problem is when I walk or make any sudden movement with my upper body." He turned his head down to inspect the wound himself.

"Well, luckily down here there won't be any need for sudden movements. And we have enough food for a couple of days!" I hoped I was right and the brutes would not find the secret passage.

I went to collect the bag that the witch had left for me. "We'll wait here for a while and hope Naghnatë returns. In the meantime, we should recover our strength as much as we can and pray the brutes don't pick up our trail."

"So she came too?" he asked surprised.

"Of course she did and I am sure Ghaeloden has done his best to save you from punishment!" I replied, deciding if it was the chunk of wax he'd have first.

"Is that what I think it is?" he exclaimed, his eyes sparkling as he extended a hand to grab the piece of Iprorim-food.

"Yes, it is, and it's all yours." I chuckled, settling for a piece of cheese and a hunk of bread.

He devoured the wax in no time and licked all of his eight, oily fingers. The feast appeared to have reinvigorated him and the fact only gave me hope. While I continued eating, he started talking again.

"I have my doubts about it…" he started.

My face betrayed my confusion.

"Ghaeloden I mean," he added.

"Oh."

"Drakhahouls are very proud creatures and honestly I wouldn't jeopardise my prestige for one like me either, if I were a dragon." There was a heavy trace of disappointment and hurt in his voice, yet he continued before I could put together a reply. "It's not that his life depended on an Iprorim or that his conscience would be damaged if he allowed one like me to perish. Besides, Felduror told me exactly what the dragon had said, you know! When he had met Ghaeloden, that is. And it was not a nice thing to say."

Now it was my curiosity that prevented me from replying.

"He said that the dragon did his duty, obviously, and reported exactly how things had developed, and that I alone had come up with the rebellious plan of going against the wizard's words. Felduror insisted that Ghaeloden was convinced that I did such a thing not for the forsaken tokens, but solely because I desired freedom above all else. In his opinion I wanted to rid myself of the wretched string that binds my wings together so I can be free again. I've always felt the Drakhahoul was onto something." The imp let out an angry puff.

I took the long pause as a sign to intervene, "Nuuk, don't you see? He said that to protect you!"

"Protect me? Lorian, look at me! How was I protected?" He flinched in obvious pain as he tried to turn himself towards me.

The sight of his bruised, sad face and tearful eyes made me swallow with remorse. "You are alive, Nuuk! If Felduror had found out about your magical abilities, he most certainly wouldn't have allowed you to live. I'm sorry it had to be you to suffer as you have, but I am glad nonetheless that you're alive. And when Naghnatë returns, I will make sure she heals you, magic or no magic, you've got my word!"

I wondered if Naghnatë would have something to say for the fact that it was his own fault that he found himself in this quandary. If he had followed her instructions, and brought back the herbs, most likely we would all be sitting here and contemplating our move for recovering the tokens instead of just trying to escape alive.

"Nuuk, what about the herbs you were supposed to bring for me?" It occurred to me to ask.

"All gone! The sceptre and my bag are with the wizard. Speaking of which, the sceptre does not work in his hands."

"You mean he cannot become invisible like you?"

"Exactly so! I'm certain of it. Although, he can hit pretty hard with it." He sighed.

"I see." Now I understood what had caused the perfectly straight gash above his brow.

The herbs could have restored much of his strength as well as mine, a crucial detail if we wanted to escape. The brief memory of how the witch had rubbed the curious plant of Drakholia on my knee, made me consider the possibility that soon I might need another cure myself. Although I had walked and climbed with much ease, my knee felt nothing like it had when the witch had mended it. During my recent exertions, I had managed to ignore the signs of my deterioration. Now that I looked at it, I wasn't sure anymore. The previous, minor stings of pain that had issued and died hastily from behind my knee and travelled up towards my spine, were more alarming now that I was resting. The signs were obvious; I would soon need help myself and I did not know if rest was helping or making things worse.

Nuuk sensed my uneasiness and looked at me questioningly. I ignored him. The last thing he needed to know was that I could not carry his weight anymore in case we needed to run.

"Where is Naghnatë anyway?" he asked.

"I don't actually know. She said she'd distract Felduror and hoped that we'd succeed on our own before she had to reveal herself, otherwise there'd be no chance of returning here for the tokens. We're supposed to wait for her here!"

"That makes sense, besides, I don't think she would have fitted in that tiny hole," he replied with a smile.

His joke made both of us laugh at length. An unexpected and healthy way of breaking the tension.

"Damnation!" I burst out when all laughter had ceased.

"What?" Nuuk's face became serious.

"The cloak! I forgot the cloak on a chair near the cell you were in. How stupid of me!" I lifted myself and cupped my face, while looking aimlessly to the ceiling.

"What cloak?"

"Before I ventured to save you, Naghnatë had given me her cloak. She said it would conceal my steps and aid my furtiveness. I'm not sure it did, but it was really warm and itchy when I was breaking down your door and I threw it on a chair. I knew there was something missing all the way down and yet I couldn't remember what. Darn it!"

"Oh," the imp said with a soft voice, "we can only hope they won't find it, although brutes as they may be, they make for pretty scary hounds!"

He was probably right; there were few chances that the orcs would miss it, they could easily have smelled me from behind a wall.

"Who is Quick?" My frustration made me recollect his first question.

"Oh, Quick! Quick is another Iprorim, poor soul!"

"So there are other imps at the castle? That is very good news Nuuk, isn't it?" I tried to cheer him up.

"I know, master Lorian. Hurt and with poor memory, I barely rejoiced having met him. I am happy that there is another one like me hereabout. Alas, I fear for his soul; he's very poorly-shaped, thin and old. And somehow, he still managed to cheer me up and wanted no pity. I would really like to save him, Lorian. He saved my life, I think!" Nuuk interrupted himself briefly, pensively. "Right before Felduror caught me, Quick cast a spell on me to befuddle my memories. I could not remember a thing until moments before your arrival. I therefore could not betray myself when that angry, old man tried to force words out of me!"

He swallowed and dried his eyes with the back of his thin hand and continued between sobs, "Before you ask, it was not his fault that I got caught. His magic came after mine. He has no tongue, thanks to our master, so he had to reply to my words someway. It was entirely my fault; I used a tiny spell to communicate with him and now that I think about it, I might have also used a fire-spell inside the armoury. It is entirely my fault!"

The viciousness of Felduror became clear. Driven by the sadness in Nuuk's eyes and filled with repulsion, I clutched my fist as if the poor, old imp was someone I knew.

"I shouldn't have shifted to the citadel. I know it was wrong of me, I don't know what I was thinking, trying to outsmart the old wizard. Still, I do not regret it, Lorian! Not for an instant. Firstly, I've found out that there is another imp that is enslaved in the same tower. Who knows how many others are trapped here within these walls? And…" he paused briefly, "I think there's something else!" His voice was rich with emotion, his face unyielding.

"What?"

"I think someone was aiding me this all time! I found the armoury's door unlocked, when I am utterly certain I locked it twice, just when I left with Ghaeloden. And the sceptre must be altering –" his voice died suddenly.

A distant but distinctive crackling sound caught both of us by surprise. Some small rocks tumbled down the tunnel where the gallery conveyed into the narrow and steep corridor that went upwards.

With my heart already racing, I pulled Winterhorn from my belt and jumped into my feet, gesturing at Nuuk to keep quiet and still, while I slowly advanced towards the noise.

Quickly the sound amplified and turned into something more recognizable; muffled steps. Someone was descending to the big, steep gallery.

With stealth, I moved faster towards the mouth of tunnel and hid myself behind the sharp corner, awaiting my moment to jump at whatever came out from the darkness.

The steps intensified and I confidently increased my grip around the knife's handle. Whoever was descending was not aware of me behind the corner as the steps never decreased their swiftness. I took a slow and long draw of air; the last one before my body went still as a rock. My arm and dagger lifted high in the air readied my whole being to strike the intruder down. Though, before I had time to do anything, the intruder slipped on the steep terrain and skidded all the way down.

The yelp she instinctively let out gave her away – it was the witch! I relaxed and exhaled, realising I was shaking. Her long, unconventional descent brought her right in front of me, on her bottom.

"Naghnatë!" I leaped to her aid, making haste to replace the dagger back in my belt.

"These cussed rocks…" her lengthy imprecation turned swiftly into a mumble I could no longer understand.

"Are you well? Here, let me help you!" I said as I lifted her up with a hand on her arm and one around her back.

Though as soon as she was up, she stepped away from me, almost pushing me to the side. Her quick gesture made me wonder if my touch was mistakenly perceived as too brazen.

"I hope you haven't compromised yourself just yet." I ignored her confused face altogether. "I found Nuuk and we've escaped. Unfortunately, now they know about us. Not that we are here in the cave, they thought that we escaped through magic. But they do know it was a human; the orcs picked up my trail. And also…" I paused briefly, weighing the magnitude of my confession, "…I've lost your cloak! In the rush, I've left it on a chair and there was no time for me to go back. Nuuk was really hurt and I couldn't risk…" I stopped myself mid-sentence.

My words changed her face expression to a heavier attitude and she took some time before she replied. "I guess that is that then. First things first, now!" She darted quickly through the boulders and holes on the floor and moved towards the imp.

I followed silently.

"Oh dear!" she exclaimed as she knelt next to Nuuk, dropping her bag carelessly on the floor.

Her thin fingers moved gently as she started inspecting the imp's face, mumbling all along. With every new bruise she found, her voice hissed a bit higher or lower, based on the gravity of the discovery. I gathered that she had recognised the most urgent injuries when she stopped abruptly.

"Wet a clean piece of cloth in fresh water and bring it to me. Soak it well!" she commanded.

There was no point in mentioning I had already cleaned it; perhaps my efforts weren't anywhere good enough, so I obeyed, happy to have her with us.

Once satisfied with her cleaning, she made Nuuk chew on a root she pulled from a bundle in her bag and made him drink aplenty from her waterskin – one of the few sentences that she addressed me after our initial encounter, had been to return her waterskin so she could prepare more of the cleansing, cold herbal-brew. Besides the face the imp pulled when he had to masticate the dry root, which also made me grimace in sympathy, the help she provided seemed to have immediate, positive effects.

Nuuk's face was not knotted anymore, his body freed from the many grips of pain that had contorted it since his capture. He appeared reinvigorated and was now able to move more freely, without wincing or gasping for air, although some of the wounds still looked like they hurt. I wondered if the herb she had used was still Drakholia and how long its numbing effect would last, considering all along if I should ask for a tiny bit for my leg.

I never got the chance, however, as Nuuk was eager to recount his adventures. His long recount took us back at the moment he had shifted and landed in her pots-and-pans' trap in the mountain's hut, which saw us all share a laugh or two. He then related about the moment he had lost his memory and had encountered Quick and finally had been rescued by me.

It filled me with joy, hearing him voice what had appeared to me more like a clumsy intrusion and frightful escape. I had not for a second stopped to reconsider what I had achieved and what weeks ago could have been and unthinkable undertaking for one like me. The more he continued, the more I did not recognise the character he was portraying; a brave and bold version of me that did not flinch or falter against the danger of the citadel, while all I could think of was the raw sense of fear and shock, conveyed by those guttural Gholaks' voices and growls. Even thinking back to those brutes made my blood chill. Why did they have that effect on me? I did not remember being that scared when I met Ghaeloden, I had passed out, sure, yet I still considered him less frightful; inexplicably so as he was a lot bigger and stronger and his capacity to fly and wield magic could tear apart an army of orcs.

"That's why I'm indebted to you! Both of you, but especially Lorian!" Nuuk's voice was directed towards me, interrupting my momentary absence.

I concluded there was no need for him to know how really scared I had been and still was. Maybe it was best to allow his aching eyes and mind think of me as the fearless redeemer he depicted. At least for the moment.

"What's important is that you are safe now and we're all together. Yet I cannot lie, I'd like Ghaeloden to be with us as well." I smiled at both of them.

"He's well alright! I saw him with my own eyes, flying about the lands with the white Drakhahoul. I suppose he was summoned to report back to the king himself, though I doubt they were alone!" Naghnatë's mocking tone allowed little interpretation on what she meant.

"I am sure he tried his best to delay Felduror," I said, more convinced now than before.

"Felduror had no intention to keep hurting me, not for a while at least. But…" Nuuk suddenly lifted himself to his feet, staring at me with his eye wide open against an obvious trail of pain.

"What?" I asked nervously.

"Lorian! It just came to me!" His tone and face promised nothing good. "Felduror gave me time to think and tell him the truth until his Gholaks returned from Sallncoln!"

"What? Gholaks?" I exchanged glances with him and the witch. "Why Sallncoln?

"That was supposed to be my bad news, and thanks to the imp it is not anymore! However, I didn't think it'd be that bad news." The witch tried to alleviate my tension. "I saw them leaving earlier, from my tree. I was on my way towards the main entrance, where I thought to distract the wizard by using a spell to disarm the guards at the gates. And when I heard the horns ringing I decided to wait. Not long after, I saw a host of orcs, daggers and axes at hand, leaving towards south."

Her words felt like needles in my heart. She continued talking, yet my ears were clinking with a sharp noise that muffled any exterior sound, making it impossible to understand a word. Like a strike that had been delivered well, I was accusing its devastating effects. My body refused to move and felt like it was trapped in a stream of drying-concrete and, while it kept me still, my mind could only focus on the words *Gholaks* and *Sallncoln*. I stopped seeing the witch and the imp, and the bodies of the three tall brutes that have chased us in the basements were foremost in my mind as if summoned from a nightmare.

Why Sallncoln? What do they want with my village?

"Lorian, are you well?" It was Nuuk's voice that became clear enough to distract me from the cacophony of noises, smells and hallucinations I was surrounded by.

I gulped and blinked repeatedly until I saw both of them staring at me.

"Why Sallncoln?" I managed to say, wondering why had the imp had waited so long to tell me about it.

"It must be the reason Felduror sent me and Ghaeloden before; to look for Naghnatë!" Nuuk felt eager to respond, while the face of the witch appeared clueless.

"That would have been a good sign if you hadn't forgotten the cloak in the cellars, Lorian, which I do not blame you for it, let's be clear!" Naghnatë started.

I was not following.

"None would've done better than you without any aid nor magic. I'm only thinking out loud and stating the facts here. So, if he hadn't found the cloak, it would've meant that he did not know about me and he sent his Gholaks to take a proper look."

"Are you sure he will know it is your cloak? Couldn't it be just anyone's?" I asked.

"If he puts his hands on it, we better assume he knows than being unprepared," the witch replied sharply. "So, assuming he knows about me, he most likely will think that I have ventured here. Then –"

"Why is he sending the Gholaks to Sallncoln?" Nuuk and I said in unison.

Naghnatë pondered her answer.

"To wipe out every trace that a dragon had been there! And I'm afraid that's not the only thing. The orcs are not travelling alone; a few acolytes accompany them. I counted at least four."

"Acolytes and orcs?" My empty words trailed faintly in the air.

"Acolytes accustomed in wielding magic and Gholaks that are eager to prove what they are worth to their master and in desperate need of blood," Nuuk added. "Whenever the wizard recounted such deeds, he behaved as if possessed, never once feeling any emotions of sorrow or sympathy towards those that perished. I doubt this will be any different, as orcs are not beasts of idleness, which is what they have been for quite some time now."

Orcs and acolytes.

"Felduror has grown careless of what the others think and is too keen on showing off his brutes again. If that is the case, it can only mean he will soon make his move on seizing the throne for himself!" Naghnatë added.

My family, Elmira!

"As I feared, we are too late! Perhaps he has already found enough tokens and stones to bind them and reach for the power that would secure his place." Naghnatë's voice was passionless.

If that was true, then the people in Sallncoln were not the only ones in danger; every human and creature that stood in the wizard's path was equally threatened. Perhaps the dragons too, if they dared not rise up against him in an attempt to aid their king. And most certainly Ghaeloden, who nurtured fervent hatred towards the old wizard.

The thought of the young, spiked dragon made me imagine an improbable airborne fight between him and his mother, Sereri, who, according to the witch, would serve Felduror until her death. An imaginary fight I could not comprehend and in which I could not see a positive outcome for Ghaeloden.

Gholaks, Drakhahouls and wizards! My mind continued to convey and balance the possible ends that innocent people and creatures might have to suffer.

I did not know what would be worse and what I could do, if indeed there was anything in my power to do at all. The face of the tall orc from the basement kept returning in my mind, tormenting my soul with a blusterous cacophony of heartbeats.

If a few of those warriors were marching for Sallncoln there would be no one able to respond to their rage. None of our people had the skills and the weapons to fight back at such soldiers of death; we might have some brave, strong men, yet unfortunately, they were not people accustomed to fighting. Besides, they don't even believe the existence of those they would fight against. Who would? Everyone knew what the old stories recounted, and nobody believed them to be true. Not even me, the hopeless, daydreaming boy, who always hoped for something to be true. And even now that I was in the middle of it all, it felt overwhelming and unreal at times.

How would someone in their right mind believe such nonsense?

People's lives were already hard enough, with little to drag them on and add sense to their modest existence. Too many years had passed since the age of elves, dwarfs and dragons had turned into legends and legends into bed-time stories. None would spare a second thought that orcs, wizards, imps and dragons still existed. And certainly no one would be able to face them.

One thing was certain; the boldness of Felduror seemed to have overwhelmed his desire to keep his existence hidden. Ready or not, no one would stand a chance. It seemed plausible that he felt ready to reveal himself to the world. His move for Sallncoln would not only show everyone that the forces of hell were once more walking the earth, but would also expose him as a new ruler, a wizard nonetheless − a wizard, right hand of a Drakhahoul king. It would shatter the frivolous stability that existed among human clans of all regions. The north and the south would see a new challenge; one they could not overcome.

It was worse than I feared. There was one thing I could do and one alone; I needed to return home and warn them and get ready, ready for war.

"Naghnatë, I need you to shift me back to your hut in the mountains that surround the Lament Valley. From there I can walk a day towards Sallncoln and still be ahead of the orcs. At least I can try and make the villagers aware of what is coming!" I spoke fast and agitatedly.

"But −" Nuuk tried to argue.

"Naghnatë, you promised!" I enforced my demand, my nails digging achingly inside my blistered fists.

"And so I will," she replied, "although, I warn you, lad, this is bigger than what you can achieve on your own. You are not ready for such an endeavour."

"Probably I won't ever be ready!" I did not care how weak I was. "What I do know however, is that I shall not stay idle while my family and those I care about are being butchered!"

"What about the tokens? There will be no better opportunity for us to come back here and surprise the wizard?" said Nuuk with concern.

"Nothing has changed from what we discussed, except it'll only be me and you. We shall both stay, Nuuk. I will take Lorian back and return here promptly." She shot a strict look at the imp, allowing no space for argument even though their chances had been drastically reduced now that the wizard was alerted to our presence.

"I hope you understand, Nuuk!" I tried to pacify the imp's confusion. "I wish I could stay, but not while my village is in danger. I can't let them die because of those artefacts, not now, not ever!" I placed my hand on his shoulder and crouched in front of him.

He seemed lost and confounded. A sad sight that made my determination waver. I did not want to leave him; he was too weak still. But, I could not stay either. I had to attempt and deliver the news to my people. As awkward as they might find it, I was their only hope of survival, if they agreed to abscond.

"I'm ready when you are!" Naghnatë interrupted our moment.

"I understand, Lorian." Nuuk overcame his sorrow to offer his compassion and support. "You do well to look after yourself. I hope to meet you again sometime!" He gulped with sadness and placed both his hands over my shoulders. His big, green irises pierced through to my soul.

I lifted myself rather quickly, the sight making me feel uncomfortable.

"Very well then, I'm ready!" I said to Naghnatë.

She then took my hand and fixed my eyes and, before I could even look back at Nuuk, we were gone.

I felt dizzy upon landing, yet I was standing, and most importantly, I did not feel the urge to puke this time.

"You are getting better at this!" Naghnatë offered a sincere smile.

I let out a small smile too, weakened by how miserable and torn I felt. I was happy to breathe the comforting air of home's vicinity, coldly tinged with autumn's arrival. Alas, I felt abnormally sad for having to leave the witch, the imp and the dragon to their unknown fates.

The sight of the multitude of pots and pans scattered about the wooden-floor, brought back the humorous, imp's recount which lifted my spirits a little.

"Would you tell master Ghaeloden I wish him well?" I thought how much I would have liked to see him one more time.

"I will!" she replied coldly.

"And would you look after Nuuk?" I continued, my eyes wet already.

"I will!" she said with the same soft but cold voice.

I took a long deep breath then and without her consent I pulled her into a hug. I expected at any moment to be pushed away. Though she did not do it this time. She allowed me to linger for a moment.

"Do not fret, young Lorian, we shall meet again!" she said as she pulled away with a wry smile upon her face, keeping her eyes on mine.

A nodding moment and she was gone.

She vanished from between my arms, making me vacillate feebly back and forth. Her last words turned to a deafening silence and I found myself smiling at an empty space, surrounded by pots and thinking how I would have liked this to end another way. But, perhaps, this was already a better way; I had met a witch, I had met a dragon, I had met an imp and I had wielded magic.

With a strong grip around Winterhorn's handle, I was ready to return home and ready for whatever else fate might bring.

ABOUT THE AUTHOR

Ovidiu Nicolae Baiculescu is the author behind **Winterhorn**, book I of the epic fantasy series **Tokens of Benevolence**. He is a Romanian-Italian traditional artist and a 3D/Vfx computer artist, that lives between Romania, Italy and UK.

Graduated in Traditional Arts of the Academy of Fine Arts and Master in Product Design (Firenze, Tuscany), Ovidiu works keenly across multiple platforms and disciplines, both digitally and traditionally, fact which allows him to envision fantastic sceneries and characters that are a vibrant proof of his ancient history passion.

www.oxhid3.com

CHARACTER MAP

Lorian Garr — *Human*

Naghnatë — *Human/Witch*

Nuuk — *Iprorim/Imp*

Felduror — *Human/Wizard*

Dharamir — **F**elduror

Quick — *Iprorim/Imp*

Henek — *Human – Lorian's brother*

Kuno — *Human – Lorian's brother*

Allarea — *Human – Lorian's grandmother*

Dhereki — *Human – Lorian's grandfather*

Elmira — *Human – Lorian's promised love*

Alaric Eamon Beorth — *Human*

Bilberith — *Human/Wizard*

Medoris — *Human – owner of the first token, the Blood-Stone*

Takahok — *Human – owner of the Rose of Ice*

Ghaeloden-Three-Horns — *Drakhahoul/Dragon*

Belrug-The-Black — *Drakhahoul/Dragon – King in the present year*

Sereri-The-White — *Drakhahoul/Dragoness*

Jaro-The-Venomous — *Drakhahoul/Dragon*

Yrsidir-Two-tails — *Drakhahoul/Dragon – King before Belrug*

Irridae-The-Brave — *Drakhahoul/Dragoness*

Algudrin-The-Bold — *Drakhahoul/Dragon*

Guzheraak — *Gholak /Orc*

Pakto — *Gholak /Orc*

Barakhuul — *Gholak /Orc*

Hegor Strongfist — *Dwarf king of Mount Nrom*

Ghorimm — *Dwarf / owner of the token Cinereus*

Loreeia — *Elven queen*

Printed in Great Britain
by Amazon